"Every girl dreams of the man she w [...] less than God's best. *Fairytales Do Come True* reminds us that God's plan is worth waiting for, in every way. This book takes a candid look at the struggles and temptations many young women face today, along with the guilt brought about from poor past choices. Through an engaging story, Amy McCart teaches the value of purity and addresses sensitive issues in a delicate manner. Any young woman who wonders if the wait is worth it will be encouraged by this book."

—Amie M. Weir
Founder of Liberty Preparatory Christian Academy
Marketing Entrepreneur

"A beautiful true story that is a must-read for everyone that has dated, will date, or is dating. (Including Marrieds) I went on this journey with Emily feeling every single emotion. A Fairytale Revival! Gripping! Powerful! Life Changing!"

—Sharelle Hall
Executive Producer, Allegentsia Productions

"A beautiful picture of true humanity, love, and grace. A must-read for every young girl who desires true love (which I believe includes ALL of us). I was encouraged in my own journey in so many ways. Amy's vulnerability is so refreshing and relatable, and I believe it sheds light on issues that are rarely touched on in Christian circles today. I guarantee that every girl will be encouraged and inspired."

—Breyanne Noelle
Singer, Model, Actress

"*Fairytales Do Come True* has been one of the most enjoyable reads I've had in quite some time. Amy's lighthearted, warm, energetic, and descriptive writing will grab your attention, allowing you to share in a journey of love, heartache, faith, pain, waiting, redemption, renewal, and hope all while sharing some hard facts and truths of the ins and outs of Christ-centered courtship, the pitfalls that young single men and women often are caught in, and the misunderstood concepts of dating and relationships taught by our culture from a very personal place in the character of Emily. I found myself constantly anticipating the next chapter, hoping and praying with the character, anxious to see each new season in her life. And, at certain points, I found the character utterly relatable, as if bits of my personal life were being told in her story. It is a must-read for those who feel that they've lost hope in love or a chance at a Fairytale ending the way God intended, for those who need encouragement to keep being faithful and trusting God's beautiful plan, and for those who need the reminder that God is a redeemer and loves giving second chances. This book, coupled with the study guide, will inspire, teach, bring growth and healing, and give personal insight to those desiring the life and relationship God really desires to offer. He is the author of real life Fairytales."

—**Laureen Alexa Trujillo**
Personal Fitness Trainer

Fairytales Do Come True

When God Writes Your Love Story

AMY J. McCART

HIGH BRIDGE BOOKS

HOUSTON

Fairytales Do Come True
by Amy J. McCart

Printed in the United States of America
ISBN (Paperback): 978-1-940024-56-1
ISBN (eBook): 978-1-940024-57-8

High Bridge Books titles may be purchased in bulk for educational, business, fundraising, or sales promotional use. For information please contact High Bridge Books via www.HighBridgeBooks.com/contact.

Published in Houston, Texas by High Bridge Books

CONTENTS

DEDICATION

To my real-life Knight in Shining Armor, my husband, Tyler. This book would not have been possible without you. When we met, your love for Jesus is what captured my heart, and years later that same passion and vigor pursuit in your Christian walk has been a daily encouragement. Thank you for always growing, learning and changing! You are proof that *Fairytales Do Come True*! I love you now and forever!

And thank you to my Lord and Savior, the one Who gives breath to my lungs. You are the reason I rise each morning, dream big dreams and pursue the extraordinary. I look forward to life's adventures with You, until the day I go to my eternal home with Jesus.

ACKNOWLEDGEMENTS

To my sweet friend and sister in Christ, Stephanie Rice! Thank you for the hours you spent reading through the original, unedited manuscript and pouring out your thoughts, prayers, and constructive criticism. I appreciate the hours you spent with me in the process of creating, editing, and perfecting the *Fairytales Do Come True: Study Guide*. What a testimony as our thoughts and ideas were seamlessly in sync. You are an iron sharpener in my life! Thank you for encouraging this project and seeing a need for it to be completed!

My publisher, Darren Shearer. Thank you for your patience, wisdom and direction with this project. You have been priceless!

To Deb and Jim Ellis, Aimee Trammell, Amie Weir, Laureen Alexa Trujillo, Sharelle Hall, and Breyanne Noelle. Thank you for reading the manuscript and providing feedback. Your words and encouragement made my heart smile.

A SPECIAL THANKS

Paige Ewing, my sweet cousin, thank you for using your photography gift to be such a blessing to me! The portraits you captured for my book and website were perfect. Love you Paige!

Check out her amazing talent: www.paigeewingministries.com and www.paigeewingphotography.com

To Genesis by 124 – Hamilton Mill and Michaela Dodd, thank you for providing your amazing salon services as I prepared for my photo shoot. You were all a true blessing! www.salon124.com

INTRODUCTION

Fairytales Do Come True is a story that will heighten your hope and strengthen your stand to wait for your dreams to become realities. People often question if their dreams are possible or even realistic? They second guess themselves because they are ridiculed for setting their hopes too high. This story takes you from the valleys to the mountaintops that only seem possible in fairytales.

As Emily goes off to college, she experiences a newfound freedom with no rules, no curfews and no parents to oversee her choices. She is allured by the parties, unsupervised dorm life and even the bar scene which goes against her conservative Christian roots.

A gradual betrayal takes hold of her, as college life is far from the way it is portrayed in the movies. Her life quickly becomes empty and filled with regrets. Emily is left dwelling on her poor choices, overwhelmed with guilt, and drowning in a sea of loneliness. Is forgiveness for all that she has done even possible?

Like most little girls, Emily dreamed about living like a princess. She longed for the fairytale romance. She dreamed about her handsome knight, riding on his white horse to rescue her from a mundane life and shower her with a pure love and affection. She loved the story of Cinderella. When all things looked hopeless, Cinderella's destiny changed and her Prince Charming came to rescue her. A life in rags did not destine her to stay there, and Emily clung to a hope, that her life's mistakes would not destine her to stay there either.

Will Emily be able to turn things around embracing grace and forgiveness in a surrendered life to Jesus? Read and find out if all of her mistakes cause her to give up on her childhood dreams of a fairytale romance. Could it be possible to have both, a fairytale romance and Jesus?

Enjoy as you read...

Fairytales Do Come True:
When God Writes Your Love Story.

1

A TROPICAL PARADISE

The breeze off of the Caribbean caught the wide brim of my crocheted white hat, blowing it back and nearly off of my head. There I sat, soaking in the wonderful fragrances of the pink hibiscus and other tropical flowers surrounding the outdoor cafe. The breeze brought with it the smell of coconut and pineapple suntan oil worn by the guests lounging at the adjoining pool. Blissful in a marriage of now 25 years, colorful umbrellas comforted our fruit smoothies while we finished a light, mid-afternoon lunch.

"Sweetheart? Sweetheart?" My husband paused waiting for my response. "Earth to Emily, earth to Emily!" he said as he waved his hand in front of my face. .

I snapped back and quickly looked up at him, "Oh, I'm sorry! I was just thinking."

"Thinking about what?" he questioned.

"I was remembering how things used to be, the countless times I sat behind my desk, just dreaming of the day I wouldn't have to go to my corporate job. I constantly dreamed of a day when I could actually live out what I was passionate about, versus sitting in corporate meetings and always playing catch-up on voicemails and emails. I would sit back and imagine myself speaking at different conferences, encouraging people, sharing truths I had learned." Pausing, I pointed to the surroundings, "This conference is better than anything I ever saw in my office daydreams. It makes me glad I didn't settle, that I never gave up on my dreams."

His soft smile and nod as he listened told me he knew exactly how I felt. Not only was the scenery a dream but as I looked across the table at my handsome husband, I realized he was a main part of my fairytale coming true. His blonde hair, short and in a trendy, spike, graced his rosy cheeks. The outline of his muscles showed through his white linen shirt. He definitely did not look his age. He still looked like a Greek god to me. '*Thor* had nothing on my husband,' I chuckled to myself.

The Caribbean rays of sunshine danced off of his watch as the colorful beams reflected from it's oyster-colored face. His right hand was a reminder of great servitude. It housed a giant ring of accomplishment. Though many had asked if he had been in a Super Bowl, his ring was actually part of a brotherhood of leaders who had helped people succeed in business and in life. The ring was a gift, a small token of the many people he had served all over America.

As we finished our lunch, I was thankful that my long, white cover-up was breathable in the humidity. I looked forward to a relaxing day by the pool, soaking in some rays, doing a little reading and most likely dosing off for a short catnap.

My thoughts were interrupted, "You are right, Sweetheart," my husband said. "It's definitely good to remember where we came from. God has brought us a long way from where we started. Not able to pay our bills or even buy other Christmas gifts, meeting for lunch in the mall food court for a packed peanut butter and jelly sandwich. We could've followed the path of all of our peers, but instead we chose to learn some valuable principles that certainly changed our life." My pursed lips and nod signaled my full agreement.

He smiled with a yawn, "I'll let you continue reminiscing. I'm going to head back up to the room for a nap. You are welcome to join meeeeee," he sang as he tried to sell me on skipping my pool time.

I cocked my head smirking and gave him a teasing glare. He knew his sales pitch wasn't working.

"OK, fine," he pouted playfully, "Let's just meet back in the room later. Remember, we have reservations for dinner at 7 o'clock."

"Okay sweetie pie," I played back.

He stood up, bent over, tucked the long loose strand of blonde hair back behind my ear, and pushed my hat aside enough to give me a gentle kiss goodbye.

"You are still my Princess. You look more beautiful today than the day I married you," he said. "Now, don't get too much sun down here. We still have several days before we leave," he reminded me. With that, he stood up, grabbed the room key off the table, and said, "I love you."

"I love you, too. Thanks for being so great. You're my favorite!" I smiled as I thought about all the times I so fondly said this to him. Putting my white sunglasses back on, I blew him a kiss. "I'll see you after a while."

He walked off, and I followed him with my gaze. All the money, houses, jewelry, or cars in the world could not replace the blessing God gave me when he gave me this man.

The waiter interrupted my stare, "Miss Emily, may I refresh your Diet Coke, or may I bring your favorite smoothie? The pineapple coconut sure looks delicious today."

"Oooh. I'd love a smoothie. Thanks Duncan!"

"Yes, ma'am," he said with his Caribbean island accent. "I'll add some extra whip cream and toasted coconut on the top, too. Just the way you like it."

"Thank you so much, Duncan. You are such a blessing."

He gave me a playful wink and disappeared.

As I waited for Duncan to return, I noticed a young lady a few tables over, maybe in her early twenties, sitting by herself. Though the umbrella of the tiki hut provided nice shade for her, it could not hide the tears that streamed down her face. As I watched her sobbing, my heart went out to her. I noticed the glimmer from a small cross necklace that hung on a delicate chain from her neck. What could be troubling this beautiful young lady?

My thoughts raced to all of the possibilities. Could it be a death in the family? An argument? A break up? She fidgeted, continually rubbing the dainty cross. I was reminded of my own life, and the turmoil I faced before I met the man of my dreams.

I thought about how hard I tried to make good choices as a young Christian. It seems like I always fell short. I knew I was disappointing God, but I was so naive, I didn't know how to change the direction my life was going. I didn't understand God's grace and *redemption*. I wasn't able to grasp the truth of God's forgiveness. My life seemed full of despair, disappointment, and unworthiness. I wondered what caused this young girl to be so distraught.

Duncan returned with my smoothie and receipt. I quickly scribbled my name and room number.

I was curious about this stranger's story. While I didn't know her, I felt drawn to her. I didn't want to intrude, but part of me just wanted to embrace her and make whatever "it" was, better. I wanted her pain to go away and to remind her that joy *does* come in the morning. Joy would come!

I longed for the opportunity to minister to her so I prayed and asked the Holy Spirit for wisdom and guidance. I knew if I was supposed to go over and talk to her, the Lord would bless me with more sunny afternoons later in the week to work on my tan.

"Father, how would you direct me in this situation? Should I go talk to this young lady? She looks so sad. Should I go comfort her? Listen to her?"

I sat, quietly, just waiting to hear the still, small voice that had directed me countless times before. The direction was clear: *"Go. Listen. Minister. You are just the person she needs to talk to right now. You have your story for a reason and for such a time as this. You were meant to be here and to share with her."*

Over the years, I had learned to become obedient more quickly than I once had been. I placed my sunglasses back in their case and dropped it in my white canvas bag. Tucking my room key in the outer zipper pocket, I tossed my bag over my shoulder, grabbed my fresh smoothie, and began to walk over to my *new* friend.

I approached the table. "Miss, I couldn't help but notice your tears. Are you okay? Can I do anything?" Biting my lip, I'm sure she could tell her sadness made me sad.

She quickly wiped her eyes with the cloth napkin, trying to hide the trace of tears. "Oh no. I'm fine. I'm fine," she waved. "Just going through some things, but it will all be fine. Thank you, though. That's very considerate of you," she said, trying to compose herself while politely giving me a way out, a dismissal.

"Alright. Well, I just wanted to check on you. If you need to talk or just need a friend, I'll be at the pool the rest of the afternoon. I'd be happy to at least be a listening ear," I said with a half smile.

"Thank you. I appreciate it. That is very sweet of you. Have a great day," she said, waving a slight goodbye.

I began to walk away. Immediately, I had this feeling that God wasn't done working, that He wanted me to minister to her. In my heart and head, I was being prompted to go back.

I heard that still, small voice, *"What are you doing? You are supposed to talk to her."*

"But, I did talk to her," I argued silently with the Holy Spirit. "She dismissed me. It didn't work out. She didn't want to talk."

"I want you to talk to her. She needs you. She was just being polite."

I sighed, the uncomfortable sigh I had done often when I knew the Holy Spirit was directing me to do something that seemed awkward. I stopped in my tracks, determined I would be obedient. I didn't know what I was going to say yet, but I would just open my mouth and let something come out, uncomfortable or not. Ahhh. I shrugged and quickly turned around to walk to the table before I convinced myself otherwise.

"I apologize. I don't mean to interrupt you again, but as I was walking away, I just felt led to come back. I felt like the Holy Spirit was telling me that you really needed a friend right now. Someone to talk to. Would you mind if I joined you for a while?"

At first, she just looked at me with a blank stare. I felt completely uncomfortable. Then, her bottom lip started to quiver, and she pressed the cloth napkin to her eyes to try to keep the tears from coming. "Sure, I would actually like that," she said with a partial smile, putting her hand out to open an invitation to the chair next to her.

"My name is Emily. It's good to meet you."

"It's good to meet you, too. My name is Elise," she said, reaching out her petite hand to shake mine in a gesture to be polite.

"As I finished my lunch, I noticed you wear a cross on your necklace. Are you a Christian?"

She nodded quietly, without looking up. I could tell she was fighting back tears.

The fact that I didn't even know her disappeared. I was compelled with compassion and just wanted to help. I rested my hand on her forearm. "Awwww, do you want to talk about it?"

The floodgates had been released. Placing the napkin over her eyes didn't seem to slow the salty shower of tears streaming down her cheeks. "I wouldn't even know where to start," she cried. "I just feel like such a failure."

Even with her tears, she was beautiful. I could tell if she smiled and was happy that she would be gorgeous. Her eyes looked glassy from the tears, but the piercing blue color could surely melt a person. She didn't look like a failure. She looked too beautiful to be a failure. Her eyes showed a gentleness, a softness, a goodness. How could she be so distraught? Surely, things couldn't be that bad?

"Well, start from the beginning. Nothing is too big for God to figure out. Sometimes, at least for me, talking about it out loud often helps me figure out answers."

Her head was down, and tears were still streaming down her face. I placed my hand on her back in attempts to bring some comfort. I wanted to be a friend that she surely needed during this time.

I noticed she did not have anything to drink and flagged Duncan down for a cold drink. "What would you like, Elise?"

"Thank you. I'll take a Diet Coke."

Duncan nodded. Moments later, he appeared with her drink.

"Well," Elise began with a sigh, "it's funny that you, of all people would come and sit with me. I leave tomorrow, but for the last several days, I have noticed you."

"Really?" I said as my voice jumped a bit in surprise.

"Yes. Well…" she paused. "I've been noticing you and, I'm guessing, your husband?"

I nodded.

She explained, "My boyfriend and I planned this trip months ago, and when we had a huge fight he decided not to come. I have had days to think without distractions. It seems like lately we fight about everything. I really love him, and I've always thought that he was the one I was going to marry. Then, I see you. The way you and your husband hold hands, how he pulls out your chair for you and pushes it in, how you two pray before meals, and how he kisses you when you part. Everything about your relationship seems so great."

Elise began to cry again, tears streaming down her face as she continued to talk.

"Even how you two talk to each other. I hope it doesn't sound like I've been totally stalking you," she chuckled through her tears, "but I just couldn't help but notice so many things. When you talk to each other, I haven't heard the words, but I could see how attentive you both are to each other. It's like you're both actually listening, not distracted."

"And, that's not all," she continued. "The days I've seen you, you look successful. It's like your life encompasses perfection," she said with a little sound of frustration in her voice. "It's what I would want my life to be like with my husband one day. You both laugh a lot. You're beautiful and without even knowing you, you seem like some of the nicest people I've ever 'not' met! The waiter even likes you, and you know him by name."

She paused, tears still streaming down her cheeks as she acknowledged the Diet Coke that Duncan had brought earlier.

"Well, Elise," I said, and then I paused, nodded, and bit my lip. "I'm not sure if that means I'm supposed to say, 'Thank you?' But, I'm glad that we could leave a good impression on you," I said, half not knowing where all of this was going.

"I know. I'm sure it sounds weird. It all goes back to my boyfriend. He just gave me the ultimatum over the phone. Because of what I chose, he decided to break up with me. I thought I was going to marry him. Two months ago, I went to church with a friend. I didn't realize what I was in for. That night, everything changed for me. I cried a lot. All the bad things that I was doing just seemed to be flooding my mind with guilt. I ended up accepting Jesus as my Savior."

Overjoyed, I leaned in to her, "Ohhhh, that's great, Elise."

"Well… it sounds great. But it seems like, ever since I made that decision, things between my boyfriend and I have been terrible! I started to go to church every week and read my Bible. It was all so new and so refreshing to me. Everything I was learning just seemed so exciting. My boyfriend hasn't been interested in hearing about it. He's always just seemed annoyed.

"The straw that broke the camel's back for him was when I told him that I didn't feel right about sleeping with him anymore, and I didn't feel right about doing some of the other things we were doing. I decided I wanted to wait until I got married. I just didn't feel right.

He was so mad. He's yelled about this whole 'Jesus thing' since. Here I am by myself, and I've been late for my period Even though it's been a few months, my nervousness got the best of me so I went ahead and took a pregnancy test. Thankfully, it was negative, but when I told my boyfriend about that, he was furious.

"Then, this morning was when he gave me the choice: him or this new 'Jesus,' like I've been cheating on him or something. We've been together for two years, and I really do love him, but when he asked that question, something inside me just told me that I couldn't choose him. Inside myself, I felt like I had to choose Jesus. So, I did. That's when he broke up with me."

Her sobs got heavier. I could tell she wasn't trying to hide her tears any longer. She just let them come. She held her hands up to her face with the cloth napkin covering it and just cried. Her shoulders and body shook as she sobbed.

I moved my chair closer to hers and embraced her. For a moment, I just held her without saying any words. Then, I said, "Elise, God will bless you for the decision you made. I promise. It may seem horrible right now, but God will give you something better than you could have ever dreamed. Sometimes, the decisions that we make seem hard, especially when someone we love gives us such an ultimatum, but God will bless you for it. He will."

She brought the napkin down from her face and continued to cry as she talked. "But, I really do love him. How can I love someone and it be right that we broke up? I thought I was going to marry him."

"Sometimes, letting go is the hardest but best thing we can do. In the Bible, it talks about not being 'unequally yoked' to an unbeliever in a relationship."

Elise interrupted, "What's that mean?"

I explained, "Well, 'unequally yoked' is talking specifically about relationships. Paul is talking about the relationship between a believer and non-believer. He later goes on to say to 'separate yourself from them.' Paul knew that when a believer was not together with another believer, there would be problems. Although your boyfriend gave you a hard choice, you chose God, and you were obedient to what the Bible says to do. For example, if a farmer would hook a large horse and a goat together, it would be very difficult for the two to work together and pull in a straight line, at the same pace. Right? Because the horse is so much bigger?"

"Right," she agreed.

"That may be a bit of a far-fetched analogy in today's culture, but Paul's point is this: being unequally yoked is going to bring problems. If a believer is dating a non-believer, like the horse and goat, they are not able to be unified. And, unity is a key to making a relationship work."

"That makes sense," she responded, "because nothing has been the same since I accepted Jesus. When my boyfriend saw that I was really serious about going to church and learning about being a Christian, things just continually got worse between us. The hard thing is that I've been thinking he's the man I'm going to marry because we had been so happy. Now, everything is so different. When I saw you and your husband, I couldn't help but notice your relationship. You two seem like you are on such a different level of happiness than I ever really knew existed. It's like he is your completion, and you are his. In losing my boyfriend, it just makes me wonder if there is anyone out there who will ever be my completion. You know?"

I nodded, and Elise continued.

"I'm probably like most girls my age. I want to find Mr. Right. I want to find the man of my dreams, but one who won't ask me to compromise my beliefs," said Elise. She sighed and continued, "I never thought about it, but after seeing you it would be awesome to marry a man that even encouraged me in this new journey with Jesus. I feel like I have so much to learn. Are there even guys out there in this world like that anymore? Did you get the last one?" she jokingly nudged. "Honestly, I've never even met a guy who loved Jesus. Do they even exist in my age group?"

Her head had been hung low. You could tell she'd given all of this quite a bit of thought. She raised her head and looked at me with intent and said, "Do single men that love Jesus even exist anymore?" Her blue eyes were piercing, looking at me in all seriousness. Her tears dried up, and she sounded as though now she was just clinging to a hope, a wish, a dream that God truly did have someone perfect for her, for the new person she was becoming.

"Elise, I don't want you to think that everything in our lives has always been perfect. We've had our rocky times, too. Like you, I came to a crossroads where I had to choose. It was either a relationship with this non-Christian guy or God. I was so wrapped up in this relationship that I nearly chose the guy! I almost decided that an earthly relationship was more important than my relationship with my Heavenly Father. I remember vividly that if I would have chosen the guy, it would've also been a choice to say, 'Bye-Bye, Jesus.' So, Elise, I can relate very closely with what you are going through.

"I thank God that, on that day when I had a choice, I chose Jesus. My life would most definitely be different if I hadn't, and I wouldn't be married to the amazing man that I have. Sometimes I do feel like I have to pinch myself, like I am living a real-life fairytale, but it's all because of God, because I chose Him first. Don't get me wrong, we have had our challenges. The strength in our marriage has always been in the foundation we set on Jesus and that is what has ultimately brought us success."

"Will you tell me about it? Will you tell me what happened?" she said as she leaned up against the table, placing her elbows on it and her chin on her hands. "Do you mind? Would you tell me?"

"It's quite a long story, Elise. Are you sure you want to hear the whole thing?"

"Yes, pleeeease. About right now, I could use any good story to know that there is still hope. Not to mention, it would be nice to take my mind off of my life right now! Really, if you don't mind, I would love to hear it." She sat back trying to regain her composure, and hold back the excitement of a potential story. Though her half smile and lifted eyebrows showed a hope, almost a desperation that she would be able to believe in a pure love.

"Sure, I suppose," I smiled.

Elise sat up, almost clapping her hands in excitement before tucking them both under her legs and settling back into her seat.

"Well… my story is similar to the story of Cinderella. 'Why?' You might ask? Because in the beginning, things really stunk. My life was dirty with stuff. Poor decisions, relationships, parties… the list goes on. But, like Cinderella, it's like a fairy godmother whisked her wand and a fairytale came true in the end." Leaning over the table, I whispered, "But you and I know that God is the one who really did it all. There's no such thing as fairy godmothers," I winked.

"It all started before I really committed my life to Jesus. I was getting ready to go to college..."

PART 1

DECISIONS

2

LIFE SHAPING. FINDING ME.

Flashback to 1995. I wrapped up the summer after my senior year of Pippen Junior and Senior High School. Pippen High was a tiny "farm town" school in our apple town of Pippen, Pennsylvania. We were known for our apple festival, apple butter, apple ice cream, apple pie, apple cobbler, apple turnover, apple chicken casserole, apple peanut butter, apple tea, apple cider, apple wine, apple coffee, apple syrup, apple sauce, and apple cider vinegar. If you could make it with apples, someone in our town was bound to try! Our mascot was the Apple Axe-men. That's right. A man in overalls, carrying a bag of apples, holding an axe. As the story goes, way back before my great-grandparents, the early settlers went through our town, cutting down all of the trees so they could plant apple trees. We are now known for the biggest apple orchards east of the Mississippi.

The summer following my graduation from Pippen High was the first that had consisted of partying and drinking—secretly, of course. I was good at keeping things from my parents. At least, I thought I was. I had been a pretty good kid in high school. As a three-sport athlete, I didn't drink because I did not want to jeopardize being kicked off of any of my sports teams. Now that I was graduated, it was as if a whole new world had opened up. It was fun, too! The parties. The guys. The drinking.

I was probably a little bit unique, maybe different from a lot of girls my age. Despite my promiscuity, I had a pact with myself. My goal was to remain a virgin until I got married. Thus far, I was successful. I wasn't really walking or living a Christian lifestyle. Though, something deep inside me knew that sex was to be something sacred and reserved for marriage. It could have been the subtleties from growing up in a Christian home. My parents, Mark and Jean, were still married, and my family attended church. Pippen High was probably more tame than most other public high schools. If my friends were having sex, they didn't really talk about it, nor was it considered the "cool" thing to do. Most couples kept what they were doing in their relationships to themselves.

Here was my chance to be whoever I wanted to be. Now, I was going into my freshman year of college: a whole new group of people, new guys, new fun, new friends, new experiences, new memories. My new school, Bordeaux University, was literally only minutes up the road from my parents' house though I had never even been on its campus until it was time to move into my dorm. Part of me allowed my mind to race with the "what ifs." Would my college experience be like how it is portrayed in movies? I pictured pink and green "sorority" Greek letters, the fun girlfriends, frilly parties, and fun outfits. The movies showed the hot guys, big muscles, and nice cars. They showed guys that carried your books and kissed you gently while their arm rested on the wall behind you. I had pictures in my head, ideas of what college could be like.

I quickly realized Bordeaux was not what I saw in movies. There was no Greek system at B.U. No pink and green. My athletic scholarships brought me to this "Christian" university. Seeing what happened on- and off-campus quickly made me realize this college was far from a *Christian* college. Yes, we had to attend chapel three times a week. Yes, we were required to take some basic religion courses. But, wow! These people were very liberal and, based upon how they could party, I sure couldn't tell there was anything different from the so-called "Christians" and a non-Christian. They took the "apples" of Pippen and made them famous for the apple martini on the campus of Bordeaux.

My misconception about a Christian college? I thought that because it was "Christian" it would encourage me to change. In chapel, I was kind of hoping to feel a draw toward Jesus and a hunger for "something more." To my disappointment, even there, I felt no pull. In chapel, they rarely even mentioned Jesus. They spoke often of diversity and acceptance. They talked of cultural awareness and unity, all of which had no appeal to me. I just heard, "blah, blah,

blah." Right, wrong, or indifferent, I'm sure some of it may have been good stuff, but I thought it all sounded like fluff.

Before college, I wasn't aware of what "liberal arts" meant, but this is where I ended up: a Liberal Arts University. Bordeaux University was known for its spectacular law program, which trained law students to think very scientifically, logically, and—of course—liberally. Going into college, I was so naive and unaware of things that were important. I even had to ask my dad whether we were democrats or republicans. I didn't know. I knew what I "thought" was right; whether it was right or not was another question. As a result of the upbringing I received from my parents, I felt I understood what they believed. For the most part, I agreed with them. What they believed, to me, just seemed to be common sense; it seemed to be right. I still wanted clarity on what "classification" *my* beliefs fell into: democrat, republican, conservative, or liberal? I had always thought "liberal" meant "more" or "to have a lot." College was teaching me a whole new meaning of the word.

What it boiled down to was that there were some things that I didn't yet have a firm handle on. I felt naïve. I entered into college with such a shapeable mind. Who and what would shape it? How would I turn out after four years here? Where would my stance be on important issues? And... would it be right?

Some issues didn't seem as clear yet—like abortion. What were my beliefs on that? I would hear both sides of the issue. On my campus, there were those shouting, "Pro-Life! Don't kill the baby!" On the other side—louder, more aggressive, and with more signs—they were saying, "Freedom of Choice! It's the mother's right! It's *her* body. Let her do what she wants!" At that point, abortion wasn't anything that affected my life nor my daily decisions. I could honestly see both sides. I felt somewhat neutral.

My neutral feelings lasted until I found myself in that clinic with a friend of mine from school. She was 19 years old and still had her whole life in front of her. A pregnancy was not part of the future she saw for herself. In order to live a normal life, she didn't feel like she had any other choice but to get an abortion. Her boyfriend encouraged the abortion. They fought constantly, and their relationship was like a roller coaster of chaos. She frequently caught him in lies and knew deep inside there was no future with him.

So, there we sat in that clinic. I couldn't help but curl up my nose at the smell. It smelled like the sick ward on a hospital floor, not an inviting place that I wanted to spend much time. Before that day, before *the* time of the procedure, I was on both sides of the fence.

This day changed things. She thought this was the only way out. The only reason I was asked to come along was because the clinic said someone would need to drive her home. She didn't appear scared, but I could tell she seemed nervous about what was going to happen. The unexpected. I didn't know how the procedure was actually going to go, and I wasn't too sure that she had really done much research on it either.

The doctor and nurse escorted us to the room where the procedure would be done. I was told I would only be able to be in the room with her until they began. Then, I would be asked to wait in the adjacent room. The room was white. I felt the doctor had most likely informed my friend about the procedure he was going to perform. As the time drew nearer, I could see so many unanswered questions in her eyes.

The doctor and nurse seemed sterile in both personality and uniform. The doctor appeared callous, like this was just a job or a paycheck to him. For that reason, it seemed unlikely that he would want to try to discourage my friend from her decision. For her, this pregnancy was an accident and an inconvenience, and I was there to support her.

On the counter, I saw a long, clear tube that looked like a vacuum hooked up to a machine with a switch right next to it. I was asked to step out of the room and told it would just be a few minutes before they would be done.

As I stood in the other room, I heard what sounded like a very loud "shop-vac." I then heard the revving of a vacuum and then what sounded like a normal purr. Then, I would hear the machine revving up again, followed by a release. I was starting to realize what those sounds really were. I later did find out that the loud suction sounds were the release as body parts were pulled off this unborn, but living child.

When I got home that afternoon, I looked up clinics that performed abortions. The whole experience was a pivotal point in my life and my belief system. One website showed piles of aborted body parts laying on a counter. I was so shocked. Surely, this could not be right. Did people really know how this worked?! Did people really know that the baby had a heartbeat within the first 4-5 weeks? This baby inside my friend had been alive. At 10-11 weeks, the baby had arms and legs, fingers and toes. The baby even already had eyelids and earlobes! The baby had skin and a brain.

Thinking back to the sound of the suction made me want to cry. This helpless baby had been pulled apart by its limbs, and I stood in the next room in silence. From that point on, I believed that people who shouted, "Pro-Choice," had never experienced the impact of seeing the tiny arm or leg laying on a clinic counter as I had seen on one of the websites. I was shocked to read about clinics who aborted babies even at 36 weeks when a baby weighed between 5-7 pounds! That was a full grown baby. I knew I was now most definitely "Pro-Life."

During my freshman year, I realized that this Christian University I had chosen to attend had "Pro-Choice" people lurking everywhere. I began to see and hear what I could not have imagined at a Christian University. Sure, my hidden hope had been that I would find a "deeper" walk in my shallow Christian life. I quickly realized that, through the loud and bold cries on campus of Pro-Choice and homosexual rights, maybe this wouldn't be the place where I would have that "kum-by-yah" experience. I became very familiar with words and terms like *awareness*, *acceptance*, and *diversity*.

What I thought and silently hoped for in a deeper relationship with this Jesus I barely knew seemed farther and farther out of my grasp. There had to be more. I desperately wanted to experience pure love, something I knew existed but had not yet found—not a dirty love but a pure love. The disgust of watching others and their views opened my eyes to what I felt was an error in their beliefs and helped me to see more clearly what I believed was right and wrong.

I was finally establishing my own beliefs, and they were getting stronger. The "opinion board" on campus enraged me and was even causing me to be extremely dogmatic and verbal in my newly found voice. I was beginning to see why my family believed as they did and why they had chosen the "political" stance they had chosen. For the first time, I began to understand some of the differences between democrats and republicans, conservatives and liberals. Through my naive, young mind, I was starting to piece things together and understand the beginning of me.

3

FRESHMAN INITIATION

Aside from the drama on campus and the beginnings of finding myself, I was happy to finally find a friend, someone who I really clicked with and could just be myself around. She was fun and lighthearted. She was a breath of fresh air and didn't condemn me. She even shared my name! Her name was Emili Michaels.

We made our mark at the bar downtown. Even with our fake IDs, they still announced our real names when we came in.

"Awwwww! Look who just got here! It's Emili with an 'i' and Emily with a 'y.' Let the party begin; they're here!" It was fun to be announced and known when we walked in. It was a good thing they didn't look at the names on our IDs because our IDs, of course, showed our fake names.

The DJ liked us. What can I say; we were fun people! We could be goofy and friendly. We weren't afraid to get up to the mic and have a good time doing some karaoke, and we definitely knew how to turn it on when we wanted to be sexy. When we showed up at Martini's Pub, we had no intention of buying any drinks for ourselves. We would find some hot guys, make eye contact several times, and act a little shy. Eventually, we would be able to talk to them and begin to work our charm. It didn't take long until Bud Lights in a bottle were flowing the rest of the night!

I began to enjoy the taste of beer. The first swig of the ice-cold, bitter beer went down a little hard. But, with each additional tip of the bottle, it eventually went down smoothly. Sometimes, I felt like I was living in a beer commercial. You know, the ones that show all of the hot guys and pretty girls laughing and drinking beer. Those commercials seem to imply that the beer is what creates a good time, and that without it, there would be no fun. The beer brought all of these single guys and girls to a place where they could meet, get too friendly, spend the night somewhere strange, and wonder how they got there when they woke up the next morning. They never showed that part on the commercials.

Dorm life at Bordeaux proved to be quite interesting. My dorm housed mostly athletes. Along with the athletes came a lot of big egos. Most of these guys were the big shot, super-star athletes at their high schools. On scholarships, they brought their "big shot" attitudes over to college.

Cameron was one of those scholarship athletes. His muscles rippled and were very noticeable in his cutoff t-shirts. He was good looking, and he knew it. He started to say "hey" to me whenever I walked past his room. At first, it was just a "hey." Then, it began to escalate into what seemed like harmless flirting when I walked by. I didn't mind the flirting. Being noticed by such a great athlete and someone who already appeared to be popular made me feel special. What seemed wild to me was that, not only was he a great athlete and great looking, but he was flirting with me! Of all people… me! It felt good to be noticed. I longed to feel important and special. His attention made me feel like I fit in. Though, deep down, I felt very insecure. I was still trying to figure out if I could just be "me" and fit in, or if I would have to manufacture a different version of myself in order to fit in. His attention seemed to make some of those insecurities go away.

During open dorm hours, I would go down to his floor and conveniently pass by his room. If he was around and his door was open, sometimes, he called out to me and asked me to come in. We would typically shoot the breeze and laugh together. Flirty one-liners were becoming a regular part of our conversations.

One eventful afternoon, things happened a bit differently. What had seemed like innocent flirting led to things I was not expecting.

It was the weekend, and the dorms were quiet. Weekends often took people off-campus or out-of-town to visit friends or family. As I was walking by on my way to the REC center, from inside his room, Cameron yelled to me, "Hey! Come keep me company!"

"Hi there," I smiled as I walked in. "You solo this weekend? Did your roomie go home?" I asked, noticing Cameron made a special effort to close the door when I walked in.

"He did," he paused as he brushed past me. "He should be back later," Cameron said as he clicked the TV off. Coming closer, I could feel his breath on my face. "You look hot in your running clothes," he said and smiled. His blunt compliment was out of the ordinary. I felt my cheeks turn red. This was the closest he had ever been to me, and cutting all the small talk, he kissed me. This was my first "kiss" as a college freshman. I must admit; it got me excited.

It felt fast, and I was taken back a bit but tried to appear like it didn't bother me. I didn't want to seem like a stupid, naïve little freshman. I didn't want to seem like a "little girl." I began to feel apprehensive and nervous as he started getting aggressive. In his aggression, he pushed me up against the door and was clamping down on my wrists. For a split second, I didn't know whether to think it was fun and wild or dangerous and too forceful. Then, the more forceful he became, he started hurting my wrists. I now was ready to be done and get out. This wasn't fun.

My mind began to wander, and I was hoping that his roommate would get back and barge in. I imagined that could be my escape. I was no longer impressed with his "popularity" or his athletic skills. He pushed me into the closet and my back hit the wall with a thud. Out of fear, I continued to kiss him. He was bigger and stronger than me. At this point, it seemed that my resistance and pulling away was barely noticeable to him. He pushed me on the bed and climbed on top of me. His kisses got harder and he pulled me over on top of him. Without any hesitancy, he began forcing my head down. I tried to protest and stay up by his face, but he continued to push on my shoulders and my head. I just wanted to leave. I just wanted out of the room. I hated it. I just wanted out. I was disgusted. I felt ashamed and used. How could I allow this to happen?

A flash of naïve thoughts came. I had envisioned the flirting leading to the two of us being an "item"—not this. I had been hoping that, just maybe, I would find that awesome college boyfriend with whom I could spend all of my spare time, a boyfriend with whom I could go out on dates, go to parties, hold hands on the way to class, and snuggle up and watch movies. That was the reason I smiled at him and walked past his room, hoping he would notice me. The star athlete… my boyfriend? How far off was I?! How naïve and blind I had been?

I had learned the basics from my old boyfriend. Unlike Cameron, Nathan was never too aggressive, nor did he ever seem out-of-control. He never pushed me to do things I didn't want to do. Though we messed around, with him, at least, I felt justified; after all, he was my boyfriend. Unfortunately, what I had learned with Nathan, I could use with Cameron to get out.

As he continued to push my head down, I finally consented and gave him what he wanted.

Cameron opened the door and let me out. I said nothing. I just wanted to leave. I ran upstairs and burst into my room. All alone and in silence, I cried. I felt dirty and used. I hated feeling like this. I was afraid of what other people might think of me if they found out what happened. I wondered if I could have done something different to discourage him. Here I was, starting my freshman year of college, and look what I allowed to happen. I was hoping that things would be different. I was hoping I could break the mold and be classified as a "good" girl. I did care about my image. I wanted to be in the "cool" crowd. I wanted guys to think I was pretty and fun. But, how could I be that girl? Who was I, anyway?

As I laid there on my bed crying that afternoon, I desperately wanted to know how to be the "me" that I desired to be. I wanted to know how to avoid getting myself into bad situations where it seemed like there were no good choices. I had no idea who the "cool" people even were yet. I wanted to know if they managed to avoid being pressured into doing things they didn't want to do. If they did avoid it, I wanted to know how. More than anything, I wanted to be like that. I wanted to be strong enough to say "no" when I didn't want to do something.

Elise was sitting, leaning into the table, listening intently. "What a jerk!" she interrupted, shaking her head in disgust.

I responded, "Yes. In that situation, he was a jerk. But, before that, he had always been a pretty nice guy. Later on in the school year, we were able to be civil toward one another, but I avoided visiting him. I think that made him realize he had crossed the line.

"In hindsight, I learned a lot from that experience. I was young and pretty. I probably had on my athletic shorts and a sports tank top because I was on my way to workout. Though a guy never has the right to do anything like that, in my actions and probably the way I dressed, I was unknowingly putting off an image that caused Cameron to assume things. At the time, I just saw it as harmless flirting, but I learned there is nothing harmless about flirting. Flirting can lead a guy to do things that he otherwise would not do! Flirting can alter one's judgment, causing their emotions and feelings to take control. Looking back, the valuable lessons I took away can help my own daughters and other young ladies that are put in similar situations."

Elise nodded. "You're right. I've had friends in similar situations. Many of them have had much worse things happen. But, go ahead, continue. I want to hear more," she prodded.

4

UNANSWERED QUESTIONS

My parents never really had "the talk" with me about the birds and the bees. There were instances when they may have mentioned it in a passing conversation, but there was no real, direct discussion about sexuality. During the occasional times I frequented church, I heard very little on the subject. Every once and a while, I did get some bread crumbs about the topic. No one ever talked about the subject. It was avoided like the plague! Maybe adults were just afraid to say some of the words out loud that needed to be said. I, for one, would have appreciated some guidance in the area of physical relationships.

My mom said I accepted Jesus into my heart when I was younger, around age four or five. Continual seeds of Christian beliefs were heavily sprinkled into my heart, causing me to want to do what was right. Although, a real relationship, something deep and concrete with Jesus and the Holy Spirit was missing from my life. I believed Jesus was the Savior, that he died on a cross for me and rose again. I knew the basics and believed the basics, but was that enough? Would that get me into heaven? If someone had asked me, I would say I was a Christian, but I had no remembrance of when or where I had made the decision to accept Jesus into my life.

Like most people, I got excited to celebrate Easter and Christmas. To me, it was a great opportunity to get chocolate, money, and, of course, gifts! We often read the stories from the Bible about Jesus' birth, death, and resurrection, but the central theme in my head for the two wonderful holidays was *presents*: Easter baskets, stockings, chocolate, and lots of presents! I loved it!

Growing up, I did believe that, if I died, I would go to heaven. Although, I definitely didn't want anyone to look to me as an example to follow. My life was far from a good representation of Jesus, I thought. Jesus seemed more like a stranger than someone I actually had a relationship with, just a man out of a book that was written a long time ago. I believed he lived and did good things and that he even died for me, but the idea of it being more than just words on paper was still foreign.

I didn't read my Bible because I had a hard time understanding it. When I was in high school and captain of our cross country team, my dad would often point out verses that were great for athletes like Philippians 4:13: "I can do all things through Christ who strengthens me." As a runner, I also really liked Psalms 18:33 in the Contemporary English Version: "You make my feet run as fast as those of a deer." I would repeat that over and over before a race and while I was racing: "I have feet like the feet of a deer. I have feet like the feet of a deer. I have feet fast like the feet of a deer!" I also gave verses to our team. We all felt like they brought comfort, especially right before a race when our nerves were so jittery. However, I only knew verses like these because my my mom and dad told me about them. I didn't really know how to find them or search them out for myself.

A secret part of me longed to believe that there was more to Christianity. I didn't want it to be shallow. I wanted something real, something that would move me.

What about real life? I had so many questions that no one freely answered, and I was too afraid to ask. I had questions about physical things. Because I knew pre-marital sex was wrong, what else was wrong? Or, better yet, what wasn't wrong? Kissing? Fondling? And, what about oral things? I had never classified that as "sex." According to the Bible, would that fall in the lines of "sex" also?

Though I had many questions, I continued living in the shadowed, hazy bliss called my life. Summers consisted of being at the lake, parties, drinking, hot guys, being intoxicated, and having fun. At this point, I had lost count of who I messed around with at parties. Because I wasn't having sex, I kind of felt like I was still "in bounds."

From my limited Bible knowledge, I knew this: "no sex before marriage." I was resolute to hold out until I was married to have sex. Isn't there something to be said for that? Almost everyone I knew, by this time, had already had sex. Isn't there something to be said for waiting? Shouldn't I save what I considered to be the "major part" for my husband? I was proud of myself for at least that.

But, what about the other stuff? Was it all wrong? Would I look back with regrets when I got married? Would I wish that I had saved everything for him? Would there be any other repercussions from my actions? I had so many unanswered questions. If I could only fast-forward in life and ask the married version of me. Would there ever really be a black and white answer? If there even was a black and white answer, would I ever know about it in time? Was it too late?

Elise grabbed my arm. "So, I can't wait until the end of the story. You've got to tell me now!"

"Tell you what?" I asked.

"Tell me whether you had regrets when you got married? Do you wish you would have saved everything for your husband?"

I sighed a great sigh. I couldn't help but just sit quietly as I thought back to the beginning of our marriage. Just remembering my feelings almost brought tears to my eyes. "Elise, I wish there was an easy way to say it. I wish there was an easy answer. If I could've saved everything—and, I mean *everything* for my husband—I absolutely would go back and change it!"

"Really? Everything?"

"Yes! Everything! Just think about it. Picture the man of your dreams. He's pure and like a knight who rides up on a white horse. He is perfect in every way. He's honorable, handsome, and respectable. He loves you more than words can describe. He loves everything about you. He makes you laugh. He treats you like a princess, buys you your favorite items, is passionate about the Lord, and is intense about studying God's Word. He's your best friend. He makes you better." I watched as Elise's eyes were closed, the corners of her lips turned up as I described this dream man.

"Not only has he been praying for you for years, he's been writing you letters. He's been writing you love letters, even at 16, 17, and 18 years old. As he falls into temptation, instead of giving in to it, he writes you a love letter and pours out his heart instead. He loves you so much that he is saving every part of himself for you. The thing is—with his looks, his personality, his charisma, his athleticism, his business mind—he could get any girl he wanted. He did not save himself for you because of lack of options. Quite to the contrary. Women flock to him and his blue eyes. He saves himself for you. He saves every part of himself because he loves you. Without even knowing you yet, he loves every part of you. God created him to love you. Imagine this man."

Elise's lips were no longer curled up in a smile. Tears were streaming out of the corners of her eyes. She kept her eyes closed. Her nose was squinted up, and she was biting on her lips, trying to cry silently. She couldn't help but put her head down as she rested her hand on her temple and tears flowed.

Elise wiped her eyes. "Do you really think God has someone like this for even me?" she said, almost in a whisper.

"Yes. I do. I know He does. I think God has someone like that for every believer who chooses to wait for His best."

"So, did you ever think about some of the other guys after you got married?" Elise probed further.

"I wish the answer was 'no.' But, I did think about some of them. I hated it when they came in my mind. Even though I was forgiven, I still had not forgotten all of the things I had done with other guys when I was single. I was fairly seasoned in a lot of sexual activities; my husband was not. Granted, as a married couple, you come together and learn each other, what makes each other happy. But, in those earlier years, it was hard for me to not silently compare. I never told my husband, and I never belittled him as he learned, but it was a hard season. I wish with every fiber of my being that we could have both, naively, just learned everything together."

I gritted my teeth, uncomfortable with what I was about to say, but it was a major truth that I wished I could turn back and change. I knew I had to share. "One of my biggest questions before I got married was about whether I would regret oral activities. And, yes, that is a major regret! After experiencing everything marriage has to offer when two become one in the bedroom, a climax is a climax, whether it's from the actual act of sex or through other acts of foreplay. I wish I would've saved every experience for my husband."

I paused.

"Elise, just envisioning this white knight, valiantly riding in to rescue me... I wish I could've saved every kiss for him. He is the most handsome man I have ever met, and he waited for me.

"I wish I had saved it all. All." The heaviness I felt came through my expression. I hoped Elise felt the transparency that was in my heart.

There was a long silence. It was almost hard to jump back into telling my story, but I knew the best was yet to come. Elise motioned with her hand and nodded for me to continue.

The year continued with some challenges. From a school perspective, I had never had this much reading in my life! These professors expected a lot! When did they think a person had time to read as much as they were asking? Not to mention, I had a part-time job at the Soda Shop to help pay for school, and I had obligations because of my cross-country scholarship. College was a bit harder than I anticipated.

It was Monday night. I could no longer take it anymore. How could I do it all?

I picked up the phone to dial the one person who I knew had all the answers.

"Hello?" he said.

"Daddy..." No longer able to hold it in, I burst into tears.

"Emily, what's wrong? What's wrong, honey?"

"Dad, I just don't know how to do it all? I don't know how to get all of this reading done plus studying, working, and running. I just don't know how to get it all done? I have so much reading to do for my history class, and that's just one class. Dad, I just don't know how to do it." My sobs continued with no efforts to control or stop them.

Surely, he knew the answers. He had done it all. He had four children while working full-time *and* attending college, yet he graduated a 4.0 grade point average. If anyone knew how to balance time, he did.

"Aww, Emily. It's going to be okay. It's all about taking breaks. Set your timer to read for 25 minutes and then take a 5-minute break or a 10-minute break if you need to."

My sobs continued while he tried to help.

"Honey, do you want to just come home tonight? I would be happy to help you. Why don't you just come home? Mom will make you some dinner, you can eat during one of your study breaks, and you can sleep in your own room tonight."

Being taken care of by mom, eating her food, and having a little of dad all to myself sounded like just what I needed. I felt a weight lifting off of my shoulders just at the thought of being home. Peaceful. Quiet. Familiar. And, the smell of mom's cooking lingering through the house. I agreed and told him I'd be home in the next 20 minutes.

Walking in the front door, the wafted aroma of home-cooked food settled into the entrance area. My dad greeted me with a hug. "Hey, sweetheart. Glad you are home. Mom is making some dinner for you. Tomato soup and a grilled turkey and cheese sandwich."

"Sounds delicious! Thanks, dad!" I hugged him back, lingering just a moment longer than normal. It was just good to be babied by the two people I loved so much.

Dad grabbed my heavy backpack, "Whoa, this is heavy! What'd you do, put bricks in this bag?" He joked. "Do you want to set up to study downstairs?"

"Yes, that'd be great." The creaking of the stairs as we walked down and the familiar smells of the vanilla air-fresheners that my mom used were more reminders that I was home. I could have my eyes closed and know where I was just from the smells and creaking floors.

I sat on the couch, pulling out my stack of books that I hoped to tackle before heading to bed.

"Okay," my dad started, "Let's begin with the class you need to have finished first. What class is that?"

"My history class for tomorrow," I said. "That's the one with all of the reading."

"Can you show me how much reading you need to have done?" my dad said.

I flipped open the boring book, and showed him the 72 pages that needed to be completed before tomorrow's class and the questions that went along with it. "The hardest part is that it's just so boring. It's so hard not to fall asleep while I'm reading it," I said. The slant in my eyes and glimpse of hopelessness revealed my desperate need for guidance.

"Emily, the key to getting through material like this is to work on a timer. Work in chunks of time. Then, you will have a five- or ten-minute break to look forward to instead of thinking that you have to read for the next five hours straight. You will figure out how long you can work per session. It may be 20, 30, or 40 minutes before you need a break. But, let's start out with 25 minutes. Then, you can take a break to eat and start again. Does that sound good?"

"Yes, that sounds good," I said and then sighed in relief. I was thankful that my dad had a plan for me to complete my piles of work.

He set the kitchen timer on the table for 25 minutes. "I'll be back in a little bit. Also, it's good to have a highlighter while you read, too. Subconsciously, it will help you to stay more alert and pay more attention to what you are reading," he said, handing over a pink and green highlighter. "I'll see you in a little bit with dinner."

The corners of my lips curved up in a forced, half-smile, my eyes staring concretely into my dad's eyes. "Thank you," I said. My heart was so full of gratitude. I didn't know how to fully express what I felt inside.

The timer went off right as I heard the squeaking of the steps and the downstairs door opening. The aroma of food settled into the downstairs before I even saw my dad. Carrying a tray, he had a plate with my grilled turkey and cheese sandwich, a bowl of tomato soup, a side of saltine crackers, and a glass of milk. Mom had even included one of her famous monster cookies for dessert. I loved being home. The freedom of college was great, but it still couldn't beat being home.

Mom was right behind dad. She smiled and said, "Hey, sweetie. We're so glad you're home. You're going to do a great job getting all of your homework done tonight. You can do it. Just let me know if you need anything," she said as she kissed me on the forehead. "I'll be upstairs."

"Okay! Thanks for the dinner, mom! You are the best!"

"So, how'd your reading go?" Dad asked.

"It went really well. The timer actually helped. It helped me to get through the boring parts because I knew the time was ticking down toward my break time."

"Yes, that always helped me. Even just getting up and walking around for a few minutes or walking outside was helpful for a brief change of scenery before biting off the next chunk of time."

The next couple hours flew by as the buzz of the timer provided continual relief. I visited with my parents, took bathroom breaks, and snagged another cookie from the top of the stove. Before going to bed, I had actually completed all of my reading. I felt so proud of myself and thankful that my dad was there to help me conquer the task.

Aside from the challenges of staying on-track academically, I seemed to get myself into more sticky situations with guys. Sure, like most single people, I liked the game of flirting back-and-forth with a guy when there was a mutual connection, an interest. I liked playing hard-to-get. I liked the chase. What did I ultimately want? A guy who, after the "chase" was over and after the "game" was done, would become my exclusive boyfriend. I wanted a best friend in my boyfriend. Someone fun and good-looking. He would be mine, and I would be his.

So began the saga of my freshman flings. My search for this "Mr. Right" led through a trail of many "Mr. Wrongs," starting with one of the college coaches. He was mysterious but very good-looking. He was older, had dark hair, and he had a confidence about him that I was drawn to. He was single, and he had a "position." The "position" made the pursuit much more interesting. The first few weeks consisted of planned, passing "hellos." Because I wasn't on the team he coached, I just wanted to get him to notice me. Then came the mutual flirting until, finally, he asked me if I wanted to come over for pizza and a movie. There, it began. Would he be different? Would I find what I was looking for? A good-looking yet nice, fun guy? No. The uncomfortable progression of the physical caused him to be crossed off of my list.

The string went on. Next was an older guy in his fifth year of college, and he was a high school coach. Our relationship was bland. It was fun at times but too bland.

From him, there was another college coach who was a no-go. He was too calculated and mechanical, not spontaneous and fun enough for me.

Then, a married police officer. Needless to say, I had not found my best friend nor my boyfriend in him either.

All of the guys I dated had a title. Maybe it was their position or what appeared to be power or authority that made me attracted to them? Maybe it was that their position made me feel more secure, like I could be protected. Would I find someone who could and would lead me through life and my unanswered questions? Partially, I knew deep down that I was looking for a man with leadership, confidence, surety, and clarity about where he was going and who he was. Maybe his clarity could rub off on me and help me figure out life, what I wanted to do, what I believed, and where I was going.

Finally, there was a guy who I really enjoyed dating, Ryan. No title, just Ryan. He was fun, spontaneous, attractive, and he had a large build. We partied together. Danced. Laughed. He always smelled good. His cologne I could recognize from anywhere. Ryan always knew what to say to make me laugh. I had finally found him. Ryan was only with me; we were exclusive. For the first time, I was in a relationship that wasn't a secret. Maybe it was because he didn't have a title. We were an official and public item. I liked that we could go out and dance or go to a bar and socialize together. We didn't have to be side-by-side all night to have fun. He could be across the room, catch my attention, and give me a slow wink while the side of his lips would curl up. I loved it! His smile would linger in the air. His eyes were slow to leave our gaze while he continued in the conversation he was having. Then, his eyes would glance back to me several times with a smile while he talked. Clear from across the room, without even words, he had his way of reminding me that he was with me. He always had a way of making me feel special. Even if the bar was filled with pretty girls, he gave them no time of day. It felt good to be secure that we were together. He was the first guy who did not pressure me to do anything I didn't want to do. I really liked him.

My initial season of freshman flings was over. When I could, many nights I spent at Ryan's. I really appreciated that, even though we slept in the same bed, he knew the line. He knew that I did not want to have sex, and he respected that. The fact that he never even tried made me like him even more. He never pushed my head anywhere, nor did he try to coerce me into anything. Because he didn't force me, it caused me to want to please him. From a physical perspective, Ryan basically became my teacher. Many nights, I willingly did things, and he returned the favor.

When it was all said and done, always the next day, I went back to my dorm not feeling violated. For this, Ryan was a blessing.

Ryan and I had a falling out. His drinking began to get out of control. I had never run in circles with people who did drugs. The parties or bars I hung out at did not have heavy drug use. I could easily pick up the smell pot because my campus reeked of pot-heads.

On this night, I snuck up on Ryan and playfully wrapped my arms around him as he stood at the back door of the bar. I noticed the end of an exchange with a guy I had never seen. The small areas of skin that I could see on the dark man were littered with tattoos wrapping around his neck and covering his hands. I could only imagine what I would see if he wasn't wearing a coat. He quickly tucked the zip-lock bag of white contents inside his coat pocket while Ryan's overwhelming stack of large bills was put in his wallet.

Ryan was dealing drugs.

Later on that same night, undercover cops took Ryan to jail for possession. I was shocked and snapped into reality. It was a relatively quiet scene by the side door that led to the alleyway. I could read

Ryan's lips from where I sat and knew he was cussing. I couldn't help but notice his wrists were cuffed behind his back in the confining silver bracelets. My heart raced, not knowing if the cops would take me just because we were dating. Could I be arrested for dating someone who was doing drugs? Dealing drugs? The naivety of my thoughts made my heart race as I saw the second officer searching the bar with his eyes. Was he searching for me? I silently prayed he wasn't. Then, the three left out the back. As they turned, Ryan caught my eye and mouthed, "I'm sorry. I'm so sorry."

For some reason, I knew at that moment that my little fairytale romance with Ryan was over. His mom had bailed him out. From what I found out, it had not been the first time.

He did not call me. I did not call him. It was a mutual knowing. We were over.

5

SOPHOMORE YEAR: A YEAR OF CHANGES

An array of orange, yellow, and red trees painted the Bordeaux campus as a backdrop, indicating that another Pennsylvania fall was upon us. This always has been, by far, my favorite season. Some trees looked as if the very tips had been dipped in sunshine. Taking in a deep breath, I could feel the crisp air in my nostrils, and I could smell the sweet aroma of the burning leaves. I loved walking across campus, hearing the crunching of leaves beneath my feet. Sweatshirt weather and cross-country season were in full-swing, but another load of classes bogged me down with a giant list of things to read. Crossing the grass, I strolled down the sidewalk toward my dorm.

I couldn't help but sometimes be surprised that my college was considered to be a "Christian" University. I didn't know exactly what to expect at a "Christian" school, but it certainly wasn't this. As it turned out, a whole year had passed, and I didn't know even *one* real Christian—at least, none that acted any different than I did. This was a bit disappointing about my college experience so far. If someone was really living out something with passion, such as their Christian faith, wouldn't they act differently? I wanted to see an example in someone. I wanted to be drawn toward something. So far, I was not.

I didn't really miss my freshman year. I didn't miss the parties or the guys, the relationships that seemed meaningless, the bars, or my fake ID that labeled me as "Marie." The blonde hair of her ID picture was helping me get into any bar I wanted. It had now been over a year since I had entered into the "party" scene, and it was starting to seem a bit overrated. Empty. Sure, it was sometimes fun, but I was starting to get bored.

Maybe this year would be different. Maybe this year, I would meet someone awesome or get really focused on running. Maybe I would focus on losing that "freshman 15" that seemed to inch its way around my waist. My desire to excel was there, but "at what?" was the question.

Emili decided not to come back that fall. I missed her. Our friendship wasn't extremely deep, but we had a blast! She took me to the edge. Though I typically just had moments of being "risqué," she lived a life of complete spontaneity! She was always having fun, always the life of the party! If things seemed dull, she would find a way to spice them up. We took wild road trips and visited people we met online. We did stuff that, to most people, was dangerous and unwise. To Emili, it was caution to the wind! At the words, "road trip," she would squeal with delight, and we were off! Thankfully, we never had a bad experience.

New freshman sprinkled onto our dorm floor and added a different flavor of excitement. With a whole new batch of freshmen, the dynamics changed. There was "new cool" arriving. New associations meant a potentially new group of friends. While I was a sophomore, my new roommate, Kelly, was a freshman. I liked her immediately. She was like an undercover cool. People were drawn to her. There was something about her that made girls want to be friends with her. She was laid back but could equally be upbeat and funny. She also had a rare confidence about her. She seemed confident in who she was and didn't try to force fitting in. She didn't get real uptight or allow things to get her stressed. I had never met anyone like her.

Kelly hung out with her sister. Early in the year, they established a whole group of friends who were upperclassmen. Though I hung out with her some, I still felt like I was on the outside, looking in. I didn't totally fit the mold to be "one of them." We went to some parties together that fall, mostly off-campus because this group wasn't into the bar scene.

Going into my sophomore year, my overall feeling was that I wanted it to be different. I did not want to repeat some of the things I did my freshman year. I didn't want to cave in to pressure. I wanted to change me. I didn't want to continue to get in compromising situations with guys, situations of decision. Most often, not only did the situation cause me to take a hit on my own self-image, but I also ended up not liking the guy afterward, either. I was losing hope, for sure. Was my dream guy really out there somewhere? Could he be possible? It surely didn't look like he was here—at least, not at Bordeaux.

Many days, as my afternoon classes would come to an end, I would sit in the bay window of my dorm room, just looking out over the lawn. My music was playing loudly to drown out all of my thoughts. The window was open, allowing me to feel the cool fall breeze and smell the fresh fall air. One of my frequent favorites would blare out of my speakers, Mariah Carey's, "Always Be My Baby." It seemed like such a carefree song. It always made me happy. I inevitably would throw my head back, smile, close my eyes, and just belt out the words like a famous singer.

Certified as a lifeguard during freshman maymester, I now had the joy of waking up early on every Monday, Wednesday, and Friday! I had the the bright-and-early 5:30am shift! That meant I would need to roll out of bed by about 5:15, giving me enough time to throw on my swimsuit, grab my whistle and guard tank-top, put on my comfy shorts, and begin my walk over to the REC Center.

As I arrived, I was often greeted by several little old ladies who were waiting for the door to be unlocked so they could warm up for their 5:45am water aerobics class. With their sweet little smiles and their grey hair tucked under sleek swim caps, they always made me smile, despite the early mornings.

Sometimes, Lydia, the instructor, would beat me to the pool. Short, stocky, and twice my age, she would begin getting everything out and ready for the one-hour class. Lydia was always pleasant but was not overly zealous or talkative in the morning either. Though it was almost ungodly early for a college student to get up, my thought was that I needed money. If I didn't take the morning shift, I would just sleep. So, I might as well wake up and make some money. Right? The three and a half hours at the pool would come and go. The hardest job was to not fall asleep in the guard chair! I didn't make a ton of money, but it would at least help pay for some of my tuition that my cross-country and track scholarships didn't cover.

Still undecided on a major, I enrolled in one of my required classes to get it checked off of the list: "American Religion." Like most classes, it was pretty boring. Strewn into the weekly lectures, Dr. Stevens talked about the importance of diversity and acceptance. Something about it all just didn't sit well with me, but I wasn't quite sure why. Partially, I felt he seemed to be missing the point. How could we accept everyone else's religion and be tolerant of their beliefs and lifestyles if those very things seemed to go against the Bible? How do you just accept it all? Isn't a Christian supposed to stand out and be firm about what the Bible says? This is, at least, what I thought good Christians should be doing.

One afternoon that fall, Dr. Stevens gave us an interesting assignment. The assignment was to visit a church two times that was outside of our own denomination and write a paper on it. Okay. That didn't seem too hard.

My family went to a "Missionary Church." Not knowing the differences between denominations, I assumed that my church was similar to a Baptist or Methodist church.

I had heard of a church that my cousin had visited, which was a non-denominational church. According to my logic, it seemed like there would be less politics in a church that was not under the umbrella of a denomination. I decided to visit that church and use it as the subject of my paper. Surely, it would be different than the cultural awareness chapels we had each week!

My parents were pretty smart when it came to the Bible. They were married very young, and they married quickly. They dated only two weeks before my dad brought my mom home and introduced her to his parents. "Mom," he said, "I want to introduce you to the woman I'm going to be marrying next weekend." Needless to say, my grandmother cried and cried. She was devastated. Her football and track superstar was turning down all of his scholarship offers to get married to a woman she did not even know.

My parents were in a hurry to marry, not because they were pregnant, but because they thought Jesus was coming back soon.

They thought his return was coming so quickly that they wanted to experience having children and a family before being whisked away to heaven in the rapture. At 18 and 19 years old, not only did they get married, they began a family. They had four kids by the time they were 23 and 24. Ashley, Emily (me), Kate, and Jacob. The church they attended was intense. Not only were we all born at home, we didn't celebrate the hype of Christmas or go to doctors.

They attended Greek and Hebrew classes at church weekly, which helped them to study the Bible in its original language. I thought of my dad as a genius! He knew so much about the Bible. I could just ask him a question about where a verse was or what the Bible said about a topic, and by pure memory, he'd whip out the verse's location. I was amazed!

My parents had some amazing experiences, seeing people healed, miracles of crippled people walking, and a ton of other stuff!

After a church split when I was only five years old, they stopped attending that church. For the first time since being married, my parents were free. They became free to begin making their own decisions and experience life. They began celebrating Christmas, going to doctors, having us kids actually attending school, and getting vaccines—things they had never done before. It seemed like, along with the split, came a lot of hurt feelings, pain, and frustration. This began the path of our family drifting in and out of churches for what seemed like the next 10 years.

For me and my siblings, growing up in church consisted of sitting quietly on the grass floor of the big tent where we attended. My siblings and I learned bits and pieces about God, but we most definitely learned how to sit quietly.

I would classify my sisters and brother as Christians. My parents recalled all of us having salvation experiences very early. Though, we definitely weren't a group of "goody-goody" kids like others we knew in high school. I wondered if a person could be a Christian, an athlete, and popular all at the same time. None of us represented that combination though. We were athletes, involved and popular, but none of us lived a Christ-like life.

My first visit to this new church for my assignment was in mid-November. I was wowed! As they began to enter into a time of praise and worship, it was different than any church I had visited. The atmosphere in the room was full and heavy. At the same time, it was light and filling.

Being in the presence of the singing, the words, and the feelings, my heart was being captivated. I had never experienced this kind of high, this kind of simple happiness. My only comparison was partying. Many times, I had gotten a buzz from socially smoking a cigarette or had gotten drunk; this feeling was similar yet so different. It was all of the good without the guilt. I had never felt this feeling before. It was hard to explain, but my heart was experiencing something for which I had longed. I was experiencing something deeper than any relationship I had ever experienced, and the pastor had not even begun to talk.

I did not realize this church would cause me to feel so vulnerable. I had been looking for something for so long. For over a year, I had been blindly searching for something deeper. Every guy was just proving that a human relationship between two selfish people would fail every time. I admit. I had been vain, selfish, manipulative, and deceitful. I had all of these traits, but, deep down, I just wanted to be good. I wanted to be a good person.

Until entering into that time of praise and worship, I didn't know my heart was this fragile with a desire for wholeness. Whatever these people had, I already knew that I wanted it. I had never experienced anything like this, but I knew that it was God. I knew the atmosphere was one that had ushered in the very presence of an Almighty God.

The pastor said, "Whether you have never accepted Jesus as your Lord, or maybe you have backslid and fallen into a life of sin… tonight is for you. No matter what sin, what mistakes, the Lord will forgive you!"

The flow of tears began down my cheeks as I sat silently, listening. How could a God so good and so big forgive me of all I had done? Would he really do that for me?

The pastor continued, "As far as the East is from the West, your Father in heaven will forgive you. Once you accept His forgiveness, He will forget what you did. It will be as if it never even happened.

You may feel dirty now, but Jesus Christ went to the cross for *you* so your sins would be forgiven. He went to the cross. He bore the pain and suffering. He shed His blood so that you could receive Him as your Savior and be saved. The blood of Jesus will cover that sin, wash it away, and you will be white as snow. No more dirtiness. Jesus Christ will fill that place in your heart where there has been a void. He will fill that emptiness. Will you receive Jesus today as your Savior?"

How could this pastor have possibly known all of this? I felt like he was talking directly to me.

"If everyone could close their eyes and bow their heads, we are going to pray. I would like everyone to repeat after me. Let's pray, 'Lord Jesus, I ask you to forgive me of my sins. I confess with my mouth that Jesus is Lord and that he died for me. I believe in my heart that God raised Jesus from the dead. And, I thank you that because of this, I am saved!'

The pastor continued, "If you just confessed that for yourself, congratulations! You are a new creation and now you are saved. Let's rejoice together." Then, the whole congregation began clapping, cheering, whooping, and hollering like I had only heard at a football game. It seemed extremely awkward but, in a way, very exciting.

The prayer seemed so simple. I may have done that when I was little, but it was nice to know that now, today, I was sure. I didn't feel butterflies in my stomach or anything. I didn't see any lights shining down from heaven like a spotlight but, I did feel happy. My heart felt better. Though I had not forgotten my past, I was thankful that the pastor said God had forgotten it, that now I was white as snow. He said I could leave here and not feel dirty, but could I really do that? He said God would forget, but could I forget?

Despite the questions that still raced through my head, I knew things would be different now. I knew that my reputation would not change overnight. I knew that I had created an image and would now have to consistently "walk the walk" for people to think differently about me, for people to know that I had changed.

Over the next few weeks, I found out that there was a "Campus Ministries" department on my campus. I learned about small group Bible studies and quickly became a part of one that met every Sunday night. The group I was a part of had only 10-15 people, but I was just happy to be with people who seemed different. These people seemed so few on campus.

As I attended each week, I could see that they were real. Mallory had a real heart for Jesus; she had a real heart to draw closer and know Him more.

Victoria, even though she stressed about her grades, had a passion to be different; she wanted to be a light on the campus. She wanted to share the love of Jesus. She wanted other people to know that there was more to life.

Then, there was Max. Max was a tall guy. It seemed like he could've played basketball if he wasn't so clumsy. Max loved the Lord. He wanted to set an example. He wanted to stand out. He often invited people to join our Bible study.

Peter was bold. Peter was good-looking. Hiding underneath his t-shirt were outlined indentions of what looked like a solid, six-pack of abs, squared-off shoulders, and a back indicated he could lift a lot of weights. He was six feet tall. His chiseled jaw line, crystal green eyes, and wavy brown hair made him officially an eye-catcher. Not to mention, he had a smile that looked like it "cost a lot of money in braces" or were perfectly, God-given straight white teeth. Sure, I was a Christian now, but I wasn't blind. Let's be honest. He was a hottie. It was encouraging that Peter loved Jesus, and it was good to know that at least one good-looking guy on this planet existed in this small species of Christians! How refreshing. I had hope.

Each week, we would come together and sing worship songs. It was amazing to hear all of the voices. It was wonderful to look across our group of people and see my new friends raising their hands in the air as they sang to Jesus, seeing them close their eyes and wanting to keep their focus on Him. I heard not only female voices but also the baritone sound of the men in our Bible study. Every week made me want to know Jesus even more. Every week, I had a greater desire to learn, read, and be a witness for Jesus.

I knew there had to be so many people on campus who shared the same void that I had felt for so long, people who were filling their void with relationships, partying, or sports. I knew there were people who would rather have what I had now. I wanted to be a light to lead them to what I now had.

6

EMOTIONALLY VULNERABLE

My Junior Year. This year, I moved from the dorms to back home with my parents. I had experienced the "college" life, the dorm life, and I was satisfied. I had made friends. Now, I would just take advantage of being able to save money and live with my parents, not to mention that they only lived five minutes from campus.

Fall brought with it my least favorite class, Accounting. I didn't really enjoy the equations and balance sheets. It just didn't make sense to me. The accounting class was in one of the REC Center classrooms. That worked out well because I spent so much of my time at the REC Center. Between cross-country, track, weight training, the off-season training, and life-guarding at the indoor pool, the REC Center seemed like a second home to me.

Class began. I made my way to the second row, far-right side. The class wasn't too big, maybe only 30 students. Two guys sat caddy corner behind me to the right. I recognized them but did not know them. They were underclassmen. Soon after class began, the professor asked us to split up into groups of 4. These groups of 4 would be study groups that we would utilize throughout the semester. Jessica and I turned around to scan the room and ended up locking eyes with two guys, Matt and Rick. We all nodded in agreement that the four of us would work together.

That was my first time meeting Rick. Without him saying a word, I could tell he was cocky. His beach blonde hair fell at his shoulders as he flipped it to the side. Looking more like he belonged in California than Pennsylvania, he was pretty. He appeared just a bit over six feet tall. Though his build was small, he walked tall. In the way he strode into the class and sat down, you could tell he did not lack a positive self-image. He puffed his chest out and pulled his shoulders back. His confident arrogance and edgy surfer long hair won him points with most people. He was so sure of himself. He immediately gave off the impression that he was a "bad boy," but he won you over with a "good boy" charm. He already proved that he was a *major* suck-up to the professor. It was evident that part of his "good grades" came from his ability to sweet-talk his professors. He turned on a quietly provocative smile and, by the blush of our married accounting professor, it was obvious his luring had made her feel beautiful and sexy. He made her feel that bit of "danger," living on the edge by having a cute college student flirt with her. Some call it manipulation. Some call it brown-nosing. Either way, he sure was able to talk his way into being our professor's friend.

The four of us began meeting a few nights a week to finish our accounting homework. Most of the time, we met in Rick's room because he didn't have a roommate. Sitting around his coffee table on the floor, we would each finish a problem and check it with each other's answers. It was a good thing Jessica was in our group. She was definitely the smartest of all of us. I was comforted knowing she was a Christian, too. She acted different, and it was refreshing to be around someone who I could tell had important values.

Day after day, my cross-country cool-down inevitably came to a completion at Rick's dorm room. My quick "drop-in" to see if our study group was meeting later that night sometimes turned into an hour or more visit. At this point, the only cell phone I had ever seen was that of a girl on the fourth floor who had a bag phone. Dorm phones were hit-or-miss in regard to people actually answering them. If I stopped by, I would be able to catch him if he was in a neighboring room or in the hallway. If it was just Rick in his room, our conversations ranged from school to classes—sometimes even about Jesus! He usually laughed when I talked about my Bible study, but I would invite him anyway. Something inside me just wanted him to come. He seemed like the impossible person. If he ever got saved, it would seem like a miracle! Right now, he was already so manipulative and such a salesman that, if he got saved, I was sure he could sell people right into a relationship with Jesus!

Rick and I were spending a lot of time together, and the countless hours seemed to continue deepening our relationship. As I would tap on the door, Rachel may come to the door, never very happy to see me as she flipped back her long blonde hair. She was "kind of" Rick's girlfriend. She was short, only around 5'4". Her long golden hair with bouncy, big curls hit the middle of her back. Her tan complexion was another reminder of what made her appear perfect as her penetrating hazel eyes met with mine the moment I stepped into the room. Jealous a little, she looked like a miniature version of Barbie, the perfect figure included. I wasn't sure how people like her could stay so skinny because I knew she didn't workout. She knew we were accounting partners and would smile like she didn't mind my presence, but we all knew that she was not a fan of me. Maybe it was the way Rick looked at me or our friendship that started to go deeper than any of us wanted to admit. I would definitely say to anyone that we were just friends, that I was not a threat to Rachel, but even I knew that things between Rick and I were beginning to get very different.

In some regards, I chose to stay different. I was one of those "Christians," and they were both partiers. I did not drink. I was not in a "relationship." I didn't even "mess around" with guys anymore. They did not even know the "old" me, I had a clean slate with them. I had stayed pretty PG for over a year since I had recommitted my life to Christ.

They both, on the other-hand, had this "image" to uphold. Rick drove a black Ford Expedition, and Rachel had a matching black, new, opulent Range Rover Jeep. They did fit well together. But, here I was, the unlikely, but somehow quickly becoming an irreplaceable friend. It's weird to even be called a friend because I was not a normal friend.

It was 11:30pm, and open dorm visiting hours had ended. This meant no one of the opposite sex was allowed on the floor. Rick and I set up our books in the study lounge just outside his floor.

"Let's hurry up and finish this accounting. You do this one," he said, pointing to the second-to-last question. "And, I'll do the last one." We sat on the floor, leaning against the carpeted wall of the study lounge. We were the only people in the small room, and the lights of his floor were now dark. Moments flew by as we worked in silence, each penciling out how we were coming to a conclusion for our answers.

My debit and credit columns of my paper began to fill up. I listed out accounts receivable, accounts payable, cash, supplies, and withdrawals. My brain was beginning to cap out. Keeping all of these numbers separate and trying to keep them in the proper columns often got confusing to me.

"Are you done?" he asked.

"Yes, I think I have it right," I said as I jotted my last number down.

We skimmed through both questions and discussed how we got to our conclusions. Neither of us claimed to be real accounting experts, but we were confident enough in our answers to call it quits for the night, so we closed our books.

"So, I have my Bible study coming up on Thursday night. Just wanted to make sure you have that on your calendar?" I half joked.

At Rick's hearty laugh, I couldn't help but laugh myself, "Uhhh, yah. Let me make sure I put that down. I definitely don't want to miss learning about the Bible because it is top on my list. *Is!*" he repeated, pushing hair out of his eyes, his voice of complete sarcasm as he emphasized *is*.

"Well, Rick, it should be! What if you died today? If you don't accept Jesus into your life, you'll spend forever in hell," I reminded him.

"I know, I know. It's something that I plan to do sometime, I just don't think I'm ready to give up my life right now to live the straight and narrow," he said, making arm movements like a robot. His face showed droopy eyes and a bored facial expression. "I mean, really, I couldn't party then and, you know, I probably couldn't keep all of my girlfriends if I became a Christian." He winked with a chuckle. "I know it's been a good thing for you, and I'm really happy for you, but I'm just not sure about all the Jesus stuff yet for me. Maybe one day, if you keep bugging me about it," he said, half serious.

The tilt of my head and raise of my eyebrows told him I didn't think that was a good answer.

"No, for real, Emily! I'm sure I'll make the decision sometime. I actually do enjoy you telling me about all the Jesus stuff."

"I guess I'll have to keep bugging you about it then. As good of a job as you did selling Professor Ravens on a shorter accounting assignment, I'm sure you would be a great salesperson with Christianity!"

"I must say, though, I do wish I would've known you before you were a Christian," he said, raising his eyebrows up and down in an attempt to give me a sexy look and a cheeky smirk.

I just shook my head.

"I talked to my little brother today."

"Oh yeah," I said. "What's going on with him?"

"Well, he was actually telling me about my parents buying two more locations for one of their businesses."

"That's exciting! What kind of business do they own?"

"They own a tax assessment business which has four locations. They also own a chain of ice cream franchises. Until today, they had six locations. According to my brother, I guess they have eight now. I usually run two or three of the ice cream stores in the summer. You know me, I love bossing people around," he laughed. "And my brother was just telling me about his new truck! He was bragging to me about the tires he bought to go on it. He knows how much I like my Expedition, so he had to poke at me a little because his tires and rims are now better than mine."

I merely smiled. I was thankful for my used orange Camry, but it certainly wasn't new or even close to it. It definitely didn't compare to his shiny, black Expedition with all the chrome detailing.

"Well, good for your brother. Knowing you and how everything is a competition, I'm sure it won't be long before you have nicer tires than he does," I chided, poking at his ego. We both knew it was true. "So, what else about your parents? Your life? Did they always own businesses?" I asked.

"Yes, since I was young. I worked at most of the locations growing up, so I learned a lot about running businesses. That's how they bought the lake house and the Florida house. My brother and I, at times, have had to work like dogs for them though, so it hasn't always been that great for a teenage kid. But, I guess we have enjoyed the benefits, finally being able to spend a lot of time on the lake in the summer. Driving around in a boat, meeting hot chicks, is the way to do it." Snapping his fingers and moving his head back and forth, Rick laughed at his own joke like he was all that!

"Aren't you just the god to all the lakers?!" I said with sarcasm filling my comment.

"Yes, thank you! I know. I have to turn so many people down. It's rough, but someone's gotta do it! Ha!"

The next hour flew by as we talked more about his brother and family businesses, the large high school he went to, and why he chose Bordeaux University to attend school. Why would a non-Christian come to a Christian University, other than having sports scholarships like me? He was far from the athletic type! He explained how the law program drew him to this college. Also, he thought that a degree from Bordeaux would look good for helping him get into the Masters program he already planned to complete at Stanford.

Looking at my watch, I stood up. It was already 1:45am. I needed to get home. "Well, hey, hate to break up the party, but I really need to get going."

"Ahhhh Emily, why don't you just stay here tonight," he stood up, drawing closer to me, trying to keep me from putting all of my books in my bag. "I have two beds in my room. You can sleep in one of them."

I grinned. His convincing eyes pierced me, telling me that it was surely a good idea to stay. As I was leaning against the wall, he continued his pitch. "Really, Emily, it's not a big deal at all. The bed is all made and everything. It's so late and cold out right now. Just stay."

He drew himself closer to me, closing his eyes until I could feel his breath on my face. As he leaned in closer, I turned my head, and his lips grazed the side of my cheek.

"See, that's why I can't stay in your room!"

He laughed and shrugged his shoulders as if the joke was on me. "All right, suit yourself if you want to go out in this cold, but I have a nice warm bed waiting in there," he motioned his hand toward the hallway that led to his room.

"Well, I don't think so. We both know I'm not at the top of Rachel's list anyway, and this would really put me on her bad list!"

"She doesn't have to know! I promise."

I finished putting my things in my bag, "Goodbye, Rick." I said with definiteness. "I'm sure I will see you sometime tomorrow."

"Okay," he said with no sign of defeat on his face, still only arrogance, like he was somehow in control, and my denial was just part of his plan to get my buy-in next time.

The more time we spent together, the more intertwined we became in each other's lives. Rachel knew it. She knew she may be Rick's "girlfriend," but I was the one who, deep down, he was tied to. I was the one he was drawn to. Our friendship was so hard to explain, but everyone saw right through it. Rick's friends knew we were more than friends, despite what we said or did. I would overhear Wayne in his dorm room across the hall saying, "Rachel may have the looks, the money, and the image that Rick wants… but Emily has his heart. Emily has him." We all knew that was true. I knew it. Even Rachel, she knew it. If she ever brought me up, brought my name into things, or acted like she didn't like him spending time with me, he would defend me. He would threaten to break up with her. And because "we" weren't together, there was no need for them to break up.

From a Christian perspective, I could tell our relationship had become unhealthy. I was getting more and more drawn to him. We had so many classes together, which meant lots of opportunities to work together on projects and homework. But, it remained that I was a Christian. He was not, but our hearts had become *so* intertwined. It was as if a steel cord tied us together, almost as if we were one. As if our hearts beat together. As if our breaths were breathed together. We were more "one" than I had ever known what "one" could be. We were so intimate without experiencing intimacy. We had given to each other in such a full way that no one could separate us. It filled my lungs. It filled my breath.

I still went to my weekly Bible study, but it now felt like my heart was competing between Rick and God. I was constantly drawn to his room. When we were tired, we had even taken a few naps together. It seemed like we were crossing all lines of what was acceptable— not because of Rachel. She had no bearings on our thoughts at all.

What made it feel like we were crossing lines was my relationship with Jesus, something I held close, but he did not. We'd lay on the top bunk, Rick behind me, his arms wrapped around me, rhythmically breathing on my neck. Steady, slow, deep breaths. His breath was warm on my neck. It was like warning signals were shooting off inside me saying, "Danger! Leave! Danger! Leave!" It was dangerous. It felt dangerous. I laid there knowing, if I would let him, he would take me over. All the feelings of my days and nights with Ryan could and would come flooding back; I was sure. I did not doubt that Rick was extremely talented in the areas of foreplay and arousal. His breathing alone on my neck was in itself a sense of foreplay. I don't know that I ever fell asleep during one of our naps. I just laid there, loving it, and hating it, knowing that I should leave. I knew that he was gradually pulling back the drapery of my, once, very protected heart. If I continued to allow him in, I would most definitely come to a crossroad that would be very difficult. A crossroad of decision. I still had not gotten there, but the bars of my heart were being moved.

Rick told me that his name in the dictionary was defined as "powerful and rich." Oddly enough, it had seemed like an accurate description. Even though I had denied his many attempts to kiss me, part of me did think he held a little bit of power over me. That made me nervous.

My internal struggle of wanting to give in to him and wanting to stay strong was becoming overwhelming. I knew I should not be thinking this. I was living a new life! I was a born-again Christian. I was walking with the Lord. I was leading a Bible study now. I had started and was the president of our university's Fellowship of Christian Athletes (FCA). I was a leader. I was a Christian. I now had a Christian image to uphold.

I had not given in yet. I could still technically say, "No, we haven't kissed. No, we haven't 'done' anything." In my heart of hearts, I knew where we had gone had almost been more dangerous than the countless "kisses" I had experienced during my early college flings. Though I did not know what it was like, it almost felt like our relationship was like sex. Deeper than sex. Without the touching. Emotionally, we were so deeply intertwined, so connected, protective, obsessed. It was hard to imagine that sex could go much deeper. Could it? The thought of sex often seemed like a very shallow act with little emotional connection. But, then again, that could just be my preconceived notion from watching Julia Roberts in the movie, *Pretty Woman*.

Each night, after leaving from being with Rick, my drive home would be torturous. As I got in my car, it would almost be inevitable that our song would come on. It played all the time, constantly sounding through the radio stations, coffee houses, and the halls of the university's post office. Savage Garden's "Truly Madly Deeply." At the first beat into the song, I would know. I would sigh deeply as my hands grasped the steering wheel, and I would just shake my head. Rick was beginning to be a constant thought in my mind. He constantly made his place there, ringing, reminding, and calling me to come. To be near him. Yes, he continued to live his life. I tried to continue to live mine, but my brain, lately, had very little free time without him in it.

The second semester was upon us. Late nights of projects and study groups would often bring me pulling in to my parent's house at the wee hours of the morning. After we were done studying, Jessica, Matt, Rick, and I would linger for a short time. The dynamics of our group were always entertaining. Rick would stand up, pull his shoulders back, pretending to point to people, "Hey, you need to do this and this and this. Yes, I need it done now!" He would bark as though he were the "invisible" people's boss. We would laugh because the silly solo role-play fit him so well. I did not doubt that he would be the boss of a lot of people one day. He loved telling people what to do.

Jessica would inevitably wrap it up, having no reason to stick around with the group. Matt, Rick, and I would goof around for a while longer, joking about something or talking about how the basketball team was doing.

Matt played guard. His looks were actually much more my speed. He had a very solid build, just shy of six feet tall. His shoulders were broad, and you could see his muscles through his t-shirt. His jaw-line was squared, and he had blue eyes, short blonde hair, and a basketball player's spike. He was very attractive. If only I were attracted to him, surely my life would be easier. I bet he would not have such a resistance toward Jesus, toward getting saved, and toward this worthy life-change. Shortly following Jessica, Matt would leave. Rick and I would remain. Just us. 2:00am. We would talk. I would most likely be sitting on the floor, leaning against the couch, my legs under the wooden coffee table.

The discussion began again about Jesus. Though often short, it always ended at the same place: "I just don't know that I'm ready to do what you talk about: 'giving my life to Jesus.' I do think it's interesting though. You are definitely the strongest person I know."

We would continue to talk, some serious conversation, some light. Not really having to leave, I would begin to get up and start packing up my things. How long would it take me to leave this time? My best friend, Rick, standing up to hug me would say, "You can just stay. Why don't you just stay here instead of driving home. I'll wake you up in the morning." As we were leaning against the corner of the bunk-beds, "You can sleep with me. I promise. I won't do anything!"

We both laughed, and, immediately, I replied, "No, I need to go home." Rick hugged me, my best friend who had somehow come to own part of what seemed to be my soul. It had gotten to the point where his embrace made my body warm and limp. The familiar goodbye routine of a long hug, which led to a playful kiss on my neck and countless attempts to kiss me.

Everything inside me wanted to stay. Rick was different. We were "unequally yoked," like the Bible describes. The daily, weekly, and monthly emotional foreplay left me wanting him in ways I had given up, in ways that I decided to forgo because of my new relationship with Jesus. My relationship with Rick was supposedly founded as an opportunity to share Jesus with him, to draw him in to know the Jesus I knew. I wanted Rick to know Jesus, to accept Him, and to go to heaven one day. My initial valiant attempts to minister were getting dwarfed.

I wasn't sure if he was any closer to that decision, but one thing that I knew was that Jesus was slowly being put on my back burner. Though we would talk about Jesus often, I could already tell that I was fighting in a losing battle. I started to notice that, lately, the still small voice that I had only known for a little over a year was becoming more and more faint. I was becoming too weak. Something would have to change and soon.

7

HEART STRINGS

Track season was upon us. I was beginning to train for my junior-year season. Indoor season would grace us with the fast laps around the short track, such a different experience than running on the normal, long, outdoor track. It definitely was nice to stay inside during those cold, snowy days! Not having to bundle up and brave the cold to plod our way up and down the side streets of my university town was nice. It would warm up soon, and then the outdoor season would begin, and the shortness of our indoor meets would come to an end.

If I could just hit some of my times, I would qualify for indoor nationals. I was clipping along around a 2:22 for my 800-meter run, and my 1500 was a moderately quick 4:53. It would be great to pull both of those times down for a personal record. Though, the curves of the indoor track were a bit tighter, and there were more of them, I wasn't sure that the indoor season would bring me to breaking my PRs. The 3 ¾ laps on the outdoor track would equal 7 ½ laps on the indoor track for my 1500. It was just different running inside. The air was stale and warm, always smelling of chlorine because of the adjoining indoor pool. Lap after lap, some fast, some moderate, we would make our way around the track, peering down into the gymnasium as the softball team avoided the bitter cold, practicing indoors as well.

I was beginning to go back-and-forth about my relationship with Rick. It was no longer a question of whether it was healthy. It was not. It was almost as if people would get out of the way when I was coming. They knew that their interruptions with Rick would not stand if I was around, not because I was going to stop them, but because Rick would ensure that no one messed with me.

Rachel and her best friend, Elisabeth, would often leave when I got there. I would get to the door and hear Rachel, Liz, and Rick laughing inside. When I would tap on the door and walk in, Rachel would say, "Oh, hey, Emily," with a monotoned, unenthusiastic voice. She would then say, "We were just getting ready to leave." With a tilt of her head, her blonde locks perfectly styled, she glanced passed me, turning to Rick, she'd say, "We'll see you later." With that, they both disappeared out of the room, not challenging my being there, nor challenging anything about me.

That was totally cool with me. Rachel knew what would happen if she raised a fuss as she did during the previous semester. Rick had grabbed Rachel's arm and pulled her out into the hall. "Do you have a problem? Because Emily is my friend, and if you have a problem with it, you can leave! You don't have to come around if you are going to have an attitude!" The "not-so-quiet" conversation in the hall told everyone who was near where Rick stood about me and Rachel. Rachel, as always, chose to keep their relationship. She didn't like my relationship with Rick, but she didn't want to lose Rick. Rick and I were so fully connected that not even his girlfriend could separate us.

Aside from telling each other everything, the fact that he could not or had not "conquered" me probably had something to do with Rick being so into me. Rick wanted to win at everything and would not stop until he did. If manipulation was needed, he would use any trick in the book to come out on top. I don't think he had ever lost in the game before. If he had his sights on a girl, I'm sure in all his past relationships, he would find a way to win. The sweet talk would begin. His eyes and his half-smile had a way of piercing you and pulling you in to want to experience the danger or the fun. Whatever was behind the eyes, whatever was behind the smile, it pulled you in to want to partake like forbidden waters. Rick always won.

Well, he had not fully won with me. He had my heart in an unusual way. He had my friendship, but he had not won me physically. Even in my party days, even when I had strayed away from my walk with the Lord, even despite the actions of close friends, I somehow had kept this resolve that I wanted to wait until I was married to have sex. Just that act. Sex. Was sex really what everyone made it out to be? Was it really something that great? Unfortunately, in my long resolve to remain a virgin, oral activities had not been part of my *pact* to myself.

In the back of my head, I had this eerie feeling that, if I allowed myself to be more to Rick, he very well could be like the others—maybe not immediately, but I felt like it would eventually come. He would get bored. After dwelling in his victory of accomplishment, what more would there be in the game, in the chase? I would just be like Rachel. A won game. A trophy that he could show off. I wasn't quite the trophy material as Rachel—at least, I didn't think so.

I felt very average. Maybe it was the fact that I was not the girl that came from a wealthy family like Rachel. She always was wearing something new, something that surely didn't come from re-sale shops. Daddy's credit card allowed her to get the things she needed or wanted while at college. Of course, "clothes" would most surely fit into the "need" category. I, on the other-hand, either looked sporty or grungy. Sometimes, I would wear baggy or loose-fitting jeans, an untucked button-up shirt with a tank, or some other shirt that not only came from the sale racks, it came from the "already owned and worn" racks of a consignment shop. A lot of college students shopped at the consignment shops around town. We were broke. Well, at least, most of us were.

I reasoned with myself that the only thing I had on Rachel was my virginity. Once that was gone, I anticipated my days with Rick would soon be over. The *game* or the *chase*, the *challenge* of trying to conquer someone would be over. I would be won. Like a trophy or prize on a mantel, Rick would have the satisfaction of winning over my God. After that, who knew how much longer our relationship would continue. I knew we needed to part ways, but I didn't want to do it on those terms, on the terms of losing my virginity and being an "old shoe" tossed aside. I wanted to do it on the terms of making the right choice. I knew that I would eventually have to make a choice. I just wasn't quite ready to do that yet. Our friendship and relationship had me so intertwined. I breathed Rick. I woke up thinking about Rick. I went to bed thinking about Rick. My life was most definitely consumed. I believe his, in a lot of ways, was equally so.

8

SPIRITUAL BRICK

Running from my car to the inside of the REC Center, I was life-guarding on yet another early morning. I surely would not miss the cold or snow! Because I didn't snow ski much anymore, I had no real use for all of this cold weather—especially when Christmas was already over, and there was no reason for the "festive white wonderland." During this time of winter, February and March, it was starting to get ugly. You could see the brown, dirty snow piling up, the snow-plows pushing it into an even bank, lining the road.

At the close of my shift, I planned on doing a little cross-training. I'd swim about a mile. That might take 30 minutes. It always seemed that swimming was one of the best ways for me to lose weight. I surely didn't want to do "extra" running right now. Outside was too cold, and the indoor track was too hot.

Hopping in the pool with my swim cap and goggles on, I looked at my stopwatch, reset it, and hit "start." Here goes! With my arms straight out, my right hand laying flat over the left, and my head cupped between my arms, I pushed hard off the wall with my legs and kick, kick, kick, kick! Stretching my body out as long as I could, I began. Right arm. Left arm. Right arm. Breathe. Right arm. Left arm. Right arm. Breathe. The rhythmic, steady sound of swimming. The constancy of breathing. Before becoming a Christian, my mind would just wander to any old thing. Classes, guys I thought were good-looking, parties, the bar scene, friends, family, what seemed like the aimless attempt to get skinny. My mind just went all over the place. Now that I was a Christian, most mornings when I swam, I would attempt to pray. I would attempt to see if God had anything to say to me. I hadn't really mastered the art of having a "conversation" with God yet, but I did experience a few times when I felt like He did talk to me.

I began to pray about the summer. During the last three summers, I had worked for a marketing company. Believe it or not, I sold knives! I definitely became a believer! They were, for sure, the best knives I had ever used. During my first summer with the company, I was a sales rep. It was totally referral-based as far as appointments went. I wasn't too thrilled about that, but I managed to do well.

During my second summer, I became an assistant manager. At that point, I started helping with classes and training. I liked doing this. I enjoyed teaching people tips and how to do things, good ways to word sales approaches or get referrals. I did some selling during my second summer and finished my total personal sales somewhere around $25,000.

Then, during the last summer, I was a branch manager. I opened up my very own office. Despite the hesitancy of my parents, I went ahead and did it. I had to find an office location, a place to live, and office furniture, and then I had to begin the advertising campaign to bring in sales reps for the summer months. My office was open from May through the beginning of September. It did really well. As a whole office, we did around $100,000 in sales. Not too bad for the first summer.

Right. Left. Right. Breathe. "Well, God," I prayed, "what should I do this summer? You know I had some bad experiences with that manager. I'm totally grossed out. How can I go back to work when I would have to answer to him? I could most likely live with Mary Catherine again. That was a pretty good experience. I just don't feel like it, God. For some reason, I don't feel like that is what I'm supposed to do. If I don't do that, what then?" I asked hypothetically, not expecting an answer. I didn't really know He was listening. If He was, I didn't know if He would talk back to me.

Then, like a giant-sized brick falling onto my stomach, I felt as if I was going to sink to the bottom of the pool. I heard His suggestion: "What about going on a mission trip?"

Would I choke, swallowing the contents of the pool? "A MISSION TRIP?!" I protested, "I'm not the mission trip type! God, you know me! I used to be a big partier! God, I messed around with a lot of people in my past. I had a fake ID and went to bars a lot.

God, I'm not the 'mission trip' type. Not to mention, this weird friendship I'm currently in," I argued.

Right. Left. Right. Gasp for air. Right. Left. Right. Gasp for air. I could not believe the very idea. I knew it must have been God because I would not have thought up that idea in a million years! A mission trip?! Was He serious?

I finished my swimming, toweled off, showered, and left the locker room. As I made my way down the hall to leave, I noticed something on the track and field bulletin board that I had never seen before. It was a poster. At a quick glance, I saw different pictures of sports teams competing. Football, volleyball, basketball, soccer, track, drama, and cheerleading. The top of the poster read, "ATHLETES OUTREACH FOR CHRIST." The subtitle said, "Have you thought about a Mission Trip this summer? Come with AOC to one of the following places: England, Ireland, Scotland, Czech Republic, Russia, France, South America."

I could not believe what I was seeing! If that wasn't a clear enough sign, I did not know what was, but the whole idea of a mission trip was still a bit "out there" for me to grasp. Though it may seem like "writing on the wall", God would have to do a lot more than that to convince me that I was "mission trip" material!

Later that night before heading to the coffee shop to study, I went up to the dorms to see if my friend, Jerri, wanted to go with me. As I knocked on her door, my knock fell on silence. I knocked again. No one. Right as I was getting ready to leave, a girl walked up, getting ready to knock on Jerri's door.

"She's not here," I said.

"Oh, bummer," the girl said. "I was going to show her some of the information about the mission trip that I'm going on this summer."

I probably looked like a freak. I dropped my mouth in awe. "Are you serious? Are you really going on a mission trip this summer?"

"Yeah, I have a bunch of information about it in my room. Oh, I'm Samantha, by the way."

"Nice to meet you. I'm Emily," I said. "Do you mind if I take a look at what you have?"

Her enthusiastic nod led me down a few doors and across the hall to her room. For the next 30 minutes, we leafed through some of the information she had. She had been looking at a lot of different possibilities and had a lot of information. The trip that she was looking to go on was to China. I never really had an interest in going to China, but "England" popped in my head again. Hmm... England. That sounded kind of neat. Though it seemed like another totally wild coincidence, I still was not sold on this whole "mission trip" idea. I really didn't feel like I was that type of girl. I knew that I was "born again" when I got saved, but so much of the old me still seemed to be there.

"God," I thought. "I know, to most, it would seem pretty obvious, but you are still going to have to do better than that to convince me. I just don't feel like I'm the type? The serving? The missionary type? Am I really good enough to go share Jesus with people?"

I thanked Samantha and left her room, letting her know I had a lot of studying to do for accounting. I was heading to the coffee shop downtown, most likely until they closed. If I was going to avoid interruptions, I would need to get off-campus.

The winter air was bitter, even in my bundled up ski coat. As I opened up the door to the coffee shop, the *ding* of the bell sounded, and I welcomed the warm air and the enticing aroma of fresh coffee. "Yum," I thought. "This is going to hit the spot." The coffee shop was unusually empty that night. Great for me! That meant I could get a lot done without feeling like I had to look up and smile at all the people who may come in. I purchased my coffee and found a seat in the empty cafe, making sure my back was facing the door to avoid any unwanted obligatory pleasantries.

My mind bounced through the unusual events of the day. Wow! Did God really want me to go on a mission trip?! I could not shake the coincidental occurrences! In the pool, the poster, and then meeting Samantha. How weird was all of that?!

An hour had passed, and I had not really accomplished much studying. For what seemed like the 100th time, I read the same sentence in my accounting book, and I still did not know what it said. I was not paying attention to what I was reading.

The *ding* of the door sounded, and three people made their way to the front counter for coffee. I overheard their laughs and muffled conversation. They sure did look happy.

Here I was, on the other hand, in a twisted friendship with this guy who was not a Christian, no progress in studying for my accounting test, and then God sends me a curve ball about a mission trip. I must say, my thoughts were neither happy nor excited. My thoughts seemed more confused and astounded. Like barbells on my brain, my thoughts were heavy. My life felt heavy. Everything seemed like it was such a big deal, like I had such big decisions to make.

The three began to walk my way. Wouldn't you know it... of all the places in the cafe, these people had to sit just one table away from me. Frustration made me want to jump out of my skin, and my thoughts were going wild: "You have GOT to be kidding! Could they not have chosen a different table? Don't they see that I am trying to study?! I mean, FOR REAL! I have enough going on as it is. I'm having enough trouble focusing, let alone having their conversation linger into my already jumbled brain."

They looked at me and smiled as they sat down. I gave them a half smile—you know, the fake kind. I was pretty sure they could tell I was annoyed. Nonetheless, I tried to get back into my accounting book for desperately needed focus.

As intruders to my ears, bits of their conversation made it almost impossible for the words on my accounting page to stand out at all. My mind was everywhere else except studying. I was now officially sitting there just listening to their conversation.

"Well," the red-headed young man said, "I will be leaving to go to China in three months. I'm really excited about this mission trip. It's my fourth one. This will definitely be the longest trip though..."

"This is ridiculous!" I thought. "You have GOT to be kidding! I get the point, God! I get it! I get it! Nothing like hitting me with a cement truck! I GET IT!"

I had enough. I walked up to the table of the three, asked if I could join them, and spent the rest of the evening talking to them about mission trips. We spent several hours just chatting and laughing until the coffee shop closed.

That was the first and last time I saw any of them. Were they really human? Or, did God just send some angels to talk about missions so I would agree to go?

I was in. I would go.

Over the next few weeks, I gathered information about this "AOC" organization. The mission trips would focus on sharing the gospel via sports, drama and music, competing in athletic events, having big assemblies, street witnessing, camps, school rallies, and more. I could not believe it. For a mission trip, it really did seem to fit me perfectly. I decided upon doing track and cheerleading. If they needed anything else, I would definitely volunteer for drama; that sounded fun!

I got my support letter together and began sending them out, soliciting for the money to help get me there.

9

THE BREAK

The cool air whisped through my hair, and the pitter-patter of my feet sounded rhythmically on the pavement as I made my way back to campus. It was late-spring, and remnants of the cold winter were still lingering as each breath came out like a cold puff of smoke. Because we didn't have a track yet, our practices resumed at the high school track. Our track team would do a one-mile warm up run to the high school track for our daily practice. As the respective groups finished—sprinters, distance runners, jumpers, and throwers—we cooled down by running back to the university in groups or individually. Then, we would go about our evening.

On one particular night, I did intervals. 400-meter intervals. 10. We were clippin'! As usual, I pulled in as the fastest during our intervals. I wasn't the fastest, but I usually practiced the hardest and was definitely not a 400-meter runner! I could sprint, but I always felt that middle-distance was more my cup of tea. Middle distance was a combination of endurance, speed, and knowing how to run your race. Middle-distance runners had to know how to size-up the competition.

My 800-meter race mirrored my dad's from when he was a runner. During the first 500 meters, stay with the leaders. After completing the front curve, come up on the back stretch of lap two. With 300 meters left, it was time to turn on the burners. Instead of waiting for my "kick" until the last 200 meters—like most runners did—I would begin mine at the last 300. It often threw runners off. They weren't used to it. If they decided to change up their game-plan and put in their kick early, they would likely burn out by the last 100 meters. As for me, I was not the fastest sprinter. I did not want to leave it up to a 100-meter dash on whether I was going to win. Pulling away from competition on the back stretch gave me some cushion in the event that there were some good sprinters who saved enough "game" until the end. My goal? To be far enough ahead to sprint into the finish line a winner.

Almost back on campus from my cool-down run, I looked both ways before running across main street. On this day, like most days, I was going to cut through the dorm, Rick's floor, and swing by his room. But, today was unlike most days. Today was a big day! My heart, my spirit, all of my insides had been uneasy and in knots for days as I thought about approaching this subject. Like taking a blow to the chest—my gut, my heart—everything inside felt like it was in knots. During the entire run back to campus, my head was spinning. How was I going to embrace this topic with belief and conviction when it was something I technically didn't want to do?

I didn't want to be on a "break" from Rick. How would I even survive being away from my best friend? At the same time, how could I survive spiritually with him? What part of me would survive? Frustrations and questions still haunted me. Who would I talk too now? I had gradually let most of my girlfriends go, simply due to lack of time spent connecting with them. Besides my running partner, I didn't talk to many people about Rick. But, I had determined it; today was the day.

Today was the day that needed to happen for a long time. How would it go? How would it work? What would I say? Could we really stay apart? Could we really take a break? Would I be able to breathe without him? In a weird way, I felt somewhat "possessed." I had heard of people being possessed or oppressed. I didn't know what that was like, but I felt like somehow in my mind and heart that was how I was. The cement bonds internally connecting us somehow had to be demolished. The idea that the talk would be difficult was an understatement. Attempting to break free would be like scaling Mount Everest. It surely would not be impossible, but I did not know how I was going to do it. I didn't know if I had the energy, strength, and stamina to actually attempt the feat. Could it really be possible to break the ties that we had already securely created?

I rapped on the door and heard Rick shout, "Come in," from the inside. I made my way in.

"Oh, hey Emily!" he said with the immediate and normal embrace. "How was your practice? You obviously have been running," he joked as he looked me up and down in fashion disgust.

I laughed. He was always so real to himself—real to who he was. Even with me, that did not change. He was not trying to fool anyone. If he could have his cake and eat it too, he'd do it and even tell you while he was doing it.

"Practice was good," I said. I knew I had to cut to the chase immediately before I lost my courage in his charm. "But, Rick," I said, changing tones. "We really need to talk." His light-hearted smile changed to something serious.

"What? What's going on? What's wrong?"

"I just know that we need to change things. We need to take a break. We need to be apart for a while. I just can't do this anymore. I feel like I need to get back to *me*. I'm going on a mission trip this summer. I just don't feel like we can continue this, whatever 'this' is. It's too much," I said. My brows were raised, my face showing the turmoil of decision, the decision that was obviously still going on in my head. It was a decision that had not been firmly decided. This decision had yet to be made into a solid resolve.

He immediately began save-mode. Sales mode. Urgent. Defensive of our friendship. An expression of a bit of fear shown over his face. Fear of loss. Would I really be strong enough to leave him? Rick? The Rick?

"But, Emily, we're fine. We are good. Emily, we are okay. We don't need a break," he said as he came to hug me with the strong scent of his cologne lingering. He pulled back and said jokingly, "I'll stop trying to kiss you if that would make it better. I promise! I can stop. I can be good. Emily, we don't need a break." He said this not wanting to appear that he was begging or pleading. The word, "please," was on his voice. His eyes showed everything he thought. His eyes were filled with a bit of fear, afraid that I was just strong enough to really go through with it, go through with our "break-up."

A *break up*?! Here we were, not *dating*. To the world around us, we were just "friends," but this was the hardest non-break-up break-up I had ever experienced. A break from each other? Could it be done? We were best friends. How could best friends be separated? How could we do it? Ahhhhh! Torment and torture were the two emotions going on internally. Inside me, all I could feel was disgust, like I was going to throw up. Knots. I wanted to scream on the inside. Despite the internal misery, I knew I was going to go through with it—at least for today. I wasn't committed to forever, but I could try a week. To get to a week, I knew it started with a day. Today.

A break from each other. Maybe that would allow some of what seemed like "strongholds" to loosen their grip. My brain was bound so tightly by the memories of the constant time we spent together. It seemed like a lifetime ago that I owned my own thoughts without Rick in them. I knew I needed to get a clear perspective and to be free from the cloudiness in my mind—at least, set free long enough so I could manage to get some clarity of thought.

I laughed at his "kissing" comment. He did always try to kiss me. It was such a joke, but the joke was getting too real for me. I was afraid that, any day, I would let it happen. I said, "Rick, thanks, but that is not enough. We are just too close. What we have right now is just too much. I really just need a break. I need time to think about things. Think about me. Think about who I really am. I feel like I'm losing part of me. I need to get things together. We are just too close, Rick. We are just too close."

He hugged me and held me. He held me close. He held me tight. The embrace was so warm. So comfortable. So real. How could I let go? His cologne lingered as my head rested on his shoulder. I drank in his smell. He always smelled so good. The arms in his Polo sweater held me. There was not even a sign of him wanting to let go. Maybe if he could hold me long enough, I might change my mind. In my mind, I knew that "no" was the answer. I had this resolve that we were, at least, taking a break.

For this moment, though, while I was still there, I would remain in his arms. I would remain in the forbidden place—in the place that I knew had begun to take the place of my God. A relationship that had been elevated to a status that could be considered an "idol." Our relationship had consumed more time than my relationship with God. My thoughts of Rick consumed more time than my thoughts about God. Our relationship had entered into a definite danger zone. Missionary dating turned bad. It was missionary dating, starting with the intent of seeing Rick saved, but hopelessly losing—losing to temptation.

I remembered the visual demonstration of seeing one person standing on a chair, the other standing on the ground. The person standing on a chair tried to pull the other person up onto it. The person standing on the chair struggled. Most of the time, the person on the chair was not able to lift the other person up. Though, on the flip side, when the person on the ground attempted to pull the person off the chair, it inevitably happened. Both ended up on the ground. That was what happened here. My intentions were good in the beginning. I was trying to lift Rick up and lead him to Jesus, but my plans had most definitely gone awry.

"Rick, I have to go."

"Please, Emily. Please don't go. We don't need a break."

"Rick, I have to go," I pulled away from our embrace and left the room. Like a baby shocked at a reprimand, Rick was left standing, his eyes filled with questions and surprised anguish. "How could this be happening to me?" I could hear him thinking. This was definitely not something that he had expected would ever come to him.

The drive home was equally torture and freedom—two feelings, so opposite. How was it possible to feel them both with such intensity?

The next weeks brought physical and mental torture. At least, summer was here, and I did not have to see Rick every day on campus. Maymester was over. Each day was still like going through withdrawals. I had never experienced drugs or addiction, but I felt like this is how it would feel to try to break one. Painful. My heart ached constantly. The desire to go to see him filled me at every moment. I knew that the feeling was not love, but it was something that felt equally as strong—not in a good way though. It was the feeling of something drawing me, something trying to pull me. I wanted it, but the very essence of it somehow felt very dangerous. Very dangerous. A type of danger that I had never felt before—not a fun or adventurous danger but a danger for my very soul. It was deep down in my spirit. I knew that I was walking a very fine line.

"Come to the lake," Rick asked on the phone. "Please, please just come to the lake. Please just come up and spend some time with me. We can just chill out. No one will be there. We can just watch TV and chill out. Please, Emily. Please, will you come?"

It was July 1st. I was only a week away from going on the mission trip. I would be traveling to England, Northern Ireland, and Scotland for my three-week trip. I had raised my support, had my passport, and was ready for my escape.

Reluctantly, I agreed to meeting Rick at the lake. Over the last several weeks since our "break-up," it was almost as if our ties to each other became stronger and more powerful. Maybe it was the sense of "loss" or possible loss that made him want to spend more time with me. It definitely felt good to be pursued and wanted.

Still, I was very hesitant to go to the lake. My emotions were doing summersaults. I felt so vulnerable to him. I felt weak and not on solid ground when I was around him. My feelings were drawing me to him. His charming smile was ushering me to do whatever, tempting me. My hesitancy lost out while I pulled up to the little white lake house. I saw his black Expedition out front. It was nearing 9:30pm on this summer evening. The sun had already set, and it was finally getting dark.

I walked up the steps of the porch, tapped on the door, and walked in. Across the room in the kitchen, he smiled and strutted over to give me a hug. "Hi," he said as he pulled me to him. This hug was longer than a traditional friend hug. This hug lingered. This hug was one that was given with a sigh of relief, the sigh of it saying, "Finally, my best friend is back. Finally, we can be together. We can just be. You were meant to be with me." It was a sigh a lover would make, a sigh knowing you had your lover in your arms. As wrong as it was, it still felt good. I felt small in his arms, his shoulders broad and his embrace warm. A feeling of security and safety in that moment raced through me. I loved the feeling of being wanted and accepted.

He let go of our embrace and picked up his bottle of beer. "I would ask you if you wanted a beer, but I know you don't because you don't drink anymore. But... do you want a beer?" He poked in fun, knowing he probably wouldn't convince me to cave and have one. I responded with the common Emily "no," so he opened the fridge and offered me a Coke or Diet Coke.

"Diet Coke," I said, making my way to the couch.

Handing me my drink, he sat on the chair right next to the couch. "So, how are you? I've missed you. Are you all ready to go to Europe soon? You can take me with you!" he said and laughed.

"Well, we do need to get you saved. We can take care of that right now. You want me to pray, and you can accept Jesus into your life?" I said jokingly.

He laughed out loud and said, "I don't think Jesus is ready for me yet! Besides, I've got you. You can tell me the Jesus stuff, and I can just keep on being me."

I didn't have much of a response other than, "Rick, I promise, despite how you roll, Jesus could handle you." I smiled, and we changed the subject, knowing good and well that he was not ready to make any big changes tonight.

He grabbed a blanket, turned on the movie, and asked if I wanted to lay on the couch with him. We had taken naps together in his dorm room and had laid down together before. It was usually pretty harmless. But, I could feel that, every time we did something like that—every time he hugged me or tried to kiss me, even if he was joking—my resistance was breaking down. And, I—me, Emily—was getting ready to go on a mission trip! Hello! A mission trip where they share the gospel of Jesus. Here I was, walking a tight rope in my own life. My walk with Jesus was almost turning out to be a walk by myself.

Rick snuggled up behind me, put his arms around me, and we covered up with the blanket. This definitely did not look like a "harmless friendship." The movie already started to play, and all I could do is lay there, my mind racing! "Ahhhhh! It feels so good to lay here. Ahhhh! He smells so good. I really like his arms around me." It was like forbidden fruit, and I knew it—something I wanted but knew I should not have or enjoy. In my nervousness, I hoped he didn't try anything because I was very weak.

The movie was pointless. I could sense he was not really watching it either. In the smallness of the couch, I couldn't help but feel his warmth against me. There was a security about being in someone's arms. I longed for that refuge and retreat, the feeling of protection in a man's arms. Sure, the 5-, 8-, and 13-mile runs had also caused me to be skinnier than normal. Far from scrawny, my legs still showed an obvious lifetime of running in their defined, cut curves.

As much as physical appearance mattered to Rick, I knew that he noticed. It was hard not to tell. My body couldn't help but be tense as I laid on the couch next to this person to whom I was supposed to be an example for Christ. The tightrope I had been walking seemed to be unraveling before my very eyes. As much as I knew it and hated it, that tightrope was down to just a thread. I hadn't totally blown it—at least, not yet.

He began kissing lightly on the back of my neck. "Hey!" I protested, pulling my shoulder up to my ear, "Stop it." I didn't put up a really good fight because he kept doing it. This time, my squirm allowed him to continue. "Hey… that tickles. Stop," I said in a softer voice, definitely not sounding too convincing. He continued. Because I was not making him stop, and I continued to lay there, pressed up against him, he continued with more aggression and more passion. I sighed in defeat. I partially turned my shoulder into him, and we kissed.

After several minutes, he got up, pulling me with him.

"Let's get more comfortable, let's go to the bedroom," he said.

I followed him, all the warning signs and signals going off in my head—the red flag, waving in my mind and the voice saying, "Stop! Stop! This is your last chance! Stop!" But, I followed him. He was pulling me to him with his hands, cupping my head, still kissing me— like he was a sailor who had been away at sea, and I, his mistress. He pushed me on the bed.

Looking at my clothes in a pile on the floor, I couldn't help but lay there in frustration. Though I remained a virgin and did not have sex with Rick, I did, however, completely blow my attempt to not be sexually physical with him. For the last several minutes, I had repeatedly said "no" every way I knew how. Though I had given in to messing around, I still wanted to remain a virgin for whoever my husband would be one day. I was successful in that resolve—barely. It was so close, though, which made me even more frustrated. How many times can a person say, "No. Please don't. No. No. No," while squirming and moving out of optimal positions for entry. Why did he continually try when I clearly did not want to have sex? Doesn't "no" still mean "no?"

Rick got up to go to the bathroom and shower while I just laid there, numb and alone. My respect for Rick had infinitely diminished. There was no gentleman in that bed. I knew him well enough to know that he was very selfish. Most decisions were based on himself before others. I knew he wasn't a Christian. In a way, I couldn't expect much more. I was just disappointed. I hoped that maybe he would be different and respectful, a gentleman, and he hadn't been. Even knowing where I stood with things, knowing my desire to wait until I was married, even with me telling him to stop *while* we were in the heat of things, he continually tried anyways?! He still tried, over and over, to go inside me while I kept moving away to keep it from happening. I guess I had just hoped for more. His main thought was most likely a selfish one. That's why he made attempt after attempt.

My thoughts raced about my own, more major, downfall. "How could I have done this? How could I have allowed this to happen?" I felt so defeated. "Though we did not technically have the act of sex, I had given in and was naked with him. I had stood strong for so long, keeping the physical part of our relationship off limits. For months and months, I had been 'unconquerable,' and he knew it. How had things gotten to this place. How did I get here? Laying in this bed?

I knew Rick had viewed me as different, and I also think he respected me for being different. I think he respected not being able to "have me." In a way, as much as he loved to win "the game," I think he liked the idea that there was a Higher Power that won out over him, that someone could love God so much that God would win over his charm. He maybe hadn't even known how his kiss attempts had been chiseling away at my resolve until now. Here, I laid—weak, ruined, and defeated.

Sure, we didn't have sex, but for all intents and purposes, he still won. I had failed and now what? Go to England and share the gospel of Jesus with people?" I laughed under my breath as only a sheet draped over me. "Go on a mission trip? How could I possibly do something so honorable." Complete heaviness and shame filled my whole body. Spotted, soiled, tainted, and tarnished, I felt like the mistake I made now completely defined me. Was there even a recovery from something like this? Where would my path lead now?

Wrapped in a towel, Rick walked out of the bathroom. I was up, pulling my shirt on, and he came over to hug me. In his voice and in his hug, it was like nothing was wrong. My hug back to him was cold—no squeeze, no warmth, just limp arms performing the act of hugging.

I was dressed. We quickly exchanged some unimportant pleasantries, and I told him some excuse so that I could leave. I needed to be alone! I needed to leave immediately!

10

CHOOSING

I didn't typically frequent Wal-Mart this late, ever. It was just past 2:00am. I pulled in, got out of my car, and began my quick but nervous walk through the dark parking lot. The doors swung open, and I headed in. So nervous. All I could think about was how much of a failure I was. "What a failure. How could I?! How could I put myself in this position, in this situation? What a complete loss of my testimony. I completely failed! Here I am, a Christian leader. I lead Bible studies on campus. I have standards. My goal is to see people come to a saving knowledge of Jesus. My desire is to see people's lives rocked by the love of Jesus, to see the lost find the missing link in their lives. That is my true passion. How could my world be rocked in such an unplanned, unwanted way as this? How could I let this happen? My goal had been to see him saved, see him come to know Jesus. My initial, valiant effort led to a slippery slope that left my head spinning. My intentions were to evangelize by my life and my character—not this."

In my mind, I was totally freaking out! I thought, "This is so dumb. It won't tell anything yet anyways. I'm totally wasting my money, but I just want to see. I headed toward the pharmacy area to find it. Ahhhhhhhhhh! How could I allow this to happen? I am a 'strong' Christian. How could I have put myself into this situation? How could I even be here, buying *this*? It's barely been a few hours. We didn't even have sex, but it was close. What if a sperm somehow happened to sneak by? I heard they were good swimmers. What if one got on me and somehow swam in? Ahhh!" Even in my mind, the idea seemed very far-fetched, but my naivety was the boss and hastened before my logical sense could catch up.

Passing by several aisles of health products, I turned down the aisle that looked like it could be right. "How would I know? It's not like I've ever bought this before!" Quickly scanning the boxes of whitening strips, condoms, other health items, my eyes came upon the section. I found them. Pregnancy tests.

Wow! Now, another decision: which do I choose? One line? Two lines? Plus or minus? A box of three? Box of one? Ahhhhh! This is *so* ridiculous! Why am I so nervous?! I hardly could believe I was even here. We didn't even have sex. I'm still a virgin. I'm going to wait for my husband. Should I just leave? No! I'm going to buy one right now and go in the bathroom right here and find out now! Could it even show yet? I'm sure I'm jumping the gun. You probably have to at least wait a week, maybe two? I have *no* idea! Could I get pregnant without having sex?

As I expected, it was only one line: not pregnant. Back at home, I was ready to go to sleep. I was exhausted. Disappointed. Still, a bit on edge. And now, I was confused. Now, I would have a choice to make. I could not have both worlds. I could not live two lives. I knew the point of decision would need to be made within the next few days. Would it be Rick? Would I finally cross over? Give everything up? Finally commit to him? Give up everything and just jump in with both feet—even have sex? Throw away completely the idea of waiting to have sex until I was married. Just give him what he seemed to ultimately want? Would I back out on the mission trip? Or, would I turn from Rick? Would I finally cut ties? Go on the mission trip? Spend three weeks getting my life and commitment to God back on solid ground?

I had only a few days to decide. But, for now, my eyes could barely stay awake. I fell into bed, thankful to escape the unfortunate reality that I had created.

Three days and all I experienced was mental anguish. I had never felt so torn in my life due to a mere decision. This decision would change everything! I was really contemplating giving it *all* up, giving up everything I believed for this relationship. Diving in head first, I would go ahead and just have sex, get it over with and be with Rick. In one hand, that was the decision I was holding. In the other hand, it was the mission trip. This was the worst day of my life. In one hand, I was holding God, my possible future, my life, my devotion, and the life that I felt really defined me. In my other hand, I was holding Rick. Choosing Rick meant giving up everything, everything that, over the last year, had become true and concrete in my life.

I sat at the lake house. Rick was not there, but I just sat in my car. It seemed like every song that came on was our song. The sound of cellos and violins introduced the next song over my car speakers. One of our ultimates: "All My Life" by K.C. & JoJo. I laid my head on the steering wheel and could only sob. The song brought floods of memories. All of the good moments, the laughing, the closeness, how we completed each other's sentences, and the way Rick looked at me when he was joking around. Rick had so much of my heart; he was my best friend. How could I go on living without him? My body shook uncontrollably as I cried, just listening to the words. Excruciating anguish filled my heart. I felt like it was going to beat out of my chest. What was I going to do? There didn't seem to be a good option.

I closed my eyes and left my head on the steering wheel as I just listened to the lyrics:

> I promise to never fall in love, with a stranger, you're all I'm thinking of, I praise the Lord above, for sending me your love, I cherish every thought, I really love you. And all my life, I prayed for someone like you, and I thank God, that I finally found you. All my life, I prayed for someone like you. And I hope that you feel the same way too. Yes I pray that you do love me...

As the song ended, I got out of the car and headed to the swing. I sat there, swinging by the calm lake waters. I held out each of my hands and stared into my empty palms. It was as if each palm represented such a huge life path, but either decision brought with it the pain of leaving the other behind. A tear dropped onto the creases of my open palms. I balled them both into fists, pulled my knees up, and rested my fists on my head. What radically different paths I had to choose from. They represented completely different life paths— like Hollywood is to the Amish backroads of my farm town. Lifestyles that represented the opposite, and I knew it. One, living for myself: things, vanity, and turning off my mind to what allowed me to experience true internal fullness. The other, a life where I was whole, complete, and seemingly happy. A life being led and directed by a Higher Power. A life that I had experienced only for a short time, and it had been filled with fulfillment, completion, and satisfaction. What would I do?

It had been three days. My mind had seemed so full, like it would explode any minute from all of the pressure. I had been avoiding everyone. I had avoided my family, my parents. I didn't want to talk to anyone, especially someone who may try to sway my decision one way or another. I had also been avoiding God. I thought, if I could block Him out, maybe He would not try to drop thoughts or decisions in my head. For three days, it was as if I put up this brick wall between me and God. I didn't want to hear from Him. I felt He was extremely disappointed in me. My predominant thought played again. As if on repeat for what seemed like the 100th time, I had set out with good intentions and lost everything. I lost everything. There was no testimony left. I fell. I gave in. I failed. Rick won. The "world" won. It pulled me right in. In my whole being, to the achy core of my bones, I was filled with disappointment in myself. How could God even take me back after this? Would I just go to Rick? Would I give it all up?

God, is there something better out there for me? God, is there really a godly man who is out there, who will not pressure me to do things that I don't want to do? God, I'm sorry.

God was silent. No answer. That figures. I wouldn't answer me either; I screwed up so bad.

So, there I sat, just continuing to swing. Staring. Looking like I was staring into a daze of nothing. I was staring at my hands. Staring at the two choices—one choice I knew I would have to make today.

I heard the sound of gravel crunching beneath what sounded like his SUV.

My thoughts were like gears in my mind, turning and beginning to spin almost out of control. They were going faster and faster in circles. He was almost here. He would be getting out of his Expedition any minute, and I still was no closer to making a decision. What was I going to do? Rushed and racing, I didn't know if he could tell how fast my head was spinning.

The heaviness of the gravel sound let me know Rick was pulling up. I continued to just sit. Not turn. Not get up. Just sit. My heart was in my throat. My eyes showed only one sign: a sign of anguish. I didn't want to make either decision.

Did I have enough strength? I was so unworthy. I was so dirty. I was such a failure. "God, how could you take me back? How could I go on this trip? I have never failed so greatly like this before. God, this failure feels like it's taken over my whole body. God, how could I be any good on a mission trip? I have failed so greatly." I placed my head in my hands. I wished God was standing there. Maybe He would answer me if we saw each other face to face. Maybe I would be able to tell if He was mad at me, too—as mad as I was at myself. I just wanted Him to know how sorry I was. I was sorry for disappointing Him. Sorry for everything. My heart, which had been clogging my throat, now felt as though I was holding it in my hands. I still didn't know the words that would come.

Rick walked up. He sat down beside me. "Hey. I've missed you. Are you okay?"

I couldn't imagine my eyes looking any more pathetic. I was sure he could tell I was really struggling. He wrapped one arm around my shoulder, the swing slowing down to almost still. He pulled me to him and wrapped his other arm around me. As my head rested on his shoulder, I thought about my best friend. His smell. If I chose him, would he choose me back? I did not even know if he would have been willing to give up Rachel. I believed he would. I believed he would walk away, but I didn't know for sure. Would he leave her if I went to him? Would he cut off those ties?

Part of me just wanted to sit there in silence before the tides changed, before my world was different, without God or Rick. My heart hurt, my head hurt, and my body hurt. I ached. Sitting so close, my head on his shoulder... his smell. I wanted to freeze time and his smell. I just wanted to sit in silence. I wasn't ready for words.

We sat. His arms around me. Warm. Close. I knew we couldn't sit there forever. Still, unsure of how I would go on, I knew a chapter had to end.

I opened my mouth, "Rick, something has to change. We can't do this anymore. I can't do this. I can't see you." Words were coming out of my mouth; I just didn't know how. "I don't even think we can be friends. It has to be all or nothing; we can't have both. Today, this is it."

"Emily," he pleaded. "We can make it work. We can."

"How can we make it work, Rick? I'm supposed to leave tomorrow for this mission trip. Are you willing to change your life? Are you ready to choose Jesus over sex?"

He said nothing. His silence was his answer.

I stared, just looking over the lake, still in a bit of indecision.

"Emily, I'm sure I will choose Jesus sometime." He emphasized *sometime*. "I just don't know when I'll be ready for that. Em, just let's stay together. We're too good of friends to split up. Who's going to hassle you over late night study sessions?" His smile and nudge, trying to lighten my mood. "Emily, we know everything about each other. We're too close to not be together. I promise we can make this work."

"Rick, I don't know. I just don't know if 'sometime' is good enough for me. I feel like it's all your life and none of mine. I'm giving everything, and you're giving nothing."

"Well, what if I said I'd go to church with you sometime, sometime when you got back from your trip. You could bring me to your church and introduce me to your church friends. I would be willing to do that for you. You've got to admit, Em... it would be a big first step for me. They might turn me away though," he joked. "In the meantime, if you couldn't resist me, I suppose I could still sacrifice my body too."

"See, it's all just a joke. To you, all the physical stuff isn't a big deal, but it is a big deal to me. The idea of remaining pure and pursuing God is important to me. All of that has gotten so diluted in our relationship."

"Emily, I was just joking. I can ease off the physical jokes and trying to do stuff with you."

"I guess I'm just frustrated that I gave in to doing stuff with you that I know is wrong to do as a Christian. And then, it didn't help that you kept on trying to have sex even though you know I plan to save that for when I get married. I just felt very used. I felt like you weren't respecting what I wanted at all. But ultimately, it is still my fault. I'm not blaming you for us messing around. I should not have been here in the first place. I've allowed all boundaries to go out the window and just disregarded them."

Rick had nothing to say. He didn't apologize for his unwanted attempts to have sex. He didn't apologize for anything.

I continued, "I can't choose this. I would have to give up everything else. Everything that I stand for. I'm sorry that I failed you. I'm sorry that I gave in. It was not supposed to happen like that. That was not supposed to happen at all. I'm sorry." I paused and added, "I'm choosing God. I can't live a double life. I have to choose God over you. I think it would be great for you to start going to church, but for me, for right now, I have to choose God over you."

That was it. I was done. I got up and began walking to my car. I couldn't believe I said it. I don't know how the words were audible over the gaping clog in my throat. I felt like I was in a haze. The words that came were a miracle because, with each step, I didn't feel like I had the strength to be walking away. I felt like my knees were going to buckle, and I would fall to the ground. I wanted to turn, to hug, to be held in his embrace. To smell his smell. I wanted to stay, but something inside me kept each foot walking, one in front of the other. My body wanted to stay, but my feet were pulling me away.

My body surged as Rick's hand grabbed my shoulder to spin me around, "Emily, please. It doesn't have to be like this." He grabbed my hand as he pleaded in the moment, his expression one of urgency. "Really, Emily. Let's go to church together when you get back. I would do that for you."

Pulling my hand away from his grasp, I kept walking. "I can't."

Rick followed me. His lips were moving fast. He was saying something, but I didn't hear anything. My mind seemed so full.

Thoughts were pressed to the top, overflowing, not allowing anything else in. I couldn't hear.

I got in my car, and I looked one last time. He just stood there. He didn't wave. He just stood there, still. I think he was as shocked as I was at what had just happened. Getting into my car, strictly out of habit, my keys thankfully entered the ignition, I put the car into drive, and began to pull away. I couldn't even look in the rearview mirror. I could not turn back.

PART 2

NEW BEGINNINGS

11

MISSION TRIP

I t was July 7th, and I was happy to make it to this day of departure. The flight from Chicago to Newark went by quickly. I found my connecting gate that would take me to London, and it was filled with young college-age-looking students. All over. People sitting in chairs and on the floor. Big bags scattered the concourse, containing necessities that would need to last the next three weeks.

Laughing echoed in the air while a group sat playing cards. I saw several "AOC" bags and knew that these would be the people I would be with for the next three weeks. These were the people I would get to know and call friends. I did not know what was in store though I did wonder if anyone could see past my fake smile. Could they see what a failure I had just been? Did the guilt I carried blatantly reveal my sin? Was it evident? I felt like I was wearing this dirty secret on the outside for everyone to see. I managed to smile anyway. I made my way over to a girl who had long blonde hair, and she welcomed me right in to sit with her and a few other girls. Here we go. It was all beginning.

Next stop, Gatwick Airport, London.

The flight seemed long. I sat next to a guy named Jason who was also traveling with AOC. For the next six hours, all there was to do was talk or sleep. Jason was friendly and asked me the basics of where I was from. To avoid him asking more about me and all that I did not want to share, I knew I needed to get him talking.

"So, tell me about you. What's your story?"

"I'm from Arkansas, and I'm a quarterback on our football team at Arkansas State. I'm also a youth leader at a church close to my college. I play guitar and lead worship for the youth group and for our college ministries group, and I love it! It's awesome to watch people entering into a time of worship."

"Oh wow! Did you bring your guitar with you on this trip?"

"No, I didn't, not this time. I figured they had people who would be doing all the worship stuff. I'm just playing football with the AOC team. What are you doing on this trip?"

"I'm doing track and cheerleading. I run the 800 and 1500. So, tell me more? What else about Arkansas? What else about you?" I actually really wanted to know now. For the first time ever, this was the first guy I had ever met who had openly talked about his passion to go into a time of worship. Not only that, he also played the guitar, and he sang? Nothing seemed more attractive to me than a guy who played worship music on a guitar. He seemed like my dream guy already, and he played my favorite sport! I *loved* football! Growing up, learning to throw a spiral with my dad and sister, Kate, were some of my favorite times. I was proud of my football skills. I was sure it would even impress Jason. Most girls don't know how to throw a long spiral.

"Well, I'm studying education to be a high school history teacher. I'm also engaged to a girl named Bethany who is an elementary education major. She is awesome! We are planning on getting married after we both graduate next year. A few months ago, we actually bought a house not far from campus, which Bethany lives in. I'm living in an apartment a few miles away until we get married. It's definitely good that she's the one who lives there because she has already started decorating. I'm sure she'll have our house beautiful by the time I move in. You girls are like that," he nudged. "If it were me living there, the walls would all be white with posters pinned up in every room."

"Oh wow! Congratulations! What an exciting time for you both," I said, mustering a sound of excitement though, inside, my heart sank. The glimmer of hope that I had was shot down at the one word: *engaged.* Everything about him reminded me of my dad. He seemed so perfect. My dad played football, guitar, and even further knew a ton about the Bible. Jason probably did, too.

Was he sure he was taken? I guess owning a house with someone is pretty serious, not that I would try to break up someone who was engaged, but the fleeting thought that he was still not married did cross through my brain. I longed for a husband like him. In the short 15 minutes I had known him, I had already secretly hoped that maybe he was my future husband. A godly man, he seemed so sure about himself. He seemed so solid in who he was in Christ. Even his quirky jokes made it seem like I had known him forever. He even resembled my dad. His blue eyes danced with a friendly innocence. His baseball cap covered his dark hair, making him appear sporty—just my type. He had broad shoulders, perfectly indicative of the position he played in football. Most quarterbacks I had met were around six feet tall and had broad shoulders, narrowing down to a thin waist. That was Jason.

Despite my disappointment, at least, Jason revealed to me that there are men out there who love Jesus. Maybe he was not going to be my future husband, but I still felt hope. There really were Christian guys out there! I would work at becoming the *me* that I wanted to be. One day, there would be a husband that would be as perfect as Jason seemed. Surely, there was someone out there for me.

My mind drifted from Jason, back in time to the one Christian guy I dated, Jeremy. Not only was he nice, he was relatively good-looking. Our first date consisted of him pulling up to my house in his shiny, black, convertible sports car. Now, that appealed to the old and new me! Love Jesus and travel in style? This seemed like a good combination. We went to dinner and a movie, and he paid. So many broke college guys often tried to do the dutch dates, making the girl pay for her half. It didn't seem very gentlemanly to me. Then again, most college guys were jerks behind closed doors anyways.

I had met Jeremy in Sunday school at church. When he brought me back home from our date, he walked me to my door, thanked me for a nice evening, and told me he would love to take me out again. Without any uncomfortable pauses, he said "goodnight" and began walking back to his car, never even attempting to kiss me. What a breath of fresh air! I did not want to kiss him—at least, not yet. I just wanted to enjoy my time of getting to know him without pressure.

I did not want to kiss most guys I went out with, but most went ahead and tried anyways. Jeremy was a refreshing change. I would definitely go out with him again.

Though Jeremy brought with him a radical contrast from the non-Christian guys I had dated, there still seemed to be something missing. I was happy he went to church, he had a nice car, he had a nice job, he was respectful, but there was something missing. To even consider getting serious in a Christian relationship, I wanted more. What he had—or, at least, what I had seen so far—wasn't enough for me. I wanted someone with fire and zeal, someone who was growing in the Lord so much that they inspired me to grow. I wanted someone who would draw me to be a better person, someone who would draw me to have a deeper and stronger walk with the Lord.

As a new Christian, I was passionate about this new Jesus I had met. At times, when I was at church, it was as if I were drinking from a faucet and couldn't get enough water. I just wanted to keep drinking. On my dates with Jeremy, my mind wandered to whether there was a guy who had the great qualities and respect that Jeremy possessed but who equally had a fire in his eyes, a passion for Jesus, and a passion for his walk with the Lord. I had never known anyone like this man I longed for. I wondered, did this man exist?

A slight bit of turbulence snapped me back. Jason was talking about a Bible study and a marriage study he was doing with Bethany. The man was doing a Bible study with his fiancé? Are you serious? Was this for real?

He said, "When you meet Mr. Right, you guys should check out that book." The direct comment caught me off guard a little and caused me to listen better.

"Oh, what was the title again?" I asked because my mind had been in other places.

"*Preparing for Marriage* by Dennis Rainey. It is a great book for preparing every aspect of your life for marriage!"

Jason just went over the top. He was already perfect before telling me about the Bible study with his fiancé! Disappointment and hope, all in one, described my emotions! The perfect but taken guy! Surely, there was more than one guy like this on the planet—but, one that was single?

Here I sat, next to a younger version of my dad. Maybe Jason was even a handyman! I admired my dad's ability to do what seemed like anything and with excellence. He built out the downstairs of our house, the deck around our pool, and a gazebo in the back simply from plans in his mind! My dad was an awesome man, hard to compare. Yet, here I sat next to someone so much like him! Jason seemed perfect, except for the small detail that he was engaged. My thoughts drooped, "Wow. This Bethany girl is so lucky. God, is there someone for me? God, I'm so sorry. Will you please forgive me? I'm so sorry for screwing up so bad."

I had a longing in my heart although it wasn't actually a longing for love. I couldn't completely put my finger on what I desired. Maybe it was to feel the fullness of forgiveness. Sitting next to Mr. Perfect caused my mind to accentuate my major failure just days before. I felt so dirty. I felt so unworthy. I felt like crying, and here I was on a *mission trip* of all things, right after completely falling and losing my whole testimony. Like a cement truck of guilt, my mind was heavy. I surely didn't feel worthy of someone as great as Jason.

"God, I really am sorry. Please, forgive me."

After hours of talking and some sleeping, we finally landed in London. It was my first time out of the country. England seemed so elite. What I had seen in movies and all the people with cool accents caused my anticipation to rise. Part of the guilt I carried drifted to the back of my mind as the newness and excitement emerged.

We all found our luggage and were making our way out to the parking garage to meet up with another group. Evidently, another group had been there already for three weeks. They had been traveling to Paris, remote parts of France, and to the Czech Republic. Our bus had arrived though we were waiting for the other group before loading. It was evident that we were the newbies. As our group of 50 stood around quietly, you could tell we all just met. Jason and I stood together; he was really the only person I had gotten to know so far.

Before seeing them, we heard them. The loud sound of what could hardly even be considered singing was in the distance. It was more like belting out or loudly yelling musical lyrics. Around the corner came 20-30 more college students, heading in our direction. Some were skipping, walking, and laughing. Mostly, they were singing really loud. "Hallelujah, salvation and glory, honor and power to the Lord our God. For the Lord our God is Mighty, the Lord our God's omnipotent, the Lord our God he is Woooonnnnnderful!" They clapped and danced as they pranced our way.

Their excitement and unity, in a way, shined some light on our uneasiness. They were all so excited, and here we were… new, uneasy, and a bit shy. But here it was. It was all beginning. They joined up with us, scattering about, talking to the new arrivals.

After a few minutes, I especially noticed one guy who looked a bit annoying, a little too outgoing for me. He was bopping around from group to group, enthusiastically introducing himself. He finally made his way over to us. "Hey! I'm David!" He beamed and stuck out his hand to shake mine. "What's your name?" he asked.

"Hey, David. Great to meet you. I'm Emily," I said, hoping my nervousness wasn't obvious.

"Oh yeah, you're the other one who is going to be doing track and field with us, right?"

"Yep. I run the 800 and 1500."

"Ok, so where are you from?"

"I'm from Pennsylvania, a little town called Pippen."

"Oh my gosh!" David exclaimed, looking like he was about ready to jump out of his skin. It almost startled me he was so excited. "I run track at school with a girl from that area! Do you know Marie Daniels? She's an awesome runner!"

"Oh my gosh! Yes, I do! She ran at a school that competed with us. She was always really good."

Well, there you have it. We had made a little click. In my mind, this guy was now Mr. Congeniality. He was so happy and enthusiastic. He definitely seemed like a welcoming committee! Mr. Congeniality made his connections with Jason, me, and another guy standing with us, Steven. He then moseyed on to the next group of people.

12

INTRODUCTIONS

The combined group loaded the buses, and we were off to where we would be spending a majority of our days: the Loft. Back at the Loft, aside from mingling, we had an introductory meeting about what to expect over the next three weeks, especially what would be happening during our stay in the quaint, English town of Ashford. The Loft was where we would be assembling for Bible studies, praise and worship, drama practice, and other meetings. Our host families would be arriving shortly to pick us up. Then, we would be off to see where we would be living for our 10- day stay in England.

After a few songs of praise and worship, the meeting semi-adjourned for everyone to mix and mingle a little more. There were sporadic announcements as families arrived to pick up their "students."

"Emily Cook. Emily Cook and Stephanie Smith... your ride is here." I grabbed my belongings and headed to the door.

Max, one of the leading AOC coordinators made the introductions for us. "Emily, Stephanie… this is Laura. You will meet her mom, Belle, when you arrive back at their flat. You will be staying with them during the next 10 days. Enjoy your time. In the morning, they will show you how to make the walk back here. We will begin at 8:30am. We'll see you then."

"Thank you, Max. See you tomorrow. Good night," I said as Stephanie nodded in agreement.

"Hiiiiii!" Laura said, embracing me with a giant hug. It was like she was my best friend, or, a long-lost best friend. She was so nice. Her long hair was beautiful and dark with wavy, flowing curls. After saying her "hello," she pulled back and just held my shoulders. "I'm so glad you all are finally here. It's going to be a grand week," she said, emphasizing *grand* like she had been waiting for this time to come for decades.

She turned to Stephanie and did the same to her. She embraced her like she was a long-lost best friend or sister. You could just tell everything about Laura was encompassed by pure, unencumbered love. Her face was just beautiful, not in a "model" sort of way but beautiful in a different way. Radiant. You could tell, just being in her presence, that she was different. I immediately wanted to be like her. She was warm and accepting but had a very confident assurance about her, like she knew who she was, and she was very rock solid in that.

We walked outside, and she introduced us to Joseph, her car. Stephanie and I both laughed. It was an orange Mini. "I named it 'Joseph' because of the color on the outside and the many colors of the interior," she laughed. "Joseph has been a very good car for me. Well... hop in!"

We scrunched into the orange Mini, Joseph, and we were off. I was taking it all in as we traveled the tiny roads of Ashford. The houses were so close together that they almost seemed connected. There were little yards in the front with iron gates. The yards were so small, maybe only a 12x12 space, enough to plant only a rose bush on each side of the entrance gate. Beyond the entrance gate of the narrow, two-story houses were bars on the doors and windows, wrought iron bars. It was so interesting. It seemed like such a quaint, perfect place. Why would it need wrought iron bars on everything? We cut onto a busier road, and I laughed as I peeked off my right shoulder to see a Kentucky Fried Chicken.

"Wow, you even have a KFC?" I said, more in surprise than anything.

"Yes! We have just about everything! But most places like that are pretty expensive," Laura explained.

I felt a little more at ease, more at home. It was comforting to know that, if I really needed a Mountain Dew, it wasn't too far away.

Laura pulled up to her house. Much like every other one we had seen, the wrought iron gate was accompanied by rose bushes on each side. We got out of the car, grabbed our bags, and made our way up the steps to the front door. Before we even got to the top step, the front door opened with a smiling woman ready to embrace us.

"It is so lovely to see you both. You must be Emily and Stephanie," she said with a voice full of love and excitement. "It is just so lovely to have you both here. I'm Belle. We truly have been excited to celebrate such a grand week." She embraced each of us in a warm, full hug, like one you would receive from a grandma. "Laura will show you both to your room. Why don't you get settled for just a minute, and I will put on some tea. We will have tea and biscuits while we get to know each other before bed. I know you have both had a long day, so I do not want to keep you up too late."

Laura got in front of us, ready to give us a quick walking tour as she brought us to our room. "This is the Parlour," she said, gesturing with her left hand. "You'll notice we don't have a telly though I don't think you would have the time to watch if we did, amidst your full schedule. Several years ago, we gave it away. We fancy reading and often found ourselves never using it." Walking a few more steps, she said, "This is the tea room where we'll meet for a few minutes before turning in."

Pointing to the bathroom adjacent to the stairs, she said, "Here is the loo. There is also another loo upstairs at the end of the corridor."

"What is that rope hanging down?" I asked, never having seen anything like that.

A laugh burst out, catching herself off-guard. "Please excuse me," Laura said, a glimmering smile innocent in the jovial moment. "I sometimes forget that simple things may be different in the United States. All you do when you're finished using the loo is pull this cord, and it will flush," she said with the wooden nob in her hand, motioning to pull down on the chain.

"Sounds simple enough." I said, looking back at Stephanie as she nodded.

"There is the kitchen. We'll have breakfast in the morning before leaving."

Turning the corner, Laura led us upstairs past the second loo to our bedroom at the end of the hall.

"Please let us know if we can do anything for you. I'll let you freshen up before we gather in the tea room for tea and biscuits." Closing the door behind her, with her eyebrows raised, she gave us one last smile as she pulled her shoulders up in excitement. She looked like a child getting ready to open Christmas presents all because we had finally arrived. It was refreshing to have such a warm welcome.

It was a nice room with two twin beds and white bedspreads, accompanied with a note and a white lilac flower on each pillow. How sweet. I sat down to open the envelope, interested to hear what would be the words from this English woman of God:

> Dear Emily,
>
> We just wanted to welcome you to England and our home. If there's anything you need, just ask us. We're here to serve you. We pray that you will have a good time here. I know God is going to do something wonderful in Ashford, and I pray that he blesses you all for your work here.
>
> Love in Christ,
> Laura and Belle

About 10 minutes later, Stephanie and I were settled in. We didn't do much unpacking because we would be there for only 10 days. It felt good just to lay down on a bed for a few minutes and soak it all in. Traveling across the world was exhausting! I could now say that I had experienced jet-lag. My eyes longed for the extended night, looking at only the back of my eyelids, but I was equally excited to meet these compelling women downstairs. From the moment I met them, I was drawn to them.

Not wanting to disappoint, Stephanie and I made our way downstairs where Belle had some hot tea and biscuits for us. We would sit in their tea room and just visit. I felt like I was in a movie. "Tea and biscuits." Even just saying it made me smile inside. "I'll take a spot of tea please." What a fun place to live. They actually do this in real life. What was even more interesting was that Belle offered milk with our tea. Do you really put milk in tea, too? How strange, but this is what they do. The phrase popped in my head: "When in Rome, do as the Romans." I converted that to, "When in England, do as the English." I added some milk to my hot tea. From the crystal glass dish, I used the miniature tongs to pick up two sugar cubes.

Hmmmm. English tea. I marveled that, here I was, sitting in England and drinking tea. This would definitely go down in my book of most amazing moments. From my "American" standards, the biscuits didn't taste like a traditional biscuit, nor did they taste like cookies. It was somehow a combination of the two: not too sweet but yummy, nonetheless.

Laura and Belle fired off several questions to Stephanie and me, questions about our families, what we studied in school, and what we were excited about. I answered their many questions: "I have an older sister, Ashley; a younger sister, Kate; and a little brother, Jacob. I'm pretty close to all of them. My dad works for a motorsports company, managing marketing and sales. My mom works at a hospital in accounting. We kids are close in age, so we've been able to grow up together, hanging out, doing sports, and for the most part, being pretty good friends. I've always competed in track and cross-country through high school, and I now have a scholarship at my university.

"I am an elementary education major, so I guess I want to teach," I said, hesitantly, because I really didn't know if teaching was what I was excited about. Here I was in my junior year of college, and I *still* didn't have a strong leaning toward a career. I couldn't stay in college forever. This was still a frustrating reminder.

Belle and Laura told us about how they were both excited to see God move in their country while our group was there. They had been praying and expecting God to do great things and were very excited that we were finally there.

"We need an awakening here. Our country needs an awakening. We know God is going to do great things," Laura said, her eyes filled with passion and her voice with equal anticipation.

I hadn't been around her much yet, but even as Laura briefly shared, her ability to just *be* had more passion and strength than I could remember ever seeing in anyone. Just to be. Her just *being* demonstrated more longing for Jesus than I had ever experienced. You could see the passion that was on her insides, displayed through her face, how she sat, her eyes, and her expressions. You could see her passion through her very being, like she was encompassed by a great bubble or accompanied by a great cloud. Even as we sat there in the tea room, I wanted to be around Laura. She was radiant. Her face shown with a glow I had never really seen. Being around her made me feel like I was in the very presence of Jesus. I longed for more of that feeling.

Being in her presence made my guilt feel lesser. It made my pain feel cushioned. It made me feel like I could eventually, maybe, experience forgiveness, be truly forgiven, and have my sins forgotten. Right now, I had no idea how God or anyone could ever forget what I had done or the horrible testimony I had left. My failures. My shortcomings. Those three days where I really did consider Rick or God. It made my heart feel heavy just thinking about it. I felt like I was accompanied by a great cloud also, but a great dark cloud of what felt like oppression and darkness. I longed for the light that I saw in Laura. I longed to experience freedom inside me, in my heart and in my mind. To be free from the heavy bondage I felt, the strong ties that linked back to Rick, even though he was across the world. Could I break free of the ties that held us together. They still felt so strong. They still felt like they had such a great hold on me. I just wanted to experience freedom. My heart ached to be free.

We finished our tea and biscuits. Belle and Laura must have been able to sense that Stephanie and I were extremely exhausted. They dismissed us to bed, and Laura let us know what time we would need to leave in order to get to the Loft on time.

After changing into our pajamas, we crawled into bed. Three weeks. I would be away for three weeks, three weeks away from Rick. I really wanted this experience to change me, to go back a different person, to go back healed and whole. Forgiven. I wanted to go back home with no guilt, free and without a stronghold of being tied to Rick. The feeling of where my life had come was almost repulsive, turning my stomach in knots. I craved happiness. I craved freedom. My thoughts must have trailed off quickly as sleep took over my tired body.

13

FORGIVENESS

The smell of bacon woke me. I wasn't sure if traveling made one hungry, but I felt like I could eat a horse. Stephanie and I finished getting dressed for our first full day in England and headed downstairs.

Approaching the kitchen, we could hear soft humming and were greeted by Belle in a white apron, her dark hair pinned up into a loose bun. I could tell by the aroma that she was a good cook.

From first glance into the kitchen, I felt an immediate peace and joy in my heart. The kitchen table was smiling with fresh flowers, including bright tulips and assorted roses clipped from the small garden. Fragile Tuscany juice glasses housed freshly-squeezed orange juice with pulp swimming inside while four empty orange peels sat aside the porcelain sink. Our teacups were on petite saucers that bloomed with elegant, bright florals and had a platinum trim around their rims. The teapot sat on an equally elegant saucer with the china sugar cube bowl at its side. Cloth napkins lay beside where our plates would be, silverware atop the neat fold. Though everything seemed so elegant just for a breakfast, it somehow seemed neatly simple and clean on the white, lace-trimmed tablecloth.

"Lovely morning to you. I pray you slept well last night," Belle said, gleaming. "Your food is hot and ready. I hope you're both hungry this morning." She placed a china plate in front of each of our spots at the table. Steam was dancing from our plates with three eggs over easy, a biscuit cut in half with butter dripping off the sides, and three pieces of bacon. To the right of our plates, she sat for each of us a tiny, china fruit bowl decorated with tendrils of buds and leaves, floral sprouts with flecks of gold, and shimmering mica. Fresh blackberries, raspberries, blueberries, and strawberries topped with what looked like a touch of powered sugar.

A feast for a princess. Despite wearing comfortable walking attire instead of a princess gown, I felt like royalty in this English flat.

Walking down the crimson brick steps of the flat, Laura let us know our walk would be only 10-15 minutes. The rose bushes lining the wrought iron fence were in full bloom with yellow and red silk-like petals. Cherry trees lined the cobblestone street. Remnants of the pink and white flowers still scattered their branches while the bright magenta and deep amethyst berries were abundantly in their season.

The weather was breathtaking. There was a cool breeze, and cotton ball clouds covered the sky. The temperature felt more like early-fall than mid-summer. It felt only 65 or 70 degrees. With the breeze and the sun's rays already beating down, it was simply perfect.

The street was quiet. After traveling a few blocks, Laura motioned for us to take the crosswalk toward the adjacent park.

"As you're walking tomorrow, just remember to stay on this footway for three blocks before crossing the carriageway. If you've arrived at the red phone box," she said, pointing toward the next block, "you've gone too far." Her English accent was like listening to music. I loved every word and sentence she said. "I will come to walk you back this evening, but if you are ever in a place that you need us, give me a bell any time," she said as she handed us each a piece of paper with her phone number. "You will see a phone box frequently. Just try to keep some coins with you. It will be much less than a pound, probably only 20-30 pence, but I doubt you will need to give me a bell. You will get along just lovely, and I believe you will fancy Ashford as much as I do!" With her arms outstretched, she spun around in a circle, the breeze catching her dark strands. Joy enveloped her with a smile that was contagious. She was made of happiness. She looked joy. She acted joy. She was joy. The very word described her much better than her real name, Laura.

"Thank you," Stephanie said and smiled. "You are such a big help to us! Thank you for walking us, too."

"Cheers, my friends. It is just such a pleasure to have you here. My mum and I have been quite excited for months. God is going to be so glorified on this trip. Our country needs this. Our country needs a revival. Our country needs Jesus. To see a lost bloke and imagine him living a life without knowing my Jesus makes my heart cry." In that split second, her eyes welled up with tears. "But praise the Lord," she declared, "you are here! The English love Americans. In the schools you will be going to and clinics where you will be serving, the little ones are so impressionable and think Americans walk on water. To influence a nation, you need to influence its young people. The heavens are going to be rejoicing at the great revival that will happen here."

The overflow of happiness made me speechless. I felt speechless around her. I just wanted her to talk. I had nothing to say that would be remotely as exciting as what she talked about. Jesus was clearly the love of her life. Because she had not yet mentioned a boyfriend, I imagined Jesus was her only love.

We exited the other end of the park, reacquainting our feet with cobblestone. The remaining two blocks swallowed us with the antiquated brick buildings on both sides of the tight alleyways. To my surprise, we had arrived! The side door to the Loft was just ahead. Because everything had been so dark when we arrived, it felt like the first time I was seeing the long, three-story building.

"Here you are. Have a lovely day! I will be back to get you at the close of your day."

"Thank you, Laura!" I said, echoed by Stephanie.

"Cheerio!" Laura waved and walked off.

Stephanie and I made our way into the Loft. It looked like most people were there, still some students from our group filing in. The place was packed! There sure were a lot of people in our group.

A lady stood up front at a keyboard and announced, "Good morning! Get settled in. My name is Patricia, but over the years it seems most people now call me Mama Pat." Bouncy brown curls brushed the top of her shoulders, and glasses framed her face. She did seem like the mama type, a mama that could give a really good hug, her broad shoulders providing a beacon of safety.

Everything about me and where I was emotionally seemed unstable, but I was happy that at least the ground I was standing on was concrete. The people surrounding me seemed immovable. I knew, for the survival of my fragile and wounded Christian faith, this was a good thing.

"Feel free to call me whichever you like. Each morning, we'll start with a time of prayer and worship," Mama Pat said as her fingers were already effortlessly dancing across the acoustic keyboard.

Voices ascended in unison as Mama Pat began into the first worship song. I wasn't used to hearing such a mix of voices. There were as many guys as there were women, so the deep, baritone voices were refreshing to hear. What a beautiful sound! I have never been around this many men who loved the Lord. So many of them were good-looking, but the most attractive feature they possessed was that their eyes were closed, their hands were lifted, and their voices were praising the Lord loudly. There *really* were guys out there that loved the Lord. There were guys out there who really weren't just normal church-goers. There were some that actually had a passion for Jesus?! It was a refreshing morning.

I saw Jason. He was one of them. His arms were lifted, focused on his singing, focused on the Lord. It seemed like just another prick of a pin; this perfect guy was already taken.

Praise and worship was followed by a short devotion time, led by one of our leaders, Max. His Canadian accent rang as he began. "What a great time of worship, eh?!" Max led us in a time of clapping as he glanced over at Mama Pat. "We will become a family over the next few weeks to come—in times of worship as well as while we're out and about. Look around at your brothers and sisters." I enjoyed being around different accents. Max saying "out and about" sounded more like "oat and a boat," such a distinct difference from my friends back home. So far, the English and Canadian accents just made me smile.

Max then laid out what the day would entail. Today, there would be two groups of people. The morning would be filled with sports and drama practices. Then, we would meet at the Stour Centre for lunch at noon, followed by an afternoon of street ministry. Then, a small group would be going to a school to share testimonies during their general assembly. How amazing. He explained that, here in England, we were free to share about Jesus in schools. We were free to talk about it in their school assembly; we just could not give an altar call at the school. Although, we could share with them how *we* accepted Jesus into our lives.

Mama Pat and Max split us into our respective groups. We would be running sports clinics at the Stour Centre after dinner each evening. This event was designed to draw in the community. Our athletic clinics would be free. We would usher kids and adults into the Stour Centre for an assembly. Each night would offer something different: a band, drama skits, and praise and worship. But each night would somehow include a salvation message, an opportunity for people to invite Jesus to be the head of their lives.

As Max detailed where each respective group would go, I noted that the cheerleaders were getting together to prepare for the evening's clinic. Though it was only Day One, we had to prepare what we would be teaching the kids who attended the cheerleading breakout session at the sports clinics. Though clinics would not begin until tomorrow, we definitely had a lot to do in a short time.

It was late in the afternoon, and I found myself in the shade of a tree, parked on a cold, iron bench. Overlooking a small channel, blossoms of pink flower petals floated through the air and into the water. I had only escaped my mind for a few hours, and here I was again; there was no escaping myself. I sat in the midst of the beauty of the rose bushes and flowers, the green vibrant trees draping their branches over the finely bricked paths, and the trickle of the channel. It looked like a portrait. Here I sat, feeling not like a magnificent portrait but like a canvas with wet acrylics dumped into a cesspool of black, brown, navy, and red chaos, deserted to be alone and smeared into something unrecognizable. I felt far from a masterpiece, and I couldn't run from me. I was always there.

My exhaustion had caught me, and all I could do was cry. I felt such a heavy weight about Rick. I felt the dirtiness of disappointment, the guilt of letting God down. I couldn't hold it in any longer. The shame I felt was overwhelming. I sat there and just cried. I did not feel worthy of being on this trip or being with these great people.

Chip walked up and sat down beside me. He was tall and lanky, his skater attire reminding me of his home state of California. "So you're having a good day then?" Chip's eyes widened. Veins in his neck were bouncing out, accompanying his large yet fake smile. His tone was facetious.

I couldn't help but laugh. In the short time I had known Chip during our intro session and lunch, his jovial wit and laughing stamped him as the group's comedian. His personality was lighthearted and refreshing. I wished it could be that easy. I wished I could laugh myself out of this gloomy pit.

The sun was bright, and the park was open. "Do you want to talk about it?" He said, changing to a serious tone.

I burst into tears; I couldn't help it. Like a rampage, I began to spill everything. I shared about how I initially wanted to witness to Rick, we became close friends, and how I blew it all right before I left. I screwed it up. I lost my witness. Worst of all, I had known better. I rattled off how I just wanted to experience freedom. I wanted to enjoy the trip. I wanted this trip to change me—not just others... me. I wanted to be new. I wanted to experience forgiveness. I knew it was available, but I seemed so undeserving. Rivers of tears streamed down my face.

There on the park bench, Chip put his arm around my shoulder and was a friend. Patting my shoulder, he said, "Everything is going to be okay. God had a plan for you to come on this trip, during a time that you would need it the most. Emily, if you have asked Him, He has already forgiven you. You just have to forgive yourself. You just have to believe that He has forgiven you and receive it. He is in the business of forgiveness. Think about it. If He didn't forgive, how could *any* of these people we are sharing the gospel with get accepted into heaven? If He didn't forgive, why are we even here? He will forgive you, Emily. Just ask Him."

I knew what he said was true. He made it sound so easy, but through my tears, I just didn't know how to come to grips with it all. I still felt such a great heaviness, and I couldn't imagine how forgiveness could allow it to lift.

Dragging my arm, Chip pulled me to my feet. "Let me walk you to dinner. You are going to get through this, Emily," he said as he put his arm around my shoulder with a brotherly side hug, "and you are going to be better than new when it's all done! You are exactly where you are supposed to be, and that's on this trip."

His encouragement lifted my spirits a little. Maybe before it was all over, God would use me.

Back at the house after dinner, Stephanie made her way to bed while I sat down in the tea room with Laura. Our chat began with Laura sharing about her love for Jesus and about what they were doing at her church.

Though, as full of Jesus as Laura was, a heaviness still filled the room. I believed we both could sense it. Could she see the black cloud that accompanied me? The cloud wasn't allowing me to forget, let alone forgive myself. It just hovered over me, everywhere I went, following me.

"Emily, if you need to talk about anything, I just want you to know that I'm here to listen," she said. Compassion filled her eyes as if she knew there had been something weighing on me.

In such a short time, I had come to view Laura as a spiritual giant. As we sat and talked, her eyes were so intense as if she was looking right into my soul to the core of my being. She seemed to have an ability to discern things. With my limited knowledge of the things of God, I assumed her gift of discernment came from her close relationship with Him. Even though Laura couldn't have been more than 5-6 years older than me, she seemed years advanced. Her spiritual maturity made her seem grounded and solid. At this point of my fragile walk, I would have believed almost anything Laura said.

"I guess I'm not very good at hiding my emotions," I responded. For the next couple of hours, we talked. I cried. She listened. I poured out my heart, replaying the horrible details of my fall. My heart laid there on the carpet, so broken into pieces. Un-repairable, I thought. Was there hope for even me? Could God forgive me?

I explained how—for three days, the worst three days of my life—I stood there, overlooking the lake with God in one hand and Rick in the other. I kept running and running and running from God. I wanted to choose which it would be. I wanted to choose. I did not want help from God. I did not want persuading. But, there I stood, one decision away from choosing a life without God. I cried at the fact that I was such a fine thread away from denying a life with God. I considered it for three long days! God was *shut off* from my life, and I almost walked out on Him. I almost turned my back completely on

Him. I was sure that many disappointments would've accompanied a decision to follow after Rick if I would've chosen him.

Compassion filled Laura's eyes as she just listened. You could see the pain on her face. It was like she was feeling the pain with me, like she was feeling the guilt and carrying it with me. Her eyes and face showed such great compassion as I just sobbed uncontrollably. I sobbed, and I sobbed. I sat there on the carpet, drinking my tea. The hot tea was comforting, mixed with milk and honey. I felt that Laura knew the whole story. There was nothing else to tell. I was empty and exhausted. I didn't think I could cry any more.

Laura didn't try to answer me with her own words. Laura just laid her hands on me and began to pray. Her prayer to God was so filled with heart, so filled with passion, so filled with longing and a desperate need. She was not asking Him to do things that she questioned whether He would do. She was asking Him to do things that she sounded confident that He *would do*. She thanked Him for healing me. She thanked Him for forgiving me. She thanked Him for mending my broken heart, for putting it back together. Her passionate words were so comforting.

I could feel a presence in the room like I had never felt before. I could feel a presence in the room like light. The light of the presence was so great that it was pushing out the dark cloud that hovered around me. The dark cloud was being choked out. There was no room left for it. Though my eyes had been closed during the entirety of her prayer, the room felt completely filled with His full presence, with light. A cloud of white. I didn't want to open my eyes. I just wanted to sit in it, sit in this presence forever. It felt so good. The heaviness was gone. The blackness clouding my heart was no longer there. I felt free! For the first time in months, my heart was smiling again. Shining and glowing, my heart was happy.

I didn't even hear the words that Laura was praying anymore. Or, I didn't understand them. I just felt better. At some point during my loss of time, she closed the prayer. I was unsure if we had been there for hours or just minutes. Time seemed to be lost. With her sweet embrace, she said, "Emily, you are forgiven! He loves you so much, and so do I!" She held me in her embrace, repeating in a whisper, "You are forgiven. You are forgiven." Her hair was soft and smelled of lilacs. I felt like I was bouncing on clouds.

I was forgiven. I knew it. I felt it. I felt forgiveness. I felt loved. I felt clean.

I also felt exhausted. All of the tears, the emotions, the great white cloud, experiencing such a presence of God... I knew my sleep would be sweet. We said our "goodnights" and headed to bed.

14

THE CHALKBOARD

I felt revived. On my first day as the new, forgiven me, I was assigned to the street ministry group.

We stood around in our green matching shirts alongside other bystanders as we watched this man paint and narrate the story of Jesus. The initial strokes were three simple, plain strokes of black on the canvas. It did not look like it was going to turn into an awesome painting. At the end of the gruesome, retold story of Jesus' death on the cross, the completion of the canvas showed an amazing picture. The painting depicted three crosses, sunbeams shooting across the canvas, and a glorious resurrection! Jesus was no longer on the cross but had risen.

From where we stood on the cobblestone streets, hope and joy came even to me as I gloried in my newfound forgiveness. Jesus really did go to the cross to defeat sin and hell for *me*! A feeling of such gratefulness came upon me. Could other people feel what I was feeling just from a mere picture? At the completion of the story, soft worship music began to play as the AOC members dispersed into the crowd of people. The opportunity to talk to on-lookers was ripe, and in our own individual ways, we began conversations, praying we would be able to invite and welcome a new believer into the family of God.

I sat down next to a woman named Sarah. Like everyone else, her English accent sounded like it was from a movie, but her tone was downtrodden. I could tell that the story made an impact on her, but her life challenges were getting in the way of her making a decision. We talked through things. We discussed how Jesus, through the Holy Spirit, was a great Comforter. I shared how this decision would give her access to a Helper, One she could commune with, pray to, and receive direction from. We talked about how much Jesus loved her and how, if it would have been just her, he still would've gone to that cross like the artist so beautifully described. He loved her that much. Jesus cared about her so much that he would've even done it for just her.

As we talked, I was thankful that I finally felt the guilt-free freedom to share with her. It was amazing that—for days, weeks, and months—I had been carrying such a strong weight of bondage. I had allowed entanglements of the world to cloud the fact that Jesus went to the cross for every sin—even mine! I sat there, knowing that sometimes words were easy to say but harder to experience for ourselves. I hoped that Sarah would be able to feel even a portion of the freedom I felt when Laura prayed for me.

Sarah sat in silence. Tears streamed down her face. I said, "Sarah, God desires for us to one day live in eternity, walking the streets of gold with Him. Dancing, shouting, and laughing. His love for you is so great, and nothing you have ever done nor will ever do will separate you from the love of God. He thinks you are beautiful, and He wants to walk every day with you, guiding you, blessing you, and loving you."

"I want that. I need that," she said as tears continued to stream down her face. "I need direction and comfort. I don't want to be alone. How can I have Jesus with me?"

There, on the bench of the cobblestone street, we prayed. She simply repeated my words to invite Jesus into her life:

> Lord Jesus, I thank you for dying on the cross to give *me* the opportunity to live. Today, I confess to you my sins and ask that you would forgive me. I confess that *You* are Lord. I believe in my heart that God raised You from the dead. I thank you that you defeated death, hell, and the grave and that today you *live*. I thank you that, because I have confessed and believed that, I am saved! Thank you for saving me! Please guide me in my walk and relationship with You. I love You. I pray all of this in Jesus' mighty Name! Amen!

Sarah embraced me. Through tears, she thanked me and said she felt better already. She said, "I knew there was a reason I walked this way today. I didn't know why, but now I know that this is why I was led down this small path instead of taking the road today. Thank you, Miss Emily."

Before we parted, I invited her to come to the Stour Centre at 7:00pm. I handed her a flyer with details of the night of praise and worship and a short message. I also mentioned that I would love to get her plugged in with other Christians in the area. She thanked me for the invitation and told me she would do her best to make it. Our "goodbyes" left me feeling wonderful. Angels right now were rejoicing in heaven! They were having a party!

I was in awe of God. Just a day had passed since I, myself, had been bawling like a baby, needing forgiveness. I was amazed that in such a short time the Lord could use me, newly-mended, to lead someone to His saving grace. Praise the Lord that we only have to be willing and not perfect. He can even use us who have messed up. I sat, thankful.

I didn't see many of the other AOCers. Many of them had most likely headed over to the Stour Centre for lunch. I saw that David was still around. I hoped that maybe we would be able to walk over together. I liked the whole rule of "ladies need to be accompanied by a guy when going to or from the AOC facilities." That was a great rule. Right now, it gave me a good excuse to get to walk with David.

David saw me sitting on the bench by myself and made his way over. "Do you want me to walk with you to lunch?" he asked.

"Sure. That would be great!" As we began to walk, I shared my new excitement. "So, I just prayed with that lady and led her to Jesus! I'm so excited! What an awesome opportunity! It was so exciting to see how the Holy Spirit led the conversation!"

David did a little jump-skip out of excitement as we walked. "Emily, that is so exciting! Congratulations! You led someone to Jesus! How awesome!" I couldn't help but laugh at his positive response.

We were both excited. We turned to walk through one of the parks that would be a more scenic route to the Stour Centre. The park was beautiful and so green. The lawn was meticulously manicured, tall hedges lined the wrought iron gates of the park and were trimmed to perfection. Rose bushes filled with white, yellow, and red roses guided each path and sidewalk. The middle of the park was expansively open with green, plush grass enveloping it, accompanied by sidewalks on each side that crossed in the middle. Further ahead were paths and gardens filled with more rose bushes. Benches arrayed different sections of the peaceful gardens. The only description of this place was an *oasis*. It was opulent. This park was more beautiful than any park I had ever seen. A fountain was off to the right where another entrance could usher more people into this oasis of vibrant flowers, green grass, and majestic trees that were hovering over and hiding this magical place.

David and I walked slow. Though I had not talked to him much, I longed for this time to continue. It felt good to walk with him and talk with someone whose fervor for the Lord seemed to exceed my own. Aside from our first meeting at the airport and the impression he left on me as being the "Mr. Congeniality" of our group, the only other real interaction I had with him was at one of the schools where he was throwing the hammer.

He was great with the kids. One young boy specifically took an interest in David's coaching. They boy had blonde hair sweeping over his eyes, attentive as David instructed him. David had his khaki hat on backwards, covering his own sandy blonde hair. David was pretty tall, about 6'2". With his broad shoulders, he seemed to tower over the boy. His green FCA shorts hid his muscular legs.

David had shown the boy how to hold the handle of the hammer. A long wire came off the handle that attached to the heavy ball. Gaining momentum, David began to slowly spin to show the boy how to get the hang of the hammer's weight. Spin, spin, release. I enjoyed watching. The hammer seemed neat. Being a track athlete myself, I obviously enjoyed the sport.

There was something about him. It just felt good to be around him. I had never been around a godly man like him. A "cool," godly man—not like some crusty old, boring Christian. I mean, David was really good-looking, had an upbeat personality, and he was fun! There was nothing "crusty" or "boring" about him. He kept just enough of an edge or mystery. In my old days, I may have called it "a chase." He left "a chase" in him that caused him to be even more appealing.

We continued our stroll through the park, walking toward the Stour Centre. As if out of nowhere, David stopped, turned to me, and hugged me. Right at a cross-section of paths, we stood, David hugging me. It seemed so spontaneous, even a bit awkward because I did not know David well, but it was still nice.

In that moment, what seemed to only be a split second of time, God revealed something amazing to me. Hovering over David's left shoulder, my right side, I could see a big, green chalkboard only an arm's-length away. A large hand holding a white piece of chalk wrote these words on the chalkboard: "This is your husband. This is the man you are going to marry."

I knew it was God's hand, and I knew that David did not see it. It happened so fast. It was almost hard to believe it even happened, but the picture was engraved immediately in my spirit. It was so clear and crisp. It was so evident that it was God's hand.

My mind raced with questions. "Had God really been instructing me? How could this be? Right now? During this time? I had just experienced the lowest point of my life. It had barely been a week ago, and God was going to show this to me? I still did not even know David well. Could he really be my husband though he was almost still a stranger?" This was definitely life-altering. Life changing. I did feel like I was on the upswing, climbing my way out of the pit of despair, but this was indeed the *very* last thing I would have expected or anticipated. It seemed surreal. It was overwhelming.

The chalkboard was gone. The hug was over. David looked at me and simply said, "I just wanted to give you a hug. I hope you didn't mind."

"Uh, mind?" I thought, "Are you kidding me? I loved it!"

I simply replied back with, "I didn't mind. It was nice."

David grabbed my hand. For the next 100 yards to the exit gate of the park, we walked hand-in-hand. What was going on?! My feelings were racing. I was trying to get my feet back on the ground. This amazing, godly man was holding my hand! This was so strange but awesome! I felt so small next to him. He was so tall. He initiated and was holding *my* hand. He hugged me. I felt like I was not walking but floating on cloud nine.

It was July 14th, 1998. The morning was filled with practices. During the afternoon, our group would split up with half going to a nursing home and the other half doing street ministry. I noticed that David was in the group that would be going to the nursing home, and I was in the other group. I was a bit bummed, but I knew it would be a good day.

On this particular day, I just wanted to read the Bible. It already felt like a peaceful day; I expected great things. I found a little cafe and bought a hot tea—prepared the "English" way—and a hot blueberry scone. I took my purchases and headed to the park. I remembered seeing a secluded little pocket hide-away that was set apart from the main traffic of the park. That was where I wanted to be. I just wanted to read and pray. I wanted to seek the Lord and hear His Voice.

I walked in through the main gate. The park was breathtaking. I wished we had something like this back home. It was just so peaceful. I turned immediately to a hideaway pocket of the quaint oasis and found the tucked-away nook in the park to be empty. "Perfect," I thought.

I set up camp, getting out my Bible, my journal, and my pens. I placed my scone and tea on the bench. There, I began to search out Scripture, seeking the very heart of my God who so graciously forgave me. Though my fall with Rick was just over a week ago, he thankfully seemed like a world away. As I sat in this utopia, I was so thankful for God's forgiveness. I was so thankful that I felt His forgiveness. When I arrived in England, I didn't know if my heart would ever recover from the black hole it was in. My entire world and existence felt dark. Would there and could there be a recovery from falling into such sin?

Joy rose up in my heart with a resounding *yes!* "Yes! Yes!" was the answer! There I sat, forgiven! God had really forgiven me, and I knew it! I felt it! On the night Laura prayed for me, I received a forgiveness that I didn't know existed. It was as if God Himself recreated my heart into one that was white as snow. The darkness was gone, and my new heart resided. Ahhhhhh. To feel whole again. I longed to please my Father. I longed to know Him more. I paused from my thoughts and just looked around.

The cobblestone path swept into a horseshoe walkway. Trees were shading the area, allowing just enough blue sky and sunlight to peek through. Rose bushes and flower bulbs were scattered about, adding the perfect splash of color. I most definitely felt that I had found a wonderful, quiet little haven. In this place, I believed God Himself would come to spend time with me. It was like a piece of heaven on earth.

More than an hour had passed as I was lost in the Word. Digging in, devouring, highlighting, and jotting notes as I read, I was enjoying my quiet time—my time with me, the Lord, and my Bible. Then, out of nowhere, I got a sense that I needed to hurry. "Get up. Go. Now. Get up. Get your things. Go out to the middle of the park. Go sit out in the middle of the park. Go now."

The urgency seemed so great and direct. I assumed it was a prompting from the Holy Spirit, my friend whose presence I had sensed only a handful of times before. Without questioning, I quickly gathered up my belongings and left my oasis, left my haven and made my new camp out in the openness of the park. The fairway of the open park had beautiful green grass like you would see on a nice golf course, trimmed tightly to perfection.

Less than five minutes had passed, and then I saw the reason why I was in the middle of the park. A woman dressed in a business suit was passing through the park on the far sidewalk. The red flag went up in my spirit, almost as if a spotlight was pointing her out. I knew why I was ushered so quickly to make my way to my new camp. I knew I was placed there just for her, to talk to her.

I bounced up—my newfound obedience a bit nerving—and headed to chat with my park friend. Our conversation led us to sit on a nearby bench. As we talked, the opportunity opened for me to share Jesus. Within a few short minutes, we were praying, and she received Jesus into her life as her Savior. It was the fastest time of sharing I had ever experienced. It was so quick. We embraced and, as quickly as she appeared, she was gone.

Praise the Lord. I was so thankful that I was obedient. Wow. God was so amazing. "Simply amazing," I thought.

I spent a bit more time reading, and I then made my way out of the park to the main cobblestone street. I saw that the other group must have finished with the nursing home as many of them were scattered about the street. Then, there was David.

"Hey!" he said.

"Hey there," I responded.

"I'm heading to the Stour Centre. You wanna go with me?" he asked.

"Sure."

We began our walk through the park once again. I was excited. I already loved being with him. As we walked, I told him about my day: the park and the oasis, the quick prompting of the Holy Spirit, and how quickly the lady appeared. I was so excited about being able to lead her to the Lord. David shared in my excitement.

"Hey, do you want to go back and check out the rose gardens?" he said as he pointed toward the manicured maze of flowers off the path's sidewalk.

"I'd love too."

We walked through the intricacy of beauty, red, yellow, and white roses perfectly positioned. They were bigger than any roses I had ever seen. They were beautiful. A garden of perfume filling the air, I only wished I could bottle the smell and the moment. We knelt over and smelled many of them.

David stood behind me and wrapped his arms around me. For a moment, it felt nice to be held. As quickly as the innocence of this hug came, in one movement, it seemed to be gone. It didn't feel right. He held me for a moment longer, and then we made our way out of the garden. I just didn't feel good about it.

I wanted David to be different than the guys I had dated, the guys I was with before I was walking with the Lord. I didn't want David to be like them. The mere thoughts of them reminded me of the cheapness I felt when I was around them. I knew the worldly relationships I had experienced were not based in purity but were based in self, fulfilling the desires of the flesh. I knew David was only human, but my desire was for someone who wouldn't even consider doing anything with impure motives.

Maybe my dreams were too far-fetched? Maybe it was lofty to think that, in this day and age, true purity was a virtue that was still held in high regard. The real, underlying lump in my heart was that I did not want to feel dirty. It seemed I had lived a whole life of feeling dirty and guilty, and I wanted to avoid those feelings at all costs. I wanted to start over. I wanted my actions to be pleasing to Jesus.

Outside of the garden, David had me sit me down on a bench. "Emily, I'm sorry. That was wrong of me. We need to set some guidelines. I think maybe we should not be together alone. If we are together, it would be better if someone else is with us. I know that, on this trip, the focus needs to be on Jesus and seeing people come to Him. I just don't want the temptation to be with you to take our focus off of why we are here. Please forgive me, Emily."

"I forgive you." I nodded in agreement and said, "And I agree with you. That sounds like a good idea."

A breath of fresh air. David wasn't perfect, but the action he took to sit me down and apologize was refreshing. No guy had ever apologized for anything! It seemed a little middle-schoolish because we hadn't technically even *done* anything, but I would take that any day over the alternative that the world offered!

A recollection of my first kiss as a sixth-grader flashed in my mind. It was a planned event as I got a restroom pass and met by the lockers. The awkward moment of silence came. My sixth-grade boyfriend stood there by our lockers with his eyes closed. As fast as I could, I kissed him on the cheek and sprinted back up the stairs and into my classroom. I decided that, if I had a "middle-school" physical relationship with my fiancé until we were married, I would be delighted! To save everything else for the honeymoon would be, to me, amazing.

We got up from the park bench and walked toward the exit. This time, our hands were empty—not hand-in-hand—just pleasantly but longingly empty.

15

MINISTRY

July 15th. It was a busy day. Two days ago, I barely noticed David. Now, I longed just to be in the same room with him. So far, though, he did not sit by me at meals or even go out of his way to talk to me. I anxiously awaited our next interaction.

I couldn't get the vision of the chalkboard out of my head. Why would God show me something like this? I highly doubted that a chalkboard floated down from heaven, appearing to David and labeling me as his wife. Even though the experience was now hidden in the depths of me, deep in my spirit, I felt that he could actually be "the one."

It was a bit hard to believe that God would write on a chalkboard. Why a chalkboard? Was God being old-fashioned? We didn't even use chalkboards anymore. Did God really work that way? This experience was foreign and something I had never experienced before, but it was certainly something I could not make up. How would one even imagine God writing on a free-floating chalkboard in the sky? The weirdness of it made me believe its message even more.

Our morning cheerleading practice flew by. We were preparing cheers and dances to teach in our sports clinics later that evening.

After our practice, it was time to hit the cobblestone streets of Ashford for a run. If I was going to compete in our upcoming track meets, I needed to keep my conditioning up. I didn't know exactly how far I was running, but I would just run for time. The track athletes were going to head to the track to train later this week in preparation for our meet with Northern Ireland. I would feel at home with the familiar feel of the rubber track beneath my feet, the gentle curves sweeping me into familiar straightaways. Every track was the same. Every track felt good. Every track had memories.

In the afternoon, I, along with six other AOC attendees, went to a school. We would participate in their general assembly and would then be split up into groups, doing different activities outside. As the quarterback on our AOC football team, Mike was chosen to give his testimony in the general assembly. Tall and good-looking, his square jawline and thick auburn hair made him look more like a model than a summer "missionary." His straight, white teeth and piercing chocolate eyes softened as he laughed and talked with the little kids in the primary school.

Mike was introduced and smiled as he began talking to the kids tightly seated in the assembly. He said, "I've always been an athlete in America. Football and basketball were always the most important things in my life until I met Jesus… I'm sure there may be a few of you who have experienced your parents getting separated. Well, a few years ago, mine did, too. These seemed to be the darkest hours of my life. My friends didn't know what I was going through or how to relate. I tried to just play more basketball or more football to avoid the pain that I was feeling, but I couldn't escape it. I laid in bed at night and just cried. I wondered if there was anything I could've done that would've kept my parents together. Was there something I did that made them choose to get a divorce? Honestly, it was the hardest time I had ever faced."

Mike continued, "I wasn't sure if my buddy, Kip, could tell I was acting differently or that I was in a lot of pain, but he invited to a youth event at his church. Before everything got started, we shot some hoops outside, and the kids at this church seemed pretty cool. I didn't know what I was in for that night. We headed inside to sing a few songs and listen to the youth leader. I realized I longed to have what he shared about."

Walking back and forth on the assembly stage, Mike said, "The pastor told me that this Jesus would help me with anything I was going through. He said that Jesus loved me. Not only that, Jesus died for me so I would not have to go to hell. All I had to do was receive Jesus into my life. That night, I got out of my seat and went to the front. There, on my knees [Mike knelt down on the stage, folding his hands in front of him and closing his eyes], I asked Jesus to come into my life and be my Savior."

After the long pause of reflection, the kids started clapping, and so did we.

"Sure, life hasn't been a walk-in-the-park with my parents getting divorced, but it has been a lot easier with Jesus. I still experienced tears and pain, but Jesus has brought a lot of comfort. Since that time, Jesus has really helped me with my athletics and direction in my life. When I pray, He's even answered questions that I did not know the answers to. Jesus became a best friend to me. He even brought me here to England to meet all of you kids," he said, bending over to rub a boy's head as he laughed.

"But, hey! Who wants to go outside and play?!" he shouted, raising both fists into the air. The kids' shreeks, cheers, and screams rang through the auditorium. "Okay! We're going to do that! Let me tell you one more thing. Do you want to hear one more thing before we go outside?" He waited for their response.

"Yesssssssss!" the voices of about 300 elementary-age kids sounded in unison, happy at the opportunity to yell at the top of their lungs!

"Well, we are going to play some sports this afternoon, but I want to invite you tonight to hang out with all of us Americans! We are so excited to be here in England! Tonight, we'll have sports clinics, a live band playing music, and a special message at the Stour Centre. It will be at seven o'clock, so come out and join us. We are going to have a blast! Let me hear you if you are going to try to come out to be with the Americans tonight!" Mike invited more cheers and screaming!

"Wooooooo yahhhhhhh!" The kids yelled and yelled until their faces were red!

"Great! Well, we'll see you tonight! And we'll see you outside with your teachers in just a few minutes!" Mike exited the stage. Excited for the temporary permission to not be proper, the kids continued to cheer.

I smiled at what a great job Mike seemed to do, connecting with the little kids. What a breath of fresh air and a bit overwhelming to be among so many guys who loved the Lord! It was such a rare thing. I truly had never experienced a group like this before. It seemed more common for women to be outspoken about their love for the Lord, and here more than 40 guys in the same place that had a passion for Jesus was unique—to say the least!

I still wanted to keep my eyes on Jesus. The mess with Rick, though I was forgiven, was still fresh in my mind and heart. I felt like the wounds and the hurts were still healing. I was too fragile to even like anyone romantically. I would just be fun, have fun, focus on seeing people saved, and make new friends. Guys or girls... just friends.

Over the next couple of hours, we spent time outside, rotating groups of kids through our stations. The kids were so excited to run and jump on the guys. They would try to tackle them but didn't have a chance. The guys showed their strength as they picked up the feisty boys. Now, they were not just Americans. They were superheroes to these boys. It was cute to watch the big football players play with the kids.

In one group, the kids were learning to pass a football, catch a football, and do a short scrimmage. In another group, they were learning to pass, bump, and set a volleyball. In my group, they were learning to do a short cheer. At the end, we went over and did our newly learned cheers for all of the AOC guys and kids playing in the football scrimmage. The kids picked things up rather quickly, smiling from ear to ear. This would no doubt be the highlight of their week and month, having the Americans at their school.

Our time wound down, and we said our goodbyes, hug upon hug upon hug. We even signed countless autographs. We all said we were excited to see them tonight if they could come.

The next few hours did not leave much "down time." We got back in time for dinner, a time of prayer, and fellowship before heading off to begin the sports clinics. The evening had begun. So many kids and adults gave us definite opportunities to minister, make friends, and help create memories.

Kids from our school ran up to embrace me with big hugs, obviously having talked their parents into bringing them. Our cheerleading clinic had as many boys as it had girls, far from what we'd experience if we were in the States. I was sure the macho programming of American boys would keep them from learning cheers and dances.

Our hour flew by quickly. As our time came to a close for the sports clinics, we ushered the kids and adults into the Stour Centre. It was like we were having a big party. Excitement filled the air. Everyone was smiling and happy. The Americans were here. It was so funny that it was such a big deal. I wondered if all of England liked Americans or if it was just this little town of Ashford. We seemed like a novelty.

I enjoyed being around the English. Their accents were so… royal. With all the attention, hugs, and signatures, I felt like I was playing the role of a princess. We should be in big fancy dresses, curtsying to those we passed by, waving the "princess" wave to the other aristocrats, nobles, and peasants. Didn't every girl dream of being a princess when she was younger? It was so fun just to listen to them talk with their dignified accents that I had practiced during my childhood.

The evening began with a band. Everyone was having a great time, jumping around, laughing, and singing. The gymnasium was filled. Most of the young people stood on the floor in front of the stage. The stands were scattered with people. As things quieted down, most kids joined their parents in the stands.

The drama team took the stage, and "Do You Feel Their Pain" by Steve Camp began to blare through the Stour Centre speakers. There were about 10 AOCers on stage. Eight of them were frozen in different positions, dressed completely in black with black scarves, representing the sin that was binding them. On one, the black scarf was around her eyes; on another, around his ears; on another, her hands in the air with the black scarf binding her hands together like handcuffs; and around yet another, the scarf was wrapped tightly around her mouth. As the music started, each actor had an expression and stance of anguish. They looked like they were in pain or experiencing torture, their expressions so real with despair. One sin-bound person with his black scarf binding him in a drunken position had an invisible bottle tipped back to his mouth. Alcoholism had him bound to a world of sin, a life of sin. His life was in a bottomless pit, ashamed, sad, and empty. The lyrics rang throughout the auditorium.

> Do you feel their pain? Has it touched your life? Can you taste the salt in the tears they cry? Will you love them more, than the hate that's built? Will you love them back to life again?

You could see what looked like real emotions. Anguish. Lonely souls. The onlookers watched, some with a tear sneaking out of the corner of their eyes as they witnessed the bondage.

As we watched and listened, the music told a story as we witnessed the silence of the drama team, acting out their roles. Missi began making her way around to each person imprisoned by sin. As she acted out, you could tell she was sharing passionately about how much Jesus loved them. How if they would receive Him as their Savior, they could be free and leave behind their life of sin. Their bondages could be broken. He loved them so much and died for them. He desired and even longed for a relationship with them! One by one, the black scarves binding each actor were loosened. Individually, they chose to be set free.

Center stage, our eyes were drawn to a man dressed completely in white, representing Jesus. His arms were outstretched like he was hanging on the cross. His body jolted, showing the pain Jesus felt as he hung on the cross, his face showing an expression of torture and pain as he turned it from one side to the other. His arms were outstretched as if they were saying, "Come! Come to me! I'm doing this for you! Come! Come child! This is for you. I'm dying so that *you* would have life! Come! Turn your sin over. Give it to me. Be set free!"

We watched David writhe in pain as he played the role of Jesus. The lyrics continued to call to the lost: "All empty eyes and lonely souls, standing for love, and praying for hope." The music escalated, the volume loud. "And Jesus said, bring them all to me. I will make them whole. I can set them free!" Throughout the stands, people stood up all over. The magnitude of the freedom was great. Some in the stands lifted their arms in the air, thanking Jesus for what He had done on the cross.

One by one, those bound by black scarves, bound by sin, came and hung their scarves on Jesus' outstretched arms. Once free, they bowed at the feet of Jesus and worshipped Him, each experiencing freedom for the first time. Freedom! Release! Freedom from their sin, the sin that had been binding them! Freedom in Jesus. Jesus' favor, mercy, grace, passion, and sacrifice allowed them to be free.

Will you care for them? Will you lend a hand? Will you cast a stone? Do you feel their pain? Has it touched your life? Can you taste the salt in the tears they cry? Will you love them more, than the hate that's built? Will you love them back to life again?

The end of the song brought each person bowing and worshipping their newfound Savior, Jesus. Freedom. Life. Forgiveness. Wholeness. Jesus took all of their pain. Jesus took all of their sin. Jesus brought wholeness. Jesus loved them back to life again!

My heart felt so full. What a powerful drama performance. What power. What an amazing way to show what we can experience in Christ, the freedom that is available no matter what bondage, no matter what sin. "Praise the Lord," I thought. "Praise the Lord that God sent Jesus for me. For all the sin and shame. For all the guilt. That God sent Jesus so that I could be forgiven even for my relationship with Rick."

The last notes played and great applause filled the arena. The drama team waited just a moment before exiting the platform. Laura's pastor came to the microphone and thanked AOC for such an amazing drama performance. He offered another round of applause for the Americans and Canadians who had come over with AOC in order to minister to their town. A great applause went up through the arena, and he invited up the next speaker, David.

I was taken aback to see him walking up onto the stage. David had a lot of surprises I didn't know about. I just found out he was amazing at acting. And now, he was going to speak?! My interest was sparked even more. Frozen in disbelief as David began to speak, my thoughts were simple: "Wow, this guy is quite talented. Mr. Congeniality had more than just a pretty face and an athletic build."

He took me off guard. Upon meeting him, I had no intentions of liking him. Where I referred to him in my mind as Mr. Congeniality, he was now becoming David—a very appealing David at that.

His ability to communicate with the audience had everyone hanging on his every word. He began to share about his relationship with a Savior, a Savior who had suffered and died so that he could have life. A Savior who had given up everything for him, for us. He told us of a Savior, a Savior full of love who desired to have a relationship with each of us.

David shared the details of what Jesus went through on His journey to the cross. The betrayal and torture as Jesus received a beating like none other, with the "cat of nine tails" whip. Not just a common whip, these tails had charred glass and stone woven into their leather-like braids, the nine tails tearing flesh from His body at each of the 39 lashes.

To hear about what Jesus went through made me cringe. I could hardly believe it myself that Jesus did this for me. He endured it for me. I wasn't sure that I could handle even one lash from such a horrific object. Simply hearing about it made me queasy.

"Jesus was an innocent man. The soldiers proceeded to club a crown made of thorns onto Jesus' head," he said. With a ferocious beating motion, he pretended to have a club, beating Jesus like the soldiers did.

David continued, "The needlelike thorns, piercing his scalp with each blow, blood pouring down his cheeks." Standing in silence, David paused, waiting, allowing people to take in the depth of this gruesome event. Silence.

"At any moment, Jesus could have called it off. He could have stopped this torture. He had legions of angels at His beckoning call. At one command of His voice, He could have been free from this pain. But, no! Jesus endured this for you. He endured it for me. An innocent lamb had to be sacrificed for the sins of the world. Jesus was that Lamb. Jesus was innocent. As He was being beaten, He knew that, in order for you and me to receive forgiveness from our sins, He would have to pay the ultimate price: death."

David continued, "The good news is that Jesus rose again! Today, Jesus is alive. Not only did He defeat death, He defeated hell! He defeated the grave! He defeated it so that *you* would have the opportunity to confess and believe in Him and be saved. His blood that He shed that day was enough to cover any sin you have committed and any sin you will ever commit. Jesus' blood was enough. Receiving Him gives us the opportunity to enter into heaven when we die. All we have to do is make the decision. All we have to do is choose Him. Choose to believe. Choose to hope. Choose to trust. Choose..." he said, pausing, "...to follow Jesus."

Passion filled David's face. A yearning encompassed his expression. His face was enveloped with an agony of desire as his words grabbed us like a hook. Tugging at the hearts of everyone who was in listening distance, the gymnasium was quiet. You could hear a pin drop. The air was thick and heavy. You could feel it. I had an ache and yearning in my own heart. I knew that today would be the day of salvation for many.

The band began to play worship music softly in the background, and the mood was one that pulled you in. Pulled you in to Jesus. A longing to come was there before there was even an invitation. There was a feeling in the air that people were ready to do whatever they needed in order to meet this Jesus.

David closed, "Today is the day for you to receive Jesus. Today is the day for you to meet Him, to receive Him as your Lord and Savior. If today you are saying, 'I want to meet Jesus. I want to have Him in my life,' then I'm going to invite you to come down here now. I'm going to invite you to get out of your seat and come down front. We are going to pray together. I'm going to lead a prayer to allow you to invite Jesus to come into your life. If that is you, if I have been talking to you, I'm inviting you to come. Come down now. Come down and meet Jesus. Get out of your seats now and come."

I noticed the first person who stood. It was a thin young man. He was in the bleachers and began running down to the stage. The sound of other feet on the metal bleachers filled the air. David stood on the stage, his eyes closed and his hands reaching toward heaven, praising God. I looked around in tears. Tears and tears flooded my cheeks. People all over were coming down to meet Jesus. People were hungry. Some were running down. Some couldn't get there fast enough. Children, young people, and adults. People flooded toward the stage.

David said, "Continue to come. If that is you, if you want to meet Jesus tonight, continue to come. For those of you still in your seats, I want to ask you this question: Are you 99% sure that you are going to heaven? You feel pretty confident? Well, friend, if you are 99% sure, then you are 100% unsure. I invite you to become 100% sure that, on the day that you are taken from earth, you will spend it in eternity with Jesus! I invite you to come. I invite you to be 100% sure that YOU are going to heaven. I invite YOU to come."

More people got out of their seats and began to come. Older people, distinguished people. More people began to come. Some immediately, some slowly, but they got out of their seats and made their way down front.

"Praise the Lord. Praise the Name of Jesus. People, just praise Jesus tonight! There is a party going on in heaven tonight!"

There was a long pause as people continued to come. The sound of footsteps on the bleachers rang through the sound of the worship music. The feet on the bleachers was music in itself as more people were coming. They just kept coming. Some were crying; some were smiling. All of these people were coming to meet Jesus! What a blessing.

"Well, let's go ahead and pray," David said as he led everyone standing in the sinners prayer.

At the close of the prayer, those still sitting came to their feet and *erupted* with applause. People began shouting. It sounded as if we were at a football game. The cheers were filled with excitement. You could hear through the audience people shouting, "Hallelujah!" "Praise the Lord!" "Hallelujah! Hallelujah!" All over the gymnasium, gusts of applause continued. The newly saved stood in front, some tears streaming down their faces with an expression of relief, like a heavy burden had just been lifted off of their shoulders. Some smiled and laughed, appearing overjoyed. Others simply looked overwhelmed as they turned and looked at everyone on their feet, standing and cheering... cheering for them. Cheering for the decision that they just made. Many on the floor smiled, turning to the person next to them, embracing them in a hug. The applause across the gymnasium continued. All over the gymnasium, people in the stands, people on the floor, and the newly saved believers had their hands lifted to the heavens, praising the Lord.

The words from the band began to rise in the auditorium as believers joined in worship, greeting the very presence of the Lord, singing,

> We fall down, we lay our crowns at the feet of Jesus. The greatness of his mercy and love, at the feet of Jesus. We cry holy, holy, holy. We cry holy, holy, holy. We cry holy, holy, holy, is the Lamb.

The band continued with the chorus. The air was filled with awe. I left my eyes closed and could almost feel the presence of angels in our midst. I knew that God was so overjoyed with what had just taken place. I remembered hearing about angels in heaven rejoicing when just one person came to accept Jesus as Savior. I knew that, right now, there must be an amazing party going on up there. There was such a feeling of joy and peace in the air. I had never felt as close to God as I did in those moments. What a victorious time. What a time of praise! With my hands lifted, I just thanked the Lord for an amazing night.

As the evening closed out, the band completed their chorus, some short announcements were made, and people began making their way out of the Stour Centre. Many people stood around and just talked. I walked by David and told him that it was an amazing night.

"Yes! It was so grand! Did you see the first guy to come down? The guy who ran?"

"Yes. That was so awesome!"

"Well, that guy was someone I had met in the park today. His name is Leon. He came! I'm so jacked that he came tonight! Praise the Lord, and he accepted Jesus into his life. He was rescued from the grips of death. How glorious!" David was so excited. "God led me to sit next to him today. He and another guy were in the park, just sitting on a bench. As I listened to him, he sounded like he was at the end of his rope, so I invited him to come with me here. He did and what a glorious time!"

"Praise the Lord!" I said. "That is so awesome, David!"

David was bouncing with excitement. The night had been anointed. In every way—from the music, drama, and message—the night had been completely blessed. How could any event top what we had experienced here tonight?

16

NEW EXCITEMENT

It was July 16th. I was still amazed about the previous night. What an amazing evening. My eyebrows were raised about this David guy. Sure, he was Mr. Congeniality, but wow, was he an anointed speaker! He had an extraordinary passion, like none I had ever seen before. What a wonderful ability to be able to share a love so deep for your Savior and in such a vivid, transparent way. He was now on my radar. I knew we were not supposed to date on this trip, and that was fine, but this was the type of guy that I would like to know. Never having experienced a vision before, I secretly hoped the chalkboard message was true about my future.

I had always been attracted to the football player build, and if I hadn't know better, I definitely would have thought David was a football player. He looked like a running back, lean and muscular with broad shoulders. He looked like he would be fast, too big to be a sprinter in track but perfect for a running back because he looked strong and fast. Though I had never written out all the qualities and features that I liked, if I had, I was now seeing it in the flesh: David! David was almost a whole foot taller than me, which made me feel small.

I couldn't help but reflect on the staggering series of events that led me to this place! Up until recently, I never really had "heard" from God. The several incidences that caused me agree to come on this mission trip seemed more than just coincidences. I knew that those things had to be orchestrated by God. But, the whole chalkboard thing? Now, that was still a bit surreal. I had never experienced anything like that before. The chalkboard hung freely in the sky for what seemed like minutes. In reality, it may have been only a split second. The more I was around David, the more I hoped it was real. I hoped it was God that said this man would be my husband. In my life so far, I had never met a Christian who was anything like David.

I enjoyed some time in the park. As I laid there on the grass, I saw Leon. David's Leon. How exciting. He was sitting on a bench, reading a little book. I made my way over to see him. "Hey, Leon! I'm Emily. I'm one of David's friends."

"Great to meet you," he said.

"Great to meet you, too. Congratulations about an awesome decision last night. That is exciting!" I noticed the book he was reading was called *The Decision* which they handed out for all the people who made Jesus their Lord. I was proud of him for reading it.

"Thank you. I'm excited about it. It is just such a good feeling and such a weight lifted off my shoulders. I have so much to learn," he said as he held up the booklet.

"Well, you are welcome to join me on the grass if you want. I was just studying my Bible. If you have any questions, I'd be happy to answer them for you or show you where the answer is in the Bible."

Leon joined me. For the next hour, we sat, talked, and looked things up in the Bible. It was great to help him in this next step of understanding.

Later that night, Stephanie and I got back to Laura's and Belle's house. It had been a long but good day. After getting a bit settled in, Laura announced, "I have somewhere that I want to take you two. It is somewhere quite lovely. I really think you'll fancy it as much as I do."

Stephanie and I hopped into "Joseph" with Laura, and she was off! The Mini was indeed little! The word, "Mini," was a great name for it. Not only was Joseph small in size, but it looked like—with the help of someone—we could almost pick it up. The doors were paper thin, maybe a bit stronger than a cardboard box, not that I had ever ridden in a box before. It was all the more reason to be thankful that Laura was such a good Christian. She seemed to be at such a pinnacle in her Christian walk that angels most likely accompanied Joseph and kept the passengers safe from harm. The several stoplights and windy roads were taking us out of town. There were no more lights. There were few houses, and it was dark. Laura kept driving.

Laura pulled off the road and turned left into a small little parking lot that was in the middle of nowhere. Joseph rested as the only car parked in the tiny lot. We got out of the car, and Laura led us to cross the street, eager like a little kid. In the darkness, we passed through a small iron gate and could tell we were up high. In the blackness, we still could make out the rolling of green hills, steeper in some sections than others, a faint cow "mooing" in the distance. I imagined they were beautiful in the daytime. We walked through the grass and made our way to a bench.

Gleefully, Laura announced, "We're here!"

As we sat down, Laura continued. "I have always loved this place. At night, it's so dark and peaceful. The hills overlook our little city of Ashford, so when you look down into the valley, you can see everything! Because we are away from the lights of the city, the stars look so grand up here. Their brightness is accentuated. I have always fancied this as one of my favorite places to talk to God. It's like God is so close that you could reach out and touch him. I like to just look up and marvel in what He has made. I come here to think. Just me and God. Looking down to the city lights twinkling and seeing the smallness of everything makes me feel like I'm a world away." Laura leaned back into the bench, sat, and just stared.

It was so dark. We did seem so far away from everything. I had never seen this many stars before. We could see thousands and thousands as they covered the sky. I imagined it may have been what Abraham saw when God told him his descendants would be as numerous as the stars in the sky. Glittering and sparkling, the dancing lights above were breathtaking.

As I looked down from this small mountain, overlooking the little town of Ashford, I thought of the memories the little town had filled my heart with already. The memory of experiencing forgiveness, true forgiveness from what seemed like to me an unforgivable sin. Praying to receive direction and the Lord directing me to the people who were ready to receive salvation. Personally helping to lead people to the Lord. Walking in the park with David and receiving a hug, the chalkboard, and the Lord revealing that he would be my husband. As I looked down on the small town of Ashford, my heart was filled with love and an astounding sense of fullness.

Stephanie got up and walked further down the small mountain. Laura and I remained on the bench, just staring out into the expanse, the endless sky.

"Laura, I have something really exciting to tell you."

"Oh yah?! What is it?"

"Well, I know this seems abrupt... but Laura, I believe I have met the man I'm going to marry. Laura, he is so wonderful. When I got here, this was the last thing I was expecting from this trip. I was so broken and still feel like I'm healing. But Laura, I can't explain it. It's like from the very depths of me, I feel like this is the man I'm going to marry."

"Wow, really? So, tell me about him. What's his name? What's he like? How did this all happen?"

"His name is David. Laura, he is amazing! We went on a walk in the park the other day, and he stopped and hugged me. It was just different. He spoke the other night at the event at the Stour Centre. You probably remember him; all of those people got saved. Laura, he is just so awesome! I don't know how to explain it, and I know it may sound dumb, but I really do believe he is the man I'm going to marry. I believe God set him apart just for me. I can't explain it. I've never been this sure about something. I mean *sure*, Laura! I feel so sure about it," I said with my excitement was spilling over. I was so excited about David, but I also thought it surely sounded rushed to anyone who knew what I had just been through.

"Emily, that's great! I'm so excited for you! Just go slow, Emily, and let God be God. If this David really is the one for you, God will work it out, and you don't need to."

It was good advice. I would take it. I leaned back on the bench and just stared up at the stars. We sat and just stared. In silence, slouched down on the bench, our heads resting atop the old wood, we just stared. It was so much to take in. I had never seen anything so amazing. The stars shined above, sparkling, each with thousands of friends by their side. I knew God knew how many stars were up there. As far as the eye could see, there were stars! Like a blanket covering us on this little mountain, a blanket of twinkling stars. I wished I could take them all back with me to Pennsylvania.

Friday, July 17th. We were going to get a little bit of a break from a long, full week. We were going to take a trip to Canterbury! Wow! I had heard about this place in the famous *Canterbury Tales*. I didn't know anything about the *Canterbury Tales* other than that they were famous.

We passed lush green grass on the way. As we rode, our driver pointed out a famous castle in the distance. A real castle! I would love to stay in a castle one day. Even though I was excited about going to see the Canterbury Cathedral and all of the little shops in the city, I was a little bummed. David went to Canterbury with his host family, the Wrights. I hoped I would see him while we were there.

In the meantime, I sat with Lily on the trip there. Lily was fun, bubbly, and extremely beautiful. She had a tender heart toward God and a remarkable talent in drama. Her long, flowing red hair was stunning, the kind of red hair that turns heads. We sat on the bus, giddily talking like schoolgirls. It was unlike me to laugh and chat so much. She brought out the lighthearted side of me that few people knew. Lily was the only girl on the trip that I opened up to about David. How my heart longed to be around him. David was the unofficial leader in our group. Everyone looked to him with automatic respect. There was something different about him.

Tom had also raised himself above the crowd in leadership. It was his passion for the Lord. Tom, like David, had innate leadership qualities. They stuck out in our group. People looked for someone to lead, and those were the two guys. Of course, Lily liked Tom. Sure, she didn't say she was going to marry him, but she liked him nonetheless. Tom was about 5'10", and he had blonde hair and blue eyes. He was also a runner. He and Lily did look cute together.

As much as Lily and I were transparent with each other about our crushes on David and Tom, we still had a passion for the lost, a hunger to see people saved. We had a desire to see God move in these countries, to see God be glorified. She was refreshing, a total girl with her make-up on and hair always done. She was equally as fun. Her passion and desire to see people saved gave me a new desire. She caused me to see the value in having a Christian girlfriend, a girl in my life back home who would sharpen me. Where we could encourage each other but also have fun being the girls God made us to be.

It seemed like a lifetime ago that I was home. It seemed like so long ago that I had questioned, God or Rick? Astounding that it had been only 2 weeks. Praise the Lord that I had chosen God! Who could have guessed that God would bring me all the way to England to meet my husband? Not only that, it happened during a season of life that was my all-time low. I had been in a pit of desperation, dismal with little hope of bouncing back, let alone hope to thrive as a Christian. I was hurting when I arrived in England. My heart was like sand slipping through fingers. No shape, no depth, no joy... just loose sand flowing out into nothing. Before coming, I was unsure that my heart would ever take shape again. My heart seemed weak, but somehow, God breathed life back into it, back into me. God had somehow taken what was weak and broken and brought me back to life! I felt like Lazarus: for a time, dead, but now alive in Jesus.

It was Friday, and it felt good to be happy. If I thought about it for too long, some of the oppressive feelings would try to come back, but I would force them out. I didn't allow myself to feel oppressed or guilty. When Laura prayed with me, I received forgiveness, and I was bound and determined to stay that way. God had forgiven and forgotten; I was doing my best to do the same.

I enjoyed this feeling of freedom and joy. It was such a new feeling for me. I had almost forgotten what it was like. The moments of joy and freedom I was now living in revealed to me the great bondage I had been in when I was with Rick. I wasn't truly happy around him because I wasn't being true to myself. I wasn't being true to my first love, Jesus.

How refreshing. I leaned back in my seat on the bus and just closed my eyes. What a great feeling. This is what freedom feels like! This is what happiness feels like. I like this.

We arrived in Canterbury. I glanced down the cobblestone street past a few quaint shops and bistro tables and chairs that sat outside a small café. Intricate stonework decorated many of the buildings, each one different. Structures arrayed in brick, white stone, and cobblestone. Some had a Swiss look, cream, accented by dark chocolate beams. Every structure was so unique, creating such a picturesque view as we walked the streets. Statues of kings and princes perfectly accented the historic town. Sections on the outskirts of the little town had trees adorned with purple and white flowers.

If not already magnificent enough, the oldest and most famous Christian structure in all of England towered over the town: the Canterbury Cathedral. It's original completion dated back to 1077, embracing the whole city as a monument of history and beauty. The perpendicular, gothic architecture was defined by its pointed arches and vaulted roofs, emphasizing the vertical lines of this colossal superstructure. The lancet windows—tall, narrow, and pointed—formed an arch at the top. It held one of England's earliest and largest collections of medieval stained glass, with over 12,000 square feet of colorful images that depicted inspirational stories of men and women. Grand and majestic, I knew that touring this cathedral would be a highlight of my European adventure.

One of my goals was to get a souvenir in Canterbury. I had bought only two keepsakes so far: a jacket and a scarf, both with the words "England" on them. Other than that, I hadn't really spent any money. I wanted to find something that would be practical, something that I would use and that would last. I wasn't sure what that would be yet, but being a college student, I had somehow acquired the ability to be very frugal. I didn't spend money quickly. When I did, it was well thought out.

Several of us girls, accompanied by a few brave guys, enjoyed shopping on the streets of Canterbury. In and out of shops with an occasional stop for a quick snack or something to drink, we were having a great time just taking it all in. I found one of my purchases. I walked in a store, and the whiff of leather overtook me. Nice, new leather… what a pleasant aroma! I needed some shoes, so this was it. This was the purchase. Because Doc Marten shoes was first established in the UK, not only would a new pair of Doc Martens be a nostalgic purchase, they would be useful as well. I was excited about having nice shoes, leather and lasting. I would definitely get a lot of use out of these in the Pennsylvania fall and winter seasons. I found the perfect pair, exchanged my English "pounds" for a pair of shoes, which were placed neatly in a keepsake bag. I was happy and proud of my purchase.

Our next stop was the long-awaited Canterbury Cathedral. It would finally become more than words from a trifold brochure.

Breathtaking. Magnificent. The cathedral ceilings went on forever. The stained glass was flamboyant in color, light beaming through, causing the colors to dance in the wide expanse of the open cathedral. Stepping back hundreds of years, the stale smell of old books and antique wood drifted in and out of my nostrils. It was hard to believe people were capable to complete something this magnificent almost 1000 years ago. Simply amazing!

Stephan, the cute coach, accompanied Holly, Lily, and me as we explored. Holly, with her long blonde hair, was almost as bubbly as Lily. Three fun girls in England. Could it get any better than this? Our goal was to get to the top of the cathedral where we could look out over the city. My secret goal was still to steal away a few minutes of this memorable day with David. In such a romantic, historic town, it only seemed appropriate for the fairytale I had begun in my head. To my disappointment, we had barely spoken since his "sit-down" talk in the park.

We reached the pinnacle of the cathedral, kissing the clouds as we stepped onto the cobblestone landing. Suddenly, breath left my body. For a split second, my heart stopped. There he stood, with the four AOC students and their host family, the Wrights. To conclude an already momentous day, for an instant, the penetrating turquoise of David's eyes connected with mine. Just as quickly, my heart sank as David fully rejoined in the conversation, commencing in their laughter.

In general, I knew guys were different than girls, but the girl in me wanted David to jump up with glee and stroll to my side. Needless to say, excitement did not overtake him when he saw me. He just continued in his conversation. My heart, on the other hand, felt like it was going a hundred miles a minute. Could he tell? He had a unique way about him. He seemed so distant, so far out of reach. How could he be so calm and not even act excited to see me when it was him who had hugged me in the park?

I had not been asking for this, this disturbing romance. For the most part, from a relationship standpoint, I had been minding my own business before he whisked in and turned my heart upside-down! If it weren't for the hug in the park, he would probably still just be "Mr. Congeniality" to me. Then, I could enjoy my time peacefully without my heart being so involved. Was he always this aloof? Or, was this what made him a leader, maintaining a firm hold on his emotions, showing little excitement, and just remaining steady?

A little frustrated and feeling a bit "wrote off," we did at least manage to get a picture together. Then, David and his host family were off to their next destination.

17

OPPRESSION IN NORTHERN IRELAND

July 18th. Leaving Ashford, clouds were raining in my heart. I never imagined only ten days could allow me to grow so attached to Laura and Belle. The English "goodbye" of "cheerio" sure didn't feel very cheery today. Far from cheery, my heart was so sad to leave, but I was so happy that the impact they made on my life now made up an essential aspect of the new me. The new me that I was developing into. The new me that desired to have Jesus pour out of my being without having to say a word.

Like Thomas Jefferson—a hero to America, spearheading freedom and change, and the principal author of the Declaration of Independence—these two women were heroes in my life. These two women brought change and freedom to me. These two women represented the "Thomas Jefferson" in the life of Emily Cook.

Belle—a motherly, loving, and compassionate woman—opened her home, providing a place of peace that invited the Holy Spirit to be welcomed permanently. A hug from Belle was like an embrace from heaven itself. You felt unconditional love in her arms, and for someone fragile and broken, unconditional love is exactly what I needed.

And Laura, words could not explain. She got me back on my feet. She helped bring life to the limp shell that I had brought to England. She was a friend. She listened, prayed for, and loved me without condemnation. Ultimately, without Laura, I don't know if I would have experienced forgiveness. Let there be no mistake, God planned out the housing arrangements long before we arrived in England. Laura now upheld a new standard that I didn't even know existed. She embodied what a Christian woman should be. A woman of passion, love, and a full heart toward God's will and plan. I had never met anyone like her before. Knowing her left me speechless. Her wisdom and knowledge of the Bible. At the same time, she was a woman of such grace. Laura left an imprint on my life that would forever be unforgettable.

"I love you, friend," Laura said as tears streamed down her face.

I knew my tears were soaking her long dark strands as we stood in a firm embrace. I didn't know when I would see her again or if I ever would. The angel in my life. "I love you, too. Thank you so much. Thank you for everything." Biting my lips in a smile, we looked at each other and hugged one more time. What more could I say? Mere words could not explain what she had done in my life.

"Cherrio, friend. Cherrio. Have a lovely trip, and help those Irish chaps meet Jesus." Tucking a strand of hair behind my ear, she held my shoulders at arms-length, kissed her hand and touched it to my forehead. "Love you," she whispered with a smile, then turned and walked away.

Back at the Loft, we loaded onto the buses. I hoped that I would be able to sit by David or close to him on the bus. Of course, I didn't want to appear like I was looking for or wanted to sit by him. "Desperate" was not what I was going for, nor did I want it to seem like I was chasing him. Instead, I ended up sitting next to Conner. A whole trip, hours and hours on a bus, and I wasn't even on the same bus as David. How disappointing.

Conner was such a super guy. I would anticipate that if God had not revealed that I was going to marry David, Conner would be a great catch. He was super good-looking, a football player, had a big build, and was an Alabama boy. He had a southern Alabama accent which I couldn't help but think was cute, and he was very much a gentleman. He responded with "yes, ma'am" as we talked.

Most places in Pennsylvania were similar to New York. People would knock past you, not even gruffing out an "excuse me." And here was a southern gentleman, saying, "Yes ma'am," and opening doors for me? Good manners were quite an attractive feature! If I didn't make it at the top of David's list, Conner sure had his way of impressing and could be next in line for marriage material.

The line for the restroom was long, so we pulled out the football to play a little catch while we waited.

I put my hands out, motioning Conner to toss the ball to me. Only feet apart, he pitched it underhanded, and I grabbed it. I took off in the opposite direction, giving myself good distance for my first throw. After separating myself, Conner yelled in hesitant unbelief, "Are you sure you can throw it that far?"

Lowering the football and grabbing it like taking it from a snap, I took a few backward strides as a quarterback in a game. Tapping the football and looking for the open man, I side-stepped a few paces to my right, pulled back, and with my fingers perfectly positioned down the laces of the football, I released the ball. The spiral flew effortlessly through the sky, a beauty ascending in perfect precision into Conner's hands.

"What?!" Conner said as he fell to his knees after catching my throw, shrieking in awe. "What?! What in the world?! Guys!" he said and pointed, "Did you see that? She throws like a guy—actually, better than most guys!" He laughed as he got ready to toss it back. "Can you catch it, too? If you can catch it, now *that* will be impressive."

He tossed a long throw to me. Running a few paces toward the ball, I caught it with ease.

"Oh my goodness! She can catch, too!" Conner laughed out loud. I smiled. My quarterback dad had taught me well.

A note that Conner had given me held no mystery that he liked me. It was a sweet note, and I felt honored that he thought highly of me. I knew that, once the trip was over, I had the opportunity to keep in touch with all of my new friends.

Aside from Conner, Stephan had been giving me extra attention, too—unsolicited, but subtle attention. Also a 'Bama boy, he was attractive but was more on the quiet side. Despite the opportunity, both had a missing ingredient. Ultimately, when it came down to wedding bells and "I do", the number one quality I desired in my future husband was an evident, deep desire, and passion for the Lord. I wanted the Lord to be number one in his life, even above me. I wanted him to have leadership qualities that would shine through in the way he carried himself.

David just walked in a room and carried a mantle of leadership. I was unsure of how to explain it, but he carried a weight with him. It was different. It was dynamic. I wanted to be with someone who was dynamic. Conner was awesome. Before this trip, he would've been the most "spiritual" guy I had known. But David... David took things to a whole new level, making it almost impossible for anyone else to compete. I didn't know there were men out there who were so passionate about the Lord, who even put the Lord above a relationship with a girl. It was the most appealing and attractive quality I had ever seen.

Our next stop was Belfast, Northern Ireland. We had been prepped about Northern Ireland. There was so much controversy in the city, such a division between the Catholics and the Protestants, a religious warfare. We were told about the armed guards that would be standing along the wall that separated the two sides of the city. There was truly a wall that separated them. A week before, three young boys had been killed, burned to death. A newspaper article read, "12-year-old boy found himself in the back bedroom... dazedly watching over three small white coffins holding all that remained of his three younger brothers. They burned to death when Protestant thugs, angered by a ban... tossed a fire bomb through the window of the Catholic family's home..."

The place where we were going held great hostility and division, immense pain and anger. It was so hard to believe that people who served the same God could be so hateful toward each other. I did not fully understand their hatred. It made me sad though. I was not Catholic, but my heart mourned for the family that lost their three boys, all over religious division. Surely, Christ would be saddened. In the comic section of another newspaper, it showed a comic with a picture of Jesus sitting on a rock with his staff. It merely said, "Jesus wept. John 11:35." Beside the rock where Jesus sat, it showed a newspaper with the front page that said,

THREE BOYS DIE
IN N. IRELAND
Protestant - Catholic
Violence Continues

We were going into a place that has experienced indescribable pain.

Traveling had been exhausting but interesting at the same time. We took in the rolling hills of the English and Irish countryside as we went from town to town. We also met a lot of interesting people as we stopped for gas and bathroom breaks.

As we pulled in, it was nice to finally be there at the Solid Rock Center. All the guys and girls would be staying in the same location this time—the guys, upstairs in a large room while the girls would stay in two smaller rooms. Settling in, we all claimed a cot, making our beds with the sheet and thin, gray, wool blanket that was provided. This was where we would call home for the next week.

Out front, Brittney and several other AOCers were attempting to make friends with some of the neighborhood children. Glass was scattered throughout the streets and sidewalks, and barefoot children ran about as if they hadn't noticed the charred glass. A yelp came from Brittney as she got hit with a potato. Several of the children were shooting potato guns, not easily swayed to friendship. A heavy, thick feeling of oppression filled the air. The atmosphere was so different from the oasis we had just left. The armed guards on the rooftops in the distance was just one shred of this proof. The quaint and lovely, small town of Ashford seemed a world away from the warzone of battle we were in. The sad part was that it was a war that continued, and children were involved. Like someone squeezing my heart, I could feel the pressure. I could tell that this would be a very different week than the one we just had.

In the world of David, I felt like a fly on the wall—invisible. My heart hurt, and I longed to talk to him. I saw David and several other people sitting and talking in the great room. The "dining" and "meeting" area were both set up in a big open room, like a gym with carpet. I pulled up a chair and began to listen to the conversation. David just seemed so smart, so wise. His leadership was apparent as people sat around listening to him. Even the leaders of the trip saw it.

Often at lunch, or going to and from events, there seemed to be a buzz among the girls about him. Not to mention, if David walked by, most girls turned their heads to watch as he passed. He was certainly the catch of the trip though I think most of the girls felt that he was out of their league—me included. Some other guys tried to "take" leadership, but David didn't even have to "take it." It was automatic, whether in his silence or in well-thought-out words. In his spare time, I couldn't help but notice David was not part of the group of guys playing and goofing around. He was with Mama Pat, helping to set up, listening, asking questions, and completely separating himself from being a mere carefree participant. He seemed to thrive on learning, and he was such an intent listener as she spoke to him. Her wisdom, knowledge of the Word, and motherly kindness caused David to want to learn more from her. Everything about him was different from everyone on the trip. You could tell that he was going to do something significant, something great with his life.

As I listened to the conversation, I gathered they were talking about relationships and what made a relationship a "godly" one. I listened for a while until David asked a question, "What should a girl do to get a guy to notice her?"

Several seconds went by and everyone remained silent. Seated at the back of the metal chairs, I responded, "Nothing?"

David acknowledged, "That is exactly right! Absolutely nothing," he said and paused, waiting for those around to really get it. "If a girl wants a guy to notice her, she should do absolutely nothing to get his attention. If she is a godly girl, pursuing and seeking the Lord, following her calling, she will be noticed. The guy will notice her. The guy will find her. It is not her job to try to be noticed," he emphasized. "Her job is to pursue the Lord and His will.

By doing that, she *will* align herself in a position for God to bring that 'perfect someone' into her life."

What David was saying made complete sense even though, at the present moment, I did not like it. I just wanted David to notice me. I wanted him to see me. I wanted to spend time with him. But listening in to this discussion gave me some important insights into who David was. He seemed to be most definitely "old fashioned."

Maybe it was not "old fashioned." It was just the way it was actually supposed to be, the Biblical way for relationships. It was so foreign to me. To not "try" to get a guy's attention? In my party days, I had learned to master the art of getting a guy's attention. This "not trying to get a guy's attention" seemed so far in the other direction. The Christian way was so different from what the "world" does.

I had always been so focused on my actions and drawing attention to myself, positioning myself in a favorable light to the guy I wanted to impress. Positioning myself so that he would see me. Sometimes, I would set myself up to be where he was and "oh, what a coincidence that you're here!" It would appear that *he* was following me or that *he* ran into me and not the other way around. I had learned. I had become a master.

The life of a godly girl, a godly woman, was much different than the life I once lived as a partier, as a woman of the world. What a different life! What did all of this mean to me? What it all meant was that I couldn't use my learned and perfected tricks, manipulation, and plans—whatever you want to call them—I couldn't use those on David. It wasn't right. In a relationship that was based on the Word and on God, I wouldn't be able to use the world's tactics. I was now treading on new water. New ground. I had never been in a situation like this before. Not trying to be noticed when I *knew how* to get noticed?! Whoa! This was definitely new.

It kind of made me sad. I wanted to pursue David, but deep down, I wanted to be *the pursued*. I longed for the guy to pursue me. I wanted the "knight in shining armor" to come riding up on his horse, to be seeking me, to search for me, and to find me! I wanted to be pursued. I wanted to be romanced. I wanted to be the one who was called. I wanted him to come and knock on *my* door, holding a rose to take me out on a date. I did not want to have to use the tactics I had learned from the world. I did not want to manipulate anymore to get my way. I craved to be the "princess in her tower," destined to be rescued by her knight, her savior, her prince. I longed for him to sweep me up, carry me off, and place me on his horse. Saving me from a world of unkindness, pressure, un-gentleman-like conduct, and "worldly" relationships based upon sexual acts and selfishness. I wanted to enter into a "white glove" world, a world that I sensed was pure and unblemished. White. Lovely. Nice. Perfect. Proper. A world that a princess would live in with proper conduct, proper dress, proper etiquette, and respect. That was it. I wanted to live in a "white glove" world.

My conclusion? If I wanted this *new* romance, I would need to do it a *new* way. I remember hearing that the definition of *insanity* is "doing the same things but expecting different results." That's what all of my relationships had been up to this point in my life. I had done the same thing, hoping someone would be different, but the results always ended up the same. I had been walking down a path leading to "insanity." For things to change, for things to be different, I would need to do what David had talked about. What should a girl do to get a guy to notice her? Absolutely nothing.

I guess I would have to truly pursue God. Because my heart longed and almost hurt for David, that meant I would just have to pursue God more. I would have to pursue God with more passion, more fervor, and more diligence.

My conclusion? I would pursue God on a level I had never been. He would be my first, my last, my all.

Our group maintained a full schedule, participating in sporting events and hosting various outreaches. In Belfast, not only was the air thick and heavy from the religious oppression, it felt heavy to me because I felt so invisible to David. How my heart longed to just talk to him, but when I walked past, his glance didn't even come to meet mine. "That was okay," I reasoned. I would focus on being led by the Holy Spirit, growing spiritually, and seeing people saved.

The sports complex where we conducted clinics, the Shankill Leisure Centre, was barely 200 yards away. Bars housed the windows on the front door of the Solid Rock Centre. Chains wound tightly on the door, keeping us safe inside and keeping intruders out. Being chained in like prisoners was actually for our safety. The drastic difference from our utopia in Ashford was bluntly before our eyes each day as we tried to leave the centre.

I led the cheerleading camps, which encompassed several days of teaching the children of the area a hip hop dance. They were doing so well. Even the boys were doing a great job! I was happy to see that they all had shoes on during our practices on the outdoor pavement. We were preparing for our final night's performance where the children would invite the friends and family, and our group would also have an invitation to meet Jesus.

Thankfully, cheerleading camp for the afternoon was over, and I had some down time before dinner and our evening worship session. Though butterflies filled my stomach, the gnawing ache I felt was greater. I was desperate. Despite my nervousness, I had to talk to Mama Pat.

Mama Pat had spent a lot of time with David. She was truly what her name revealed: "Mama Pat." She was like a mama! She had a "mama-ness" about her. Her presence was a safe place. Her warmth made you feel that you could open up to her about anything. She had eyes that did not judge and a spirit that did not condemn. She was a safe haven.

We tucked inside the little glass booth right inside the door. A solid wall on the bottom half and glass on the top. I wasn't sure if the private room was a ticket booth or a sound room. I was just thankful to have a few moments closed off, alone, and secluded.

"Mama Pat, I just had to talk to someone. It's about David."

"Yes?"

"Well... back in England, I felt like God revealed to me that I am going to marry him. And now, my heart just hurts to be around him. What do I do?" My tormented facial expression pleaded in total submission, anticipating what I was sure would be the right recommendation.

"Awww. Well, Emily, David is a very special person. He is definitely a leader and a man after God's heart. God has very big plans for him. Emily, if he truly is the man you are going to marry, God will work it all out. Though you will both return to your own lives when the trip is over, if it's meant to be, distance will not matter. God will make a way."

"Do you think so?" I asked. My eyes filled with hope.

"Yes. If it is meant to be, it will be. In the meantime, while you are here, let's see how many people we can invite into the Kingdom of God. Together, let's allow this time to be a focused time to watch God move in this city. What do you think?"

"You're right. I just need to stay focused. Maybe that will help my heart not want to be with him so much." I knew she was right. I just needed reassurance. God would work it out if it was meant to be. Truthfully, I knew I couldn't do anything to rush it along, besides walking in obedience. If I had really heard from God, on that special day when I hear wedding bells, at the end of the aisle, there… I would meet him. There, David would be standing, waiting for me. I felt confident that he would be my husband. I was just unsure of how I could wait when the longing in my heart hurt so badly? I knew God would work it out. Somehow, I would figure out how to wait.

18

DESIRED ATTENTION

July 22. It was a rainy day in Belfast. It rained and rained and then rained some more. Finally, we were going to a track meet. This was the only actual meet that we would participate in. It was against some other provinces and several nations. It was my first international track meet. Anticipation raced through my veins from the moment my eyes opened as I laid looking up at the dingy white ceiling panels. I had been running consistently on the trip though my focus felt very thin. The laser focus I normally had leading up to a race was not as prominent due to our busy schedule. Nonetheless, I would do my best and run as fast as I could.

We took the mini bus over to the meet. There were only about 10 of us that would be competing. In between and after events, we had tracts about salvation that we would hand out, openly sharing the gospel as we felt led.

Being at this Ireland track caused my adrenaline to race as the last call for the 1500 sounded. Despite my self-coached training over the last two weeks, I was eager. Standing on the grassy surface inside the track, I felt something different in me today, an unusual drive. Maybe it was competing against other nations or because David was there to cheer me on. Maybe it was the sheer fact that we were in this meet to glorify God. I wasn't sure what caused the unusual stirring, but in the depths of me, I felt I would run fast today.

They called us to the line. As the official announced our individual names, we each took our position on the arched curve at the back 300 meter mark. The waterfall start meant, once the gun sounded, lanes did not matter. We would be able to cut in immediately.

"Runners, to your marks… Get set…" the official took a long pause, "Go!" And the gun went off!

We made our way quickly off the start line, jockeying for a position in the front. I felt great. Quick steady breaths, taking in the misty air. It was a quick start, but it felt good. I was looking for a nice comfortable spot on the inside lane. I wasn't as concerned with being in the first place position—yet. The first place position this early in the race just put a target on your back for everyone to focus on. I tucked in behind first place and clipped at her heels. I was sure she could feel me breathing.

I heard David on the back-stretch by the 200 mark cheering. He was leaned over, yelling, "Come on, Emily! You can do it! You look good. Keep it up!"

That made me happy. Extra motivation. I did hear him.

Crossing lap one, I remained right on the heels of the girl leading. Inches separated us as I held the second-place spot intentionally. Down the back stretch, stride for stride, we continued, almost breathing at the same pace. The rainy, cold air passing through my lungs and back out in a puff of smoke.

We crossed the line for lap two with a consistent speed going into our third lap. Still remaining on her heels, I was content to follow her until just the right time. I would patiently keep her pace and wait.

Finishing lap three, we were on the last lap with only 400 meters to go! I still felt good and very strong. The leader was too slow to stay with right now. As we crossed the finish line going into our final lap, I surged out to pull ahead of her before hitting the first curve. I quickly began opening up the gap. She did not stay with me. We pulled onto the back straightaway, and I opened up the gap further. There was David, yelling and cheering, motivating me even more. I pushed my legs to go further, to turn over faster. My breathing was steady, and my arms were even, strong, and pumping fast. 250 left. 200. The last curve. I was going to lay it all on the line now. My final kick. My arms were pumping strong and steady. Hard. I was kicking. 150. 100. The last straightaway. 100 yards to go! I could sense that second place was too far behind me to catch up, but I was going to give it everything I had anyways. This last 100 meters was going to be quick, and I was determined to leave it *all* on the track. The words of my high school coach, Coach Claude, rang in my head: "Form, keep your form. Arms at a 90-degree angle. Pump. Go hard. Hands in a loose grip, not tight to steal energy. Set yourself up to have the most energy to run fast. Form! Form!" I felt like my form was strong and efficient. 75 meters! 50 meters! My legs were rolling over fast! 25. 5 more strides. My strides were lengthened and fast. Right left, right left, push in to the finish. Lean quick. Done.

I had won. On this rainy, not totally optimal day for conditions, I still won. A bit out of practice and without competition on my last lap, I somehow managed to tie my PR. Tying my personal record in the off-season at 4:53 on a slippery track made me very happy. I was still working toward my ultimate goal of 4:45 before completing collegiate track days. I had a couple of track seasons to get my time down. I was pleased.

Locking my fingers together behind my head, I walked a quick recovery to catch my breath and stretch out my cramping abdomen. I turned around before getting to the first curve and walked back to shake hands with those still finishing.

It felt good to win. I won. I smiled. I loved a race when I just felt good. Before and after, I felt good and strong.

Our ride back to the Solid Rock Centre was a cold one. Most of us had not brought a change of clothes, and it had rained almost the whole time we were at the track. The discomfort I felt from being in wet clothes was completely masked by the excitement I had to be sitting in the back of the bus by David. Not only did I have a good race, but I was *finally* noticed again. For the first time since England, we talked. I felt I had come from being invisible to visible! Granted, I respected David for wanting to stay focused, but it was still nice to have a little of his focus back on me.

While the other athletes faced forward, David reached over and touched my hand. I almost jumped. My arms immediately filled with goosebumps! Slowly, he drew circles on the top of my hand with his index finger, until he finally intertwined his fingers with mine. *He* reached over to hold *my* hand.

Jeri, the other hammer thrower, sat in front of us. Like David, she had also been in France with the first group. It was evident that the time they had spent together at track practices in France had created a unique friendship. Occasionally, she turned around to talk to David. Each time, he quickly pulled his hand back. Though she wasn't flirty with him, to me, Jeri still gave off a subtle vibe that she liked David. She didn't seem his type, but I didn't doubt she may have liked him.

There was almost a thrill of not wanting to get caught, like being on a field trip in elementary school, and Jeri was the principal. I felt like a little kid. Rush and excitement filled my veins, and here I was 21 years old! It was slow, PG excitement. This tortoise-like speed was refreshing.

Jeri settled in, facing forward, and David reached over to hold my hand once again. The warmth of his masculine hands encompassing mine was an overwhelming completion to an already great day! The calloused edges on the palms of his strong hands was most likely from the countless times he grasped the handle of the hammer and endless repetitions of lifting in the weight room.

I was on cloud nine! I didn't know if my feet would touch the ground when I tried to walk. Would I just float off the bus?

Back at the Solid Rock Centre, it was just track athletes who occupied the facility. Everyone else was at the AOC football game. Our team played Ireland that night, and those who weren't playing were watching. The Solid Rock Centre was so big. With such high ceilings, it felt empty. Like a needle in a haystack, I didn't know where anyone had gone. Everyone was off doing their own thing. I assumed many were headed for a hot shower after our cold, wet day.

For some reason, I found myself downstairs in the big assembly area. Still excited from my hand being held, I walked over to the kitchen where I thought I heard someone. As I popped my head in the door, I saw David standing at the back entrance of the kitchen. At the back entrance, there was a door that headed outside as well as a back set of stairs that went up to the guys' room. There he stood, in the dark. With only small illumination from the exit sign, I noticed his hands partially in the air.

"Hey," I said. "What are you doing?"

"Hey, yourself!" he said, smiling with his hands still raised. "Well, there seems to be a leak right here from the rain. There might actually be a few leaks."

"Oh?" I said. In the long pause, we were talking about nothing to try to cause the space between us to disappear. How do I seem interested in a leak? "Wow, it's leaking?"

"Yep, it's leaking," David said, lingering with his hands in the air, not attempting to fix it; just stalling.

I slowly walked into the kitchen a few steps, sounding interested. I honestly couldn't have cared less about the leak. I just wanted to be near him.

David continued to stand there at the back door, still acting interested in the leak. Looking up, he motioned up toward what must have been several holes. The moment was brimming with the awkwardness of me wanting to be there, him seeming like he wanted me there, but neither of us knowing what to say to make that happen. So, there he stood, still *interested* in a leak. He continued to stand there as if just waiting.

Somehow, the space shrank to nothing. The awkward space and time was gone. I stood there, stating the obvious. "Yes, it is leaking."

I took a step back, and his hands immediately went around my waist. At that moment, adrenaline captured my whole being. I stepped up onto the first step. He drew me closer to him, his hands feeling strong and secure around my waist. There were no words now. The space between us had disappeared, and I was now standing in his arms. He softly touched my cheek with his hand, brought his lips to mine, and kissed me.

The slow-motion moment came to an abrupt stop when we heard someone in the kitchen. David quickly pulled away. The light in the kitchen turned on, and I slipped up a few more stairs to avoid being seen. David walked out into the kitchen. "Oh... Hey, Stan," he said in a nonchalant tone.

"Hey, Man. What are you doing?"

"Oh, just checking out a leak. Heading to the bathroom. Good to see you man." David patted Stan on the back as he passed, not lingering to talk.

Could my heartbeat be heard? I stood there, hugging the wall of the back steps, trying not to move or breathe. The kitchen lights finally turned off. I waited about a minute and then zipped through the kitchen and snuck up the front stairs without being seen.

Upstairs, I fell onto my cot to gain my composure. I could breathe. I could finally take a breath. What had just happened? My mind was racing. Was this good or bad?

I walked out of my room and was met by David with a blunt, "We need to talk."

"Ok," I followed him. We walked into the small common area upstairs, and he pulled two chairs together facing each other. I sat and he sat.

"What just happened was totally inappropriate. I apologize. That never should have happened. I just wanted to ask for your forgiveness. That is not why God called us to this trip, and it will not happen again. We will for sure just have to make sure someone else is around any time we are together. But, I assure you, it will not happen again." His voice was sure and stern as he emphasized *will not*. It was kind of cold. Direct. Not like how you would talk to someone you just kissed. Cold and business. As if to wipe your hands together and say, "Done."

"Uh, yah. I forgive you," I said, partly in question. It was definitely a nice gesture, but I was not sorry that it happened.

"Thank you. Again, I apologize. It won't happen again." That was it. That was all. He got up from his chair and disappeared into the guys' room.

"Whoa! What just happened?" I thought. "What just happened?" I didn't know what to think now. Sure, we weren't supposed to date on this trip, but I didn't think it was too horribly bad. Maybe because I was so in love, I was blind to something obvious? Had I missed something? Granted, it wasn't a perfect kiss, but it was a kiss nonetheless, and I didn't look at him any differently. My heart was still full.

The next five days were a blur. Kids were saved, and good things happened, but my disconnected mind raced nowhere. I hardly could think straight. I could hardly think about anything.

True to his word, nothing with David happened again. I was now, once again, the invisible girl. Even as I walked past him, he didn't even look at me. I was sure no one else noticed, but for me, it was as if you could announce it to the world! Get out a megaphone or a microphone: I was totally being ignored! I hated it. I just wanted to talk to him. I wanted to feel his hand. I just wanted to be around him. How my heart hurt. Maybe things would change. I mean, after all, when we were in England at the track, he did say, "There are always plane tickets." He mentioned planes! He planted the seed of hope that we could visit each other. The seed he planted remained in my heart. I prayed things hadn't changed. He would fly from South Carolina to Pennsylvania, or I would fly to Bayside Island where he went to college. He was right. There were planes. We could visit.

Though I felt so invisible, I held on to the hope that David was just trying to be focused on the Lord. I secretly prayed he was just being valiant in his avoidance of me. I appreciated him being strong even though my heart was already putty in his hands. I knew I would have to let him pursue me. I thought that, after the trip was over, we could talk. No rules. No restrictions. We could get to know each other. That was my silent hope.

July 27th, 1998. It was time for goodbyes. The trip was over. Back at the airport in Newark, New Jersey, we awaited our baggage. Everyone would now go their separate ways to catch their next flight. I stood there with David as we waited for our bags. On the six-hour flight from London, I had ample time to prepare how I envisioned our fairytale parting to be. The goodbye I had planned in my head was magical. He would get my bag off the carousel, and we would walk slowly, hand-in-hand to my gate. He would tell me how sad he was to see me go, reminding me that there are plane tickets and that we would see each other soon. At my gate, he would kiss me goodbye, and I would float away, down the corridor to my plane. It would be like a climax in a movie. I remained anticipant of our long walk together.

We stood by the baggage pick-up. It was very crowded. David already had his backpack on, ready to collect his other luggage. The carousel went around, and I made a comment that I saw my bag coming. As we stood there, David aloof, not attempting to engage in a conversation. As my suitcase approached, closer and closer, it didn't appear that he was going to grab it. Disappointed, I walked to the side of the carousel, lugging it over the edge myself. What happened to this debonair gentleman and my magical ending? Nothing was playing out as I had envisioned. That suitcase was all I had. I technically could leave.

Stalling, I finally said, "Well, I have a card for you. I'll tuck it in your backpack." I unzipped a pocket and slid the card in.

"Great. Thanks. I guess you better go catch your next flight," he said, waving me on. "It was good to meet you," David said with zero feeling. He looked forward again like he was just going to continue looking for his bag.

For real? That was it? "Good to meet you?" You have got to be kidding. What about walking me to my gate? What about holding my hand? The mission trip was over. We no longer had rules.

I stood there for a minute, feeling alone, stupid, and awkward. I could tell he was not going to walk me anywhere. Jason and Hank were waiting for me because we were on the same next flight.

"Okay. Well, I guess I'll see you later."

"Yeah. See ya," David replied.

No hug. Nothing. As I turned to walk away, the floodgates started. I didn't turn to look back. I just began to bawl. This had gone nothing like I had expected.

PART 3

WAITING

19

BREAKING UP

I'd been home for a week. Hosting a bonfire, my Aunt Betty wanted the whole family to come over and hear about the summer mission trip adventures. My cousin, Kristin, had been on a mission trip for the entire summer with World Evangelism Ministries. I had been on a shorter trip but much further away from Kristen's stateside summer. We were both filled with excitement about what God had done with us and through us during our trips.

I shared about all the experiences I had on my trip. The schools and assemblies, the street ministry, the bondage and warfare of Northern Ireland, and interweaving the gospel with athletics and clinics. God had touched hundreds of lives during our three-week European trip, and we rejoiced about the salvations. I had kept track of the individual people I had prayed the prayer of salvation with—14 people in all. My aunts were both in tears.

Finally, I shared about David. "If that is not all climactic enough, I also met the man I'm going to marry. His name is David."

"Wow! That's awesome, Emily. So, have you talked to him a lot since you've been back?" Aunt Cindy asked.

"Actually, no. I haven't talked to him at all," I responded.

"Well, if you are going to marry him, wouldn't it be good if you talked to him?"

Sure, that made sense. I was not going to allow her mere question to get me discouraged or make me start to doubt. "I'm sure that will happen. We will talk. I'm just going to wait for him to call me. He's kinda old-fashioned. *He* likes to be the pursuer. So... the time will come. I'm not sure when, but he will call me."

Aunt Cindy's courteous smile was one that told me she was simply humoring me as she nodded her head. The look behind her smirking eyes said, "Yeah. Right. Sure you're going to marry him. He hasn't even contacted you. It will be okay. You will get over him soon." She definitely did not appear optimistic. Her masked smile may have revealed a glimmer of hopefulness for my sake that, at least, he may let me down easily.

I was resolute about what I saw, tenacious in my faith about something that could not be touched or seen with eyes. I believed that I really *did* see God's hand. That I really did receive in my spirit the words that David was going to be my husband. I couldn't put everything together. I didn't know how it would all happen. I didn't know when. I just believed. Deep down, in the depths of who I was, I believed that, one day, he would be my husband.

The phone at my parents' house rang. "Hello, Cooks," I answered.

My heart dropped at the sound I heard on the other end of the phone.

"Emily, Hi. I miss you." Rick knew I was back. His voice brought a flood of memories. I could hear his heart drawing me in, calling me in. I could hear the truth in his voice. He really did miss me. He had been my best friend. We knew everything about each other. We had become connected, intertwined at the soul, almost every part of us. My feelings were trying to betray me, momentarily luring me back in, falling into the entanglement of his voice and the strange soul tie. A piece of me knew I had some sort of love for him, a twisted love. In a split second, just hearing him say my name, *Emily*, was like a giant magnet, pulling me to him.

"Hi, Rick," I said, trying not to sound too excited or disappointed. I had such a mix of emotions with him. Here, I had met my husband. On the other end of the phone was a man whom I had barely escaped. For the past three weeks, I was free to breathe, no longer captive in a relationship. Now what? His voice already drew me to him. I did long to see him. How could things ever be the same?

"How are you? How has your summer been?" I said in my nonchalant tone. I tried my best to act normal and regain my composure.

"It's been great. I want to see you though. I want to see you, Emily. When can I see you? Let's get together. Let's catch up." The initial reaction in me was wanting to run. There was something about him that was almost mesmerizing, something that could captivate my heart, my insides. Part of me felt like I should just run, run fast the other way. Another part of me felt like I needed to tell him about David, tell him about this man that I was going to marry. I knew we would have to see each other again sometime. We still had about a month before school would start back, and I couldn't escape forever.

"Okay, let's get together," I said. "When do you want to get together?"

"How about tonight? I'm still at home, so maybe we could meet halfway? How about Saginaw? Would that work for you? Would 10:00 work for you? We could do the park at the edge of town?"

"Sure. I can do that. I'll see you then," I said.

With a long pause, it took Rick a minute to respond, "Emily... I really missed you. I'm glad that we can see each other tonight."

"Yeah, it'll be good to catch up. I'll see you tonight."

"Alright. See you at 10."

We hung up. Wow. His voice rung in my head. He had such a large piece of me. Would I ever have it all back? Would I ever not feel so drawn to him? Would I ever truly and completely be free? I felt the strength of our bond. Though it wasn't as strong as it was before, I could still feel it's power. How quickly I could be brought back to this place, to these feelings. I had forgotten how it felt. My heart felt split. My heart felt pulled.

I pulled in to the parking lot and saw Rick's black SUV. At the sheer sight of it, memories and feelings that had been suppressed quickly came flooding back. His shiny, clean Ford Expedition preceded him with an *umph* as if ranking him, showing his importance, and saying, "I've shown up, I am on the scene." I still held to a desire and belief that everything we had been, everything we had experienced somehow wouldn't all be in vain despite my great fall. I knew that, tonight, my road with Rick was over. It would end here, under the stars in this small park along the river. This great power that he walked around with would be amazing if it was backed by Jesus, if it was encompassed with Jesus.

I longed for him to meet my Jesus, my Savior. How different he would be. If and when he finally did make that decision, he would be like Saul in the Bible. Powerful and influential, Saul persecuted Christians in great power and strength. Saul was as far from a believer as one could be—until one day.

The light beamed down on that glorious road, and Saul had what we know of as the "Damascus Road Experience." He had literal blinders on his eyes, *scales* as the Bible said. He was blinded, and the truth of Jesus opened his eyes, allowing the scales to fall from his eyes. Saul became a believer, and his name was changed to Paul. It's amazing to think that the greatest enemy to Christianity became the person who wrote a good majority of the New Testament.

I knew that God was no respecter of persons. If Saul's life could be changed so radically, I believed that Rick's life could be changed, too. There was hope. I didn't know how it would happen, nor could I continue with him. After tonight, my prayers would have to be enough. Although Rick represented a bondage that kept me from Jesus, there was a part of me that really did love him deeply, a deep love.

I no longer wanted both. I no longer wanted Rick and God. There was a unique but incomparable intestinal fortitude in both David and Rick. David carried a similar weight of his presence upon arriving on a scene, though radically different in purpose. Unlike a grim vehicle, carrying in a luring darkness, David walked in a room carrying light, like an army drawing you to light. As if accompanied by grand, translucent angels, his straightened backbone and stance for what was right trumped the arrogance of the world as I silently paralleled the two. David, in such a short time, revealed to me that everything I longed for could be mine. He allowed me to realize that true, godly relationships were available and that they were not just a figment of my wishful imagination.

In my newfound revelation, I still knew Rick's salesman-like influence would be world-changing if, like Saul, he had that radical Jesus-moment. He could affect the world positively for Christ, and what a day that would be! I held to a hope that Rick would decide to make Jesus his Savior, but tonight would end my journey of trying to make this happen on my own.

I got out of my car and saw the dark shadow of Rick sitting on a picnic table, overlooking the river. When he saw me coming toward him, he immediately got up and walked toward me. He immediately embraced me. His arms felt strong, and his embrace was tight. His embrace was long. We stood there for a moment and held each other. I drank in the smell of his cologne and quickly remembered why his embrace was dangerous. I loved that he smelled good. He always smelled good, and that was something I felt like I had always been a sucker for. A long hug from a good-looking guy. An embrace that said, "I want you. I miss you." A big SUV that I liked. An amazing smell. To be wanted. It seemed that so many things were stacked in his favor. So many things. But the one thing, the most important thing, was missing. He still did not have my Jesus, nor was he ready for Him. He was not ready to make that commitment.

Rick pulled back just a little bit and looked at my face, his arms still embracing me, "I missed you so much. It's so good to see you." He turned his head slightly, with a look of surprise, and said, "You look good, but different." He quickly embraced me again and said, "It's just so good to see you, Emily," he said, resting his chin on the top of my head, easily enveloping me in his arms.

I smiled. His hug was warm and comfortable. For the moment I was in it, I enjoyed it. I knew he could tell it was over, really over. Something in me was different. I had a different resolve.

We sat on the top of the old wooden picnic table, overlooking the river. It was dark, and the air was crisp. It did feel like a Pennsylvania fall evening. I could tell fall was approaching by the chill in the air. It even smelled fresh when you drank in a deep breath. Sitting to my left, Rick playfully nudged while I leaned forward, my elbows on my knees.

"So? How was the mission trip? How was England? Did you have a good time?" Rick asked.

"I did. It was definitely a life-changing time. It was pretty amazing. We saw a lot of people saved. So many people came to know Jesus. It was overwhelming."

"Wow! That's great, Emily!" he said with as much enthusiasm as a non-believer could muster. He was excited about it only because I was excited.

"Rick," I said, excited and serious at the same time, "Rick, I also met the man that I am going to marry. I met him! I met my husband." My tone was absolute, no doubts or wavering.

"Wow! Really? What's his name? What's he like?" A surprised disappointment sounded in his voice, a pitch higher than his normal inflection.

"Well, his name is David. He is a track and field athlete. He attends a division-one university in South Carolina on a track scholarship. He throws the hammer. He's a big guy. Blonde hair, blue eyes, and amazing." I wasn't trying to rub it in his face; I was just describing David. In description, he did sound amazing, and he was even better in real life. "He spoke one night when we were there, and I could hardly believe it. He has an incredible way of communicating. As he gave a salvation message, people just kept on going down. People just kept getting out of their seats, flooding the front to accept Jesus as their Savior. It was so amazing." As I spoke, it was almost like I was getting lost in what I was saying. Rick just sat back and took it all in. His demeanor changed. He leaned back on the table and continued to listen.

"And, along with all that," I continued, "along with his passion for the Lord, he had an amazing ability to lead people. One afternoon in England, we went on a walk through a park. As we walked, he stopped and hugged me. It was so amazing. When he hugged me, in that instant, I saw a quick vision of a green chalkboard hanging in the air, and I saw a hand. The hand wrote, 'This is your husband. This is the man you are going to marry.' I knew immediately that it was God's hand. Rick," I said and paused, "I knew I had met the man that I'm going to marry."

"Wow," he said and then sat in silence. He believed enough in God and in my relationship with Him to know what I said was true.

We both sat in the silence of the somber night for a few minutes, looking over the river. I could almost feel the weight of my words sinking in to Rick as each moment passed. The thick darkness encompassed the twinkling of the stars. Though the sky was black, I felt such brightness, such light. The silence continued. We laid back on the table and just looked up in silence, in darkness. What freedom I felt in my heart. It felt so good to tell Rick about David. It almost felt like, for the first time, I began to experience a release from the bondage I had felt for so long. I sensed that Rick, in that moment, knew the game was over; he had lost. God had recaptured my heart. Just for choosing Him, He also gave me a glimpse of what would be my future, my husband. Rick could tell my voice reflected surety. He knew that I had met my husband. One day, David would marry me. An aimless attempt to get things to be "like they used to be" would be futile.

Rick sat up, his shoulders drooped and his posture unusually slumped. He knew it was over.

"Wow, Emily," he said. "I really do believe you. I can tell that you are going to marry David. Wow."

We sat for a while longer in silence and then got up to leave. Rick's long embrace made me miss him already. We had shared so much together. This, though, was the end. I was saying goodbye to my best friend. His embrace felt good and felt sad with his head tucked in tightly to the side of my head and his chin resting down on my shoulder. I took deep breaths, smelling him. I knew that this would be the last time I would be held like this by Rick. We lingered there, just holding each other. We knew that, once we let go, it would be over. This was our goodbye embrace. I would miss his smell. His cologne was strong and rich. I was saying goodbye to my best friend.

Tears welled up in both of our eyes. When we released, we stood back, his arms still around my waist. We looked like lovers. We looked like more than what we were. We were saying goodbye. No more words were needed. We looked at each other with the silence of our words saying everything. We both knew it was final. This was goodbye.

20

WAITING

August had come and gone. I had not seen or spoken to David since that last moment at the airport on July 27th. It had been over one month since that final day when I cried as I walked away from him. How I longed to hear his voice and get to know him. Each day, in my prayers, I pleaded constantly, "Lord, *please* let him know that he's going to marry me! Lord please let today be the day that he contacts me! Please, Lord! Please!" I just hoped that God would hear, that God would answer my cries. I longed to hear David's voice. When would he call? When would he write? E-mail? Something? I ached. My whole body longed to hear from him.

September had come and gone. No David. No call. No e-mail. No word. "Lord, pleeeeeease have him call me. Please have him e-mail. Lord, please!" My heart hurt. It seemed that, every day, my prayer was the same. Every day, a day of painful longing. The mundane life of classes occupied my time but not my heart and mind.

Fall semester was in full-swing, and the Pennsylvania leaves had been falling for several weeks. This was my favorite time of year. So beautiful. Perfect weather. And it was time to wear my favorite clothes: sweatshirts and jeans! The only way it could be better is if the computer lab would reveal an e-mail from my future husband. Obsessively, I went out of my way every day to go to the computer lab. I would find an empty computer and, with anticipation in my heart, quickly put in my login and password. Today was going to be the day. I knew it was. Today would be it. I would zip to click on the e-mail icon, scanning through the e-mails. Nothing. Like clockwork, my head would fall limp into my hands again. Bent over with my elbows on my knees, I could only shake my head as it was cupped in my hands. "Please, Jesus," I whispered. "Please." I didn't need to explain my plea to Jesus. I was sure he knew. My continual reminder to Him surely had to be getting annoying. I know if I were sitting at the right hand of God and had to listen to me, I would have given me what I wanted by now. Surely, everyone up there was getting tired of my draining repetition.

Monday, there was nothing. Tuesday, nothing. Wednesday, nothing. Thursday, nothing. Friday, nothing. Week after week, I had been met with disappointment. Nothing.

My heart dropped. There it was. It had been so long. Rick's Expedition was parked in front of the post office. Why did it seem I would be doing so well and then, just seeing him or his Expedition, my heart would drop. I hoped I'd see him, but I hoped I wouldn't.

I parked my Camry and headed toward the post office. After wiggling my key into the bronze box, I found no fun mail—only campus junk mail. So far, no Rick. Walking down the hall, I turned the corner to head downstairs to the computer lab. "Please, Lord. Please let there be an e-mail from David."

I found an open computer and rushed to sign on. I pulled up my e-mail. For what seemed like another countless time, I quickly scanned down through all of my new e-mails. No e-mail from David.

My heart hurt. My whole being was sad. Another day had come. One day, one glorious day, I would hear from him. I knew I would. I had to cling to the hope that what I saw was true. That what I saw was real. The chalkboard that revealed my future. That this, this man, though hundreds of miles away, would be my husband one day. I just wished God would hurry up and reveal it to David, too.

On countless nights, upon getting home late from studying, I found myself looking up at the black country sky. Living in the country provided a beauty people in town didn't get to enjoy. The hundreds of twinkling stars as far as my eyes could see arrayed the sky like a dark blanket overlooking the cornfield and my parents' house. The late-October nights were getting cold, easily dipping into the 40s at night, but I was drawn to linger in the brisk air.

Leaning against my car, I stared yet again into the great expanse. It took me back to England, sitting atop the hillside, gazing down to Ashford, spilling my heart to Laura about how I was going to marry David. As I looked up, I found the tiny group of stars that reminded me of a tea cup. Like many times before, I repeated the prayer I heard Jesus pray in the New Testament, "Lord, please take this cup from me. Not my will but yours be done." I continued, "Lord, I really believe that I'm going to marry David, but if it's not meant to be, I completely give him up to you. Not my will, Father, but *your* will be done!" I truly meant it. If David was not meant to be my husband, I would love to know. Then, at least I could escape the misery I felt each day that passed without hearing from him. If he was not supposed to be mine, I just wanted to know.

But I got the typical response from the Lord: nothing. I heard nothing. No assurance that David would be my husband but no decline that he would not.

The minutes leaning against my car caused the metal to match the warmth of my body temperature, making the cold air easier to dawdle in longer. The tea cup was a continual reminder of surrendering David to the Lord again. I felt that was all I did. He was constantly on my mind. I couldn't escape thoughts of him though, on many days, I wished I could. My heart was so heavy, longing to hear from him. July 27th seemed like an eternity ago.

With a sigh and seemingly no closer to my love, I headed inside for a night of sleep. I hoped that the next day would be better. I hoped that the next day would bring news of David.

Elise jumped in, interrupting, "So, it's almost *November*," she said, emphasizing November, "and you *still* haven't heard from David? How did you possibly survive? Did you just end up calling him, or did you keep waiting? I don't know how you did it. I don't think I could have ever done that!" she exclaimed emphatically as she shook her head.

The warm Caribbean sun stood above us, I held up Elise's Diet Coke glass, and I motioned for Duncan to bring two. He bowed his head down, gracing with his right hand as if he were opening the door for a lady. I knew his gestures meant, "Yes ma'am, right away."

"Well, Elise, I was miserable. Honestly, I still don't know how I was getting through each day, but I was choosing to wait. I felt I had to honor what David had said on the mission trip: 'If a girl wanted a guy to notice her, she should do absolutely nothing.' Now, sure, if he would never have said that, I'm sure I would have called him, e-mailed, or sent him a letter. I felt like I was treading on thin ice. I didn't want to ruin my chances by initiating things with him. I knew I only had one chance."

"So, you were literally miserable every day?" Elise asked.

"Unfortunately, yes. If I could go back, I believe I would have tried to busy myself for God, doing something for the Kingdom, something to help people or something. Anything, really. I was so into myself. The focus on me and checking my e-mails really made things worse. If I would've taken my eyes off of myself and helped other people or done work for God, time would have passed much more quickly. The daily focus on myself caused life to move at a torturous snail's pace. I almost think David's comment should have an addendum."

"Oh yeah? What's that?"

"'What should a girl do to get a guy to notice her? Absolutely nothing. She should assert herself aggressively in her relationship with God, listening and following the Lord's plans for her life. Then, her husband will find her!' That would be my 'David-addendum.' With that mindset, I may have been able to enjoy life during my time of waiting, rather than wallowing in misery."

"So? When did you finally reconnect? Did he call you or see you, or did he finally e-mail? What happened?"

"Slow down, slow down," I said with a smile. "I'm getting to that."

Duncan quietly placed two fresh, refilled glasses on our table, along with an icy pitcher so we could refill at our leisure.

"Alright... let's jump back in. Where were we?" I thought for a moment. "Oh, November... it was Thanksgiving."

November 26th. It was Thanksgiving, and it was also my Dad's birthday. Another day. The whole family was there. Grandma and Grandpa and all of us kids: Ashley, Kate, Jake, and me. Mom was upstairs, banging around in the kitchen. There was an aroma of turkey and gravy, buttery garlic from the mashed potatoes that wafted into every crevice of the house. Everything Mom had ever made tasted fantastic! On many occasions, we would tell her she should own a restaurant or catering company. Her typical response was to only thank us but brush it off. "I would love that," she would say. "Maybe one day I will." She truly had a gift. In the meantime, we would enjoy the fruits of her delicious gift!

Dad... well, Dad was doing whatever Mom asked him to do. He knew that, if he didn't continue to stay "busy," she would give him projects. If he wasn't busy, he at least tried to look like it. He had already been to Wal-Mart for her twice, picking up some last minute items. Now, he was getting the long table set downstairs.

Us kids? Well, honestly, we didn't jump to help like we should. We knew that, if we even walked in the kitchen, she would put us to work. Feeling half guilty, we still maintained a hidden state, staying out of Mom's sight. In attempts to avoid her wrath, we definitely stayed away from the kitchen.

Aside from the aroma filling the house all morning, the Macy's Thanksgiving Day Parade was showing on every TV in the house. Of course, Thanksgiving lunch was always the highlight! Turkey and gravy, ham, dressing, mashed potatoes, green bean casserole, mom's famous broccoli and rice casserole, sweet potatoes with the gooey syrup and marshmallows on top, and warm yeast rolls. It was almost the best day of the year.

Desserts and chocolates lined the bar. Now, the hardest decision was to choose which one or how many to try: Mom's homemade apple pie and pecan pie, the Raspberry Cream pie and Coconut Cream pie from our famous Amish restaurant, and then the array of chocolates from the Chocolate Nutte Shoppe in downtown Pippen. Thankfully, whatever I didn't try first, I could sample later because they would all be left out all day for grazing.

The remainder of our day and into the evening would be spent playing games. This was, by far, our favorite tradition that we all always looked forward to on Thanksgiving and Christmas. After everything was cleaned up, Ashley started getting the first game going while Grandpa and Jacob began this year's puzzle. Hotels was one of our favorite games, especially mine. We were all pretty competitive and liked to win. Mom always did such a great job finding new games for the holidays, but we continued to go back to this family favorite.

The next several hours were spent drinking pop and snacking on the goodies behind the bar; no one thought about diets or weight during this day. Thanksgiving brought my most treasured activity: family time. Everyone was together. I loved this. A roar of laughter was frequent as Jacob did something stupid or was being his "comedian" self. Each of us, including Grandma and Grandpa, truly enjoyed ourselves. What a blessed day and family. Everyone was together.

"Emily," I heard mom yell from upstairs. "The phone is for you!"

I went behind the bar to grab the cordless phone. "Hello," I said.

"Hello, Emily. This is David."

It seemed like every ounce of breath swept out of my body. Oh my goodness. "Breathe, Emily! Breathe! Say something! Ahhhhhhhh! Oh my goodness! Say something. Don't sound stupid or too excited."

"Wow! Hi, David. It's so great to hear from you!" I said, smiling from ear to ear. I quickly made my way back to my room. As I passed by the game table, Ash and Kate definitely could tell that, whoever it was, it was good! By my expression and the way I floated passed them, they probably knew it was David.

"I just wanted to call you on Thanksgiving. I've been thinking about you and thought it would be nice to talk to you. How are you doing? Are you having a good day?"

I mean, *hello*! Best day of the last 132 days of my life! I couldn't even begin to tell how excited I was, but I definitely didn't want him to know the full extent of my excitement! I was trying to keep my cool, trying to act normal. All the while, I felt like I was jumping out of my skin! I was ecstatic! "I've been doing great. We're having a great day. We've just been playing games and enjoying time with the family. What about you? How have you been?"

"I've been doing great. School is great. Track has been going awesome this season. I've been really trying to bulk up and train hard. God has truly been good. We've had a great Thanksgiving so far. I think we are going to see a movie in a little bit." For the next thirty minutes, we talked about college, track, family, God, the AOC trip… we just talked about everything. I had never talked at such great lengths to David, not even on the trip. For the first time, I was beginning to get more insight into who he was. Somehow, the topic came up about our future spouse. David proceeded to tell me about his "list." He had made a list of all the qualities and characteristics he wanted in his wife. He had more than 30 things on his list of what he wanted in his wife. "What a good idea," I thought. "I need to make a list."

I just laid there on my bed in my room, hoping the time would never end. Just listening to David. He was so together. So spiritually smart. I enjoyed laying there, listening to him talk. My smile felt like it extended from ocean to ocean. What a blessed time. I was so happy. I prayed silently that maybe this would be the spark that would have us talking more.

"Well, hey… It has been really good talking to you, but I need to get going. Have a great day, Emily."

The way he said my name. I loved hearing him say *Emily*. It was slow and with meaning. Most people didn't say my name, but David seemed to do everything a bit different than most people.

I was sad that the moments were ending but overwhelmed with joy. My heart was overflowing. "It was great talking to you, too. Thanks for calling. Enjoy your movie."

"We will. Bye, Emily."

"Goodbye, David." We hung up. I held the phone to my chest. I didn't know when I would talk to him again. I didn't know if he would call soon. I hoped I had said something that sparked an interest in him, something to make him want to talk again soon.

Laying on my bed, my arms draped out wide. I was so in love.

21

COSTA RICA

December and Christmas break had come and gone with no word from David. In my optimism, I had hoped he would maybe call on Christmas but to no avail.

January brought not only a new year but also a new adventure. I would be leaving for Costa Rica for my three months of studying abroad. Pulling in to my parents' house for the last time before leaving, I had said goodbye to my friends.

Like clock-work, I continued to pray on those winter nights, "Lord, please take this cup from me! Not my will, Father, but Your will be done! You know what my will is, Father. My will is to marry David, but if it's not Your will, please let me know. I will give him up." I lingered a bit longer, staring at the Pennsylvania night. Would the stars be the same in Costa Rica? Would I be able to find my little tea cup?

After hours of travel—switching flights, delays, and sauntering through airports—we were finally in Costa Rica. I laid in my new bed, soaking in all of the events of the last few days. I said "goodbyes" to my family and said "hellos" to my new family. The next three months would surely help my Spanish, but could they help my heart? I was ready for the promise in the book of Proverbs, that desire fulfilled brings joy. I was ready for the fulfillment of my desire, to just hear David's voice again, even if it was through a typed out message on the computer.

During these first six weeks, the 19 students in our group were all in San Jose, the country's capital. Spread throughout the region, we all lived with different families and would need to navigate our way to our Spanish class the next morning.

I lived in Barrio Pinto and had a new big brother, Eduardo. My mom and dad, so far, seemed very loving. Upon meeting me, my short, stout little mama grabbed me by the shoulders, held me at arms-length, and said, "Mi amor! Bienvenidos mi hija! Estamos muy contentos de tenerte aqui!" With that, she embraced me with a long, warm, strong embrace. My mind raced, trying to figure out what she said. Something about love and welcome, and I thought *hija* meant daughter or little girl, and I thought I heard the word *happy*. After the first two sentences, she lost me. My few semesters of Spanish classes proved I should've applied myself more. Trying to decipher Spanish sentences as quickly as they spoke was still a challenge. Nonetheless, I felt blessed to be placed with a family that seemed so warm. I simply smiled in response and said, "Hola. Gracias." I figured I wouldn't be messing anything up by saying "hello" and "thank you."

Although being immersed into families who spoke no English would be challenging, these first six weeks would allow me to participate in daily Spanish language, grammar, and history classes. Thankfully, it would be alongside our English-speaking classmates. It would be a long three months of silent meals if we didn't learn how to speak Spanish. I hoped that we would at least get to a basic conversation level.

Before I left for Costa Rica, I e-mailed my AOC friends, including David. I figured there was no "pursuit" if David was simply included in a group e-mail. For my Web Design class, I had to design a website, and I chose to base mine off of our summer trip to Europe. Our assignment had to incorporate pictures.

Naturally, among the dozen pictures I had posted, I included my favorite, a picture of David and me smelling roses in England. It was taken on our last day of the mission trip while we were in London for a few hours to do some sight-seeing. We saw the magnificent Buckingham Palace, Big Ben, and the London Tower Bridge. Smelling the roses together in London was my last real "moment" with David while on our mission trip. I was curious if he ever saw the picture. It was beautiful. To me, it represented more than just a picture of us "smelling roses." It encompassed our connection that we made while on the trip, the amazing moments, walks through the park, our time on the bus, and the forbidden kiss. It was the last picture we had taken together. Maybe the picture would bring back some of the same memories when he saw it? I really went back and forth about including him on the e-mail. I knew he didn't like the "girl pursuing the guy" approach, so I had to think of a way to communicate that wouldn't be seen as me pursuing him, especially because it was a mass e-mail to AOC friends. Nonetheless, if he did see it, I hoped he liked it.

I was told that there were computer labs scattered throughout San Jose. I was sure several of us would find those labs and become regulars! I couldn't imagine not being able to check my e-mail. I just knew I would have one from David soon.

After yet another day of classes, the days were finally becoming routine. I knew how to take the bus into town without getting lost or getting off at the wrong spot. My blue eyes and blonde hair caught the attention from Costa Ricans everywhere I went. I definitely stuck out. It could be very easy to get into trouble here if I were still a partier!

I didn't waste any time finding the few computer labs around town. In the ten days of our stay so far, I had managed to pop into a lab on eight of the ten days. Most days, it took the internet longer to load than the actual time I needed to be there. The circle icon was spinning and spinning and spinning, causing me to wait anxiously. Would this be the day? Would I leave elated or disappointed again? Unfortunately, each day thus far had only brought disappointment.

My Spanish was improving. Being immersed in the language and living with a family caused me to sit at the edge of my seat in class each day. It wasn't as if what we were learning was a matter of life and death though I was eager to apply what I was learning when I got home at dinner. Unlike the boring classes I had taken back at B.U. where I had nowhere to apply what I had learned, I had a sense of urgency to learn the language.

I finally saw the value and relevance of verb conjugations, an area where I desperately needed to improve. At least, if I knew the meaning of a verb but conjugated it in the wrong tense, whoever I was talking to probably would be able to reason what I actually meant. Being able to apply what I learned almost instantaneously caused my learning to accelerate. "Mi Mama y Papa" purposefully slowed down while talking to me. I was thankful. It helped me to pick up a few words to understand the gist of their comments or questions. I met Eduardo's girlfriend, Maria, who seemed very nice. I anticipated that it wouldn't be long until they were married and Eduardo would move out.

Upon the dismissal of class each day, we could zip to the computer lab. Maybe today would be the day that I would hear from David. Even my Costa Rican parents had said innocently, "If you're going to marry him, wouldn't he write or call?" After I pieced together their Spanish words, I figured out what they were saying. Their question didn't cause me to doubt. Though I hated this whole waiting process, for some reason, I knew it would all work out.

I signed on to a computer, pulling up my e-mails. My heart leapt!

Subject: Re: hello.
Date: Fri, 15 Jan 1999 12:23:59 EDT
Emily,

This is David!! I am so happy to hear from you and know that God is still working so well in your life. I visited your web page and that brought back so much joy in my life and reminded me of you.

You are so special to me, and I hope that, in God's time, we can see each other and talk face-to-face. I wish there were more girls like you. I know that God has so many big things for you to do.

I am doing awesome. Track could not be any better. My goal is to become an All-American. Also, to qualify for the

Olympic Trials. God is blessing me so much, and he is so gloriously awesome. I am growing so much, and I wish I could tell you all about it.

Tell me again, why are you in Costa Rica? I miss you.

David

Wow! He said he "missed me." Oh, how I missed him. If he only knew. He said he missed me. He really said it. Wow. I'm special to him. He wants to see me again. I took a deep breath and re-read the words again and again. The day I had been waiting for had *finally* come to pass. I finally heard from David. Oh, how I missed him! My heart just wanted to cry out. Joy filled me. Happiness. Thankfulness. A desire fulfilled. He finally wrote to me. That gave me permission to write back. I missed him still. January 15th, the day I finally heard from David, the man I was going to marry. I sat and re-read the words, slowly soaking in what a special e-mail I had received. I hit the *print* button. I knew I would cherish the words on the piece of paper, especially on any long, hard days.

February 4th. Classes in San Jose went well that day. I managed to do a little bit of shopping in the market area before making my way to the bus stop to head back home, my new home. I really enjoyed my mom and dad. They were so loving and so fun. I knew my mom would have dinner ready when I arrived. I would have just enough time to put my things in my room and goof around with mi papá a little before sitting down with the family.

When I walked in, I was greeted with a hug and kisses on both cheeks from my little five-feet tall, Costa Rican mamá. She had on her yellow apron, and I peeked out and noticed clothes, including some of mine, hanging to dry in the courtyard. I truly loved her. Dropping my bags off in my room, I also saw a neatly folded pile of clothes on my bed and freshly starched and ironed clothes hanging in my closet. She must have been busy washing, ironing, and cooking for most of the day. She was such an amazing woman. Having ironed clothes was definitely a luxury because I certainly did not iron when I was back home. If only I could just take her home with me when I returned. I enjoyed being "mamá'd."

Dinner was yummy, as usual. The typical rice and beans, some sort of chicken in a tomato sauce, bread, a unique salad blend, and guava juice. Meals were so interesting. I had never made beans nor rice like this at home that tasted this good. I wasn't quite sure what her secret was. It was probably that they cooked almost all day long, soaking in the flavor of minced onions and cilantro. I raved over how good everything was, and knew I must have hit a hot button. My little mama, red in the cheeks, responded with smiles and said, "Ayyyyyyy. Gracias, mi amor. Gracias, mi amorcita. Es un placer. Es un placer." I was quickly able to translate this in my mind: "Thank you, my love. Thank you, my little love. It's a pleasure. It's a pleasure." She put her hands to my cheeks, squeezed them gently, and kissed my forehead.

Finishing dinner, she began taking dishes from the table to the kitchen as the phone rang. "Hola?" she said as she answered the phone. "Si. Si. Es aqui."

"Yes. Yes. She is here," I overheard. The phone was for me.

"Emily, el telefono. Es para ti."

It wasn't often that I got a telephone call. Maybe it was one of my classmates calling about a Spanish assignment, or maybe I'd get lucky, and it would be my mom or dad, one of my sisters or brother from back home. My older sister had just had a baby, so I knew there was quite a lot of excitement about the first grandbaby.

Making my way to the phone, I took it from my mamá. "Hola, es Emily."

"Hello, Emily. It's David. How are you?"

His voice. Silence. My heart dropped in my chest. I must have changed to a shade of white or red because my mamá looked at me and asked, "Todo esta bien?" Is everything ok?

My eyes as large as saucers, I shook my head, expressing an excited "yes!" Yet, I had a grimaced, ecstatic, nervous smile pasted on my face. My mamá just smiled. I think she knew. I knew my body language surely appeared like I was freaking out!

"Hi. David? What a surprise!" I tried to sound as calm and non-excited as possible. I didn't want it to be completely obvious that I was totally in love with him.

"Well, I just missed you and really wanted to talk to you. I thought I would surprise you with a call."

"You definitely succeeded in surprising me! It's so good to hear your voice." I had only heard his voice one other time on the phone. That was on Thanksgiving Day. What a shock to be hearing it now while in Costa Rica. A smile took over my face.

He asked, "So, how have you been? How is Costa Rica? Do you like it?"

For the next 5-10 minutes, we chatted just about everyday life. I wasn't sure if he could feel it, but my heart was putty in his hands. As he gave me a glimpse into his life, I felt like the luckiest girl on the planet. Though happiness filled my heart and face, I couldn't help but wipe away the tears that welled up in my eyes. Knowing a bit more about what he did, what he was passionate about, and his training schedule for track, I enjoyed knowing anything and everything he told me. My heart beamed at hearing what made him tick.

"I miss you. Please be careful while you are there," he said, followed by a long pause. I hoped he didn't hear the sniffle as I wiped my nose. I couldn't help but cry. I was so happy. I quickly wiped the tears that were now streaming down my cheeks. I was happy he couldn't see me. He would surely see that I was in love with him. "Emily…"

"Yes?" I managed in a whisper, choking back any sound of obvious tears.

"Are you okay?"

"Yes, thank you. It was so good to hear from you. I will be careful. You be careful, too. Train hard now," I teased, covering up the drops of happiness leaking from my eyes. "I'd love to watch you in the Olympics!" I felt like I recovered. I hoped he didn't hear my hidden feelings.

"I will." For what seemed like an eternity, he paused. "Good night, Emily."

"Good night, David," I said and finally heard his line click. Before placing the phone back on the receiver, I held it close to my chest, hugging it. In my mind, I was thanking God for such an amazing gift!

Could I be any more excited? I felt like I was holding hundreds of helium balloons, and my feet were soaring off the ground as I stood, clinching the phone. Hanging up the receiver, I stood there, tightly closing my eyes and wiping my brow. Maybe my tears would be hidden from my family.

My papá smiled at me from the living room. He mouthed words that I did not understand as my mind was still in a foggy haze. Bringing his hands to his heart, I heard him say, "Mi amor," my love, as he smiled.

I returned in Spanish, "Yes, the man I am going to marry one day."

The rest of the evening, my parents and brother periodically laughed at me. I sat there with them as they watched TV, and every time they looked at me, I was still smiling. I couldn't help it. My heart was so happy. I was so happy. David called me. He even said he missed me. I was on a different planet for sure right now.

Our first six weeks in San Jose had come to an end. I gave my family a temporary goodbye as I would return to stay with them during last four days of our Costa Rica trip. It was still sad to say goodbye. I was excited to know that it was only temporary; otherwise, it would be a much more emotional day.

The second part of my Costa Rica stay brought me to a small town called San Isidro del General, close to the Panama border. I worked at an all-girls orphanage, teaching them English. My new parents were nice. My new little sister, Ana Sofia, was a bubbly, energetic six-year old.

I wasn't sure if I could ever get used to the cockroaches that roamed the house freely. Cockroaches seemed to be an accepted and unnoticed part of this area, unnoticed by everyone but me. I still yelped as I saw them run beneath my feet in the kitchen, the shower, and in my room. Ranking with my hatred of spiders, cockroaches seemed equally if not more disgusting.

It had only been a few nights after my arrival. As I tightly tucked the covers around me, the scurry of feet beside my head caused me to wince. I wanted to keep my eyes closed tightly. I didn't want to move. If I could only plug my ears and hear nothing, I would. Ignorance was bliss, right? I cringed, not wanting to open my eyes, remaining completely still. I peeked through the corner of my eye, not wanting to know the reality. Five or six cockroaches made their home beside my head until I moved, and they hastened past my head over my bed.

Without time to think, tears immediately began to stream down my face. I couldn't hold them back. I urgently sat up in my bed, pulling my knees tightly to my chest as I sat in the dark. Rocking back and forth, sobs came uncontrollably. There were cockroaches in my bed. I hated them. I didn't even want to touch my feet to the floor. What if they were there? I sat in the dark, just tightly rocking. If I squeezed my legs harder, maybe they would disappear?

I finally braved the floor, jumping down to turn on the light, hoping to scare them into crevices I would not see. In a tip-toed run, I ran to get the cordless phone from the living room and returned to my room.

The phone rang and rang. Please answer. Please answer, I prayed.

"Hello?" a sleepy voice replied.

"Mom," was all I could muster as I sobbed.

"What? What is it, Emily? What's wrong?" Her sleepy voice instantly woke in urgency as she heard my sobbing.

"Mom, there are cockroaches in my bed! Cockroaches!" I cried.

Relief swept over her voice as she tried to calm me down.

"Emily, can you get your Bible?" she asked me. I was happy she was taking charge. I needed someone to give me a direct order.

"Yes." Just hearing my mom's voice caused me to calm down a bit. My sobs were beginning to wane.

"Open it to Psalm 91," she instructed.

I flipped through the pages of my Bible, trying not to tear the thin pages as my hands shook. "I'm there," I said, muffled.

"Emily, I'm going to read this Psalm to you. This Psalm is a protection Psalm. You are going to be okay. Okay, Emily?"

"Okay, Mom."

She began,

> He who dwells in the secret place of the Most High shall abide under the shadow of the Almighty. I will say of the Lord, 'He is my refuge and my fortress; My God, in Him I will trust. Surely He shall deliver you from the snare of the fowler and from the perilous pestilence.'

Her voice was soothing. I felt better already. My heartbeat was slowing back down, and I wiped my face as the tears dried in my eyes.

> 'He shall cover you with His feathers, and under His wings you shall take refuge; His truth shall be your shield and buckler. You shall not be afraid of the terror by night, nor of the arrow that flies by day, nor of the pestilence that walks in darkness, nor of the destruction that lays waste at noonday. A thousand may fall at your side, and ten thousand at your right hand; but it shall not come near you. Only with your eyes shall you look, and see the reward of the wicked. Because you have made the Lord, who is my refuge, even the Most High, your dwelling place, no evil shall befall you, nor shall any plague come near your dwelling; for He shall give His angels charge over you, to keep you in all your ways. In their hands they shall bear you up, lest you dash your foot against a stone.'

She continued, "Emily, it's all going to be okay. Just try to lay back down. Know that you have angels all around you, and everything is going to be okay. Okay?"

"Okay, Mom. Thank you. Thank you for answering. I feel a lot better."

"Alright. Have a good night sleep, sweetheart. Everything will be okay. I love you."

"Goodnight, Mom."

"Goodnight," I replied.

With the click of the phone, she was gone, so far away. Thankfully, Mom had a way of making it all better. It wasn't perfect, but I did feel like I could at least sleep now.

At that moment, my Costa Rican mother knocked and said, "Que es la problema?" with great concern on her face. She saw the drying tears on my face as she asked what the problem was.

I told her there were cockroaches in my bed. I could tell she felt horrible, which was not my intention. As she looked at my tear-streaked face, she assured me that she would take care of it in the morning.

The next day, when I got home from working at the orphanage, she had scoured the floor of my room. I could not only tell by how clean it looked but by the smell of disinfectant cleaner. It was such a sweet gesture. I knew she had worked very hard to make my stay a good one.

Over the rest of my stay in Costa Rica, e-mails with David became more frequent but sporadic, ranging from every three to four days to as long as two weeks. I was elated because anything was better than the 132 days I had waited to hear from him initially.

My responses to his e-mails would be immediate, but it would often take him a while to reply. Every day, when I woke up, I looked forward to my workday at the orphanage being over so I could race to a computer lab. On the days I would have an e-mail, my heart would leap. My eyes would race through the words like a child on Christmas morning, each word brought a gift of something I could hold in my heart for that day and sustain me until the next correspondence. My heart longed for him every day. How exciting the day would be when we would finally see each other again. I dreamed about that day.

Three months sped by. My experience in Costa Rica was good, but I was equally happy to be going home. I enjoyed my host families and said goodbye to both of them. They had helped me to speak Spanish rather fluently now. I was excited to see how God would use this new ability in my life.

I was more than happy to say, "United States, here I come!"

22

ELLE AND THE BUDDY LIST

I knew that Ellie, my best friend, was excited to finally have me home. Though her name was Elle, I called her "Ellie" when we were goofing around, being girls. We had only met several months before I left for Costa Rica and quickly became best friends.

I remember walking into the singles class at church on Wednesday night. We were upstairs in a room that seemed like a loft. It was somewhat dark. I arrived a little late, and I could tell that the class had split up into small groups. I scanned the room and saw a girl who looked new to the class. Her long, lanky legs crossed in front of her as she slouched back in her chair. Her golden brown hair glowed, touching the middle of her back. It looked so soft. She smiled instantly, showing her pearly white, perfectly straight teeth as I pulled up a chair beside her. Something inside me told me we would be fast friends.

Elle and I hit it off immediately. She was definitely more bubbly than I was, and she was extremely friendly. I was nice and all but not your go-out-of-your-way extrovert nice, like Elle. I was not the bubbly, bouncy nice. She was the bubbly and bouncy that I was not.

Though Elle attended school at a college about 45 minutes from Bordeaux, we still managed to spend a lot of time together over the next several months. Because she missed my whole Rick relationship, she got updated on him and was very glad it was over.

I learned a lot about her life: her family, her background, and her boyfriend—well, she and Steve were on and off. I heard every detail of the in-between. It actually worked out well. Elle and I were both in similar situations. Both of us were trying to pursue the Lord, trying to seek Him in regard to our relationships, and we were both passionate about Jesus.

Elle was a fairly new believer. She hadn't been saved for very long. Her zealous excitement as she pursued Jesus was refreshing.

She was so excited to learn. She had a passion to know Jesus more intimately than any friend I ever had. We spent a lot of time at my house. I knew she really enjoyed my family. My parents were believers. It was a stable Christian environment that she was drawn to.

We had a continual, ongoing joke. Elle hugged me all the time, but I was not the "hugger" type. So, I would hug her back with a quick pat. I never really noticed it because hugging was so uncomfortable to me. After a while, Elle pointed it out. I suppose my patting was my way of saying, "Ahhhh! Okay. Let's hug and be done with it!"

Elle joked, "Emily! Stop patting me! Real friends are just supposed to hug. No patting! Patting is for people you don't really know or like!" I hugged her because she was my friend, and I knew it made her feel loved. That was fine with me. It was just so natural for her. She was full of innocent love and had a soft heart. So genuine. I could hug. I wasn't sure if I'd get over the whole "patting" thing, but I would try.

Elle. She was funny and such a girl, too. She would squeal and get excited at the littlest things. She was a true friend that made me laugh. Though I felt a bit out of my comfort zone at times, I had come to enjoy life more because of her free-spirited way of loving and living life with such joy. In her e-mails, she always ended with, "I love you." She was a blessing, and I thanked God for a friend like Elle in my life. It was awesome to finally have a friend that loved God and that was in a similar pursuit.

It was nice to be back home. I finished out a quick Maymester. Then, we were well into our summer. I was waitressing at a fabulous restaurant, Yoder's Dutch Country Kitchen. It was Amish-style cooking, and the food was beyond delicious. I was thankful to work there because that meant I got to eat the yummy food! I didn't think I could ever get tired of it! Home cooking. Roast beef and mashed potatoes, German Chocolate and Strawberry Rhubarb Pie. My tastebuds had reached as close to heaven as I thought they could.

The Raspberry Creme was at the top of my pie list, but chocolate always had the number one spot in my heart when it came to dessert!

David and I didn't talk much on the phone, but I had him on my instant messenger. *BIUmen* was his name online. He and his roommate, Todd, shared the logon name. We had a computer downstairs in the family room. Any time I was home, I almost always would go by the computer to see if BIUmen was online. If he was, I would pop on and say a quick "hello." My quick "hello" often turned into long conversations of typing back and forth. How I loved every minute of talking to him. Elle shared my excitement about our relationship and always wanted to hear all the details whenever I chatted with David. It was fun that she was almost as giddy about it as I was.

I couldn't wait to get home from waitressing. I just wanted to check the computer; maybe David was online. The frequency of our chatting was increasing. Partially, it was due to the greatness of technology because I knew when he was online. I tried to tell myself that I was not being obsessive about it, but part of me thought I was. My excitement would be up or down based upon whether I saw BIUmen online in my "buddy list." I loved talking to him. We had gotten to know each other really well through our messaging over the summer.

Fall classes started, and it was a weekend I had off work, so I went to spend the night at Elle's. We got back from dinner and were hanging out in her dorm room until her roommate wanted to go to bed.

"Let's just go sit in the stairwell. We can stay up and chat there," Elle suggested.

We headed to the stairwell in our pjs. Both of us had so much to fill the other in on about our guys. David and Steve. I knew that

Elle had been in a similar situation with Steve, doing her best to not pursue him and to be a godly woman.

As we chatted about David and me, I shared some of the things he had mentioned in our recent online discussion. He told me how special I was and how much he enjoyed talking to me. She was super excited with me. I knew that this was the man I was going to marry. Finally, he was telling me I was "special."

Ellie was excited with me. "I do have a question for you, Emily."

"Okay, what is it?" I responded.

"Well, when you and David are online, who is the person who usually initiates the conversation? Is it David or you?"

At that moment, my throat was stuck and time stopped. My head knew the answer, but I didn't want to choke it out. The lump in my throat was indisputable. There was no denying the answer. There was an answer. "Well," I stumbled, "Uh... well... umm... well, I guess I usually do."

"Emily, I think you should do something. I know you may not be excited about this, but..." Elle stopped talking for a moment and, in all seriousness, just looked at me.

"But what?"

"Well, I think you should take David off of your Buddy List."

My head screamed, "Ahhhhhhh!!!!!" My thoughts were racing. The words were trying scale my throat, but nothing was coming. "But... but... but, uh..." My thoughts were blank. I had no answer. Even in my defense, I couldn't come up with one. The words in my defense were trying to clear the ledge. They were lodged in my throat, and I couldn't talk. I couldn't even come to my own defense. I had no rebuttal. My mind raced for a reason why I should not take him off my Buddy List, but I came up with no good reason. Nothing.

"Ellie!!!! Ahhhhh!" Sadness came from within me. She was right.

"I know. It seems impossible. But Emily, you need too. *You* are the one who is contacting *him*. He can still IM you when you are on, but it would be good for you *not* to IM him every time you see him on. If he is not on your Buddy List, you won't know when he is on. You won't even be tempted."

She made a very good point. I knew she was right. The weight of the idea sinking in was difficult to bear.

For the first time, really thinking about it, I knew she was totally right. If I really wanted to be honest with myself, each time I messaged him, I was pursuing him! Over the last several months, deep down, I may have known this truth if I had allowed myself the time to dwell on it. I think my mind had been avoiding the revelation. How obvious it seemed! I was pursuing David every time I messaged him first! I had been really good at avoiding the obvious pursuit: not calling, emailing, or writing him. Whenever the whole "Instant Messaging" thing came out, it was so new and different, like it took on a different meaning. "Oh, I'll just message him." I convinced myself that it was like saying "hi," walking past him in the hallway. But it *was* different.

"Ellie. I know you're right. I will take him off," I gravely responded, a hole already seeming to pit itself in my heart.

Several months had passed. David was *off* my buddy list. It was the hardest thing I had ever done! My obsession for the computer faded, which almost lifted a little pressure from my shoulders. I no longer felt I had to constantly walk by and glance at the screen. I no longer had to obsess over when David would show up because I couldn't see him anyway. Now, when I was online, it was simply to do homework. As hard as it was, I knew it was right.

Upon removing him from my buddy list, it took three weeks for me to hear from him. Where we had been talking every two to three days, the time stretched to every couple of weeks. Weeks seemed like an eternity when I had grown so accustomed to our frequent chats. But I knew Elle was right. For some reason, I knew that taking him off my buddy list was a very crucial move.

Elle and I both were both in the same spot of misery. We were doing the right thing in our lives and relationships, but why did it have to be so hard and lonely? Both of us felt deserted. How did we end up being in the same situation with our guys? Like a silent time. When I heard from Elle, I knew she was hurting too as she waited for Steve to call or e-mail. If we only went to the same school. It would be so nice to have a friend like Elle so close. At least, we could experience our loneliness together.

E-mails from David were sporadic at best. I knew he was busy. He was training and was very serious about track. His goal was to go to the Olympics. I didn't want to be a distraction. I was doing good about not messaging him. The only time we messaged was when he messaged me first.

There was something strangely refreshing about him initiating conversation with me. I enjoyed the surprise when I saw "Hello, Emily" pop on my computer screen. As far as e-mails, the only time I emailed him was when he e-mailed me first. It was official. I was 100% letting *him* pursue *me*! Even though it was hard and completely foreign to me, it felt good. It felt good for our contact to happen because *he* initiated it. This behavior was a far cry from what the old me would have done, what the world had taught me for so many years.

Back at my parents' house on those late nights, I still frequently found myself looking up at the stars when I pulled in late. I found my little "tea cup." I reminded the Lord, "Lord, please! Take this cup from me! Not my will, but *Yours* be done! Lord, you know my desires. If David is not my husband, I *give* him to you! I want *your* best for my life! I recommit him and our relationship to you. Take it, Lord!" I lingered, staring up at the dark country sky. No street lights. No buildings. Just darkness, country darkness. Stars and darkness. "Lord, take this cup. I really do trust you with it. I don't want to mess things up. I really am trying to be obedient and patient. Please, help me."

23

MOMENTS ON A CLOUD

Thanksgiving came and went. This Christmas season was filled with more anticipation than normal. Ashley, Kate, Jacob, and I were going on a cruise, just the siblings—for a whole week. Departure and arrival was out of a port in Tampa. We would return on December 23rd, just in time for us to make the drive home to celebrate Christmas.

As we traveled to Florida to catch our cruise ship, the drive through Georgia was exceptionally difficult. The "Peach State." This was where David was from. It was torture to know I was so close to him. I longed to see him.

We arrived at our ship and spent the next week having a blast. Despite our heartfelt nickname for our ship, the "Ghetto Ship," we eventually got over the fact that our ship was not what it we envisioned it to be. Porting in Jamaica, we saw a Disney cruise ship. By comparison, it was a far cry from our beater of a boat. How they continued to book people onto this ship was questionable. We reasoned that we were together and made the best of it.

And so, the adventures began. We enjoyed a dance party that our ship offered, which included a few Canadians we had met. By day, we laid out, swam, and sat in a dingy hot tub on the deck. Porting in Jamaica, Kate cried upon getting her hair braided when the lady charged her three times the amount she originally quoted. It was a unique and memorable trip, but we would not miss our Ghetto Ship. We were determined to try Disney next time.

We were up by 5:30 to place our luggage outside our cabin door and eat breakfast before disembarking the ship by 7:00. The welcomed farewell would at least bring funny stories to share over our family

Christmas festivities with Mom and Dad. Kate had made plans for us to stop in downtown Atlanta to meet some of her friends from college for a late lunch.

Outside of Atlanta, we stopped at a rest stop to change and clean up a little bit. Ashley's plans included taking sibling pictures as a Christmas gift for Mom and Dad. That meant we all actually had to change from our travel clothes and look nice. Thankfully, the rest stop was very clean. I put on my striped sweater, but Ash quickly responded, "Emily, I like the red shirt much better. Wear that for the pictures. It looks a lot better on you."

"I agree, wear the red one. It looks better. It's for Christmas anyways," Kate said.

I pulled the striped sweater back over my head, trying not to mess up my hair that I just finished, all in order to appease my sisters. I thought the striped sweater looked better, but because they were both adamant about the red, I willingly went along with it.

Before leaving the rest stop, I couldn't help but ask the question that had been constantly ringing in my mind, "Ash, do you think it would be okay for me to call David? I mean, we are *so* close to where he lives. Maybe he could come and see us? Do you think that would be me pursuing him? I mean, how often am I in *his* city? I think this may be an exception? What do you think?"

"Yeah, go ahead. I think it would be okay."

That was all I needed. I called David. A young girl answered the phone. I assumed it was his sister. "Is David there?" I asked.

"No, he's not. Can I take a message?"

"No, that's okay. Thanks though," I responded. Hanging up, my face and heart were frowning. I was so bummed. So close and yet he wasn't home. How disappointing.

Almost in tears with disappointment, Ashley could tell I was on the verge of crying. "It's okay. You'll see him again soon, Emily," she said, trying to comfort me. Intertwining her arm in mine, she pulled me close to her as we walked to the car, giving me that big sister, "it's-going-to-be-okay" smile. I appreciated her attempt to ease the pain written across my face. I needed someone who would share in the hope that I still clung to. It had been a year and a half since I had seen him on that last day of our mission trip.

We parked downtown, close to the CNN Center. Because traffic caused us to be late, Kate ran ahead to find her friend. We were going to meet him at the ice skating rink in Centennial Park. Ashley, Jake, and I trailed behind, taking our time absorbing the Christmas decorations of the big city. The smell of fresh pine and evergreens danced in the air as we strolled, noticing the garland wrapping around each lamp post. Wreaths abundantly graced street lamps and signs, decorated with pine cones, lights, and bright red holly berries. Aside from Christmas traffic, the sound of jingling bells rang in the air, and Christmas music softly hummed over an outdoor sound system. It was amazing. Being from a small town, I didn't see grand decorations like this in real life—only in movies. Nothing was small. Everything was big! The wreaths looked as if they could wrap around me. Red bows and life-size candy canes decorated the entrance to the park. There was a slight chill in the air. People were ice skating in the park. The trees and street posts were adorned in lights, and every evergreen tree we had seen was magnificently decorated.

Ashley, Jake, and I stepped up to the outdoor lounge of the ice skating rink. The line to get skates wrapped around the rink's sitting area, and like the crowds for Black Friday shopping, we were packed together waiting for our skates. Kate was nowhere to be found. She must have still been looking for her friend.

Almost jumping at the abrupt tap on my shoulder, I turned to see a man who appeared to work at the rink. "Emily, these skates are for you," he said, handing a pair of ice skates to me and then disappearing before I had a chance to understand what happened. How did he know my name? What was going on? How did he know my skate size? It was too crowded and loud for me to ask Ashley what was going on. I wasn't sure why I didn't have to wait in the long line of people waiting for skates. In a bit of a daze, I put the skates on. My head felt a bit like it was spinning, maybe from all of the people. Mostly, it was from trying to understand what was going on. Jacob motioned for me to go ahead. He and Ashley were getting their skates and would catch up.

My head was still spinning a bit. The metal of my skates clinked on the ice, causing a flicker of snow to spray. I gained my my balance. Happy that ice skating was similar to riding a bike, my body remembered what to do almost immediately. Skating down one side of the rink, I managed to be simply one of the crowd.

As I turned to skate down the far side of the rink, in one glance up, I felt my breath escape me. Suddenly, the crowds of people around me seemed to fade away into a blur. There he was. Across the ice, holding a bouquet of red roses, there David stood. Waiting for me. Smiling.

Goosebumps immediately traveled up and down my arms. Could this be real? Was I dreaming? Was I really seeing David? His smile showed his beautiful, white, perfectly straight teeth. It really was him! It was David! Amazing! I felt like I was just going to float to him on air. Were my feet really touching the ground? Was I floating? Would this be what cloud nine felt like?

I skated to meet David. How did this happen? Was I seeing an illusion? Everything around me went cloudy and silent. All I saw was David. We were in a bubble, just us. As I met him on the ice, he handed me the roses and said, "hello," as his arms wrapped around me. Encompassed in his big embrace, I had forgotten how tall he was. On the ice, we stood, hugging.

God had not forgotten me. He had heard my prayers. He had seen my tears. God created a movie-moment, and now, I only wished I could freeze time. If I could, I believe I would stay in this moment forever. I didn't think anything could be better than the intense satisfaction of finally being in David's arms.

"Hello, Emily," he said with his deep voice, smiling as he looked down at me, handing me the roses.

"Hello." I almost laughed. Shaking my head, I was still in shock.

"Would you like to skate with me?" His charming, southern nod and arm motioned toward the long stretch of ice ahead of us.

"I would love to." Hand-in-hand, we began to skate.

I knew my smile extended across my whole face. I felt like it was glued in position. My face couldn't hide my extreme pleasure. "Please, Lord. Don't let this moment end. Please, Lord."

David looked shockingly handsome. I remembered he was good-looking. I had just forgotten how good-looking. His strong frame carried us while we skated. He took my breath away. He was beautiful. His piercing, baby blue eyes were mesmerizing, causing me to blush each time he looked my way. Short, blonde hair framed his square jawline and made him look more like he had just walked out of a GQ magazine than a guy holding roses for me. Though he wore a lightweight, forest green jacket, his wide shoulders still protruded, showing the indentions of his muscular upper body. He looked amazing. He was tall. I felt so small. I could hardly catch my breath. Was it possible to forget to breathe?

I snapped back into somewhat of a reality when I saw Katie skating toward us. I had forgotten I was with my siblings. Katie was beaming with excitement as she reached us. "So?! Are you surprised?"

Then, the questions quickly rushed through my head! Wow! Yeah! How did this all come about? How was he here? Who worked this out? How did they even meet? "Yeah!" I said. "How did this all happen? How did David know we were going to be here?"

"Well," Katie said, "We have been messaging, and I mentioned we were going to be coming through Atlanta today, and we just worked it out for him to meet up with us." Katie was grinning from ear to ear. You could tell she was very proud of her accomplishment of surprising her big sis. For real, this was the greatest surprise I had ever experienced in my life! I owed her my happiness. I had already been silently thanking the Lord. He had heard my cries for so long. It came natural to internally scream my excitement to Him.

"Wow," I commented. "Yes! This is definitely a big surprise!"

Ashley and Jake skated up to us. Introductions were made with David to Ashley and Jake. The look on Ashley's face showed immediate approval. She was already convinced of what I had repeated countless times: this was the man I was going to marry. Even just his presence brought a sort of peace. He seemed so together and confident. He was such a gentleman and was so polite. He was unlike anyone we had really ever met or known. A combination of his walk with the Lord, his southern way of being a gentleman, and his confidence made him uniquely stand apart.

After introductions, Katie proceeded to give us the "instructions" in the way only Katie could do. She was the "take-charge-of-the-situation" kind of sister. Growing up, she was always telling us what to do, telling Dad he was going to play football or catch with her. She was a definite choleric. She talked fast, relaying the series of events. "Okay, we're going to go ahead and meet my friend, have lunch, and do some things. We'll just plan on meeting you guys back here at 7:00 for dinner. Sound good?"

David said, "Sounds great!"

What? Another boost of surprise surged through me! I had barely grasped that I was actually with David, let alone that I was going to be spending the next six to seven hours with him. I had to breathe. I felt like I just needed to catch my breath. All of these surprises were overwhelming.

"Alright then," Katie said. "You kids have a good time. We'll see you at seven." She smiled and gave me hug. Her discreet but tight squeeze told me she was excited for me, and she knew how excited I was. I loved my little sister! What a gift that couldn't carry a price tag. I was indescribably excited.

Ashley, Kate, and Jacob skated off, leaving David and me. Alone. Skating across the ice. The other kids and families, couples that skated around us, were invisible to me. All I saw was David. Wow. Just David and I, hand-in-hand. We skated for a while longer. I just soaked in the time, the closeness, being with David. I had waited for this day for so long. I never could have imagined it would be this magical.

"Well," David said, "I thought we would go have lunch at one of my favorite restaurants. It's only a few blocks from here. It's called Mary Mac's and has wonderful, southern home-cookin'. How's that sound to you?"

"That sounds great!" I said.

After returning our skates, we headed to the parking garage to where David had parked. He opened my door to the navy Tahoe. First of all, I definitely liked his ride and that he opened my door. It seemed that chivalry unfortunately was in decline with guys in our generation. I was very impressed. The inside of the Tahoe was extremely nice and clean. The luxurious smell of the leather seats caught my attention. I could hardly believe that I was in a vehicle with David! Wow! Inside, I was screaming, "Ahhhhh! Thank You, Lord!"

He returned to his side and got in. Before starting the vehicle, he reached around to the back to grab something. He pulled out a beautifully wrapped box. "I just wanted to get you a little something for Christmas. I hope you like it. Go ahead, open it," he said as he handed me the package.

Like a school girl, I was so excited! I *love* getting gifts, but this gift was even more special because it was from David! What in the world could it be? As I tore into the paper, the plain white box gave me no indication of what he had gotten me. I opened up the box. As I pulled back the tissue paper, it left me speechless.

"Wow," I finally said. "It's beautiful. Thank you." I was in awe. I was impressed that David could do something that was so sentimental. It was a glass picture frame with two ceramic red roses on the frame, a perfect frame for a picture of us together. Wow. I really was speechless. It was so perfect. My mind raced back to smelling the roses with him in the park in Ashford, England; then, in London; and now, here I am, finally with him again and holding a bouquet of roses.

"It's my pleasure. I thought it was perfect when I saw it. I'm glad you like it."

I was still speechless. "Wow, David. This really is perfect. I really like it!"

"Well, good. You are worth it!"

When he turned the key, I was shocked again! With heavy bass, the speakers blared, "Come on ride that train, ride it!" I laughed. "I didn't know you listened to dance music!" That was the last thing I expected. I figured it would be some Christian CD or radio station, but it was some pure booty music! What a shocker! I laughed out loud.

"Well, I listen to Christian music a lot, but I like dance music, too. I like lots of types of music," he said as he hip-hopped along with the song, singing and dancing.

How funny. I, of course, knew all the words from clubs and cheerleading. What a day full of surprises of all kinds! Not only was he an awesome Christian and good-looking, but fun, too!? What a combination. I was pleasantly impressed.

He turned the music down a little so we could talk. We drove a few blocks while David told me about a dating fast he was doing. I was impressed. Wow. A dating fast. I had never heard of that before. I guess this "day out" was a bit of an exception to the dating fast.

We pulled up to Mary Mac's and headed inside. They got us a table right as we got there. David ordered sweet tea. Sweet tea. I remembered I was totally in the South! We didn't have "sweet tea" up North! It was just one more thing that I thought was cute about him.

"Anything you get on this menu will be good. They have great collard greens, turnip greens, black-eyed peas, fried okra, buttered beans. Everything here is good."

I had never heard of or eaten *any* of the vegetables he was talking about. "So, I guess all those are 'Southern' foods? We don't eat any of those up North. Fried okra? Sounds interesting."

David laughed and proceeded to tell me how amazing it was! "This is *real* cookin'," he let me know.

We sat through lunch and talked about everything. He told me all about his vision of opening his own business, "The Rock," a gym that would encompass helping the body, mind, and spirit. It would be a gym that would not just focus on physical fitness but would focus on helping the whole person. He knew that he eventually would want to own his own business and not work for someone else. He grew up in a family of entrepreneurs. His parents, aunts, and uncles... everyone owned their own business. Everything he said fascinated me. He seemed so sure of everything. He seemed so planned. His ideas were thought out and new.

"I was thinking, from here, we would go to Stone Mountain. It's a pretty neat place. I think you would really like it," he said as he paid the waitress.

"Sounds good to me. Thank you for lunch. It was really good."

"My pleasure."

Another one! He did it again. Who says, "My pleasure," anyway? That was such a pleasant but unusual thing to hear. I liked it. The whole "southern gentleman" thing accompanied David well. I liked his southern ways. Quite a difference from the people up north.

We parked at Stone Mountain. It was lit up with Christmas lights, and Christmas music played in the background. We walked down the street with the Stone Mountain shops. It was all so festively decorated. The cold air smelled of smoke from the outdoor fire pits. The shops mostly looked like souvenir shops. I wasn't the least bit interested in the shops. I was content strolling by. I was with David Carter! I just wanted to maximize spending time with him.

We took the sky-ride to the top of Stone Mountain and walked around more. From the summit, we were able to see miles and miles of Georgia's countryside, all the way to the high rises of downtown Atlanta. It was quite extraordinary.

We walked back through the shops and headed to the Tahoe. We saw an empty white horse and carriage waiting at the curb. The driver beckoned us over to be the next couple to warm the seats. "After you," David said, motioning with a smile and discreetly handing the driver several folded bills. During the next 30 minutes, the carriage driver told us of the history and landmarks we passed. The warmth of the white fur blanket embraced our laps, and David's fingers intertwined between mine. Most of the driver's history lesson was tuned out by the loudness of my heart beating.

When the ride was over, the driver dropped us off at David's vehicle. "I have one more place I'd like to take you. I think you will really like it."

"Great! I'm excited to see it," I said.

The short drive around a few curves took us to Grist Mill. Picturesque and beautiful. The century-old mill was lit up with garland and lights. Soft Christmas music played all around. The old, wood mill had a walkway that extended across water and overlooked the beautiful lake surrounded by trees. It was such a peaceful place.

Alone. We were at Grist Mill. No one else was around but the soft Christmas music filling the air with romance. Alone on the wooden bridge, David wrapped his arms around me and began to dance with me. A slow, close, soft dance. It felt so good to be close to David. Warm. Could I ever come down from this cloud I felt like I was on? Could this day last forever?

David leaned in to kiss me. I turned my head and said softly, "I don't want to cause you to violate your dating fast."

We continued to dance and dance. So much of me wanted that kiss, but it didn't feel right. I wanted this day to leave on a perfect note. I wanted to have kisses from him for a lifetime. One missed kiss on today would be okay. I would make him bring me back one day and take him up on this kiss.

Our time was up. We were on our way to meet back with my sisters and brother to have dinner. Then, we would be on our way back to Pennsylvania. It was such a wonderful day. I could hardly keep from smiling. Just sitting in the Tahoe, riding back to the CNN Center, I was happy. What an amazing day. December 23rd. What a wonderful day. Praise God!

Dinner was fun. David had an opportunity to get to know Ashley, Kate, and Jacob. We laughed a lot and had a good time. I could tell that Ashley and Kate especially liked him. They were cutting up a lot with David. Jacob, well, he was a boy. He was a jokester as usual, doing some of his dorky Jeff Foxworthy impersonations, repeating lines and stories verbatim. Though Jacob didn't show dramatic signs of approval, I could tell he liked David. He was just Jacob. Guys didn't give off the same vibe that girls did. I couldn't help but think of what an awesome mentor David would make for my little brother!

Back at the car, we hugged goodbye. I sat in the back seat as we pulled away, turning to wave one last time while David stood at the entrance of Centennial Park. Over the next several hours the image of seeing

David Carter standing there replayed in my mind over and over. Drifting off to sleep, I couldn't help but smile.

Part 4

The Pursued

24

AGAINST THE GRAIN

ack home, my feet had yet to reach the ground. The cloud I
was on was a comfortable change from the months of
longing. To simply reside there would have been euphoric.

Adding to this blissful state, it even appeared that David was
now officially pursuing me. David finally began to call me. Not only
that, I could tell that he liked me. On the day after Christmas, we
talked for two hours. He was driving from visiting a friend in South
Georgia—a girl, actually. She was a girl he had been pursuing to get
to know better. Though they had not been dating exclusively, after
seeing me, he decided to break it to her that their relationship would
have to end. My heart was beaming on the inside. As I laid on my
bed, I was happy he couldn't see my elated smile.

"Finally, God. Finally." I prayed, "Maybe he is getting closer to
knowing I will be his wife one day?"

David said, "Well, there were two things that I felt like the Lord
impressed on my heart when I saw you skating across the ice.
Number one: Wow! I had forgotten how beautiful you are. Number
two: Lord, don't let me screw this up this time!"

David's heart had engaged. He didn't know the extent of it, but
my heart had been fully engaged for the last 18 months of waiting
for him. I knew every day that I wanted to marry him. I pleaded with
the Lord daily to reveal to him that I would be his wife. My starry
friend, the little tea cup, heard my pleas often.

I was willing to give David up, but with all of my being, I felt
that he was made for me. He was my other half. He was my soul
mate. He was my completer. He brought out the best in me. Just
talking to him, I wanted to deepen my walk with the Lord. I wanted
to set goals. I wanted to grow and improve. Just talking to him
sparked the desire inside to me to want to do really *great* things for
the Kingdom of God. He sparked inside me a desire to make a

difference in the world, not just to go through life with a "nine to five" job, cut grass on weekends, have kids, and live a "hum-drum" life. Just hearing his voice, his passion, and his sense of direction made me want to be more. And... I really liked that feeling.

Into January, a surprise e-mail came from Mr. Briscoe, David's mentor. Mr. Briscoe and David met bi-weekly, assessing David's progress toward his goals, discussing life issues, and discussing job or business ideas. He had helped David establish his life values and goals, something he called a "Pro-Vision," and David even had business cards made up with his vision statement on the back. All I had heard with regard to Mr. Briscoe made me view him as someone who could almost walk on water. When I received a personal e-mail introducing himself, I was beyond shocked. I was speechless. He simply wanted to open the invitation for me to e-mail him at any time, and he was excited to get to know someone that was a friend of David's.

Over the next several weeks, we began the process of getting to know each other. As his mentor, he knew David's goals and knew David in a way most people did not, so I found it extremely interesting to gain another perspective into David's life. I also appreciated the sounding board he became as I most definitely did not want to be a negative distraction.

Indoor track season was in full-swing. I was running well, but I needed to continue to improve in order to hit my goal of qualifying for indoor nationals. David and I were communicating on a regular basis. To intensify my preseason workouts, he even put me on a brutal weightlifting program. His Division-One training was much more specific and vigorous than the general preseason training recommendations I received from Bordeaux's coaching staff. Snatching the weight bar from the ground to my chest, "cleans," was only one example of an exercise that my coaches never asked me to do. I wasn't sure if it was the awkwardness of the motion I didn't like or if I simply babied my knee from my ACL knee surgery early in high school. As any good protégée would do, I did them anyway.

Indoor nationals were scheduled over my spring break at the end of February. During my last few upcoming meets, I had to run a qualifying time. My best chance was to qualify in the 1500. A 4:49 was my goal time to qualify, which meant I'd have to trim four seconds off my current indoor time of 4:53. It would be a stretch, but I felt optimistic. The 800 indoor qualifying time of 2:15 would be a long shot to achieve as my best time had been a 2:22. I would have to shave off seven seconds! That was a lot to shave off an 800 time, so the 1500 was my true focus.

As David and I talked on the phone, he was very encouraging about me qualifying. I was excited about making my best attempt. In the back of my head, if I didn't qualify, I had also considered flying down to Bayside Island to surprise him. At this point, it was just a thought and a far-fetched idea at that. I was still unsure about it. I didn't want to be a distraction to David, and so many factors would have to work out. At this point, my top goal was to qualify for indoor nationals. Doing so would eliminate the possibility of going to Bayside Island over spring break. I only had two meets left to run a qualifying time.

Thoughts continued to turn over in my mind about my progressing relationship with David. Though we were not officially "boyfriend and girlfriend," I assumed that, if we lived in the same place, we would be an "official" couple. Even the thought of going to Bayside Island made me nervous. I knew it would be pressing the envelope, going against letting him stay in complete control, me submissively following. If circumstances led to the opportunity, I knew I would have to be 100% led and directed by the Holy Spirit. I was finally walking on thicker ice and didn't want to jeopardize my newfound relationship.

Valentine's Day had come. I decided to send David and Mr. Briscoe a care package. I enjoyed baking and thought chocolate chip cookies would be a nice treat. It was also Mr. Briscoe's birthday, so it provided an extra reason to send something special. Around the same time, my mom excitedly shared an e-mail she had received from

David. She bubbled at the fact I finally had this godly man in my life, pursuing me.

From: BIUmen@gmail.com
Sent: Sunday, February 13, 2000 9:23 PM
To: jeancook
Subject: Re: Thanks!

Ms. Cook,

WOW! You daughter can cook really good cookies! I was really impressed. I was shocked to receive the package. But I am not complaining at all.

Thank you for telling me how I can pray for you and Mr. Cook. It gives me the opportunity to lift you and him up and do really the only thing I can do, and that is pray.

I will share this with you… the more and more that I speak with Emily, the more I am drawn to her. Each time we get off the phone, it always seems like we have taken a step and the relationship has grown deeper.

Well, have a great day and week!

David

I completed my second meet and did not hit the qualifying time to go to indoor nationals. I was now at the point of decision. I decided my litmus test would be to *mention* the idea to Mr. Briscoe. His response would weigh heavily on my decision. He knew David almost better than anybody, especially from a coaching and focus perspective. Dropping the idea wouldn't hurt, I reasoned.

From: coachbriscoe

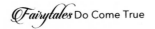

Date: Mon, 14 Feb 2000 12:02:31 -0400
Subject: A Joyous Valentine's Day!

Emily - WOW! What a FANtastic care package you sent me. It was a complete surprise! The cookies are ALL whole! Not a one of them broke. That must be a special batch - from the Lord. What about the Tupperware container?

You certainly made a new fan in Josh, our 12-year-old. He loves your cookies. We all like them, but Joshua is especially fond of them. You added to my already special Valentine's Day Birthday. The birthday card was outstanding. How long did it take you to find it? Thank you, Emily. You are a very thoughtful person.

Saturday, I went up to see Dad in Kempton, about 150 miles inland. As I shared with you before, today is his birthday, too. I took him out to lunch. He said he quit celebrating his birthday last year at 80! But I got the nicest card from him. It was good to spend time with him. Josh has a basketball game tonight, and I help coach the team, so it would have been tough to see Dad on his birthday, celebrate mine, and coach.

Five years ago, I started writing myself a letter on Valentine's Day to review the past year and put in prayer items I was concerned or interested in for the next year. It's really amazing to see God at work. I would recommend the practice to everyone. Now, on Valentine's Day, I always open that next letter. Later this afternoon, I'll write one for this year.

You asked me last week about the FCA at Joshua's middle school... I keep forgetting to respond. Forgive me. It was wonderful. 20 young people came from the 6th, 7th, and 8th grades. This week, we are going to elect officers. Thank you for your continued prayers on this.

Now, on to you... How was the meet? How are your knees holding up, especially during workouts? Yes, I will be in special prayer for you about your non-trip! I hope you understand. I believe it would be a blessing to David, but I won't mention it or get in the way. Oh, if you need a place to stay - let us know. We have loads of room with our two oldest daughters gone - seriously. Just a thought. Our number at the house is (892) 837-5732. Our place is about 6 miles or so from David's. I know you are a big girl now, but it might be better to stay with a family rather than at a hotel or at David's - another thought.

Isn't that something about him sending you my other book. Let me know what you think. I hope you will find it helpful as you are not only searching God's will for your career and life, but a mate as well.

Have a Special Valentine's Day - you certainly added to the enjoyment of my day.

The Best - Coach B - Pro 14:22

Shocked! Wow! Did I just read what I think I read?! Mr. Briscoe said, "If you need a place to stay - let us know!" If he is offering for me to *stay* with him and MaryAnn, then he must not be against the idea of me coming.

The green light from Mr. Briscoe for the first time brought this far-fetched idea into a place of actual consideration. In a million years, I did not anticipate Mr. Briscoe being so open to the thought of my visiting. Fleeting questions of where I would stay had occurred to me, but with indoor nationals, I had not spent any focused effort on planning a solution. I only knew I wouldn't stay at David's apartment. I assumed I would stay at a hotel nearby, thinking that would be my only option. I was so thankful that Mr. Briscoe was on board with the possibility, and I knew that my parents would be much more comfortable knowing I would be staying with a nice Christian family. I still needed to commit the idea to prayer. I didn't want to jump into something if God was not directing it.

The potential of seeing David again so soon caused my mind to race. Wow! How exciting! Mr. Briscoe had just added a whole new sense of optimism about this trip. Maybe with his support, I would actually go.

From: coachbriscoe
Date: Tue, 15 Feb 2000 20:49:50 -0400
Subject: Sunny SC

Emily - Yes, I can understand about different cultures and ages. Just continue to mentor and work with McKenzie and see how the Lord blesses.

I can't promise you exactly how David will feel - I don't want to blow the surprise if the Lord does lead you to come on down. I get the impression David thinks you are a special young lady - even though he's NOT dating! MaryAnn and I would be delighted to have you come next week. Sunday or even later is fine to let us know. I know plans change. That's a mighty early spring break, isn't it? Tell your mom we'll take good care of you while you are here. We understand the concerns of a parent quite well. Keep praying and see what your heart and the Lord and your parents say. Whatever answer comes back is the right one.

Hang in there with your workouts. Certainly, they are no fun, but the discipline is wonderful. Especially in the fast, have-it-all-now society we live in. This discipline will pay big dividends later in your life - trust me. Sometimes being a Christian doesn't appear to be fun, either, but if you will be faithful to the Lord, He will honor your faithfulness.

Thank you for the words of Solomon from 1st Kings. We would be wise to learn from him.

Have a super day tomorrow.

The Best - Coach B Ps 75:2

"Wow." Moments passed as I sat, thinking about what this meant. I had a peace about going. I felt God had been opening doors, not closing them. The people in my life whose spiritual advice I valued—Mom, Dad, and Mr. Briscoe—were all for it.

Overwhelmed at the shock, I realized the decision was made. I would be flying to Bayside Island. I would arrive Wednesday, February 22nd, and I would fly out on my birthday, Monday, February 28th.

I was going against the grain. Nervous excitement permeated my being. I was going to surprise David.

25

IS PURITY POSSIBLE?

My flight arrived in Bayside Island where Mr. Briscoe would pick me up. The weather was refreshingly different from Pennsylvania this time of year. A warm 70 degrees was a welcome contrast to the dirty, melting snow we were experiencing. The aroma that greeted me when I got off the airplane was even fragrant, like tropical flowers in bloom. Palm trees in the distance added to my excitement of this mini-vacation. I couldn't imagine going to school here. It would be like a long spring break! With the beach and palm trees, it might be difficult to fit in classes.

I spotted Mr. Briscoe immediately. Though I had never met him in person, I recognized him from the picture on the back of his book. He greeted me with a smile and a hug.

"Emily, so glad to have you here. Did you have a good flight?"

"Yes, it was great. Thank you so much for picking me up. I'm so excited to be here."

The luggage carousel quickly spit out my luggage, Mr. Briscoe retrieved it, and we made our way to his truck. Outside the front entrance of the airport, more palm trees and flowers adorned the sidewalks, driveway, and sign that read, "Bayside Island Airport." It was all so pretty. Before long, I would finally be able to see and surprise David. He still didn't know anything about my trip, so it would be fun to figure out how we were going to surprise him with my arrival.

As Mr. Briscoe and I left the airport, he informed me of the tentative schedule. "Well, this is what I was thinking. David has classes this afternoon. Then, he will be at track practice. Todd and David come over to our place every Wednesday night for dinner, so they are scheduled to come over tonight. If we surprise him at dinner, that would give you time to get settled in and rest. Then, we can have you come out sometime after they arrive. How does that sound?"

I tried to cover up my disappointment and mustered, "That sounds great!" My true feelings and heart slumped as I thought, "You mean I have to wait for almost five hours until I even get to see David? What wasted time. I just wanted to see him now!" I would deal with it, and it would be fine. I'm sure I could find something to do at Mr. Briscoe's and MaryAnn's. Maybe I would go for a run, sleep, or anything to pass the time that would surely drag on.

After hours, minutes, and seconds of looking at my watch, 7:00 had arrived at last. Todd and David would be there any minute! I sat nervously in the back bedroom where I was staying. I had already primped and primped, and there was no more primping to do, so I sat, fidgeting and awaiting the sign. The plan was that, once David and Todd showed up, they would proceed like normal, get their food, pray, and begin to eat. Then, Kerrie, Mr. Briscoe's daughter, would come and get me from the back bedroom. In the meantime, I just sat there, anxiously waiting.

"Ding-Dong."

My heart leapt. They had arrived! I quickly got up to press my ear against the door. I didn't want to miss anything.

I heard the door open, and MaryAnn's cheerful voice welcomed the boys in.

"MaryAnn!" I heard David say, "It's so good to see you! Hey, Mr. Briscoe... Kerrie... Joshua!"

Just hearing his voice made me nervous. My heart was beating so fast. I actually would be going out there soon. Oh my goodness. I still did not fully know what I was going to say or do. I just hoped words would come out. I guess I would wing it.

Muffled conversations of everyone chatting and getting their food made it seem like I was waiting for an eternity. When would Kerrie come and get me? When would I finally get to come out? I knew it would be soon. I could tell they were finally sitting down at the table.

The door cracked open, and Kerrie whispered, "Come on; it's time."

My heart fluttered, and my smile extended across my whole face. Finally, I would get to see David. Kerrie and I peeked through the hallway door, waiting for the official sign from Mr. Briscoe. I could see him. I could see David. His back was to me. Ahhhhhh! There he was! I was so excited!

I noticed Mr. Briscoe with the video camera, and he was standing on a chair near the far door. "Okay, David. I have a surprise for you, and I want to have it on video."

"Oh? Okay. This aught to be fun! It's not even my birthday!" David said and laughed.

"Okay, David, I will need you to close your eyes before we bring out the surprise." David sat at the dinner table, evidently now with his eyes closed, and Mr. Briscoe waved me out.

I quietly walked up and stood behind David, gently putting my hands over his eyes.

Mr. Briscoe began, "David, who do you think it is?"

"Uh... I don't know. Is it Penny? Is your daughter home from school? I have no idea."

"No, it's not Penny," Mr. Briscoe said.

"Guess who?" I said with a quiet giggle.

With my hands still over David's eyes, his head was facing down at the table. For several seconds, he just waited. He said nothing. He silently shook his head. Under his breath, I heard him say, "No way... There is no way..."

I giggled again. I could tell he now knew who was behind him. "Is it Emily?"

I took my hands off his eyes. Without moving, he just stared down at his plate, shaking his head, still obviously in shock. Several seconds passed until he finally turned to look at me. Still shaking his head, he said, "No way... No way!"

I took a few steps back, and David stood up. David looked at me in unbelief as if he were looking right through me, like he was seeing a ghost. The glazed look in his eyes penetrated me as he stood motionless. It seemed as though I was a figment of his imagination as if he could reach out his arm, and it would pass right through me. After what seemed like forever of David standing in shock, staring at me, he finally reached out and hugged me.

"Surprise!" I said, looking up at him, "I'm here!"

He stood back again, shaking his head in complete awe. "Oh my goodness!"

After we hugged for another moment, MaryAnn pulled up a chair for me to sit beside David. I got a plate of food and returned to the table where David just sat there, not eating, just sitting there. He looked up and said, "I can't believe you're here! Wow! And Mr. Briscoe was involved! I would have never guessed that!"

I laughed. "I knew Mr. Briscoe's involvement would be something you never have expected."

"Wow! I just can't believe you are here!"

The evening was filled with laughter and fun. David was merely poking at his food, leaving a plate full by the end of dinner. It was fun to surprise him. The victory of completely taking David off guard left me gleeful.

The next few days were filled with fun! David typically picked me up at Mr. Briscoe's before he went to his classes. I went to track practice with him so I could continue to train, running intervals while he spent time throwing the hammer. We typically wrapped up our workouts with 45-60 minutes in the weight room.

Our evening plans were taking us to a social event put on by one of the sororities on campus. How I could pack a whole suitcase of clothes and nothing long sleeved; I didn't know.

"Why don't I just take you to the mall. I know there is a Gap there. I can just buy you a few shirts. I don't want you to be cold."

Gifts had a way of making me feel special. Maybe it was because I rarely spent money on myself. Little did David know, what may have seemed like a small act to him went a long way with me.

"Pick out whatever you want. You probably need to get a couple of shirts or sweaters in case it's cold on another night," he said, motioning throughout the store like spending money on me was not a big deal. On the inside, the giddy girl in me wanted to squeal with excitement. *David Carter*, the man I was going to marry one day, was taking care of me! I could have bought my own shirts, but he insisted.

I chose a long-sleeved baby blue shirt and a long-sleeved red shirt, shirts I would cherish forever.

The outdoor, Sorority Social had booths, games, dancing, fundraiser pie throws, and even a dunk tank with a beautiful bikini-laden sorority girl behind the plexiglass. I had a chance to meet a myriad of David's friends and acquaintances, some of them partaking in the fullness of the festivities, including the free punch! Though David had never drank alcohol, he appeared to be a nonjudgmental friend, cutting up with people as he introduced me. When we finally had enough socializing, we headed back to his apartment.

We were going to hang out a little bit longer before he took me back to Mr. Briscoe's house. The conversation on our drive was filled with an interesting topic. I was both interested and nervous to know what David would think about it.

"So, I wanted to get your opinion on my summer."

"Okay. What do you have planned. I'd be happy to give you my thoughts," he he said and smiled.

"Well, because I'm graduating in May, I'm considering going on a mission trip for the summer before beginning life in the working world. I know that, once I start a real job, it would most likely be challenging to take several months off to go on a mission trip. I was looking at two options.

"Option number one is with Teen Outreach Ministries. Parts of it really seem to fit well with me. I would be responsible for leading a group of young people on a trip in Mexico. I would be in a leadership position and would be able to work on and develop my Spanish skills further.

"Option number two is with World Evangelism Ministries, WEM. The program is called LT, Leadership Training. My cousin has been a part of the program for about three years, and one of my best friends from high school has also done a mission trip with them. I like the fact that it would be leadership training. All the drama at Bordeaux has got me spiritually drained," I said and sighed.

"Okay, what else?" David nodded for me to continue.

"If I go with Teen Outreach Ministries, because of the timing of the trip, I would have to miss my college graduation, which is obviously not appealing. The kicker? LT will be here in Bayside Island. It would start at the end of May," I explained.

"Wow. Bayside Island," his voice sounded surprised. I couldn't read whether it was just surprised or if his tone indicated any excitement. "Well, I know that you will make the right decision. God will direct you to what you need to do, and whatever you choose, I'm sure will be right. That's exciting, Emily! What an exciting summer and trip, whichever one you choose."

I was really wanting him to tell me which trip he thought I should go on, but he didn't. He remained neutral. Though, I did not want my choice to be swayed to go to Bayside Island solely because David was there. I obviously wanted to be around him because I fully believed I was going to marry him. I would just remain very prayerful about the decision. I wanted to choose the direction God wanted for me, not simply where my heart longed to be.

Everything about LT seemed to line up with what I wanted for the summer.

We arrived back at the apartment, and when we walked in, we noticed that Todd was not there. David sat on the arm of the couch and embraced me. Typically, I was not taller than he, but with him sitting on the couch arm, we were of equal height. The warmth of his arms pulled me tight into his chest, and he kissed me with passion.

In the excitement, mixed emotions flooded my thoughts: nervousness but an overwhelming euphoric sense of joy at the same time. Questions raced in my mind. What was right from a Christian perspective? I knew the situation could escalate quickly to us moving to the couch, laying down and allowing our lusts and desires to continue. I didn't want our relationship to fit into the same category as relationships from my past. I wanted our relationship to be different, to be pure and right, pleasing in the eyes of the Lord. I wanted to keep David in the bubble I held him in, respectable and godly. I wanted to believe that there was at least one guy left on the planet that held purity in a high regard—over self.

We stopped kissing, and David just held me. I longed to stay in his embrace and to be safe in his arms, but I knew the desires that filled the air in this moment also laid out a dangerous path. As he held me, I knew we had two paths before us. We could either go down the road of promiscuity, or we could go down the road of purity. We stood there, embracing. The warm feelings in my body were still strong. My body wanted David, but in my mind and spirit, I wanted what was right: purity.

At that moment, I felt as if the Holy Spirit said to me, "Sing."

Surely, the Holy Spirit didn't just tell me to sing. I reasoned back, "Sing?! But I don't sing in front of people. I love to sing, but Lord, that would be embarrassing. Sing in front of David? Right now? It would be just me. I would be a cappella."

But then I heard it again, "Sing."

I continued to reason back, "Are you sure? Sing now?"

"Yes. Sing now."

The song that was in my mind was "Sanctuary." There, in the silence of David's apartment—in the comfort of his embrace, in the midst of two paths, two options—reluctantly, I began to sing.

> Lord prepare me, to be a sanctuary,
> Pure and holy, tried and true,
> With thanksgiving, I'll be a living
> Sanctuary, for you.
> Lord prepare me.
> For I have found greater strength,
> Than man has ever known,
> And I know you will come again,
> And take your people home,
> And I want others to see,
> The presence of your love in me.
> Sanctuary for you.
> Oh, Lord prepare me, to be a sanctuary,
> Pure and holy, tried and true,
> With thanksgiving, I'll be a living,
> Sanctuary for you.

As I finished singing, the feelings of passion subsided. Lust no longer filled the room, but the presence of the Holy Spirit captivated the moment, a welcomed presence that was refreshing.

"Wow…" David said. A long pause stilled the room as if frozen in time. Words were on David's tongue, just not coming out. "Wow. I hardly know what to say." He paused again. "That was amazing, Emily. I never knew you had such an incredible voice." He held me close.

"Thank you," I whispered, my head still tucked on his shoulder.

We still stood there for a moment longer, and then David stood up. "Okay, let me take you back to Mr. Briscoe's. It's getting late."

We left. A good ending to what could have been a spiritual downfall of a night. He took me back, and that was it. It felt good that we were good. It felt good that we did not give in to what our bodies may have wanted. The intensity of physical desire in those moments before I started singing was powerful and luring, filled with memories of feelings I should never have known. I was thankful that the Holy Spirit was present and changed the mood completely. It felt so much better to call it an evening without being accompanied with the guilt of things we should not have done.

The rest of the trip went well. We celebrated my birthday on the day I flew out, and I was surprised with a FedEx package that arrived for me at David's apartment. It was from his mom, Gloria. She sent a birthday present to me! In her note, she wrote about how excited she was that I "defied" David by coming "without his permission." She also included a stuffed duck and a CD by Barbara Streisand. It was so funny and seemed like two very random items. I laughed. I looked forward to meeting this woman who I already liked.

The trip to Bayside Island definitely brought David and I closer together. It was the first time we had ever really spent an extended amount of time together without a mandated focus. I was also thankful that I had come "without his permission."

26

MEETING THE COOKS

Back home from Bayside Island, the correspondence began. My relationship with David felt deeper than ever, and for some reason, he felt very comfortable sharing information with my mom. I was okay with that because she always cheerfully let me read what he had written to her, not to mention that my mom loved being in the know about everything. What he shared with her gave me more insight into the thoughts he was not sharing with me.

"Hi, Emilyyyyy," my mom said, playfully drawing out my name when I answered the phone. "Guess who *I* got an e-mail from today"

Without even a *hello*, I responded, "David?! Did David e-mail you again?"

"He sure did," she taunted. "It was a very nice e-mail."

"Wellll, do you mind sharing what it said? What did he say, Mom? What did he say?"

She knew I was bouncing with anticipation. She seemed to like him almost as much as I did. She sensed the growing communication between us could lead to the strong potential of him becoming her future son-in-law.

"Well, I don't actually have time to read it now. I'm stepping into a meeting. I just wanted to let you know I already e-mailed it to you. I knew you would want to read it."

"Awwww! Thanks, Mom! You're the best!"

"I love you, Emily. I'm excited for you," she said. I could hear her smile on the other side of the receiver. "I'll talk to you later. Have a great day, sweetie."

"Thanks, Mom! You, too!"

Rushing to the computer, I signed in quickly to my e-mail and opened the forwarded message.

From: BIUmen@gmail.com

Sent: Tuesday, February 29, 2000 8:50 AM
To: jeancook
Subject: Re: SURPRISE!

Mrs. Cook,

How are you doing? Well, the past five days have been wonderful! It was the first and best surprise that I have ever received. I was speechless, as you could see in the video. Plus, after the surprise, I could not eat my dinner. So, yes, it was a wonderful surprise. I am so glad that the Lord woke you and me up to start praying for Emily during the night. God is so good!

Mrs. Cook, I really do not know how to describe what I feel about Emily. I am not sure where God is going to lead her and me in the future. Please, pray that she comes here this summer. I want her to come here this summer so badly!

She told me that you almost started crying while you watched the video. Why? Just wondering. Well, thank you for bringing Emily into the world, so that I could have the opportunity to meet her and share some of her heart with me.

Have a great day!
David

I sat there, re-reading the e-mail again. He wants me to come to Bayside Island. My lips curled in happiness; my heart beat with love. He talked about our future. My continual silent prayer to God rang in my ears: "Thank you, God. Please let him know that I am the woman who is going to marry him. Let him know that I am the one."

The deadlines approached for the summer mission trips. I had to decide and send in my application. I had waited until the last minute, prayerfully seeking God about where I should go. The decision made me nervous, but with the stamped envelope in hand, I walked it out to the mailbox to finally send it off. Tucking it securely into the black box, the red ink I had used stood out, reading, "World Evangelism Ministries."

I closed the box and walked back in the house to e-mail David with the news.

My mom informed me that she had received another email from David. Having finally made my choice to spend my summer in his city, I was excited to hear his thoughts.

From: BIUmen@gmail.com
Sent: Friday, March 03, 2000 11:11 PM
To: jeancook
Subject: Re: Looking forward to the summer

Mrs. Cook,

I am going to try and answer your question as best as possible. Please feel free to clarify anything that does not make sense.

1. What are my intentions?

I will say that this is an excellent question. I cannot place my finger on exactly what my intentions are because I am looking to the Lord for guidance in this really. On an earthly level… I would love to pursue Emily. I am unsure when (God's timing), but I would like to ask Emily if she would like for her and me to become an item. I hope that this gives you an idea of my intentions. I am trying my best to stay God centered.

2. What attracts me to Emily?

Another good one, I will begin by saying that, before this past Christmas, I really was not attracted to Emily. I had not seen her for about a year and half, and I really did not think that there was any way that she and I would be able work things out. My rational thinking at work. Well, when I saw her skating across the ice rink… something changed inside me… it had to be a God thing… because I really cannot explain it. My whole attitude just changed toward her. I am not sure how to put it into words what attracts me to Emily. It could be her zeal for the Lord, and that is one thing… it could be how she and I are so much alike… it could be how beautiful she is… but deep down in my heart, there is something… I do not know what it is, but there is something. Does that make sense?

3. Meeting the whole Cook family?

Well, I am unsure about this… I am praying about coming up there for about three days. March 11-13. But I am unsure? You will meet me though. I promise. Lord willing.

I hope that I answered your questions and that they made sense. My interest in Emily is growing. I really do want to be with her and spend time with her. I really feel robbed of the time that I am not spending with her. I really do not like it. I am so thankful that God answered my prayers about her coming to Bayside Island for the summer. Praise Him!

Well, Have a great day!
David

After some more discussion, it was official. David decided to come visit for a weekend. *Elated* hardly described how I felt. Though the trip would be short, it would be long enough for him to meet my parents. Kate was at college, so he would be staying in her room.

My mom was really excited to finally meet him though she felt like she already knew him. I knew she liked him a lot already. I could tell just by her limited correspondence with him that she easily knew why I was in love with him. He was a classic southern gentleman and loved the Lord with all of his heart. What more of a combination do you need? Not to mention, he was tall, muscular, and he had blonde hair and blue eyes. It was like he was out of a dream. A man out of a story that every girl dreamed about and... he was coming to visit me!

I sat outside the gate in the Kherington Regional Airport as I waited for David's flight to arrive. I was excited and nervous. One thing I was definitely nervous about was for him to see my car. I wasn't pulling up in an immaculate Tahoe like he had. Though my car had been a blessing, my 1987 Camry was still over 10 years old and had over 150,000 miles on it. It was a gift from my grandpa, so I did not have to make any payments on it. Lacking the sleek innovative curvatures of the new Camry's, my boxy, brick-red dinosaur may have been a stunning deal in its time with its power sunroof, windows, and locks. However, the paltry square vehicle couldn't compare to a new, mint condition SUV.

"Oh well," I thought. "This is who I am, and this is what I drive. David has to find out sometime."

From the time I met David, I sensed he came from a financially affluent family. Maybe it was just intuition because, within the first 10 days of meeting him in England, I noticed something was different. The khaki Abercrombie cargo shorts had been the only thing I could tie to money because he didn't act like a snobby rich kid; actually, he acted quite the opposite. His overly friendly, yet easy-going personality was welcoming to people of every background. He seemed to be the life-of-the-party sort of guy, and everyone liked David Carter. He was easy to like.

My middle-class upbringing wasn't a huge deal. It was who I was. I was sure he wouldn't judge me for my car, but I couldn't help but be a little self-conscious. What was he going to think about my car, my house, family... everything? I assumed these were fairly normal thoughts for someone to have before bringing that "special someone" home to meet the family for the first time.

More than anything, this whole visit would be a very big deal to my family. After a year and a half, my parents would finally meet David. For the last eighteen months, I talked about meeting the man I was going to marry. I talked about my husband. I had told them that David was going to be my husband one day. I did not know the time, but I knew he was *the one*. For the longest time, there was absolutely *no* manifestation that this would ever take place. When he did not call, write, or e-mail, the only proof my family had was the one-sided convictions of my heart. The biggest difference was that I was in complete faith that he was the one. Now, 18 months later, it was the first time they were going to actually meet him and see that he was real. I did not make him up.

Thus far, the only relationship my parents had been a part of was the dating fiasco of my sister. Far from a "godly" relationship, the long saga encompassed chaos, anger, lies, betrayal, and frustration. Her relationship was on one day and off the next. It had taken a toll on my sister and on my family. So, this was a refreshing turn of events for my parents. They were going to meet a godly guy who was courting their daughter. This person could be their first son-in-law.

I clung to what I knew in my heart. I envisioned the chalkboard. The green chalkboard. I could close my eyes and see it: "This is him. This is the man you are going to marry." That is all I needed. God said it. I believed it. However, for my parents, this would be their first visual sign that what I had spoken of for so long could actually come to pass. What a faith story and testimony. Patience. Waiting.

I could only imagine how much my parents desired for each of us kids to marry and be happy, in love, in a godly relationship, successful, prosperous, blessed, and to raise up godly children. I didn't want to get ahead of myself, but I knew this visit could also show my siblings that God has great things for them, too, if they will wait for His best and not settle for less or second best. It was a testimony to my siblings that there are men and women of God out there who would be the perfect match and compliment to them as well. My relationship with David could encourage and inspire them. It could lift them up to grow and trust in the Lord daily. A godly spouse, even in this day and age, was still possible.

The airport's gate door opened. People were coming out, rolling their carry-on luggage. I quickly stood up, my heart beating fast. Any minute, David could walk out that door. I was so excited. Ahhhhhhhh! Nervous excitement. And, there he was! Rolling his carry-on, his eyes met mine, and he smiled! I ran up and gave him a big hug. He kissed me softly and said, "It is so good to see you. I missed you, Princess."

Melting in his arms, "I missed you, too. It is good to see you. Did you have a good flight?"

"I did. Thank you. Just glad to finally be here."

We walked hand-in-hand down the corridor as we chatted about his trip. He did not check any luggage, so we could go straight to the car and get on the road.

Though winter was coming to a close, we still had mounds of snow lining the streets. The cold temperatures in the 20s and 30s would be a drastic change from David's tropical life. The absence of the sparkly, white glitter of freshly-fallen snow had been replaced with dirty, brown and white, melting slush that lined the streets.

We approached my car. I unlocked the doors, David put his luggage in the back, and then he hopped in the passenger seat. He looked like a giant in my little Camry. I felt weird driving him around.

Rubbing his hands together, he said, "Burrrrrrr! It is cold out here!"

"Yes! Welcome to Pennsylvania! We were hoping you would bring the sun!"

"I should have!" he said while blowing on his bare hands.

"Oh... you'll have to pardon my car. It's not new, but it is paid for."

He laughed and said, "Well cool! I didn't come here for your car. I came here to see you."

"Well, thanks," I said and smiled. That was all that was said about my car. He didn't make me feel uncomfortable, but he didn't say anything more. We began the drive home with lots of catching up to do.

The welcoming party was there as we pulled in. Mom, Dad, Jacob, and Ashley—with her one-year-old daughter, Bailey—opened the front door as we pulled down the long drive. I could see their smiles as they waved.

In the car, David laughed with amusement at the sight of them all, and we made our way inside.

In the entrance, my mom hugged David and said, "It's so good to finally meet you, David. I'm Jean."

My dad extended his hand, saying, "I'm Mark. Great to meet you, David."

"It is great to finally be here. Thanks for having me, Mr. and Mrs. Cook."

We had approximately 48 hours together before David flew back out of Kherington Regional and home to Bayside Island. The whole weekend, it was "Mr. and Mrs. Cook." They told him several times that he could call them by their first names, so he did call mom Ms. Jean, but his southern raising still kept him with a respectful approach.

"Ms. Jean, if my grandmother caught me calling you both by your first name, she would tan my hide," he said and laughed. "My granddaddy has always taught me, 'Respect your elders, Davy.'" David repeated in a gruff grandpa voice, "'Hold your shoulders back, boy. When you talk to someone, you look them in the eye, you give them a firm handshake, Davy. You understand, boy? You always say "Ma'am" and "Sir" to anyone that is older than you, Davy," he explained.

"Well, we don't want you getting into trouble. It does sound pretty cool."

Not growing up in the South made us all feel a bit oblivious to "southern rearing" and "southern hospitality." It was so different from our northern way of responding to a simple question: "Do you want something to drink?" "What?!" or "Yeah!" Such responses sounded so disrespectful after hearing David's response that was always accompanied by "Ma'am" or "Sir."

Sitting around the table, my dad asked, "David, can I get you some tea or something to drink?"

"No thank you, Sir. I'm good thanks."

We continued chatting as David watched my dad make his tea. Dad pulled down the jar of instant Nestea and spooned out one tablespoon of tea and two tablespoons of sugar, filled his cup with water, stirred, and added ice.

"Oh my." David responded. "I will have to teach y'all how to make our southern sweet tea," he chided.

"Okay. Well, you can make it now if you want," my mom said, jumping up.

"Alright. Do you think you're ready for my special sweet tea, Ms. Jean?" He smiled at her with a cheeky grin.

"Let's do it!"

David told her what he would need and began his craft. He put the water on the stove to boil, added the tea bags in the water, and then prepared the pitcher. He scooped *two cups* of sugar into the pitcher! We all about flipped out as we watched!

"Oh, my goodness!" we repeated to each other, our mouths agape. Shocked.

David just laughed.

When the water was dark, David poured the hot tea over the two heaping cups of sugar in the pitcher, and the granules of sugar began to melt. He filled up the pan again and poured another equal amount of water into the pitcher.

"There you go! Stir and voilà! Southern sweet tea!" he said. We tested it out, gasping after tasting it! It was like drinking syrup! It was definitely *sweet*! We all enjoyed seeing David tower over us all while moving around mom's kitchen. We enjoyed every minute of it.

Back at the airport, I walked David to his gate. As the final announcement for his flight's boarding was called, he hugged and kissed me goodbye. It was so sad to see him leave. As he began down the corridor, right before he turned the corner, he looked back to wave. I stood there, tears streaming down my face, and waved. I could see the expression on David's face turn to one of sadness and compassion as he lingered, looking at me for a few seconds. He waved one last time and then disappeared around the corner.

27

A SEASON OF FIRSTS

The next few months were accompanied by many late nights on the phone. David and I could already tell that it may have been God's plan for us to live at a distance from each other. Talking on the phone, the longing to be together was evident. We were physical touch people. The countless nights talking confirmed we were going to need boundaries this summer. If we did not have boundaries, we knew that, physically, things could get out of hand. We could go places that, as Christians, we knew we had no business going. In a moment of passion or lust, we could experience things that we wanted to experience only with our marriage partner. We kept coming back to Ephesians 5:3, which reminded us, "Don't let there even be a *hint* of sexual immorality." It was so hard because just being around David made me want him even more. I was thankful that my Christian beliefs kept me grounded, but that didn't always make it easy. Knowing what was available made me long for the day I would experience it the right way, the godly way.

I partly wished I had not known or experienced anything physical in other relationships. If I hadn't, I wouldn't know what I was missing, and maybe my body wouldn't long for David in such a way. Nor would I carry around the shame that accompanied my memories. Some days, I felt dirty. The more I got to know David, the more I realized how "clean" he was, how much he really had saved for his wife. He had barely done more than kiss a girl.

My heart continually prodded, bringing me back to 1 John 1:9, when I confessed my sins and my past, God was faithful to forgive. He not only forgave me, but He forgot. He blotted my sins out of His remembrance. I was "white as snow." I wished I could have blotted it out of my memory like God had! I prayed that, on the day that David and I did get married and consummate our marriage, the vision or picture of my college fling would not be in my head. I knew

David had not experienced all that I had. I knew that he truly had saved himself from *all* forms of sexual activity. I wanted the only intimate memory in my life to be of David, not the memories of other relationships.

As much as I wished to change my past, it was too late. Things may have been different had I known what God had in store for me. There really was the "knight in shining armor," waiting to sweep me off my feet, pure and unblemished, who would rescue me.

Unworthy would definitely be a word to describe how I felt to be with David. I would've never thought that, with my background, God could bring me to a place of such great blessing with a man like David. Sure, technically, we were not even an official item yet, but I was sure that we would be soon. I was grateful that David was a man of God that was focused on obedience to the Word and to purity. Not only was he a Christian, he was a godly man who truly wanted to follow the Lord in every area of his life.

Sure, I could not turn back the clock and take back what was gone, but I could start today. I could start now. I could save myself for my wedding day—if only someone would have told me when I was younger. I don't know how they could have relayed the feelings in a way that would have stuck with me. If I would've known what I know now, I may have made kissing the boundary in all of my relationships. How different my memories would be.

May 28th. My summer was officially under way. I packed my car and started my drive for Bayside Island at 5:00am! It would be an early morning and a long day behind the steering wheel, but my excitement to finally see David literally drove me. I didn't stop except to get gas, an impressive 13 hours on the road, and my energy level was on high. I knew David would be at the church to greet me. I was beyond excited!

I pulled in to the church parking lot. It was a pink church! Not something we see in Pennsylvania. Pink stucco. I got out of my new graduation present, my Nissan Altima, and stretched my legs. It felt so good to walk around and to just *be* in Bayside Island.

LT. I had decided Leadership Training would be how I would spend my last summer before getting a "real job." Only a few weeks prior, I was at my college graduation. Now, I was on a mission trip for three months! I had great anticipation for the summer. I didn't know all that God would do, but I knew He had great things in store for our summer.

I walked into the church and stopped at the front check-in table. I was greeted by two nice ladies behind the table who gave me a packet of information and then pointed me toward the next table. I got my work assignment. I quickly glanced through some papers to find my summer employment information. A campground would be my workplace for the summer. This was all coming together.

I took a moment to let everything sink in. This was really real! I was going to be here for three months. My packet even had directions and keys to the apartment where I would be living with five other girls.

I took a deep breath. I didn't know anyone there. I would be meeting everyone for the first time. Some feelings of anxiety rose up, and I was a little nervous. As I remembered that I would be seeing David any time, a warm peace swept over my anxieties.

"Well, Emily, you are all set. We are excited to have you as a part of Leadership Training. We are excited to see God move this summer. Please let us know if there is anything we can do for you or anything you need."

I snapped out of my daze and thanked the lady that was sitting behind the table. I had everything.

I walked out of the church and across the parking lot to my car to put the packets away.

In that moment, I saw the navy blue Chevy S10 pickup truck. Leaning against the side of the truck was a tall, blonde, muscular beach model. David took my breath away. He was so handsome. My insides screamed, "Ahhhh! There he is!"

Just seeing him made the pace of my heart pick up and beat rapidly. I just wanted to skip or run to meet him. I wanted to jump, but I didn't want to seem too excited. I laid my things down in the passenger seat of new Altima and started walking to meet him. As he approached, we embraced.

"Hello, my Princess. It is so good to finally have you in Bayside Island." His arms wrapped around my waist, and he pulled me in tight to him. I wrapped my arms around his neck, and just having my head laying on his chest felt like a piece of heaven. I was finally with my Prince. I loved how tall he was. It made me feel so small to be held by him.

"It's so good to see you, too! I'm so glad to finally be here," I said.

He pulled away from our embrace for a moment. His smile gave away that something was up. "Well, Princess, I have a question for you. Are you ready?"

"Yes what?" I said in nervous excitement.

"Well, Emily, I knew this day was coming, and I have planned to wait until today. I wanted to make it official, so I'd like to ask you a question.

"Ok? What is it?" Excited confusion appeared on my face. What was he going to ask?!

"Emily Cook, would you be my girlfriend?" His soft eyes and knowing grin told me he knew my answer before even asking.

I giggled at the cute question. I didn't think anyone had asked me that since I was a sixth-grader, but I loved it. I loved everything about our relationship. The innocence of even the question made me appreciate "old-fashioned" dating. I felt silly but answered, "Of course I will be your girlfriend, David! I've been waiting for this day for a long time!"

He swept me up and gave me a simple, soft kiss on the lips as he swung me around, my feet dangling gleefully.

On May 28th, I was finally David Carter's girlfriend. Emily Cook and David Carter were officially an item.

Elise bounced with excitement. "Awwwwww! I'm so excited for you! He's hugging you and spinning you around! It seems like a movie! I can totally see you spinning around in the sunset... with palm trees in the background. Were you soooooooooo excited?!"

"I was! Finally, I was one step closer to my dream coming true!" I said.

"And I love how he asked you to be his girlfriend! That is soooooo cute! Even though it would feel a little cheesy, I would love that too!" said Elise.

"I know. It was cheesy, but I loved every minute of it," I said and smiled.

"Okay, what was summer like with him? I bet that was interesting!"

"It was, indeed," I said with a sullen tone, nodding. "It was, indeed."

"Uh, oh… what happened?"

"Well, let me jump back in and tell you."

David participated in a lot of the events that we did with LT. On Tuesday nights, we had a time of praise and worship that was followed by a sermon. Everything about LT had been refreshing. I had been needing to be poured back into. The drama at college had become so spiritually draining, and I desperately needed to get my batteries recharged.

On Thursday nights, we did street ministry. David frequently joined us on this. Our group was assigned to the Beachwalk. It was a strip along the beach with countless shops, a roller-coaster, and lots of people.

One of the recurring themes, a gap in his armor, that I began to notice was his desire to help improve me, to fix me. Hearing about the most recent John Maxwell book on leadership or another self-help book and how I needed to apply it got exhausting. I was happy he enjoyed growing and reading, but I was not interested in his books. Maybe one day, I would change, but at this point in my life, I had no one I was "leading," and I just wanted to relax.

David sat on the couch, waiting for me to come out. Several of my roommates were ready. It was Thursday night, and we were heading to the Beachwalk for street ministry.

As I walked out, David simply looked at me and said, "You're wearing that?"

The first thought in my mind was full of sarcasm, "No. I'm not wearing this… I just walked out in it for the fun of it. Yes, I'm wearing this!"

The huff of my breath and my glare told him what I thought about his comment, and he immediately went into save mode: "I mean, you look super cute. I just don't want you to look too cute out there. Because we'll be sharing Jesus with people, I just didn't want people to get the wrong idea. You look very nice, Emily." It was a very good attempt, and his face looked like a puppy dog, trying to win back my approval. But I was still ticked.

I stormed out of the room, determined to put on the ugliest, frumpiest outfit I had brought with me. My outfit had been either too cute, too short, too this, or too that. Was I right to storm out? Probably not. But I was just mad. The recurring theme of David trying to "fix Emily" was getting a bit annoying. After changing, I stormed past David as he was sitting on the couch in our living room and went outside to join the rest of the group.

On the sidewalk outside, David whispered, "Emily, I'm sorry. I didn't mean it how you took it. Will you forgive me?"

What else was I going to say? No? Of course I would forgive him. The steam was simmering down. I was still annoyed, but I knew I would get over it. "Yes, I forgive you," I said in a plain tone, reaching out to hold his hand just to prove I would get over it.

"Thank you," he said and smiled.

What an amazing time sharing the gospel down at the Beachwalk. Almost every time we went out, David and I had the privilege of leading someone to the Lord. That night, I sat down and began to speak with someone in Spanish. My time in the Costa Rican orphanage paid off because I worked with the girls daily on memorizing scripture.

Sitting on the bench with a young woman, I asked if she would like to make Jesus her Lord? I proceeded to tell her "Romanos 10:9

se dice, 'Que si confesaras con su boca que Jesús es el Señor y crees en tu corazón que Dios le levantó de los muertos, serás salvo!'"

She responded that she did believe Jesus was Lord and that God raised him from the dead. "Quiero se salvos." Her big brown eyes locked with mine, sadness and longing filled them. "I want to be saved," she said.

"Orremos," I said, which means, "Let's pray."

There on the bench, for the first time, I prayed with someone in Spanish to receive salvation. Tears streamed down her face as she hugged me after praying.

"Gracias. Gracias," she thanked me through the tears.

"De nada."

We parted ways, and I noticed David and another guy hopping off the board walk onto the sandy beach. I jogged to catch up.

"Hey! Where are you guys going?"

"Tom just accepted Jesus, and we were talking about his next step, to get baptized. He didn't know of anywhere to get baptized because he doesn't have a church, so I said he could get baptized now… in the ocean. That's where we're headed."

"Oh my!" I jumped, sand kicking up from my feet! "Tom! That is sooooo exciting! How awesome! Congratulations! What a day this will be in history for you! The day you got saved *and* got baptized in the ocean! How cool!"

"What a night." I thought, "despite the bad start to it… our first fight. Man, Satan really wanted to derail us tonight." I looked up at the stars. "Thank you, God. Thank you for still turning this into such an amazing evening. Wow! What a glorious night to celebrate!"

28

TIME WITH FAMILY

y days consisted of waking up, pulling on my dark green polo and khaki pants, and heading to the activity center at Palm Island Campground. I worked behind a desk, answered phones, rented out activity equipment, announced BINGO letters, led children's activities, and played games… a fairly easy job for the summer. Our once-a-week dance party attracted camp kids, elderly, and my favorite, David. Seeing him interact and play with kids was insightful as they would swing on him, begging to dance with him, and he would twirl them back and forth.

David and I planned to meet for lunch because we both had the afternoon off of work. "Why don't you just meet me at my place, and we can go together. I'd love to take you on a lunch date," he said from the other end of the receiver.

"That sounds wonderful. I'll head your way now."

"Alright, I'll see you in a little bit. Drive safe, Princess."

I pulled up to his apartments, parked, and made my way up to the third floor.

"Knock, knock. Hello? Is anybody home?" I joked.

The door swung open. "Well, hello to you! It's good to see you. You look beautiful as always," he said as he gave me a hug.

"Thank you," I smiled back.

"Well, hey, I need to go grab my shoes, and then I'll be ready to go."

"Okay." I grabbed a seat on the couch, happy to be in his presence.

David returned and sat beside me, bending over to slip on and tie his Nikes.

"How did you get so beautiful?" He brushed his fingers through my hair with a smile and leaned in, giving me a soft kiss on the lips.

With his lips almost touching mine, I replied, "I don't know. How did you get so cute?" His breathing was warm on my lips.

"I don't know, God, I guess," he said in a whisper, leaning in to kiss me again. This time, the kiss was longer. Sinking back into the couch cushions, the passion of his kiss swept over me. Within seconds, we were laying down, intensely kissing, his body pressed hard against mine. In the heat of passion, his hand went behind my head, our bodies breathing together while he pulled me closer.

Then, he abruptly stopped. David jumped up. "I am sorry! We need to go!" He grabbed his keys and was standing with the door open almost before I sat up.

"You are right."

"Let's drive separately if you don't mind. You can follow me."

"Okay."

We had our food and were sitting in the corner of our favorite Chinese restaurant.

"Emily, I'm sorry. Sometimes, I'm just not strong enough to be around you. We really need to reestablish our boundaries. I don't want to fall with you. I don't want to drag you into sinning. Emily, you know how much I care about you, and I care about you enough to honor your purity. Please forgive me. Lord, forgive me."

He bowed his head and began to pray, "God, please forgive us. God, please help me to be a strong leader, to be a boyfriend that holds You at the number one spot. Help Emily and me to remain pure even when we feel so passionate about each other. Father, please help us." He paused. "God, please direct us. In Jesus Name, I pray. Amen."

"Amen," I responded.

Pulling out his Daytimer, he opened to his notes section. "Emily, I really feel like, together, we need to write out our boundaries. We need to put up safeguards because, even though not a ton just happened, I promise you, I wanted more! Just because I am a Christian does not mean I don't have strong desires. Emily, I wanted a lot more. I just don't want to fall with you. I don't want to bring you down. I want to respect you for the godly girl you are. Please forgive me."

"I forgive you. Please forgive me, too. It takes two for things to happen. I'm at fault, too." David knew some of my past but not all of my un-proud details. His behavior was so radically different than what I was used to. It was refreshing.

"But, it ultimately falls on me. It should be my responsibility as the leader to lead. So… I'm going to lead now." He grabbed his mechanical pencil from the leather holder. "Let's come up with a list of boundaries. You are my girlfriend, and I want to be with you this summer. At the same time, Jesus is still number one. I want to honor Him by honoring us, remaining pure."

"Okay, good idea."

"Okay, number one… " he said and started writing.

Over the next 30 minutes, our lunch became a working lunch of reestablishing boundaries and setting new ones because we were living in the same town. Things were different now that our relationship was more than just a phone conversation. We came up with 12 guidelines to remaining pure.

David had been talking to Brent, the leader of our group, about the possibility of taking me to meet his family one weekend toward the end of June. David's sisters were participating in a similar mission trip for the summer in Kokomo Beach, Florida. They were working jobs, learning a lot about the Word, and doing evangelism outreach activities. Because David's parents and grandparents had scheduled a trip to go to Kokomo Beach to visit Jenna and Macy, he thought it would be a great opportunity for me to meet his whole family.

Everything worked out with Brent. I got the green light to go out of town to meet David's family. In the back of my mind, part of me felt like this was probably a pretty big deal. David was bringing me to meet his family. I was excited and nervous, but from what I knew of them so far, they all seemed like people I would really like.

We met up with David's parents and grandparents. Pulling up in a big, white Suburban, David's granddaddy got out first. His oversized, gold belt buckle and cowboy hat stood out. His button-up white collared shirt was pressed with a strong starch, the collar at sharp points. Without introducing himself, he said, "So, Emily, did you ever work at Hooters?"

"Now, Howard!" David's grandmother chided, swatting his arm in a scold.

I laughed, caught off guard. "No, I never worked at Hooters. I heard they have good wings though." David had prepared me to just be ready for whatever granddaddy might say. Sometimes, it was off the cuff. I was okay with that. I wasn't offended. I did think it was funny though, an awkward first question from someone who I thought would be my future grandfather.

"I'm sorry," Ms. Edith said, hugging me gently. "You will have to forgive him. It is good to meet you, Emily."

"It's good to meet you, too, Ms. Edith," I said and smiled.

Granddaddy burst out laughing. "Good to meet you, Emily. Now, David," he said gruffly, turning to look squarely up at David. "This girl seems like a nice girl now," he barked. "You may need to keep her around, you hear?"

"Yes, Sir." David nodded in submission.

Grandmother Edith and Granddaddy Howard seemed to operate in the "old-fashioned" way of doing things. Edith was an example of an elegant, submissive, yet strong woman. She was tall. Her white, silk blouse was tucked into her black-belted dress pants, and she wore a silk scarf, pinned together with a brooch. Her short red hair was set in perfect curls on her head. She seemed to be the perfect complement to Howard. I could tell she was a very strong woman, and it appeared she had to be to put up with Howard and his blunt nature. Her frequent reprimand of a tap on his hand while he would respond, "Well, Woman. It's the truth!" It was evident they had probably been married around 40-50 years. They were so in sync with one another, complementing the other in unique ways, a perfect picture of the South!

Meeting David's parents was great. They were so sweet. Dennis was about 6'4" tall, and Gloria was on the opposite end of the spectrum. She was barely 5'0". I loved it though. Hugs from Dennis were great. He was like a big teddy bear. Gloria and I hit it off immediately, like we could be best friends. She had a way about her that, even though I had just met her, she made me feel like I had known her my whole life. It was amazing. She avoided all the "small talk" and got right to whatever she wanted to talk about.

"Emily," Gloria said. "Really, Emily, I was so proud of you for going to visit David without him knowing. He needs someone to defy him sometimes. He doesn't need to be the boss all the time," she said, looking at David.

Looking down at her, he just gave her a half smile and nodded as if she were the boss.

Her soft red hair was almost a blonde, beautiful and very curly. She had a wonderful smile and laugh. She had been the one who had planned the trip, picked out where we were staying, assigned rooms, had all of our restaurants picked out, and scheduled the times we would be going. Reservations had been made, and she quietly made people aware of when we needed to be doing something. I enjoyed everything about her, her mannerisms, the way she spoke to me like I was already a daughter, her smile, and how she was so in charge without being bossy.

I immediately felt a kindred spirit with Jenna and Macy as they were both pursuing their relationship with the Lord. Macy was the baby of the family though she was still much taller than me. Her long, curly red hair was amazing. Strikingly beautiful, Jenna, the middle child, was also around 5'9" or 5'10". Flipping her long blonde hair over her shoulder, she bent down and greeted me with a hug. Their height accentuated my short stature. I was taller than Gloria though.

Based on my quick assessment, I liked the whole family. There was a warmth about them. I easily felt at home in conversations. I felt that maybe it was the Christian nature of their personalities, welcoming and kind. I would enjoy getting to know them.

The weekend went fast. Rooming with Jenna and Macy allowed me a great opportunity to get to know them. We shared late nights of laying on our beds, talking about God, their mission trip, my trip, more details about how David and I met, and about their friends and boyfriends.

After a few trips to the beach and going together to meals as a family, our weekend was over. It flew by, and it was time for David and I to say our goodbyes. Though I wasn't sure what David was looking for out of the weekend, it appeared he felt it had gone well. I knew he had spent some individual time visiting with his grandparents and parents. I hoped I received their approval. From their loving responses, I felt I had.

The weeks following our visit to Kokomo Beach brought visitors! My parents were in Bayside Island for a week-long vacation, another opportunity for them to be around David. I always loved being with my parents, so I was ecstatic that they were in town. When we weren't out doing ministry, working, or at a meeting, we spent time showing my parents around. David even had the opportunity to have some one-on-one time with them, which was good. I knew my mom was thrilled to get to know David, and in my dad's quiet way, he seemed to like David.

A week after my parents left, my older sister, Ashley, arrived. She stayed with me and the girls at our apartment. It was already crowded without her there, so she had to sleep on the couch.

As I showed Ashley around our small apartment, she replied, "I don't care where I sleep. I just want to be with my sister. I miss you. I hate having you gone this summer!"

Ashley and I had always been really close. Because we cheered together in high school, we spent countless hours in practices and at games. We were only one grade and 15 months apart, so it allowed us both to be on the same squad most years. She knew me better than almost anyone. She knew how much I was in love with David. Not to mention, I had been with Ashley through a lot of what seemed like a never-ending saga of break-ups with her most recent boyfriend. I always knew there was a really awesome man out there for Ash. She was so beautiful. Her blonde hair was always in a trendy style. Her personality was so fun and free-spirited. Though I was a bit more spontaneous, she could be coaxed into almost anything that was fun.

David and I showed her the highlights of Bayside Island: Palm Island Shops, the Beachwalk, and of course, the beach itself! Aside from spending one day at work with me, Ash spent her days at the beach or shopping, waiting for me at the apartment by the time I got off. That gave us time to go out to eat, catch a movie one night, and have ice cream at the pier. I was glad she felt so at home with my busy schedule. Just having her around made me smile.

On the last night of her stay, I got a knock on the door from Brent, our group leader for LT. Rain was pouring down, and his coat was soaked as he entered. "Hey, Brent. What's up?"

"Hey, Emily. I just wanted to let you know that, tomorrow, you and Melissa will be getting out of work a little bit early, around 2:00. I already have it worked out with your boss. Life Group leaders will be going on a scavenger hunt. Melissa already has the video camera and first clue. So, have fun!"

"Awesome! That sounds like fun! Thanks, Brent!" He pulled his coat back over his head and disappeared into the dark, pouring rain.

"Ashhhhhh," I pleaded. "See, you could stay and probably go on a scavenger hunt with me. It would be fun. You don't have to leave early tomorrow."

"No, I really need to get on the road and get back home. You will have fun though. I'm sure! You'll have to let me know how it goes."

"Okay," I said, pouting that my sister was leaving.

29

THE SCAVENGER HUNT

I woke up and said goodbye to Ashley. We prayed for safe travels as she left Bayside Island and made the long drive back to Pennsylvania. It had been raining non-stop for the last 24 hours, and the area was under a flood watch, so we prayed an extra hedge of protection around her as she got on the road.

I got to work that morning. Melissa and I rode together because we were going to be leaving early for our scavenger hunt. We parked in the back and sloshed our way to the front. There was no way to avoid the overflowing puddles.

2:00 - "Okay, Emily. Are you ready to go?" Melissa asked.

"Sure! Let's do this!"

"I have the video camera. I'll be in charge of video-taping, and I'll let you narrate and read the clues. We have to have everything on video. The first clue is in the bag, so I'll go get it."

"Sounds great," I responded. I was excited. A scavenger hunt! How fun! I was curious about whether we would meet up with the other Life Group leaders while we were out. Nonetheless, I was just excited to be getting out of work early!

Melissa picked up the video camera bag and reached in to grab the first clue. She pulled it out and handed it to me. "Here's the first clue." The outside of the envelope read, "Project #7: Clue #1."

"Okay, here's what it says:

Clue #1: How interested are you in the "Father's Time"?
Gen. 2:24 / Est. 4:14 / Gen. 17:4 / Hos. 10:12
Ex. 20:12 / Rom. 9:9 / Luk 23:24 / Ps. 31:15

This location is at Palm Island Shops. Find the words in the verses that match and are mentioned over and over. Go into the store and ask for Marge and present the clue to her.

"I have my Bible in the car. We can look up the verses and see what they say," I said.

"Sounds great! Let's get going!"

We left, the video tape rolling in Melissa's hand. When we got to my car, water came half-way up on my tires, and there were ducks swimming by my door. I guess the flood watch had been serious! We were in for a fun time, but it looked like we were going to get wet. I was glad we didn't have to look nice because the rain poured down steadily and we were without an umbrella.

Melissa jumped in the passenger side of my car with the video camera in hand, opened the Bible, and began to look up the verses that were listed. I backed up through the foot-tall, standing water to head to Palm Island Shops.

"Okay, here's Genesis 2:24: 'That is why a man leaves his father and mother and is united to his wife, and they become one flesh.' Esther 4:14: '…And who knows but that you have come to your royal position for such a time as this?' Hosea 10:12: '…for it is time to seek the *Lord*, until he comes and showers his righteousness on you.'"

"Hmmm… So, what do you think the running theme is here?" I asked as Melissa studied the verses.

"It seems like it's talking about God's timing or God's perfect time… Queen Esther being in place at the 'perfect time.' Hmmm… I'd say something about God's timing."

"You know what? This sounds wild, but now that I think about it, David and I shared the gospel with a lady at a clock shop at Palm Island Shops. I think her name may even have been Marge. This may be where we are going. I think the clock shop name is even something like, 'The Father's Time,'" I said. "Wow. Amazing that Brent would be sending us here," I said in awe.

Melissa smiled and shook her head in amazement.

We got to Palm Island Shops with no umbrella, so we knew we were just destined to be soaked. That was okay. Thankfully, this was a scavenger hunt and not a beauty contest. Not to mention, we were both dressed a little frumpy. We had on our khaki work pants and our green Palm Island Campground shirts. Definitely stylin'!

Finding a store directory, we searched down through the list of store names. "Bingo!" I said. "There it is, 'The Father's Time.' Let's go. It's down this way." I pointed as Melissa kept the video camera rolling like we were instructed to do.

We walked into the clock shop. It was very nice. It had huge grandfather clocks, wall clocks, little clocks, big clocks... clocks that made noises, coo'ed, dinged, and sang. Clocks of all kinds! We immediately made our way toward the back where we saw a tall lady standing at the counter.

"Hello," I said. "We are on a scavenger hunt, and we think there may be a clue waiting for us here." I quickly glanced down to see if she had a nametag on. Indeed, it said *Marge*. "Oh! Our clue says that we are supposed to ask for you, too!"

She smiled from behind the counter and pulled out a bag with a box in it and handed us an envelope. "You can read the clue now, but you are not supposed to open the box until the designated time. You will know when you are able to open it," she said with a warm smile.

"Okay," Melissa said with a giggle.

"Okay. Sounds good," I said as I began to open the envelope:

> Project 7: Clue #2. Here's what Clue #2 says:
> Clue #2: Are you wanting to be clothed in Christ?
> Ps. 45:3 / Is. 52:1 / Rom. 13:14
> This location is at Bayside Beach Mall (One mile away from Palm Island Shops, go down 21st Ave toward the beach to the mall.) In the store's name is a *N*, and it ends with an *S*. Show this clue to the sales associate at the first counter inside the store.

We left the store and ran through the rain back to the car. Melissa opened up the Bible and began looking for the verses as I started up the car and began to drive. She read the verses aloud, one by one. The recurring theme was "clothing yourself in Christ, girding yourself in Christ."

We made it to Bayside Beach Mall, hopped out, and ran inside. The mall directory was right inside the door, so we quickly scanned through the store list.

"Well, the only places that start with an *N* and end with an *S* are Norberto's Pizza and the Neiman Marcus clothing store. I'm going to go with Neiman Marcus! What do you think?" I said.

Melissa agreed, and we walked through the mall and made our way into Neiman Marcus.

Upon arrival, Melissa browsed the clothing racks, and I went directly to the cashier counter where I saw two sales associates working. I got the attention of one of the ladies. She had long red hair. As soon as we made eye contact, she gave me a slight smile. "We're on a scavenger hunt and have a clue to pick up. I believe the clue is here?" I questioned. Her facial expression immediately went from a bored employee to inquisitive and interested.

"Yes, we have a package for you." Her smirky smile was a bit unusual, like she knew something I didn't know, a secret. She turned her back and walked to the back side of the circular sales counter. She grabbed a bag and began to walk back to us. The bag looked bulky. "You cannot open the boxes now. You need to wait until you are told to open them. Also, here is your next clue." She handed a zip-lock bag to us. "You can't open your clue here. You need to wait until you are in the car," she instructed.

"Okay," I said. Melissa just giggled.

"Thank you!" Melissa said with a quick wink to the sales associate.

"Yeah, thanks!" I said.

"No problem," the associate smiled. She watched us as we walked out of the door. As I turned back to glance at them, I saw her whispering to the other sales associate as they watched us leave, both smiling.

It was still pouring rain. Melissa and I were already both pretty wet, but I offered to go pull the car around anyway. "I'll pull up to the front door," I said as I jetted through the parking lot, hoping the leather of my Doc Martens would recover from all of the rain.

When I pulled up, Melissa jumped in the passenger seat with the two bags. We opened the zip-lock bag and pulled out a clue and a CD. I read out loud:

Project #7: Clue #3
This CD of the Newsboys is your next clue. You will be taken
to your leader. Listen carefully to song #2. At the next stop,
you will open the first box you received. So, who is the leader
of project #7? Then, take me to your leader.

Well, that was easy. Brent was our leader. I guess we were going
back to the apartments. "So, back to Brent's?" I said to Melissa,
already knowing the answer.

"Yep! He's our leader!"

As we drove through the still-pounding rain, I wondered if we
were almost done with our scavenger hunt. It was getting late, and
both Melissa and I needed to clean up for our regular Thursday night
church service. This was fun, but I didn't want to be late, and we
were already pushing it.

I parked the car outside of our apartment, and Melissa and I ran a
few doors down to Brent's and Lisa's. We knocked, and Brent came
to the door and opened it! "Great, you guys are here! Right on time,
too!" he said. "Come on in!"

We came in and laughed a bit about our day as Brent read down
a list. "Okay, go ahead and open the first box that you received."

I opened the box and pulled out a brochure for a place called
Athena Gardens, which included a car pass to get in. I leafed through
the brochure. It looked like a really nice place with gardens and
flowers. "So? Melissa and I are going here next?" I said, though my
thoughts were racing. Boy, this was really going to make us late for
tonight's service.

"Yes. But first, you need to go back to your place, open the other
two boxes, and get cleaned up a bit. You need to be at Athena
Gardens by 5:30 so that doesn't give you too long to get ready. It will
take you about 20 minutes to get there from here."

"Okay?" I said with a questioning look. Melissa smiled. She
didn't look confused. Why did I feel so confused?

"Oh, I almost forgot," Brent jumped in, "Here! Show this rose to the guard at the gate when you get to Athena. He will give you your next clue." Brent handed a long-stemmed red rose to me. It was beautiful. I immediately brought it to my nose. The fragrant smell was as rich as a perfume, but I couldn't help but think that things were starting to get a bit strange with this scavenger hunt.

Melissa and I went back to our apartment. Video camera rolling, I began to open the other two boxes. The first box was heavy. I opened it, and out came a cute pair of shoes. They were summer sandals with a tall heal, something I would have very easily picked out to own myself. "Hmmm… Cutie shoes! What in the world?" I commented.

I continued to open the second box. I pulled out a long, silk and satin sundress. It had flowy chiffon as the top layer, with soft pink, peach, and cream flowers on the silk layer beneath the chiffon. The back of the dress had a series of spaghetti straps. It was a very cute dress. "So? Who is supposed to wear this?" I asked Melissa, raising my eyebrows.

"Well, I can already tell it doesn't look like it would fit me! What size is it? That will tell you immediately who is supposed to wear it!" she said, laughing.

I glanced at the tag. "It's a 5/6."

"Well, it ain't gonna fit me!" Melissa said.

"Well, let's just call Brent to make sure."

I hopped on the phone. "So? One of us is supposed to wear this?" I asked Brent and then heard his response. "I am supposed to wear it? Yeah… Okay…" Brent reminded me of our time schedule. "Alright, we'll be there." I hung up the phone with Brent and then definitely felt like things were getting more weird.

"Well, he said I'm supposed to wear this." A half smile and a bit of confusion showed on my face. I was sure there was something that I did not know. "Okay, I guess I better start getting ready."

Time was of the essence. I didn't have a whole lot of time to get cleaned up and put on this cutie dress. I immediately plugged in my curling iron so it could begin getting hot, and I got out my blow dryer. I walked into our bedroom to change, trying to piece together what was going on in my mind.

I thought, "Okay, what is today? Today is July 13th. Let's see... I know pretty much every important date with David. Does this involve him? I met him on July 7th. Our first kiss was on July 22nd. I saw him for the last time on July 27th. I talked to him the first time after the mission trip on Thanksgiving. Hmmm... got an email from him when I was in Costa Rica on February 4th... What is significant about today?" I racked my brain trying to piece together what was going on.

Things went from strange to stranger. Now, I was getting ready, going to be looking all cute, and Melissa was still in her mostly wet clothes and looking ragged. Something was going on. I continued thinking about what it could be.

Okay, in England, I met David on July 7th. It was about a week after I met him that we went on a walk through the park in England. That was when God told me I was going to marry him. Though I never wrote the date down, I knew it was about a week later... Oh my goodness! *Today* is that day! Exactly two years ago, God told me I was going to marry David! July 13th! Oh my goodness! I can't believe it! I'm getting engaged today! David is the one putting all of this on... not Brent! Oh my goodness!

I immediately was smiling from ear to ear. I changed and made my way into the bathroom. Melissa could tell that I had figured something out. It all made sense! The rose, showing it to the guard at the gate of Athena Gardens... and Athena Gardens of all places, a place that had garden after garden of flowers and fountains. David and I had walked through several gardens while in England. Smelling roses was where we initially began a special bond between us.

Melissa sat in the bathroom, continuing to video tape as I got ready. "So, Emily? Do you know what's going on? What are we going to do?"

I couldn't help but smile. A smile still made up my whole face. "I'm going to get engaged!" I said with joy bubbling out of me. "I'm going to get engaged today! Ahhh! David is going to ask me to marry him *today*! I'm finally getting engaged!" I was so excited I could hardly stand it!

Melissa just started laughing. I had figured it out!

The drive to Athena was like driving on a cloud. I could hardly believe that *now* was the time! I didn't know *how* it was all going to happen, but *this* was the day! I had known the feeling and what God told me in the garden that day, two years ago in England. I had only imagined that David must have written in his journal that he hugged me. I had told him that it was a *big* day when he hugged me though I didn't reveal the details of all that I saw: the chalkboard, the hand, and what exactly God had written. It was very strange but so very real to me. Somehow, David knew that today would be the perfect day to propose.

I could hardly stand the excitement. My heart felt like it was going to burst! I was on my way to get engaged! The day I had been waiting for now for two years! The countless nights of looking into the sky at my little tea cup, being willing to turn David over to God if he was not to be mine. Finally, today, one of God's promises was coming to pass. I had not made up my chalkboard. God really had revealed it to me that day. David really was going to be mine, and I was going to be his. Would I ever stop smiling? What joy filled every fiber of my being!

The more I started to think about the events of the day, the more I started to smile! David had gotten everyone in on this scavenger hunt! Melissa, Brent, and even my co-workers! Everyone knew! Thoughts flooded my mind about my parents being there and David wanting to get some time alone with them. At the time, I thought it was weird that he didn't want me around. That was fine. It was all starting to make sense now. I'm sure that David asked my parents for permission to marry me. He was brought up with very respectful, old-fashioned, and proper manners. Part of that upbringing, I was sure, included asking for permission to marry me.

I just continued, grinning from ear to ear. Melissa just laughed at me in the car. She was super excited, and we had it all on video! Wow!

We pulled up to the entrance of Athena Gardens. As we stopped at the guard gate, I showed the guard the rose. "We are supposed to pick up a clue from you I believe?" I asked.

He smiled back at me and handed me an envelope out of the window. "Have a great day, young lady," he said and winked. He waved us on, and we rolled over the speed bump onto the property.

I had never been there. Everything was immaculate. The grounds, the grass, the flowers, trees, wrought-iron gates, the statues, the fountains, and the perfectly trimmed bushes. It was amazing. How had this place been tucked away, and I did not know about it? It was simply breath-taking! It was like putting me back at one of the gardens in England. We passed some rose bushes that looked amazing, pulled into the parking lot, and rolled into a spot.

Project 7: Clue 4
Prov. 18:24
You have a friend that sticks closer to you than a brother. Who is your best friend? Now, go to her garden.

"Okay. Who is my best friend?" I said aloud. "Well, Elle? Probably Elle. My other friends..." I thought out loud. "Tara, Jodi, Emili, Ashley, Kate. But, probably Elle."

We quickly began to walk. We were looking for a garden. As we walked on the cobblestone sidewalks, we came to the first garden. On the left, we saw a sign that read, "Elle's Garden."

"You have got to be kidding!" I thought. "This is amazing! How perfect!"

Through the wrought-iron-gated entrance, I saw a fountain in the distance. On the ground in front of the fountain, I noticed there was a card propped up on something. I knew immediately that it was for me.

My pace was fast and excited. My heart was beating so fast, and I could hardly contain the smile on my face. What I had dreamed about, prayed for, pleaded for, and begged God for—day in and day out—was *finally* coming to pass. God really out-did Himself on this!

I bent down to pick up the card and noticed what it was propped up on. A scream inside my heart made me feel like a little girl. The card was propped up on a tiny, light blue, empty ring box. A box from Tiffany's. I could hardly contain myself. "An empty ring box!? Every girl knows that there must be a velvet box close by. There must be a real ring box with the real ring! There is a diamond ring here somewhere. It is really real! There is an engagement ring that came in this box! I'm getting a *ring*! Ahhhhh!"

I sat on the side of the fountain. Sounds of trickling water and the quick beating of my heart filled the air as I opened the card, ready to take in the words...

My Princess, since the moment you skated across the ice that December day, something happened to me. I was reminded of how beautiful you are and realized that God had created you special. On that day, I prayed He created you for me. Your love and passion for the Lord has attracted me to you ever since I met you in England. I love how you cry when you see someone get saved. I love to hear how beautiful your singing voice is. I love how you look at me with your beautiful, piercing blue eyes and how you love to hold my hand as I drive you places. I long to be with you every day, to create memories with you, to hold you and you to hold me. Emily, I love everything about you. When I'm not with you, I miss you. When I am with you, I just want to keep you.

I held my breath for a moment as I scanned the next few words...

Emily, I love you.

I smiled, knowing the significance of those words.

Turn around. I have something to ask you. Love, David.

Through our late night conversations, we had never said, "I love you." David felt that the phrase was overly used and used in relationships too lightly. He had always said that those words would only come out of his mouth if they were going to accompany the question, "Will you marry me?"

I melted. Seeing the words... real... tangible... "I love you. Turn around, I have something to ask you." I knew what was coming next.

I put the card down on the edge of the fountain. I turned and, across the grass, I saw David slowly walking towards me. He was dressed in a black suit, white shirt, and tie. He looked like a model walking out of a magazine, smiling brightly with his beautiful white teeth and his square jawline. I anxiously walked toward him. I just wanted to hug him. I was so excited!

My initial reaction was to want to reach out to him when he got in front of me, but he stopped me.

David then got down on one knee, held my hands, and asked the question I had been waiting to hear for two years, but with an even more beautiful spin. "Emily," he said, "Would you be willing to be number two in my life for the rest of your life? Emily, will you marry me?"

"Yes! Yes!" I said. "Yes, I will marry you!"

He opened the navy blue, velvet box, and the shimmering glare of a large diamond gleamed. The stone was in the shape of a heart. He placed the ring on my finger. He then stood up, took me in his arms, and kissed me.

The kiss seemed like I was already in heaven. It was the kiss that said, "*Jesus* is in control! Waiting for His best is truly better than anything I could have ever expected." The kiss that said, "Forever, you will be mine. Forever, we will pursue God together. Forever, you will be my Princess, and I will be your Prince." The kiss that said, "We can finally be together. We will begin life as one. A life of love and blessings. A life where dreams do come true."

David picked me up and spun me around. My smile and laughter was full of exhilaration. My excitement made me feel like I was floating.

We walked around the gardens and drank in the beauty. When we were finished, a limo waited to take us to dinner. Not just any dinner, but a dinner at the nicest place at the beach. It was the most elegant, romantic restaurant, overlooking the ocean: Isabela Grande del Mar.

30

HIS PERSPECTIVE

After coming down off the cloud I was on, my brain started going through all the questions. "How did this all come together? How did he do such an elaborate scavenger hunt, knowing my shoe size, dress size, and ring size? How did he know?"

At dinner, David filled me in on all of the details.

"Everything lined up in my favor. As I was planning everything, the prerequisite was for you to meet my family. I had to get the approval and blessing of my family: Mom, Dad, Grandmother, Granddaddy, Jenna, and Macy. So, while we were in Kokomo Beach, I snuck off to Grandmother's and Granddaddy's room to ask them what they thought about you. I asked them if I had their blessing. They gave a resounding *yes*! They really liked you!"

"Awwwww. That makes me so happy," I said.

"Then, I asked my parents and sisters. All of them also gave a resounding, 'Yes, we like her!' Get this. Mom actually told me that she knew the minute you defied me by coming to Bayside Island, she knew you were the one. She said I needed someone who was strong and could be independent."

I laughed. "Well, I'm glad she liked that! That was a tough decision. If I hadn't had Mr. Briscoe's help, I'm not sure if I would've done it. She's so funny."

"The next step in the equation... I needed to ask for your father's permission for your hand in marriage. I didn't want to do it over the phone. I wanted to do it in person. When your parents scheduled a vacation to Bayside Island, I was jacked! That allowed me to spend time alone with them to ask for their blessing to marry you. Your father obviously said *yes*."

"So, my parents *know*?!" I said in shock!

David just smiled. "Of course they know. I wasn't sure if your mom would be able to keep the secret though!" He winked.

"So what about the dress and shoes and everything? How did you work all of that out? Surely, you didn't just guess my sizes. Right?"

"Well, the details of the scavenger hunt were tricky. I had the outline and general concept in my head, but I really needed someone who could help me flesh it out, someone who could iron out the details. Then, when Ashley came to Bayside Island, I mentioned it to her, and she just took off with it! She got out a notebook and began writing everything down, line-by-line and step-by-step, that needed to be done. She also found out your dress size, shoe size, and ring size. It was perfect to have her here!"

"Wow! That doesn't surprise me! She has always been good at planning things! I bet it was helpful having her!"

"The kicker was this rain! I almost called it all off this morning because of the rain, but I just decided to go out on faith and believe everything was going to work out in my favor. Even with an outdoor proposal! Seriously, all day long, it's been a huge mental battle of what to do. Seeing on the news a flood watch going on in Bayside Island! Really?! The flood watch brought 11 inches of rain today! This morning, as I was driving around to drop off the clues, I knew I had to decide whether to have the last clue indoors or at Elle's Garden—like the original plan. As I was literally talking out loud to the Lord in my truck, I just said, 'Fine, Lord! I'm just going to go by faith on this! We're going to do it *outdoors* and *not* get rained on! I'm just going to trust you!'"

He continued, "Emily, check this out! Check out how good God is! At Athena Gardens, I don't know if you noticed, but when I got down on my knee and asked you to be 'number two' in my life for the rest of your life, it looked like rain had not even been there! How is that possible? Like there was no rain over the garden where I proposed? It was a blessing from the Lord. *God* kept it dry and perfect for us as if he sheltered that whole area from any rain."

I was amazed to hear the details of this elaborate day! What a testimony of God's goodness and a testimony of the faith it took for David to go through with everything, despite how it looked with all of the rain!

"Wow, David! That is amazing! I totally didn't notice anything about the lack of rain at Athena. I was so excited. There could have been puddles, and I wouldn't have noticed!" I laughed and smiled. The smile had not left my face from the moment I realized what would happen today.

I was engaged.

"And, do you want to know when I knew you were the One?" he asked.

"Absolutely!" I eagerly responded, excited to know any details of him finally discovering that I was to be his wife.

"You may not have known this, but when I was 17, I started a list of what I wanted in my future wife. I came up with 31 different qualities. When I started to really like you, after seeing you at the ice skating rink, I began to compare you to my list to see how you measured up. One by one, I started checking qualities off my list, qualities that you had! From the quality, "a good cook," and you sending me the most delicious chocolate chip cookies to… do you want to know the last one I checked off?" he paused.

"Yes!" I practically jumped with excitement.

"The last quality I checked off was this: *I want my wife to have a beautiful singing voice.* Do you remember singing to me in my apartment?" he asked.

Goosebumps raced up my arms. "Yes. I went back and forth in my mind and with the Holy Spirit. I felt like He was prodding me to sing, but I didn't want to. It was a very uncomfortable thing for me to do."

"Well, it's a good thing you did it. When you began to sing, I felt like I was hearing the voice of an angel. And that was the very last quality on my list. I desired my wife to have a beautiful singing voice. At that moment, Emily, the reality hit me. Chills ran through me at that moment. I knew right then that you were going to be my wife."

"Wow." Silence united us. Silence. My thoughts remembered exactly the feeling in the air the night I sang the song, *Sanctuary.* It was as if with the first words out of my mouth, you could cut the air with a knife. Not only did it eliminate the impurity that was in the air, but it was the unifying factor that would bring us to this very moment, eating together… me with this beautiful Tiffany's heart engagement ring, gleaming from my finger. In that moment, I was more thankful than ever that I had listened to the prodding of the Holy Spirit that night, that I had vanquished my insecurity of singing acapella in the loud silence of David's apartment. Praise the Lord that I sang.

I held my hand up, staring at the beautiful ring that finally rested on my finger. So many times, I had stared at the vacant, empty finger, longing to marry David. Finally, even my finger beamed with joy. I was unequivocally engaged.

We finished up an amazing dinner, talking, laughing, holding hands, enjoying great food, and especially… the company.

To top off an amazing day, we headed back to my apartment, and all of my roommates surprised us with an "Engagement Party." Wedding dress magazines, pictures, food, desserts, a sparkling cider toast, and a room full of friends congratulating us. It was so special. The journey of my dream wedding was finally beginning. The planning of it could finally start! I was engaged!

The rest of the summer was a whirlwind and sped by. I remember one afternoon that stood out because it really helped our relationship. We were at the beach, witnessing to people, and David saw some people that he knew from church. When they found out we were engaged, the gentleman said, "Could we offer one piece of important advice? This radically changed our relationship!"

"Of course!" David said. "I would love to have your advice, Ron!"

Ron looked at both of us as he stood, holding his wife's hand, and said, "Whatever you do, don't try to change each other. Leave that up to God. When we finally let *God* do the changing, fixing, and working on the other person… we were much happier. We got into the habit of casting each other onto the Lord. I would always say, 'Lord, she's your problem!'" Ron joked as he nudged his wife.

"Hey!" she said, laughing and nudging him back.

"But really, God does a much better job, and when we finally let God do the changing, we had a *lot* less fights!"

"Good advice," David replied. "Thank you, Ron. That's really good!"

After that day, I began to notice that advice actually changing our relationship. The summer had consisted of David recommending all of these books he thought would help me, but I had no interest in reading them. After the continual prodding, I took it as something that was wrong with me. He wanted to improve me and make me better. He had lunch appointments with the athletic director of his college, and they always talked about the exciting new leadership book they had read. Plucking my eyebrows sounded like more fun than the drudgery of trying to act interested.

I anticipated that, one day, I would be different. One day, I would enjoy reading those books, but that day just wasn't today. I was so thankful David took heed of the advice given and stopped trying to create a "better version" of me! I just wanted to be me! I was now planning a wedding and didn't have the time nor energy to think about who I should develop into. Because we were going to be married forever, I thought there would be an abundance of time to become a *better me* after planning a wedding.

The saying, "A word to the wise is sufficient," came to mind. David didn't need a dissertation on the topic. He simply and quietly began to apply the advice.

31

A SIN TOO GREAT?

Fall had begun, the mission trip was over, and I was back home, working full-time and planning our wedding. The remainder of our engagement would consist of over four long months of being back in a long-distance relationship. Thankfully, we decided on a winter wedding, January 6th in Pennsylvania. It would be a winter wonderland and definitely a day for me to be a Winter Princess. I was so excited about the day.

Being back home with my family brought an array of new emotions, questions, and opinions from everyone. Then, there was the question about a job search for me. Where would we live? Where would David work? I began to feel nervous. Taking in everyone's opinions and suggestions for the first time caused new feelings to emerge. With so many changes on the horizon, I began to question, "What did I want for my life? Who am I? Did I just want to follow David wherever he wanted to go?" The saga of emotions, questions, and uncertainty flooded my mind with confusion.

Because I was now a college graduate, a "real job" was at the forefront of my mind. My dad had mentioned a job opportunity that he thought would be great for me. With his connections, he was sure the job would be mine if I just said the word. It was something I already knew I was good at, a sales position outside of Atlanta. I would be making good money, easily in the six-figure range. My vision of being the "power suit" kind of woman came back to my mind. The thoughts were luring and reminding me that I could be self-sufficient, have my own money, have an important job, and be esteemed as I drove around in my nice car. The continual talk from my dad caused the position to look more and more appealing. Not to mention, I knew it would be a way I could make him proud. I saw myself as a woman in the movies, walking in with my black suit, high heels, sun glasses, and designer purse, obviously successful as I got on the elevator, heading to my corner office with windows on the top floor. I had the freedom to go anywhere I wanted, but then, the detail about David having to approve was a new caveat.

David and I talked about the opportunity. Giving it little thought, he just said, "No." He didn't feel called to move back to Georgia. He felt that life was supposed to begin in Bayside Island—not in Georgia.

This was my first battle, learning to be submissive, and we weren't even married yet. I never had to truly answer to a man to tell me what I could or could not do. I knew I was being led by my head and not my heart. I was being led by a vision of possibilities—*me*, making a great income—not necessarily by where I thought God wanted me to be. As I continued to bring it up with David, in some way, he would bring it down.

He was starting to get frustrated with me because he felt like I had changed so much just being back home. I was taking in the opinions of everyone else, and he felt like *Emily* was somewhere else. "Where was the Emily from the summer? Where is that Emily?" I could totally understand where he was coming from. Even I felt different and confused about where that Emily was.

Then came the phone conversation that made me realize how serious he was.

"Emily, I am not called to go to Georgia. That is not where I am supposed to be. I am supposed to be in Bayside Island. When I asked you to marry me and asked if you would be willing to be number two in my life for the rest of your life, that's what I meant. God is in first place and always will be in first place. He has not called me to Georgia, and if you are going to marry me, then he hasn't called you there either."

Wow. End of discussion. He was pretty clear that, if I decided to take the job in Georgia, I would be going by myself. Here it was… another decision. Choosing who to please and who to follow… God and my future husband or what my dad thought was the best thing for me and what sounded like an amazing opportunity. David was *the dream*. He was *the prize*. Through a series of what seemed like miraculous events, God had brought it all to pass. He had revealed to me in the garden in England that David was to be my husband. Here we were in the process, leading up to the day when God's Word would come full-circle on January 6th. Why was this such a hard decision?

I always wanted to please my dad. I went to Bordeaux University, not because I really wanted to go there, but because my dad wanted me to run on a scholarship in college. He didn't force me to go there. I just agreed to it because I wanted to please him. I just wanted to gain approval from my father. By gaining this *approval*, I thought that maybe he would be proud of me and even love me more. He was a great dad, and I never doubted his love, but I craved to know more that my father loved me. Here was my opportunity to please him. Here was my opportunity to make him proud by taking this job. He made these connections for me, and he would be able to watch me succeed in an industry with which he was greatly familiar.

So, my options. Option one: pleasing my father. Option two: as I knew it said somewhere in the Bible, leaving father and mother and cleaving to my spouse. Leaving my father meant that I may not be able to please him with my decisions.

As a separate aspect of this decision, I wanted to choose it, too. I wanted to take the job outside of Atlanta. It was the dream picture I had always had for myself. I always thought that I would do something like the job being offered. The job sounded like it was falling in my lap. The money, the prestige, and something I was really good at? I wanted that job as much as my parents wanted me to have it.

Why was this such a battle? I knew deep down that it was because I wanted more than what I had growing up. I watched my dad run in shoes that had holes in the sides of them, just so he could put new shoes on our feet. We kids got new running shoes every season, and here he had shoes that got his feet wet when he ran in them. I saw the money. I saw this as an opportunity to have more. More than enough. Through my contribution to my *new* family, maybe we would be able to have not only the best for our future kids but also for us, too. I wanted this job for me. I wanted this job for my future kids. I wanted this job because it seemed like it would be a way out of the middle class and, possibly, a way into wealth. A skewed perspective? I wasn't sure, but this job to me was the answer. Here David was with a continually resounding *no*!

"Why?" I thought. My only reasoning was that David grew up around money his whole life. He never did without anything. Clothes. Shoes. Vehicle. Trips. Gifts. Money. He didn't have to work in order to get through college, but I had to work my tail off. Monetarily, he never had to want for anything. Granted, his talent and hard work blessed him with a full-ride scholarship that even gave him an allowance. I was pretty sure that, when there were other needs, all he had to do was ask.

Because he grew up around wealth his *whole* life, the thought of this *job* being the source to our happiness held no water with him. It was not even a factor. He just knew God hadn't called him there. That's it. Period. End of discussion. He knew that he would be successful in whatever God led him to do and be.

He knew God would place him where he needed to be, and he would not come up short in the long line of wealthy family members. He would make it on his own and create his own success. There was not a question about whether he would be a success; he just would. The long line of family members with 6,000-, 7,000-, and 10,000-square-foot homes... first homes, second homes, planes, and new vehicles... they seemed to have it all! Even elevators in their homes! David watched as they *all* owned their own businesses. They *all* worked for themselves.

To David, a *job* was not going to be something permanent. At some point, like everyone else in his family, he would also own his own business. He saw a job as something that provided little security because they could let you go at any time. "A job controls you," David would say, "telling you when to come and go, when to get hungry, when you can or can't go on vacation, and ultimately... not paying you what you are worth... merely, what they can afford." It was a definite truth. He was going to be his own boss one day.

So, here I was... both of my dreams. Now, it was a choice? Which dream was it going to be? The picture I always had of myself... my power suit and briefcase? Or my dream and desire for the last two years? The ultimate dream of having the man that followed God more than anyone I had ever met?

I felt confused, unsure, and nervous. I felt so many emotions running through my body. I never knew how I would feel.

Sometimes, I felt like I didn't know if I was ready to just *jump*. Marriage?

On top of that, thoughts also continued to rush in about my past. My relationship with Rick. David didn't really know much about it. He didn't really know the details. He didn't really know the bondage that I had felt during that time. He didn't know that, though we didn't have sex, so much of myself was given away. Guilt was eating at the inside of me. I didn't know if I should tell him. If so, how? I didn't know if he wanted to know, but I felt like I just had to get it out. I just had to tell him about what really had happened. Would he still want to marry me after he knew the full truth about this past relationship?

My world felt so shaken. I had such a lack of peace. I would write a letter. That's what I would do. I had to get out all of my past. I wasn't sure if it was the right thing to do. I didn't know if he needed to know, but that was what I was going to do. Sit down and type a letter.

I had stayed up late through the night, typing, editing, crying, wringing my hands. But it was finished. The letter was complete... despite the details that I was ashamed of and the truths I wanted to forget about that lingered in my past. I felt I owed it to David to choose whether my sin was too great. And that was it. The letter was mailed.

By now, David should have received it. I hadn't heard from him yet. I was sure he had it. I was sure he had read it. What was he thinking? I mean, I told him everything. He now knew about the depths of my relationship with Rick. He knew of the emotional attachment. He knew about the night of my fall! The night where I almost gave up my virginity. I told him about how I continued to say "no," but after every "no," Rick just tried again.

By now, David knew of my contemplation over the three days before the mission trip. That I was truly in a position where I held Rick in one hand and God in the other. It was a decision, and I could not have both. I almost gave up my relationship with God because of my ties to Rick. I felt mentally in bondage to him. It was hard for me to escape, to get away. I felt like I needed him. We were best friends. We were in each other's heads.

David, by now, knew everything.

It took several days before I finally heard from him. He finally called. I would see. Would this be enough to make him not want to marry me? Would he decide that my sins, my past, and my pitfalls were too great? After knowing everything, could he still accept me? Here he was pure, never having done *anything* with another girl. He had completely saved himself for his wife.

And here I was, a black sheep. In this spotlight, I felt dirty and ashamed. My baggage was great. My relationships were many. How could he ever overlook everything I had done? Everything I had been?

"Well, Emily, I must say... I have never felt like how I felt when I read your letter. As I read it, I fell to my knees and started crying..." He was silent. Goosebumps raced up my arms as I wasn't sure if I wanted to know what he had to say next.

"Emily, I sat in my living room on my knees, reading over your letter. I just bawled like a baby. To imagine that you had been with someone else like you had was almost too much for me to bear. All I could do was cry and cry out to God." David paused.

I knew this would be a hard conversation. Knots had been in my stomach for days, and now, the tears began their steady flow down my cheeks. I hadn't realized how much pain the letter and my past would cause David. To imagine seeing him, a big, strong guy on his knees crying weighted my heart with his agony.

"Emily, in that time, the only thing that I heard the Holy Spirit say to me was, 'What sin?' That's all He kept saying to me, 'What sin?' Every question I asked him. His response was, 'What sin?' He repeated again, 'David, what sin?' The song, 'What Sin?', by Morgan Cryar played over and over in my mind. The lyrics go like this,

> 'What sin? What sin? That's as far away as the East is from the West. What sin? What sin? It was gone the very minute you confessed, buried in the sea of forgetfulness. The heaviest thing you'll carry is to know the guilt and shame, you'll never have to bear it, so let them go in Jesus name. Our

God is slow to anger, quick to forgive our sins, let me put them under the blood, don't bring them up again. He'll just say, What sin? What sin?'

"Emily, I just played the song over and over in my head. I even called my mom and cried. I asked her about it. I asked her what I should do. How could I forget what you had done? I had always envisioned my wife just being white. It's just hard for me to even imagine that you had done these things. I just want you for me. I never wanted to imagine anyone else having any pieces of you. Emily, I just cried to my mom. She was comforting but reminded me that all of that was in your past and, just like the song said, 'What sin?' All of those experiences in God's eyes are no longer there. They are gone. They are nonexistent. She said, 'David, those things are forgotten. If God has forgotten them, you need to forget them, too. It is Emily's past, not her present.'

"Emily, I went on my balcony and burned that letter. I never want to read it again. What sin? What sin?" David paused. The seconds seemed like an eternity.

In his pause, it was almost hard to catch my breath. Was he really saying he would forgive me. Not only forgive but that he would forget all of the horrible things I had done? He was not going to hold the dirt over my head. Was I really going to have a fresh slate with him? I was trying not to let him hear my sobs over the silence, but by this time, tears were streaming down my face. My past was so painful, especially now with someone so wonderful before me, someone who I didn't want to let down. That mercy could be bestowed upon me, and I could go from shame to a true, fresh beginning. My face was a freeway of tears. I could not stop them.

He said, "Emily, just like God has forgotten all you had done, so have I. God has already forgiven you, and I forgive you. Emily, I love you, and I want to spend the rest of my life with you. Emily, you are the white, pure bride that I want to be with. That is how I see you."

The lump in my throat prevented me from speaking. My hand just covered my mouth as I bit my lips, tears continuing to stream down my cheeks. I felt speechless. My heart writhed at the pain I caused David. At the same time, overwhelming gratefulness poured out of my soul, overpowering, engulfing, undeserving gratefulness.

"Thank you, David. Thank you for forgiving me." The thought of that song was beautiful. The lyrics were so wonderful. God truly did forget my past. My sins were as far as the East is from the West. My sins, were in the sea of forgetfulness. Praise the Lord. Praise the Lord that I could be clean. That I could be pure. Praise the Lord that I was covered by the blood of Jesus. His blood from enduring the cross covered my sins.

I was forgiven. I was still getting married. David still wanted me.

I felt like I was beginning to grab hold of my stability once again. Ever since I had been home, I felt like I was a different person. Maybe it was just all the plans and opinions that everyone had to give me. I knew my dad really wanted me to take the job with his company, and I longed to please him. David's forgiveness gave me a new perspective, a new respect for him, a deeper love.

Though the choice of not taking the job in Georgia did not make sense, being that it was close to David's family and that it was a guaranteed job. Considering that David didn't have a job yet, it seemed he could just get a job in Georgia, too. David's mind and heart were set. Georgia was not the place God wanted us to be. He knew it. He was sure about it. I had to choose my future husband over my father. I wished I could please both of them, but this was just the beginning. I was listening to David, not because I agreed with him but completely out of submission. I loved him, and this was the beginning. I would follow him to the ends of the earth if I had to. God had set him apart for me.

Wedding plans were coming along well. We had the music planned. Most of the details were in place. It was going to be a wonderful, winter wonderland! We had begun the process of our marriage counseling. Day by day, stability and surety seemed to replace the anxiousness and questions. It felt so much better not to be confused but for clarity to be back, for the *Emily* from the summer to be back to normal.

David flew in to Pennsylvania a couple of times so we could have our scheduled marriage counseling appointments with our pastor. We covered great things in our marriage counseling. Simultaneously, we were going through an amazing book, *Preparing for Marriage*, by Dennis Rainey. What good stuff! We covered everything from roles, responsibilities, holiday expectations, finances, kids, what we didn't want, expectations, and so much more! We felt like we were really getting prepared well for what was ahead.

We also had taken seriously some advice we received from Brent and Lisa that summer. They had a marriage evaluation that they did on a regular basis. We decided that we were going to put together our own marriage evaluation, completing it once a month after getting married. It covered everything! We wanted to make sure we had all of the bases covered and head off any future problems or potential causes of frustration.

32

A WHOLE NEW WORLD

I flew in to Bayside Island to attend David's graduation. Because he had to take an extra semester, he graduated in December. It was going to be a full weekend. He would graduate on Friday, and we would then make our way back to Georgia for our Saturday night Georgia wedding reception. Sunday, we would have some time to relax before I flew back home on Monday.

It was great to see David's family. There was something about Gloria that I just loved. I was so excited that she was soon to be my mother-in-law. We embraced when we saw each other as if we'd known each other for a lifetime. Her soft, red curls fell over her shoulders. It still seemed strange that I had to bend over to hug her. She was a bundle of awesomeness! She rattled off several of the details that would take place at tomorrow's reception. I simply smiled with a nod of anticipation. I sometimes felt out of my league. I did not know what to expect with this reception, but I knew it would be nice. Macy and Dennis also greeted me with a warm hug.

Jenna followed with a smile as she ducked to hug me. "Are you ready for the big weekend? You get to meet the *whole* family!" She laughed and gave me a look that said "whoa!" as we made our way to our seats.

"I guess I am as ready as I'll ever be!" I just knew I was in for quite a treat.

The graduation ceremony commenced, and my mind began to wander. I felt good about the outfit I would be wearing for the reception. My mom and I went to pick it out together. It was a beautiful, two-piece red suit with rhinestone buttons up the front, red satin shoes, rhinestone earrings, and a necklace to match. The suit was stunning. Simply wearing it made me stand a little taller. The outfit with its accessories cost around $150-$200, now easily the most expensive one in my whole wardrobe. I typically didn't spend that much money on *one* outfit, but it was breath-taking. Thankfully, my mom bought it.

I was excited. It had been a wonderful day out with mom. She was equally thrilled for me as she knew this reception was important. I think she also shared in my nervousness. Though I didn't know the details of what David's extended family was like, the idea of meeting everyone definitely stretched me. The vision of Julia Roberts in the movie, *Pretty Woman,* flashed in my mind. I secretly hoped the reception wasn't a sit-down meal with 10 pieces of silverware, forcing me to choose between one of four forks. I didn't want to stand out. Fortunately, I had been brought up in a family that emphasized respect and manners. Being somewhat of the main attraction, I didn't want to stand out in a bad way. What I lacked in my bank account, I felt that I could compensate for in my ability to be graceful. With the elegance of my red suit, I hoped I could fit in anywhere.

My thoughts continued to race until David was approaching the stage. We clapped and cheered as they announced his name and as he crossed to receive his diploma. I could see his big grin even from our seats! His teeth were so straight and white, one of the qualities I loved about him.

After grabbing lunch with David's family, we traveled back to their house. The three-hour drive seemed short with all that David and I had to talk about. He prepared me about his family. We went through some of the names of who would be there: aunts, uncles, cousins, and grandparents. I would also be seeing his parents' house for the first time. I had never been there. With summer as it was, we all just met at the airport and traveled to Kokomo Beach together.

It was already starting to get dark when we pulled up to David's house. It was a three-story brick house on about 20 acres of land. It wasn't anything over the top, but it sure was bigger than where I grew up. The property seemed massive. The yard in the front was the size of a football field. As we pulled up to park, I saw an open field of pale green grass in the back. I could only imagine it was probably even more beautiful in the spring and summer.

David showed me to my room and took me on a tour once I got settled. He did not act like his house was a big deal. He seemed nonchalant about his childhood home. The floors were a shiny, polished wood, and the house was open as you walked in. The playroom with a fire-pole coming down from the second floor was the first room we passed as he led me into a large TV room, the kitchen, two downstairs bedrooms, and a front room that spread across the whole house. A long room, two dining rooms, and a sunroom. One set of stairs by the kitchen led downstairs to another large playroom with a bathroom and a lot of unfinished storage.

Upstairs, there were four additional bedrooms, including David's, each with its own bathroom. All of the rooms were equipped with a built-in intercom system and radio, so you could talk to people in any of the other rooms. Seven bathrooms total! It was a big house. Though there were no winged cherubims painted on gold-trim-rounded ceilings, the house was immense with space, comfortably decorated and practical. There was no fancy marble or grand white columns. It was unique, lived in, and large. David had a fire-pole right outside of his room! He was definitely the first person I knew who could say that. I imagined having my own fire-pole would have been very fun growing up as a kid!

Following the grand tour, we got settled in, watched a movie, and headed to bed. We had a big day ahead of us.

I was getting ready and wanted to make sure everything was perfect, from my lip liner to my panty hose. I was determined to do my best to fit in. In a short two weeks, I would be part of this family, and the desire to make a good first impression weighed on me.

Though I did not yet know everyone by name, I was under the impression that Aunt Lillian had arranged most of the reception. I learned that it would be a formal yet drop-in reception. They expected that a few hundred people would attend. I silently thanked God that I would not have the fork dilemma of sitting down to a formal meal. The full evening would entail lots of smiling, hugging, shaking hands, and greeting people as they walked in. I was ready.

We arrived at Warwick Valley Country Club, a country club where Aunt Lillian was a member. I realized I had walked into a different world when I stepped off my plane. As we stepped off the elevator onto the second floor, I knew I was in for a treat. We walked into a reception hall that was lined with gold accents, the windows adorned with long and heavy burgundy draping. Exquisite paintings lined the room, accented by the fine trim on the walls. Round tables with soft linens were scattered about with Christmas trees of different sizes decorating the corners of the room. My eyes were drawn to the elaborately decorated central focus, a large, 20-foot tree.

Each table was arrayed with spruce centerpieces and shoots of red and gold stems, twirling up into a graceful point. Elaborate red and gold bows were woven through the spruce with ornate glass ornaments that completed each table. We heard the trickle of the four-foot punch fountain on a Christmas-laden, decorated table. Elegant china neatly sat beside the punch with a glass ladle to accompany it.

As I walked in awe around the room before guests arrived, the soft, classical music graced my ears to set the stage of perfection. The food looked too good to eat. Fine china to put it on, meats accompanied with the proper au jus, cheeses, desserts, green beans, sautéed vegetables, and a beautiful array of fruit surrounding a chocolate fountain. Even the silverware had weight to it. It wasn't plastic, and it didn't appear cheap. I felt like I was walking into someone else's life. Was this really going to be my life? Was this really going to be the family with whom I spent holidays? David had grown up in this environment, but my words could not begin to express what I thought. I was sure we would talk about it later when I had time to really show my expressions. For now, I had to keep my cool.

I felt beautiful, like a princess at a ball, and the ball was for people to meet me. I knew I would be the center of attention. I was the girl that David Carter was marrying. I was the girl that everyone was going to meet for the first time. David looked so handsome in his black suit and his blonde hair in a short, trendy spike. I thought we most definitely looked like we belonged together. Today already felt amazing. I was with the man of my dreams, attending a party that seemed like it was for the "World's Most Rich and Famous."

I stood in awe. God brought me to this place.

Guests began to come. Most stayed for quite a while. David and I stood at the door a majority of the evening to greet people as they walked in. Carrying beautifully wrapped presents, there was often a line waiting to enter the room. I hugged lots of necks, smiled, and thanked so many for joining us for this special celebration. I met so many people. I couldn't imagine having to remember the names past tonight. If only I could at least remember the aunts and uncles, that would be an achievement in itself.

As we greeted people, I noticed many people gathered in one main section of the reception hall. A large television continued to replay a video that Gloria had made of David and I as we grew up. From childhood through adolescence, to college and finally, meeting each other. The music and pictures brought waves of laughter as a periodic picture would show a silly side to David or me.

When the entry of guests slowed down, David and I were finally able to mix and mingle and enjoy the remainder of the reception. I was glad I could be a "social butterfly" when needed because tonight was filled with small talk and future new friends. I managed to keep a smile plastered on my face throughout the evening. I almost felt like I was in a pageant again. "Just smile," I remembered. "Just smile."

We woke up Sunday morning and went to church. I could tell that David was also an upstanding person with the people at his church. Many adults made a point to go out of their way to say "hello," congratulate him on his graduation and engagement, and to meet me. The more I was in an environment with people who knew David, the more I realized what I already knew. I got a special catch with him. David was going to be my husband. I was sure there were many sad hearts the day he was taken off the market.

After church, we had lunch with the whole family. Some cousins, Granddaddy, and Grandmother joined us. It was fun to be with the family. David told me that Granddaddy would often play some sort of game at the end of lunch, and the winner would get some money.

"Okay," Granddaddy said in a gruff, commanding voice. "Listen up now, ya hear." He paused as he waited for the family to quiet down. "Now, Edith is going to pass around a piece of paper. You each need to take one. Now, we're going to play the closest person to the number I write down on this here piece of paper gets this crisp $100 bill," he said, holding up the green paper. "Now, it's the closest person to the number I write down. It will be from one to 100." He held up his pencil and said, "Think carefully because the winner is going to walk away with this $100. But you've got to be the closest person to the number I write down." Granddaddy reiterated his point several times, and we watched him scratch down a number on his paper.

From the response of Jenna, Macy, David, and some of the other cousins, it appeared that this was a normal occurrence after their church lunch. Someone was going to win $100. I noticed that Granddaddy had also picked up the whole lunch tab. That appeared to be the norm, too. I imagined lunch wasn't cheap because there were about 20 of us. Amazed, I shook my head. "This was so different than what I was accustomed to. A weekly occurrence at that," I thought.

"Now, write that number down," he prodded. "Make sure you've got the right number. You've got to try to think what I wrote down now. Okay. Now, pass them on in. Pass them to Edith. Come on now. She'll collect them," Grandaddy instructed. He had a bit of a southern accent, and just by the way he talked, you could tell he commanded respect from people. It seemed that no one in the family ever argued with Granddaddy. Whether he was right or not, he was right. Even the adults were obedient when he barked orders or said we needed tables pulled together. People just obeyed.

"All right now. Everyone has their number in? All right. Now listen up. Edith is going to read off each number and say who has that number. After she reads them all off, I'll tell you which one is closest to the number I chose. Now remember, it was from one to 100."

One by one, the numbers were read off. Finally, at the end, Granddaddy said, "Okay, now, there is one of you who has it right on the money. Someone figured it out and got exactly the right number. Little Matt, you got it. Dale Earnhardt, Sr., number three. My favorite driver." Granddaddy pulled out the crisp $100 bill so the paper would make a snapping sound. "Alright, y'all, Little Matt won. He's the winner."

"Wooo hooo! Thank you, Granddaddy!" Little Matt said as he stood with a big grin to accept the money.

Filing out of the restaurant, Gloria pulled David and me aside. "Now Daaaavid," she said, drawing out his name, "I want you to just go straight to take Emily to get her outfit for the rehearsal dinner." Gloria talked in her rushed voice, a voice that said she had pre-planned everything in her head and knew that this would be the best time. "Take her down to Phipps Plaza to the Nordstrom's there. You should be able to find everything she needs right there. I know because it's Sunday they close a bit early, but you should be able to get there in plenty of time for her to try things on and get what she needs."

This was news to me. I was so excited! I loved getting new clothes! I didn't know much about upscale stores, but if I remembered correctly, Nordstrom's was a very nice store. I knew we didn't have any of them around where I lived.

We got in the Yukon and obediently did what Gloria had requested. David drove me to Phipps Plaza.

Inside Nordstrom's, we made our way to the second floor of the department store to the women's department. As we began to look around, immediately, a sales associate walked up and asked if she could start me a dressing room. She saw that we were holding a few pieces and quickly took them off our hands. "Now, what is the occasion?"

We told her, and she congratulated us on our upcoming wedding.

"You look like," she quickly looked me up and down, "a size 6? I have a few pieces in mind that I think would look great on you. Should I add those to your dressing room?"

I thanked her and politely said she was correct and that we would love any help she could give us.

The spacious dressing room housed a red velvet chair, a nice mahogany table, and a bottle of water that the sales associate had brought for me to drink. The clothes we had picked out were neatly hanging in outfits so they would be easy for me to begin trying on. In the dressing room, I looked at some of the pricetags on these pieces. Everything was separate: $80 for a silk tank top. $200 for a jacket. $180 for a skirt. I noticed that, as David was picking things out, he never once looked at a pricetag. Did he have *any* idea how much just *one* outfit was going to cost?! It did not appear that he cared or that it mattered. My mind was barely comprehending all of this. To me, it appeared like a small fortune on just one outfit!

I tried on several outfits, and the sales associate continued to bring more pieces that she thought would work well. After gathering my shoe size, she also went downstairs to the shoe department where she found some shoes that would look nice and partnered those up with each outfit. Moments later, she reappeared with the proper jewelry and panty hose. From head to toe, I would have everything that I didn't even know I needed, but this outfit would be perfect and complete.

We finally decided upon an outfit. Elegant, classy, and just the right outfit for the night before our wedding. I didn't know exactly how much the bill was, but at the end, David handed over a credit card, and it was paid. I imagined that, with each little thing that was added on, the total had to be somewhere around $700. In awe, I tried to stand up straight and confident, like I belonged and had shopped in Nordstrom's before. Each item was wrapped delicately in tissue paper before being placed into the bags. The sales associate finished with the receipt. She tucked the receipt in a fancy envelope and placed it into the bag. Once everything was perfect, she walked from behind the counter to hand our bags to us. "David... Emily... it was such a pleasure helping you find such a special outfit. You are going to be such a beautiful bride. Now please, keep my card... when you get back from your honeymoon, don't hesitate to come back in. It would be my pleasure to assist you any time." She reached out and shook David's hand and then my hand.

As we walked away, my head felt like it was spinning. I was in awe. Other than seeing the movies, I never imagined that people actually shopped like this, with this kind of help.

To really top things off, on our way out, we stopped by the men's shoe department. David found a pair of sandals that he really liked and were comfortable, something that he would be able to wear on our honeymoon. With a *small* pricetag of just $230, the Mephisto sandals were now paid for and tucked in another bag as we departed the store. Again, quite a stretch from my local Payless Shoe Store in Pippen.

On the way back to David's house, we drove by his Grandmother's and Granddaddy's. It just topped off my day. Could my head really take in more? The more and more I thought about it, the last 24 hours had to be a fairytale. I had messed up things so much and now... *this*? An amazing, kind, pure, humble, and godly man with an amazing, humble family? And... they were wealthy?

As we passed slowly so I could see, I saw the six white columns on the front of the house, which seemed like a smaller version of the White House in Washington D.C. David told me it did have an elevator, a maid's living quarters, a second garage off the house that held about 15 antique cars, and marble all throughout the inside of the house. I could only imagine it was amazing!

My weekend was more than I could put into words. How would I even go home and explain any of this to my family? How would I tell them who I was marrying? David was so down to earth. One

would never know this had been his upbringing. I knew my parents
would be just as speechless as me.

33

WINTER WONDERLAND

The Georgia crew had arrived in Pennsylvania. Freshly fallen snow sparkled, and the Southerners remained in awe of the several feet of snow that blanketed the ground. How did we operate with so much snow? The roads were plowed, cars still drove, and the wedding was indeed still *on*—despite their amazement about the weather.

The hotel that everyone was staying at had accents of Amish rugs and quilts. It had a certain ambiance about it, which showed off the charm that made the Amish community stand out. The Georgia gang broke out in snowball wars, and some of the littler ones enjoyed free-falling into the snow from the top of the wooden fence posts. It was like watching kids in a toy store with so many toys to play with that one did not know what to do. Snow angels, snowball fights, free-falling, and being buried under two to three feet of fresh powder… This was indeed a winter wonderland for me but especially for these Southerners.

On the evening of January 5th, we would have the rehearsal and rehearsal dinner. Everyone anticipated the closure of the rehearsal so we could eat the good Amish cooking scheduled for dinner. I felt very elegant in my expensive, new outfit: off-white silk shell, wine-colored jacket, and a long, silk, wine-colored skirt with intricate designs in its bodice.

The rehearsal was full. Because it was the first time the entire wedding party was together, we had a lot to do. We would all be singing one song together during the wedding ceremony. Each person had received a CD and had been practicing on their own. Now, we would finally bring it all together. My brother would also be singing a solo, and we would welcome the guests to sing several praise and worship songs with us. Things went off without a snag, everyone did well, and we were off to the Amish Inn Restaurant for dinner.

The food was unspeakably wonderful, the desserts were amazing, and the fellowship was fun. Gloria brought the video she showed at the Georgia reception of David and I growing up to show after dinner. I enjoyed it just as much the second time as I did the first. It was fun to listen to the music, see our pictures, and notice how we both went through our "dorky" looking stage at the same time: sixth grade! Both in thick-looking, big glasses, poofy hair, and funny clothes. We were meant to be together.

January 6th. Today was our big day! The sky was blue and clear, and the snow was sparkling. It was a perfect winter day! The wedding would be like it was out of a book. The bridesmaids wore long, black formal dresses that were lined with black fur along the top, custom made just for them! The Christmas decorations still graced the church: wreaths, trees, fancy burgundy bows, and candles.

My dress was perfect. White, lace, chiffon, diamonds, and pearls with a long train accompanying its beauty. My veil matched the length of my wedding dress, equally as long and with pearl accents sewn in all over the soft white tulle.

My coat hung on a hanger, ready for our exit when the wedding was over. A full length, white satin coat was lined with white fur along the front opening, and it had scoop sleeves and a fur-lined white hood. It was a coat made for a winter queen. Today, that queen was me. It was so beautiful. I was so excited to wear it. Fitted just for Emily Ann Cook. When I finally would wear it, I would be Emily Ann Carter. A new name and a new beginning.

Apart from my trip to my hair stylist upon waking up, all of us girls got ready at the church. Laughter and smiles filled the two rooms we occupied. The boys were off getting ready on the other side of the church. Our 2:00 entrance was approaching within minutes. The church parking lot was filling up as friends and family streamed into the sanctuary.

It was game time. I could hear the overture beginning in the sanctuary as Holly Miller beautifully performed "How Great Thou Art." Her soprano range was beyond anything I had ever heard as she hit the celestial notes with impeccable precision. Knowing Holly's talent and my dad's appreciation for music, this one song was what he had anxiously anticipated, especially after he heard her at the rehearsal. As Holly hit some of the final high notes, you could hear a pin drop as people silently sat mesmerized. The audience could not help but to look up from their programs as the crescendo of the song ended in an octave surely reserved for angels. Throughout the sanctuary, mouths gaped open in amazement.

The bridesmaids were in place, and "Canon in D" sounded from the piano. Such an elegant song, a portrayal of beauty and grace. One by one, the seven bridesmaids walked down the stairs from the balcony and were greeted by their respective groomsman at the base of the stairs. Waiting at the back of the sanctuary, a white miniature sleigh awaited it's cue. It was lined with burgundy velvet seats, silver trim and sparkling bells and was about to make its unique and grand entrance.

A Snow Princess and Prince sat in the sleigh. Little brown curls bounced from the shoulders of my two-year-old niece Bailey, as she took her job very seriously. Today she would be tossing artificial snow. Her hand- tailored, winter white satin dress was lined with white fur along the neck and sleeves. Bailey was accompanied by a three-year-old little boy who sat next to her, holding the shimmery satin ring pillow. Following the snowy trail of the sleigh, I would be escorted by my dad within moments.

With everyone in their places, the classic song, "Here Comes the Bride," began. The distinct tones sounded—"Da Da Da-Da... Da Da Da-Da"—and the audience of on-lookers knew that it was their cue to stand. All eyes were on me as my dad and I began our descent down the aisle. The red carpet covered with snow was a perfect entrance for us as my eyes made contact with the man who would was soon to be my husband. I was ecstatic.

So many thoughts were rushing through my head on that walk. "Wow, David looks so handsome. He is grinning from ear to ear."

My thoughts jumped quickly as I looked over at my dad. "Awww, I think my dad has a tear. I'm going to be leaving home. I'm the first to leave, his first daughter to get married. Is that a tear I see?"

We reached the end of the aisle, and I stood with my arm still embraced in my dad's arm. Pastor Bill asked, "Who gives this woman to be wed?"

"Her mother and I," replied my dad. He lifted the short veil that covered my face and kissed me on the cheek. David stepped over to be united with me as he took my arm. Here we were. Arm in arm. Looking at each other. Smiling.

The ceremony was very unique. Pastor Bill spoke briefly and then the wedding party, along with the entire party of guests in the audience, joined in singing some praise and worship songs. Our goal was to have the focus of the wedding to be Jesus. We wanted Him to be not only the center of our life and marriage; we wanted other people to experience the Jesus we knew, too. Then, David and I, along with the wedding party, sang a song. My brother, Jacob, sang a solo. It was special to have my brother sing a solo.

The ending note sounded, and that was the cue. An unusual twist to the ceremony took everyone by surprise as Pastor Bill stepped forward and handed the microphone to David.

His black tuxedo draped perfectly as David stood in silence. The silence remained in the air, causing people to be on the edge of their seats, wondering curiously, *What was about to take place? Why is the groom standing, just looking over the audience?*

Breaking the awkward hush that filled the air, in tall confidence David stood, still glancing slowly across the faces awaiting his words, and he began.

"Today, on this special, momentous day, I want to share a story. A story about an English boy named Leon." Several minutes passed as he detailed out how he had met Leon on that summer day.

"Leon was lost but was an English boy who found Jesus. On that night, when I stood on the platform to speak, I looked through the auditorium, searching for Leon, with hopeful anticipation that he would show up from my invitation I had given him earlier that day. Then, I saw him. He sat alone at the top of the bleachers. I knew that if Leon listened to the message that night and allowed the truth to penetrate his heart, it would be a day written in history for his life, a day that would surely change his life and eternity. The message that night stemmed around one verse, John 3:3, which says, "Jesus replied, 'Very truly I tell you, no one can see the kingdom of God unless they are born again.'"

David walked back and forth, sharing the details of Leon's past, being abused by his parents and abandoned on the street. Leon was broken. David would stop and pause, holding the silence yet again.

"That summer night, when the altar call was given at the Stour Centre, Leon was the first one up. His steps rang loudly on the bleachers as he stood and ran down. His steps echoed as he confidently *ran* from the furthest point to the front, not wanting to miss out on his chance to receive a love that he had missed out on… a love he longed for… to accept this man called Jesus."

Tilting his head down to discreetly wipe his eyes, David continued. "Leon made the decision of a lifetime, a decision that would change his forever, the decision that would assure him a place in eternity with our Almighty God."

David paused for a few seconds as he paced back and forth. He continued, "Jesus replied, 'Very truly I tell you no one can see the kingdom of God unless they are born again.' At that verse, people in the Stour Centre came, and Leon was the first. Today, I am going to offer that same opportunity to you. I am going to ask that everyone bow their heads. With no one looking around… if you were to answer the same question that Leon did… on a scale of 1-10, how sure are you that you would go to heaven if you died today? Are you a 10? Are you 100% sure of where you would spend your eternity? Or is there a little bit of doubt in your mind? Maybe you are a 9? If today you want to make that decision for Jesus and be 100% sure, with everyone's eyes closed, I'm going to ask, right where you are to stand. Stand for Jesus. If you want to accept him as your Savior today, go ahead and stand."

The church auditorium was dim and silent. But, in the silence of the wedding ceremony, people stood. That day, on January 6th, 2001 people around the sanctuary stood, choosing to make Jesus their Lord on that day.

David said, "Along with those who are standing, I am going to ask that the congregation join in with them in repeating this prayer together. Please repeat after me:

Father God, I realize I'm a sinner.
I cannot get to heaven without Jesus.
Right now, I acknowledge all my sins, and I ask you to forgive
me of all my sins.
I confess that Jesus is Lord.
That he lived a perfect life, and he died for me.
I believe in my heart that God raised Jesus from the dead.
And I now accept Jesus Christ as the Savior and Lord of my
life.
Thank you for saving me.
In the mighty Name of Jesus, Amen.'

An applause erupted as people sat back down. David said,
"Congratulations! If you made that decision today, you can now be
100% sure that you are going to heaven." David quietly stepped back
and turned the rest of the ceremony over to Pastor Bill.

"And the time has come," said Pastor Bill. "David and Emily, I
now pronounce you 'husband and wife.' All right, Reverend," Pastor
Bill chuckled, "here's the moment you've been waiting for. You may
now kiss your bride." A chuckle rang through the audience, and
David leaned over and kissed me.

"For the first time, I introduce to you, Mr. and Mrs. David and
Emily Carter." That must have been the cue for the music to start
because, automatically, the familiar wedding notes sounded on the
keyboard. The feeling of a celebration filled the air. The congregation
stood and began clapping as David and I and the wedding party
walked down the steps and down the aisle of the sanctuary.

We greeted the guests as they made their way to the main
entrance, each guest receiving a balloon that they would release when
we left. I was excited because now I would be able to put on my
beautiful, fur-lined winter white satin coat. After all of the guests had
exited, we made our way to the front doors to bid a short farewell. A
white sleigh pulled by two white horses awaited our exit to bring us
to the reception. Burgundy scoop ribbons and bows draped the sides
of the white sleigh.

As we stepped out, a loud cheer rang, and I truly felt like a Snow
Queen in my beautiful coat and dress. The balloons were released

and filled the sky as we left. The day seemed like a dream. I felt beautiful, people got saved, and now, I was finally holding hands with my best friend. He was mine, and I was his. This long-awaited-for desire had finally come to pass. What God told me in the garden really did come true. David had become my best friend, and now, finally, my husband.

The chill of the winter breeze brushed our faces as the horses galloped off. Draped in a white fur blanket, David wrapped his arm around me and kissed me again. We leaned back, not only soaking in the glitter of the freshly fallen snow on the fields, roads, and trees, but we sat closely, soaking in the events of the day, and one thought resounded in my head: thankfulness. I was so full of thankfulness and gratitude to the One who had made all of this possible. Snuggled up in the arms of my *knight* with his shining armor, his dapper tuxedo, I was rescued. I was his. He had come for me. I couldn't help but continue to think, "Thank You, Jesus. Thank You, Jesus! Fairytales *Do* Come True!"

Like a child listening intently to a story, Elise had her chin resting on her hands, just peering up at me. The sun was low on the horizon, and she wiped tears away with her cloth napkin. Elise had remained still for the last couple of hours, insistently prodding for me to continue.

"Well, that is it." I said.

Dabbing the corners of her eyes, she said, "That was the most wonderful story I have ever heard! It could be a movie! I feel like I just heard what I never knew was possible, but what I've always dreamed of. And it's your life! You lived through it!"

"Yes, I did. It has been a long time since I've shared the whole story. It was good to remember how God really did some amazing things in the process. Thank you for letting me share with you. I hope that maybe it helped."

"More than you know!" Elise stressed. "Thank you for sharing even the hard stuff. The stuff about Rick. For me, I know that I have been in a place that has been so difficult, and I've been living in condemnation and guilt. It's partly because I've been unsure whether I'm just going *overboard* by not giving in to what my boyfriend wants. I've gone back and forth with what I felt was right, but once I met Jesus, I couldn't get away from the feeling that physical purity was important—even though my boyfriend didn't understand. It's good to hear that it is possible to make the hard decisions. I mean, you made a really hard decision with Rick. You two were close!"

"You are right. We were. That was the most difficult time in my life," I said.

"But it is so awesome! You made the right decision, and you didn't even know that you were just *days* away from meeting the man of your dreams! The man you would marry! If you would've chosen Rick for the time being, who knows if you would have ever met David!" Elise exclaimed.

"Very true."

"It just gives me so much hope. I see you today, and you are so happy. You and your husband make such a beautiful couple. Thank you for sharing your story with me. It just gives me clarity. I know God has someone perfect for me. My job is to just pursue God with fervor, to pursue my relationship with Him. Like David said on the mission trip, it's not *my* job to get a guy to notice me. It's only my job to follow God's will for my life, and Mr. Right will find me!"

"Yes, he will, Elise! God is no respecter of persons! If he did it for one person, he will do it for you, too!"

At that, we glanced up from our conversation and noticed that David was walking toward our table.

"Well, hello, Ladies," he said with his southern charm. David smiled as he leaned over to give me a gentle kiss. "I hope I'm not interrupting anything."

"No, it's great to see you, honey. This is my new friend, Elise," I said, motioning toward Elise. "And Elise, this is my husband, David."

"Pleased to meet you," David said as he reached out and shook her hand. "Well, I had a refreshing nap. I was getting hungry, so I wanted to see if you were open to moving our reservations up a little bit if they could get us in."

"Sure, that would be fine. We actually were just finishing up. Elise just heard our *whole* story of how we met!"

"Wow!" David said, looking at Elise in surprise. "You both must be hungry after hearing that!" He joked. "That's a long story, but really, it is quite a great story."

"It is! It is so good to get to meet you. From all Emily has told me, you are an amazing man of God. I look forward to meeting a man like you one day, someone who is passionate for Jesus," Elise said with a smile.

As they were finishing up their short exchange, I reached down into my bag to grab a business card so that Elise could have my information once she got home. I didn't know if we would ever talk again, but if she did need an encouraging word from someone, I wanted her to be able to get in touch with me.

Elise and I both stood up and embraced.

"It was so good to get to meet you," I said. "Here is my card. All of my contact information is there. Please feel free to touch base with me if you need anything or if you just need me to listen to you!" I joked. "I would be happy to help in any way I can."

"Thank you so much. It was great to meet you, too. Thank you for sharing your story with me. It really did help me more than you will ever know!"

We embraced one more time, like we were long lost friends. "Have a safe flight," I said as I turned to David to begin to head into the resort.

"Thank you. I will."

Hand in hand, David and I walked away. The sun was going down, the air was cool, and the air smelled of pink hibiscus and coconut-pineapple suntan oil.

"What a great reminder," I thought. "It feels so good to reflect on how good God is and how He answers prayer. I really did marry the man of my dreams, and I am living the life of my dreams. When you do it God's way, fairytales really can come true."

David and Emily escaped into the lobby and, as the story goes...
...they lived happily ever after.

The End.

EPILOGUE

The story of David and Emily, though a fictional story, is a compilation of many true events. Many of the events happened in my life, some true and some fictional stories from the lives of other young girls to portray a more vast array of what happens in the world today.

Some of the actual events? I did meet my husband, Tyler, on a mission trip in England. God did reveal that he would be my husband in a vision on a chalkboard. Also, on January 6th, we did have a magical wedding day. Upon leaving the wedding, we enjoyed our reception and then flew out the next morning for our week in Ochos Rios, Jamaica.

What happened next? The following year? The next 5? The next 10? What happened to "David and Emily"? Really, what happened to us?

In the third revision of this book, we are getting ready to celebrate our 17-year wedding anniversary. We have four children: Tyler Jr. (11/2009), Trinity Faith (10/2011), Timothy Isaac-Josiah (12/2013), and Taylor Liberty (3/2015). We began praying for our children in 2002. We prayed specifically in order for Tyler, Trinity, Timothy, and Taylor. Though we chose not to begin our family until 2009, they came exactly according to how we prayed: characteristics and personalities. They even came in the order we prayed: Tyler, Trinity, Timothy, and Taylor. Not only are they adorable, they are an extreme blessing, too!

Over the years, when asked if I was married, my typical response has been, "Yes, we are actually still on our honeymoon," half joking. In the early years, naysayers often gave advice to me as a new wife, statements such as, "Oh, if you can make it through the first year, you'll be all right," or, "If you can make it through five years, you might just make it." But over the years, Tyler (aka: David) and I have made it a priority that our marriage remain centered upon the Lord, and when the Lord is the center, the focus, and the Rock, blessings are sure to follow. We have spent almost 17 years on a honeymoon. Every year has only gotten better.

Occupationally, my background has been in sales, education, corporate banking, and partnering in a marketing business with Tyler. God and McCart International have assisted in providing enough income for me to resign from corporate America. What a blessing!

Aside from McCart International, Tyler currently works in corporate sales and is also the host of a successful Christian podcast, *The Success Edge: for the Marketplace Christian*, where he interviews and shares stories of successful Christians in the marketplace around the world. We co-host a podcast, *Family on a Mission: with Tyler & Amy*, that dives into our daily lives as a Christian family pursuing God.

Today, due to God's blessing, I'm able to be a do-what-I-want mom. I spend my time in and out of my children's schools, writing books, blogs, and devotionals. I speak at events, and assist as a business partner with my husband.

Following God has been a continual adventure!

I'm praying the best to you on your life journey!! I'm praying you experience love, happiness, and fulfillment of your hearts desires. I'm praying your relationship with our almighty Father goes so deep that He becomes your best Friend, your "All in All," your Comforter, and your Direction. When that relationship is established, the sky is the limit.

My ultimate prayer for you and your life is that you also will be able to say...

Fairytales Do Come True
When God Writes YOUR Love Story!

"Therefore, if anyone is in Christ,
the new creation has come:
The old has gone, the new is here!"

2 Corinthians 5:17 (NIV)

ABOUT THE AUTHOR

Amy J. McCart graduated with a Bachelor of Arts degree in Business, studied Spanish abroad multiple times in Costa Rica, and completed mission trips in England, Northern Ireland, Scotland, and throughout the United States. She is a graduate of SheSpeaks, part of Proverbs 31 Ministries. Her passion to see people's lives radically impacted by Jesus led her into youth ministry in her early 20s, teaching Bible and Spanish at a Christian school in South Carolina and passionately speaking at events ranging from youth retreats and women's meetings to coliseums of more than 10,000 people. Her goal? To wake up a generation who will live for Jesus without restraint.

Born and raised in New Paris, Indiana, Amy met her *Fairytale* husband, Tyler, in England. After their wedding, she joined him in South Carolina where she began her career in sales and advertising. Later, Amy taught Spanish and Bible and ultimately worked as a Merchant Sales Bank Officer before resigning when her first son was born in 2009.

Though her early career endeavors did not involve writing, her love for writing goes back to her experience in the sixth grade when she wrote and illustrated her first book about her childhood companion, her sheepdog, Heidi. Today, she can most often be found writing non-fiction material such as Christian devotionals or topical studies.

Amy and her husband, Tyler, live in Dacula, Georgia—a suburb of Atlanta—and enjoy time spent with their four children, Tyler Junior, Trinity, Timothy, and Taylor. Together, they own a marketing business and co-host the podcast, *Family On A Mission: with Tyler and Amy*.

Amy uses writing and speaking as platform to encourage, teach, and inspire that she might glorify God for all He has done and is doing in her life. Her ultimate mission is to see the multitudes enter a personal relationship with Jesus and be transformed into confident, world changers for Christ.

Connect with Amy on social media via Facebook, Instagram, and Twitter @amyjmccart or www.amyjmccart.com.

Also, hashtag us on social media:

#FairytalesDoComeTrueBook
#FairytaleRevival
#FairytalesDoComeTrueStudyGuide
#FairytalesDoComeTrue

CPSIA information can be obtained
at www.ICGtesting.com
Printed in the USA
FSOW02n1645200917
38739FS

9 781940 024561